THE SALON IN WÜRTTEMBERG

THE SALON IN WÜRTTEMBERG

Pascal Quignard

Translated from the French by Barbara Bray

GROVE WEIDENFELD

New York

Published by Grove Weidenfeld
A division of Grove Press, Inc.
841 Broadway
New York, NY 10003-4793

Published in Canada by General Publishing Company, Ltd.

Library of Congress Cataloging-in-Publication Data
Quignard, Pascal.
[Salon du Wurtemberg. English]
The salon in Württemberg / Pascal Quignard. — 1st American ed.
p. cm.
Translation of: Le salon du Wurtemberg.
ISBN 0-8021-1317-6
I. Title.
PQ2677.U486S1813 1990
843'.914—dc20 90-43321
CIP

Manufactured in the United States of America

Printed on acid-free paper

Designed by Irving Perkins Associates

First American Edition 1991

10 9 8 7 6 5 4 3 2 1

Contents

THE SALON IN WÜRTTEMBERG

CHAPTER 1

The House in Saint-Germain-en-Laye

O du frisst mich! O du frisst mich! Du bist der Wolf und willst mich fressen!

(Oh, you're eating me! Oh, you're eating me! You're the wolf, and you want to eat me!)

GRIMMELSHAUSEN

Seinecé's room in Saint-Germain-en-Laye was extraordinarily light. It was on the second floor of a solid early-nineteenth-century house, firmly moored to the garden by a flight of steps bordered by small bay trees, tiny lilacs, and flowers. Two tall windows looked out on the garden, a few hazel trees, two fields, and the forest. Madame Aubier had kept the rest of the floor and the bedrooms above for her own use. Seinecé's room was large, and I remember the light in it as pink. Long blue drapes on English curtain rods made of brass fell in heavy old-fashioned folds, held back by yellow velvet loops. In the summer the bright daylight slowly ate away the outline of the curtains. The walls were probably painted white tinged with pink, as was the fashion two or three hundred years ago. The room had once been the dining room, and it still contained a long table with room for eight or ten people, made of wood that was now almost black. Seinecé used to leave dictionaries open on it, together with piles of books, blotters of various colors, and red and yellow pencils. He didn't leave things lying about, though: all the articles were carefully arranged. He loved the table with a jealous affection. He wanted to give the impression that several people lived there and all sat and worked at the table together. He wouldn't let anyone touch it, or even stretch out a hand toward it. That would have amounted to handling an object imbued with magic, like a flying carpet, and perhaps destroying its power. Three Quinquet oil lamps converted to electricity and placed in a triangle on the table indicated three places, as in a library reading room. When Seinecé sat in the first place with his back to the wall, he suddenly became a red-nosed old monk with magnifying spectacles, working at a Latin manuscript with gray-mittened hands. Sitting facing the window he was an Assyrian deciphering a slab of clay, conjuring up the days when the language of Sumer was still spoken, when women were beautiful and manners gentle and friendly. When he sat with his back to the bed, a Chinese mandarin slowly smoothed out a little silk handkerchief, mixed the ink, and dreamed of the face of the woman he loved, tossing in bed hot-eyed and unable to sleep.

Around the table stood six low and uncomfortable chairs with black frames and yellow woven seats. The long dark surface of the table covered with books and pencils, the three circles of light from the lamps, the white sheets of paper, the blue and green of the blotters—all combined to produce an atmosphere of mildness, radiance, warmth, and peace.

On the wall opposite the table there was a solid but slender chimneypiece, over which, tilting forward, hung a gilt-framed mirror, spotted and tarnished. A stucco nymph and satyr in the style of Louis XVI adorned the narrow mantelpiece. But the fireplace no longer functioned. A dark red Godin stove was the only thing there was to gaze into in the evening. Four very low wicker armchairs were placed around it. They creaked. We often got up to rearrange our shawls and sweaters and sometimes managed to make ourselves comfortable. We talked. Seinecé liked staying up late. I hated to miss seeing the dawn, as if being lazy enough to let the day steal a march on me might cost me eternity, or even more. We spoke very quietly. I used to leave him earlier than he'd have liked, and we always met again later than we'd have wished. I used to get back to Saint-Germain at about six in the evening, after sunset. I suddenly realize now it must have been because of the time of day that I remember the room as bathed in that strange, grainy pink glow. I slept at Louise and André Valasse's house next door to the Chenil bakery. We were both very young. It was 1964. I felt a friendship for him that everything, later, conspired to undo, and I thought his feelings for me were not uncordial.

I first met Florent Seinecé in 1963, at the staff headquarters of Army Region Number One. I was the postal officer's driver and had just had a tooth out. It was my lower left molar, and I can still feel the hole with my tongue. It's easy for me to write this page: I've only got to run my tongue over the gap and everything comes back, including the inability to bite properly. I'd gone to lie down in the little room adjoining the barbershop, where I thought no one would disturb me. Bernard, one of the barbers, claimed to have the hand that doled out passes right in his pocket, as he elegantly put it, and I did all I could to be friendly. I drowsed on the brown bunk. It was an extremely hot day.

A soldier came in, put his beret on the table in the middle of the room, and bent down to undo his shoelaces. Then he straightened up, took a handful of boiled sweets and Dutch Hopjes out of his pocket, sat down on a metal stool, and began arranging the candies on the table, first in triangles, next in diamond shapes, and finally in quincunxes. He hadn't seen me. Nor did I want to talk to anyone. I was lying holding a handkerchief to my mouth.

"Cric crac croc," he muttered to himself. "Ri-go-la, ri-go-lo."

Then he unwrapped one of the Hopjes, put the bitter little black coffee cube in his mouth, and went on absently moving his candies about on an imaginary checkerboard, still muttering, "Cric crac croc . . ."

After a little while, during which he still took no notice of me, I began to get exasperated both with his game and with the way he was garbling the song.

"No!" I called out crossly, hurting my jaw. "You've got the tune all wrong!"

The young soldier turned round in amazement.

"And not only that—you've got the words wrong too!"

He looked at me in increasing surprise. I was incoherent with fury and sat up on the bed. My explanations seemed to get more and more breathless and involved under the wondering scrutiny of those large eyes.

"You've got it all wrong," I spluttered again. "I can't speak properly because I've just had a tooth out. But it's really 'gigota' . . ."

And I sang it myself as best I could:

Rigota, Gigota,
She goes up to her room.
She breaks her leg.
She goes up to the attic.
She breaks her nose.
One, two, three.
Cric, crac,
Regina Godeau,
Rigota, Gigota.

His growing astonishment added to my confusion. I must have sounded very peculiar. My tongue felt like a glazed chestnut that had shriveled in my mouth, and my mouth tasted of blood.

"Fantastic!"

He got to his feet in his excitement.

"I've been trying to find out about that song for ages!" he said, hastily picking up the candies and putting them in his pocket. "Sing it again!" he cried. "All of it!"

I straightened up and did the best I could.

He stood in front of me, softly singing along. He offered me some candies. I told him my mouth was quite chewed up enough by itself. He was tall and thin, rather like Margrave Philip in the Baldung Grein portrait in Munich, but even more handsome with his irregular features, chestnut hair, and big bright burning eyes. Suddenly he edged me along on the bed and sat down beside me.

"Seinecé," he said, gazing at me intently. "Florent Seinecé."

"Chenogne," I answered. "Charles Chenogne."

"Your name shushes."

"It's not my fault. Yours whistles."

He took a handful of candies out of his pocket and pressed them on me again. They looked just like ordinary hard candies to me, but he told me all their different local names and varieties and explained how difficult some of them were to get hold of. It was my turn to look amazed, but I didn't let on. "Do you know 'Pimpanipole, Once Long Ago'?" he breathed. I said I did. "Sing it! I've forgotten the ending." I sang it as well as I could. "How marvelous!" he cried when I'd finished. "Just the person I've been looking for for years! An expert on nursery rhymes!" And I had found an expert on candies, said I.

But he wasn't to be distracted. For years, he said, he'd been trying to find the words that went with the tunes that came out of nowhere and nagged at him while he was walking or daydreaming. He asked me which was my favorite, then changed his mind and offered to guess. He said everyone has a song inside him that is always trying to be remembered. But you keep forgetting the one that haunts you most; the one that whenever you hear it warms you like the pierced copper pan with coals in it that they used to heat your bed with in winter when you were a child. And as he spoke of winter I remembered.

"Oh!" I cried in despair. And I sang:

Arrege harrige
Serege sirige
Ripeti pipeti
Knoll.

"H'm . . . a bit crude," he said, leniently enough. "What language is that?"

"I lived near Heilbronn as a child," I said. "Not far from Stuttgart."

"Stuttgart, after the war?"

"Just after the war."

"Are you a singer? Do you play an instrument?"

"I'm a cellist."

I corrected myself. "At least, I am in civilian life." I corrected myself again, "I *was* a cellist."

He stood up. "Right," he said. "We must celebrate. I'm going to give you a candy." For the third time he brought a fistful of them out of his pocket.

"No!" I insisted.

"I know it's childish," he said quietly, as if trying to convince himself of the fact. "I'm a qualified archivist and paleographer, and I'm working on a thesis in the archives at Beaune and Epervans. But my one passion in life is candies." Their wrappings made a rustling sound. The sound of the wrappings on the caramels was worse than those on the Hopjes. My dislike of candies in general is probably due to this racket. I tried again to explain that with my missing tooth and my dry mouth I didn't feel like eating sweets. "For later on!" he said. I finally took a Hopjes and put it in my pocket.

"Good. Now listen," he said. "I'm going to sing you something much nicer than your counting rhyme. The most beautiful song ever!

By the fountain Barbidaine
In the vale of Barboton . . .

He had a very good voice. Much better than the one fate dealt me. When he finished he looked moved. And I felt moved. He took out a packet of army Gauloises and thrust them at me. They came in a flimsy blue paper pack and had a harsh, marvelous smell. Marvelous in retrospect, that is. His long body, gauche and romantic, moved with an awkwardness he couldn't quite control.

I stood up and with some difficulty extracted a Gauloise, which I threw away as soon as I'd lit it. Smoke and the taste of blood made an unpleasant combination. I noticed Seinecé was retying his shoelaces in a triple bow (he always had great, insoluble problems with laces, ties, and belts). He picked his beret up from the table, put it on at an angle over his right eyebrow, and asked me the number of my barrack. I told him I'd gotten permission to rent a room in town so as to be able to practice the cello when I was off duty. "A room on the courtyard behind the Chenil bakery," I added. Then, hungrily: "I'm greedy."

"Don't worry, so am I," he said as if to reassure me. Then he repeated, as though it were some profound truth, "I'm greedy too." He said it with a kind of modest melancholy. He'd taken a huge room, he told me, on the first floor of an imposing villa on the edge of the forest. The house belonged to a seventy-seven-year-old spinster. "I must introduce you to Mademoiselle Aubier," he said. "She sings songs that used to be her mother's favorites."

He came over to where I was sitting on the bed again and shook hands with me at length.

"A civilized man at last," he said.

"Only because he's lost a tooth," I answered.

Seinecé was twenty-four. I was just twenty-one. We were both champing at the bit. He was married, with a little girl. His wife was called Isabelle; his daughter's name was Delphine. Isabelle was still living in Burgundy, in a little rented house in Prenois about thirty miles from Dijon, where she taught German. (The fact that she didn't know the language very well was no obstacle to teaching it. And strangely enough, after the early days Seinecé and I never referred to this linguistic link between us: admittedly, if he *had* mentioned it he'd have met with a tense, shamefaced, and irrational resistance on my part.) Originally Isabelle had been posted to Dijon only for the length of time Seinecé was supposed to spend working on the Beaune and Epervans archives, two hours' journey away. Then she'd managed to get her return to Paris postponed for the duration of Seinecé's military service, partly because of the little garden in Prenois, partly because of Delphine's crush on her schoolteacher there, and also because Isabelle's parents lived comparatively close by, near Lons-le-Saunier in the Jura. So almost every Friday Isabelle and Delphine used to take the train to Saint-Germain-en-Laye, leaving again late Sunday afternoon to reach home when it was pitch dark. To hear them talk, Prenois was a paradise, with its currant bushes and two oak trees in the garden, and the Suzon, the Ouche, and the Burgundy Canal nearby. No doubt it *was* a wonderful part of the world. I wouldn't know.

Seinecé was strange, obsessive, nervous, brilliant, inexhaustible. He wasn't very fond of music apart from those orgies, those rafts of nursery rhymes. He liked spirits but not wine; with me it was the other way around. But it's a good thing if our chief likes and dislikes isolate us. In either friendship or love you shouldn't agree with one another about important things; otherwise you'll either come to blows or get bored. I've noticed that it's only the people who disagree about everything who never quarrel.

Although Seinecé was much more than eccentric, he wasn't a

complete odd ball. But he liked what seemed to me long drawn out pranks lasting a couple of hours. One late afternoon as we lay in the sun on the lawn beside the army showers—there were no windows, so no one could see us—he tried to make me believe that when he was a child he and his father went on a trip to the Holy Land and dined at the Good Samaritan's inn, at the very table where Our Lord had sat. He appeared to them and they all had coffee together. Christ had aged, but was as bitter and dissatisfied with the world as ever. Another day Seinecé would summon up Darius, Hammurabi, Julius Caesar, or Pius XI. As a trained archivist who had studied at the Ecole des Chartes in Paris he was expert in several ancient languages, whereas I hated and still do hate Latin, which I've never been able to understand, having been taught it in an off-putting and incomprehensible manner in Bergheim. He soon noticed my recalcitrance. He didn't talk much about Beaune or Dijon, and mentioned only vaguely that he was writing a thesis on some old forgotten thing buried somewhere on the beautiful banks of the Dheune in the Duchy of Burgundy. For the moment he was driver to a very nice lieutenant colonel who didn't drink much and was almost a highbrow—Seinecé said he knew practically all the letters in the alphabet. This lieutenant colonel had the two undeniable virtues of being a stay-at-home and being in charge of the horses, which meant that he spent most of his time riding, either in the ring or in the forest.

Isabelle and Delphine would arrive nearly every Friday evening for the weekend. Isabelle was extremely beautiful—proud, amusing, and fierce, with a certain amount of affectation and haughtiness. She loathed Sundays and was always in a terrible temper then; partly at the thought of going back to a week of teaching in Dijon and being alone with Delphine in the little house in Prenois, partly because she hated stations, trains, timetables, and having to change trains in Paris, and lastly because Mademoiselle Aubier always invited us to lunch on Sunday at twelve-thirty. A long lunch lasting until two-thirty was followed by a "concert" that Isabelle or I accompanied on the piano, and that led in turn to tea, either in the conservatory—a small expanse of cement and some rubber plants—or in the garden, according to the weather. Isabelle cursed these Sunday afternoons all the more because Seinecé and I delighted in them: we were fascinated by Mademoiselle Aubier's funny ways, her clothes, her wiles, her tastes, her vocabulary, and her use of language in general. She was a spinster who had spent all her life looking after and imitating a mother whose longevity had amazed the local authorities three times: there had been a reception in 1933, when she was ninety, another in 1938 when she was ninety-five, and yet another in 1943, when she was a hundred. She died at the Liberation aged one hundred and two; this time there was no party. Mademoiselle Aubier told us her mother had devoted herself to trying to be the spitting image of *her* mother. As we contemplated that dress, that hair-netted bun, that worn, golden, silky hand, we felt as if time had stood still, as if we were looking at a woman of the ancient bourgeoisie on her way to a harpsichord lesson with François Couperin on Rue du Monceau-Saint-Gervais. A woman practically unaffected by the end of the eighteenth century, the Revolution, the Empire, the Third Republic, art nouveau, the First and the Second World Wars, except that they had all gradually opened her eyes, leaving them quite bereft of pity and almost incapable of tears.

The first time I met Mademoiselle Aubier was in her garden. It was April 1963, Palm Sunday, a fine day of bright sunshine, though chilly. Seinecé and I were coming down the steps. "Oh!" Seinecé exclaimed, pointing her out to me, "I must introduce you to Mademoiselle Aubier." In the distance, by the iron railings, I could see a little black or mauve figure with a shawl over its shoulders, a magnificent cloche hat of Manila straw on its head and a pair of little pruning shears in its hand. Mademoiselle Aubier was cutting five or six twigs from the large, almost black boxwood trees to take to Palm Sunday mass.

We went over to her.

"I'm terribly worried," she said. "I haven't seen Pilate all morning."

Pilate was Mademoiselle Aubier's dog. He was really called Pontius Pilate, I've never known why. In Magdeburg, where my father took us many times, you could see the bowl in which Pilate washed his hands. You could also contemplate Judas's lantern: I sometimes think I can see it reflected in friends' faces even now. Pontius Pilate the dog was very affectionate. He was friendly with everyone, and everyone was flattered. He was also friendly with strangers and burglars. Burglars were particularly grateful for this. Mademoiselle Aubier showed us her boxwood twigs.

"I'm all ready," she said. "At least the picture frames and the bedrooms will have a bit of company . . . And what's your name, Monsieur?" turning to me.

"Charles Chenogne," I told her.

"Welcome, Monsieur Chenogne," she said. "They say that when it's been blessed, boxwood wards off curses and bad dreams. Though *good grief*, Monsieur Chenogne, are there any curses other than bad dreams?" "*Good grief*" was Mademoiselle Aubier's favorite oath. Except if she was really furious, when she risked "Hell's bells!"

I was taken by surprise and didn't answer for a moment.

"Memories?" I stammered.

"Oh, we mustn't ask too much of consecrated boxwood!" she said, laughing heartily. "When you come right down to it, we can't keep ourselves from having lived . . ."

Seinecé interrupted. "Why not? Just as Manila straw keeps off the winter sun?"

"Yes," she said, stifling another little chuckle with her hand, like a child. "And just as the service I'm going to now keeps off a long and tedious Sunday morning."

Then she waved a little "au revoir" and teetered back to the house, calling "Pilate! Pilate!" as she went. Mademoiselle Aubier never let anyone have the last word. There are several kinds of candies and cakes, a very few men, and perhaps rather more women, made up of an indefinable mixture of provincial naivety, gentleness, timidity, distinction, and tact. Mademoiselle Aubier had this provincial side to her, despite her passion for television. She had bought a set right at the beginning of the fifties. She was always touching a little embroidered handkerchief to her upper lip, waving it about for emphasis as she spoke, putting it back to her mouth again when she stopped, and gazing doubtfully or expectantly at her interlocutor. She never spoke about herself, and to avoid doing so was always talking about her mother, whose maiden name was Fernande Paillot and who had evidently been a great watercolorist, musician, and bonesetter. These talents were still further developed in her daughter. An ant had only to crawl on little Delphine's arm or leg, or rather Mademoiselle Aubier had only to be passing at the time, and she would bear the child off into the house, grumbling that she probably wouldn't be able to lay her hands on a cool cabbage leaf as it wasn't the right time of year, but a slice of tomato would do so long as it was juicy, or a sprig of sage.

Her way of speaking struck us as wonderfully precise and vigorous. She seemed to have stepped out of a lost age, a time fallen to dust, just as easily as if she'd come in from the next room. And it was with cautious, rustling, almost mouselike steps that she arose from the depths.

And so she pattered past the railings a few moments later on her way to church, where her devotions were doubtless disillusioned but formal and respectful. She usually wore a full skirt and a blouse, high at the neck and tight at the wrists, made of dark bronze or red or mustard silk, never black. A long gold chain went intriguingly under her blouse and emerged at her waist, bearing a bunch of little jingling objects such as her watch, a small key, and some charms that had been handed down in the family for generations. This was just how her mother looked, or rather her mother's portrait, when she could be persuaded to show it to you, piously enclosed in a silver locket. To find it she had to hunt through a whole collection of such pictures; they were like the bunch of keys hanging from the belt of the portress of a convent.

Her father? She would never say a word about him, good or bad, of her own accord, and even when we pressed her she only answered our questions with a brief murmur expressing neither hate nor tension, merely a kind of impatience. You could see his portrait in the drawing room. He was like Napoleon I, only a bit fatter.

We weren't introduced to Denis Aubier, Mademoiselle Aubier's great-nephew, until the beginning of 1964, when he came to live on the third floor of the house that a few years later was to be his. Though young, he didn't look like the Bonaparte who beat back the Austrians with the shaft of his standard at Arcoli; like his uncle, he resembled the emperor in exile or even dying. He was incredibly taciturn, immobile, and wise. He became our friend. He was extremely good with his hands, infinitely patient and resourceful. He was a keen but solitary cyclist; he wanted to lose weight, but he couldn't bear anyone to see his thighs and his big blue shorts.

Unlike her great-nephew, Mademoiselle Aubier never stopped talking. This was probably because until she rented the pink room to Seinecé she had been living on her own for fifteen years and had never gotten out of the habit of talking to herself in her booming voice. "Now where did I put that pepper mill?" she would bawl, coming into the salon where we were reading or dreaming aloud. "Silly girl, you've got a memory like a sieve! Ah, here it is! It's always been rather nasty, this pepper mill, don't you think? Rather clumsy. What do you think you look like, eh, pepper mill? Aunt Antonine got you when Armel died—what a child she was, ugly as sin! Between you and me, you look rather like her." And off she'd go, still talking to the pepper mill. The peculiar thing about Mademoiselle Aubier's soliloquies was that they combined extreme solicitude for herself and her nearest and dearest with sudden bursts of sarcasm. Her face would remain mild and imperturbable while her voice became pitiless. "You!" she said to Florent one day out of the blue, "you're one of those who're submerged even when there isn't any water!" Her oddities must have been catching. When he told me about her remark, Seinecé said you could have knocked him down with a fender.

If Mademoiselle wasn't talking to herself—or to her ghosts—she was singing, singing at the top of her voice. All of a sudden you would hear

I was born in Ferrarest . . .

Sometimes you were so surprised your heart skipped a beat.

Mademoiselle Aubier's ramblings were less painful than her singing, though not necessarily pleasant, especially when she forgot and talked to herself about us as if we weren't there. "Now what am I going to give those two guys of mine?" she'd say dubiously, opening the sideboard door. "Bellonne or Dubonnet?"

Mademoiselle Aubier's most wearisome sessions were when she told us at length about her mother's memories as if they were her own. Thus we heard how Madame Aubier saw the first cabs with rubber tires, the first flush toilet, the first cigarette machine, the first gas lights. Mademoiselle Aubier would take one of us aside, lay her hand on our arm, and say, "Poor Mama used to say you couldn't imagine how delightful it was to drive along on the inflatable tires they used to make then. Much better than now! Your whole body used to vibrate! Poor Mama! And how she did love the gaslight!"

The only thing that made Isabelle Seinecé put up with her husband's landlady's maunderings was the secret hope that one day she'd agree to lease out two of the ground floor rooms until the end of Florent's military service. For nearly five months Mademoiselle Aubier temporized, thought it over, and was evasive. Instead of answering she only smiled or gave a little toss of the head that could be interpreted as either a nod of agreement or a dismissive shake. For at ground level, hidden by the steps leading up to the first floor, a little glass door led into four low but spacious rooms. As it opened, the door scraped noisily on bits of gravel, which gradually scattered and made a similar noise on the tiled floor. To the left was what Mademoiselle Aubier called the music room, where all five of us—six counting Denis—used solemnly to descend at half past two on a Sunday, together with the coffee tray, the coffee beans, and the pear liqueur.

The music room contained two folding armchairs of gray wood, which were extremely hard, another armchair, golden yellow and marvelously comfortable, an upright piano, a sewing machine made of some yellow wood like curcuma, a huge tent of a gramophone without a turntable, a big squeaky cane chaise longue with a broken footrest, a Moorish lamp, a grand piano, and, hanging on the wall in sumptuous frames of gilt and molded plaster, some stringless mandolins and miniature violins on backgrounds of old yellow velvet, between gray and khaki color. A "secret" door—one covered in the same paper as the surrounding walls—led into a large linen closet. Two large rooms on the other side of the narrow red-and-black tiled hallway served as a storeroom and cellar.

The room now used for junk covered about sixty square feet, and Isabelle Seinecé coveted it because it had a little sink set into the wall. She wanted Florent to persuade Mademoiselle Aubier to let them use it as a kitchen when she and Delphine came for the weekend. The child got on her nerves, acting up in restaurants, pretending to be an airplane or a clown or a dog baying at the moon. She was at her worst on a Friday evening, when she was tired and overexcited after the train trip from Dijon.

But what Isabelle really hated—and so, I must admit, did I, because like many musicians I loathe listening to music: it always moves you too much, and for nothing, for either you're furious at not being as good as the player you're listening to or angry because he's an impostor and has no talent at all—what Isabelle and I really hated, then, and so did Pontius Pilate, were Mademoiselle Aubier's song recitals. This ritual, inherited from her mother, took place every Sunday afternoon without fail, and ever since we'd come into her life required the consecration of our presence. She was unhappy if we weren't there because we'd gone to Paris or into the forest or on the river, but she'd go down just the same and sing to her great-nephew Denis, either providing her own accompaniment or doing without. She often sang without any audience at all, but only during the week.

"I'm all upset," she'd say. "I feel like one of the pancakes Mama used to toss so cleverly on Shrove Tuesday. I must sing myself something nice to calm me down. Perhaps Jane de Théza . . . No, I'll have a little go of Massenet's *Pitchounette*."

And as she sang she'd gradually be possessed, and eventually soothed, by a rhythm or even a laugh. But though she liked playing the piano and did so not at all badly, there was no question of her accompanying herself when we were there. And so at a quarter or half past two we'd troop down with the coffee cups, the percolator, the coffee beans, the pear liqueur, and the everlasting almond cookies, or perhaps it would be vanilla "cigarettes." Mademoiselle Aubier would then arrange the members of her audience around the "music room," in which she'd already switched on the electric heater, usually just before lunch. This heater was small and portable, dark green and rather like a cactus in appearance, but despite this link with the desert it gave out very little warmth. We never had a real fire; Mademoiselle Aubier was afraid it might damage her voice. The chairs were set out in a circle. It was like a children's class after the teacher has called the roll. Seats and duties were assigned with tyrannical firmness. Denis was always put in charge of the little spirit lamp and had to turn the strange retort in which the coffee was made. Isabelle or I had to sit down at the grand piano, though it was in much worse condition than the upright and the hammers were unreliable. Then "Mademoiselle," as we called the despotic elderly little girl, would hold her bunch of keys and trinkets in one hand, gaze at the light hanging from the ceiling, with its pink-and-yellow fringed shade, and lift her quavering voice in song. And we would all listen, including Delphine on her father's lap—all to some extent tense and resentful, but also smiling, pitying, and repressing giggles. These last soon got through to Delphine, who sat there literally exploding with laughter. Mademoiselle Aubier loftily ignored our mirth and kept her eyes on the fringes of pink and yellow beads that hung beneath the light globe and were supposed to soften its glare.

The recital lasted only half an hour; its main defect was that it was compulsory. "Shall I give us a song?" she'd say, pretending to hesitate, with her hand over her mouth and her handkerchief tapping her upper lip in perplexity.

"Just as you wish," Seinecé would reply, also sounding as if the outcome were in doubt.

"You mustn't feel you have to," Isabelle would say hypocritically.

"She's going to sing! She's going to sing!" Delphine would cry, slapping her knees without any doubt at all.

I've often thought since then how such rites awaken atavistic vestiges within us, whether at a concert, at the opera, at school, at a meeting, or at the table when one is still a child—whenever a little group hangs on the words of singer or storyteller, priest or tyrant. We're like small packs of prehistoric hunters, forever on the same eternal quest, forever fixing the prey we hunger for with the same terrible unblinking stare.

"My friends," Mademoiselle Aubier would say, "I'm going to sing you 'Butterfly' by Irénée Bergé."

And then I'd watch her, and I can see her still, as she opened her mouth and our little pack concentrated on its prey. Even if it's only a butterfly we watch it as it stumbles and falls, and our lips curl in a smile, and the hunters tear it to pieces and eat it, their eyes wide and shining, clapping their hands, stamping their feet, mouths open and lips glistening. Instead of the little invisible body of Irénée Bergé's butterfly I see a huge stag or giant aurochs with a stake driven through its side. The song of the butterfly swelled a bosom almost as ancient, though hidden beneath a bronze or dark red blouse. The gold chain emerged in the form of a great bunch of lockets, keys, and watches, like a stream that suddenly disappears underground and comes to the surface ten miles away as a river.

There's a certain kind of impulse that we find hard to resist and makes us rush into situations that don't really attract us at all. Thus we keep repeating former experiences which, although they are completely over and done with, still fascinate us like some nameless taste that is at once bitter and delicious. And we burrow into them like a blowfly on a garbage heap, or like Irénée Bergé's butterfly in the mouth of Mademoiselle Aubier, with a strong feeling that we're at home at last. Mademoiselle Aubier wasn't the only one to weave around herself a rich and complex tapestry of prescriptive rites. And it was among rites and rods, hair shirts and discipline—and even King Louis XI's little girls—that Florent Seinecé was most at ease, where he even shone. I've rarely seen a life so liturgical or a person kept so strictly under his own control. His obsessions were in a state of indefinite expansion. Nothing could wear them out, undermine them, or weaken their grip. Seinecé himself loved them above everything, and seemed deliberately to cherish, exhibit, and exploit them. Sensing that his fads and rituals sometimes irked the rest of us, he tried to make us forget them by varying them—in other words, adding to them. He collected bookends, learned periodicals, pebbles, lamps. He was particularly fond of oil and spirit lamps, and Isabelle shared this passion. Admittedly they had some very warm and colorful specimens, above all a Carcel lamp of clumsily and preposterously worked copper, which Isabelle used to fill with a mixture of olive and carnation oil. There was also a magnificent Argan light fixture, but it remained inside its cardboard box. Above all, on the table I've already mentioned, in the middle of the room, stood the Quinquet lamps with their dark and incredible curves—claret, crimson, garnet, and vermilion on a ground of yellow enamel.

"Who's been messing about with my little Minerva head?" he would shout all of a sudden, referring to a bookend in the form of a greenish stucco statuette.

"Nobody!"

"Don't tell lies! It was on the table, to the left, facing the window. And now it's looking the other way! You do it on purpose, all of you."

"You're not going to make a fuss just because I moved that horrible thing?" Isabelle would retort loudly.

"You don't understand—she can't see the light now!"

And the quarrel would gradually escalate. For Florent Seinecé wanted to control not only things but also time itself. Like Confucius. He was an expert on church festivals and the rites of nones, vespers, and compline. The three anniversaries, the four seasons, the five sounds corresponding to the five fingers, the seven canonical hours—all were carefully worked out.

"Who moved my toothbrush?" we'd suddenly hear. Or else he'd suddenly stop eating in the middle of a meal and let his spoon fall with a clatter into his soup plate, the sweat starting out on his brow, "But how is it I'm eating when it's twenty minutes to eight?"

Isabelle swore that every night and morning, either naked and shivering before getting into bed or else naked but warm after a night's sleep, he would crouch by the window pretending he was doing his deep-knee bends, but in fact indulging in interminable prayers, secret Te Deums, and experiments in magic. He'd end up by pouring a small libation—the water left in his tooth glass—onto a moribund bay tree in a pot.

Anything was an excuse for tedious repetition. Everything was a source of guilt. The slightest and most accidental circumstance acted like the yeast in the dough left to "rest" on the blue cast-iron stove at Bergheim. Hiltrud used to tell us not to speak French for fear it wouldn't rise. "The world could come to an end at any moment," he'd say, like an elderly senator in republican Rome. "Some rite not properly performed, and a star falls out of the sky." If I pointed out that the universe he lived in didn't seem all that solid anyway, he'd reply: "The human race is less solid than the universe." And then get tangled up further: "And civilizations are less solid still. My life is a tiny civilization. And a very frail one."

Seinecé read a lot, and always passionately and voraciously related the situations, characters, and descriptions he read about to the most ordinary scenes of his own experience. And this developed into something almost more than pedantry: he applied everything, connected everything, linked everything together, no matter how difficult it might be to do so. I shall never know why.

He was always surrounded with books, photographs, periodicals, and pebbles. I might be reading a musical score. He would get up, take me by the arm, and show me some picture, some reproduction he would relate to himself and tell endless stories about. Suppose it was a Crucifixion he was showing me: he'd point out some curious detail, some farfetched evidence of suffering, name the three being crucified at the same time, and observe how the centurion Longinus's hands, gripping the shaft of his spear, were covered with Jesus's blood. Then regardless of possible irreverence he would tell me what seemed to him a similar story. Of how when he was a child in Africa he and his father used to spear frogs with a fork. It was terribly hot, and they would go through the droning, quivering air to find ponds sheltered from the sun. The frogs in them were too dazed by the heat to move. "We used to go into the shade, moving slowly and silently, our forks in our hands and our trousers rolled up. The frogs would plop languidly into the pond and lie there inert. We held our forks out in front of us, then plunged them into the water, coming out each time with one of those naked, almost human creatures waving its legs about in terror. We filled up a sack with them for dinner."

I think it was Morocco where Seinecé went several times as a child, to spend the summer with his father. But it was a long way away from Morocco—in Ferryville—where his father died later on, in the early fifties. What stirred Seinecé most when he revived this memory—and it must have affected him a good deal, because he often talked about it—was the way his father used to skin the frogs with a penknife before dinner, keeping only the smooth, white, plump, human legs to throw into the frying pan. And as he spoke of it he felt the same pity and remorse as Longinus piercing Our Savior's side.

Thus everything repeated everything else. When he referred to a certain kind of window fastening as a "Cremona," it took him at once to Vergil writing on wooden tablets on the banks of the Mincio. Just as a fork was also Longinus's spear, so a book repeated a flower, a greeting a murder, a drink a deluge.

He was handsome, with a gaunt face and a rapid, low, nervous way of speaking. Usually he waved his arms about, but sometimes he'd be very calm, sitting in the wicker armchair and singing

> Shell, bee,
> Aunt and leaf and sheaf,
> Nail.

And when I remember, when I listen inside me to that fragment of nursery rhyme, I don't exactly weep, but my lip trembles.

Similarly he maintained that St. Peter wept all the tears in the world in the courtyard of Annas the priest. "If only we could write!" he used to say. "But we'll never be able to. Those who could were able to because their pens were made from the feathers of the cock that crowed when Peter wept. The most beautiful things have been written not with a ballpoint, not with a fountain pen, not with a pencil, not even with a goose quill, but between the thirteenth and seventeenth centuries, with pens made from what feathers still survived of the bird of remorse."

But I pursue these memories in vain, like the words people say they have on the tip of their tongue. When memory fails within us it doesn't always hide under some dark rock; it isn't always swallowed up in a deep whirlpool invisible on the smooth surface. Sometimes little twigs or splinters, vestiges that can't be put into words, remain embedded in a gesture, or on our faces, in our eyes, in the sound of our voices; shreds of algae, torn-off legs of little green crabs, bits of shell left behind by the receding tide. That's how I see people and things from the past now. That's how I see the sham marble statuette, made of marble dust really, that stood on the mantelpiece in the salon, reflected in the tilted mirror above. I seem to be sitting in the wicker armchair and looking up at the group—a satyr pursuing a nymph. And this memory seems to hide another. But I can't see what tide has receded, nor what it has taken with it. I can see the nymph and the god pursuing her, but I pursue in vain something beyond that nearer vision, itself pursuing itself; and unlike the satyr, who can just touch the nymph, I cannot reach what it is I seek.

The girl is naked. The sculptor, or rather molder, has given her long breasts that are tense with desire, although she is crouching down, her left hand out toward the ground, her mouth wide open. But her expression is gentle, almost sad, not terrified. The satyr is touching her plump behind, not, it seems to me, with the intention of seizing it but only to caress it. He is smiling, his lips revealing clearly defined teeth. He has long curly hair. He's much older than the girl. His body is muscular, and the mass of curly pubic hair seems disproportionate to the tiny penis, which is not erect. The girl's legs are wide apart. Her whole body is firm and plump. She turns her face toward the man pursuing her but does nothing to elude him or hide her nakedness. She just looks at him with a mysterious smile: not consenting, perhaps even mildly vexed, but sadly, almost pityingly—that is, with pitying contempt. Her smile expresses neither rebellion nor reproach. Nor does it express suffering. It is without illusion; possibly disenchanted. She turns her head, perhaps rather surprised, but her surprise seems to know by heart what causes it.

Mademoiselle Aubier, on the rare occasions when she paid us a visit in Seinecé's room, used to refer to the way the satyr was licking his chops. She had a special way of uttering expressions that seemed to her too affected or too common to be allowed to seem her own. It was as if she were using imaginary quotation marks as tongs to pluck such words out of the fire without soiling her fingers or burning or sullying her lips.

"Little harebrain!" Mademoiselle Aubier would exclaim if Isabelle played a wrong note in her accompaniment. "Not 'hare'—*here!*" This kind of joke so delighted her she'd keep repeating it until Isabelle trembled with fury. On two or three occasions she slammed down the lid of the piano, marched out, and shut herself up in Florent's room.

"It's not specs you need, it's smacks," Mademoiselle Aubier would say, at first unmoved by Isabelle's reaction. But after Isabelle had banged the door behind her, and Pontius Pilate had started to howl, and Delphine stood crying forlornly, torn between her mother's stormy departure and her father's impassiveness, Mademoiselle would lose her temper too.

"What's the matter with her?" she'd boom, turning to Seinecé. "She must have something wrong with her noodle! I can talk as commonly as she behaves, you see! Pontius, be quiet! Monsieur Chenogne, come and sit down at the piano."

I'd get up, her anger would subside as quickly as it had arisen, and she would put the score in front of me, saying languishingly: "And now we're going to sing 'Morn and Evening on the Heather.' " Delphine would climb back on Seinecé's lap, and Pontius would stretch out again on the threadbare Oriental carpet on which you could just make out some palm trees.

Pontius Pilate was goodness personified. He was all devotion to Mademoiselle Aubier, all forbearance toward the world in general, and—though he didn't keep washing his paws—as skeptical as his famous namesake. From this quality he derived a tolerance that was almost boundless as long as no one raised his or her voice. The smile hovering constantly on his lips was that of the Buddha when, as he sat in the lotus position, an ancient and sorrowful fly, previously incarnated six or seven hundred times as a man, alighted on his knee and shed a tear. Pontius had a marvelous way of looking at you, questioning and reassuring at the same time. In the midst of a heated discussion or giggle-provoking recital he seemed to be saying, ironically and somehow beseechingly, "Nothing new under the sun! Or under the lamp!"

It's said that dogs often resemble their owners, and one often notices the opposite influence. Mademoiselle Aubier did look rather like Pilate, reflecting the same amused and sometimes cruel compassion. It may be that after having been her mother's dog for nearly sixty years, Mademoiselle Aubier then became Pontius Pilate's lady companion. I often used to crouch down beside him, scratch his head, and say, "Hail, Pontius!"

I learned to read from *Baron Münchhausen.* Suddenly in the Estonian forest it's so cold that no matter how loud and shattering the calls the coachman tries to play on his horn, it gives forth no sound. Baron Münchhausen of course has a ready explanation: the horn has caught a cold and lost its voice. The coach arrives at the inn. The Baron goes over to the fire and hangs the horn from the mantelpiece. Gradually the frozen notes thaw in the warmth, and movingly, after long silence, the refrigerated calls are heard. Thus do memories crowd in on us, give rise to others, subdivide and multiply.

"Oh, you cute little thing!" Mademoiselle Aubier would cry when Delphine, usually at a good pace, got under her feet. She had turned two and a half, then three, and was a delightful child. Sitting hunched up with her elbows on her knees and her chin in her hands, she would gaze at one of us, the trees, a butterfly, Mademoiselle Aubier singing, a worm, or a sunbeam, with the same amazed intentness, as if taking aim at everything she looked at. These periods of rest lasted four or five minutes every couple of hours, and that was Delphine's favorite attitude. Her thumb would go straight into her mouth whenever the conversation grew too stormy or some emotion threatened.

Seinecé loved his daughter with an exclusive passion. He worshiped her as if she were a tiny goddess. If he got home late on a Friday evening because he'd had to drive the lieutenant colonel to some distant riding club, he would sit on the floor for hours beside his daughter's bed. His eyes must have gotten used to the dark at the same rate that the nursery rhymes he whispered in her ear, if she was awake, grew soft and faint. He stayed there watching her long after she fell asleep. He said he sat on in the dark observing the life that manifests itself so eloquently in children when they're asleep, even in their small fists.

We usually went to bed too late to suit her—or me. It was all the more painful for me to see her sitting exhausted with her elbows on the table because in fact I liked watching her like that: her drowsiness attracted me, as did her eyes, dim with the tangle of images registered during the day, like the wondrous calls frozen inside Baron Münchhausen's horn. She valiantly propped her chin in her hands as she gazed before her, already asleep, digesting her supper, and dreaming with her eyes wide open.

On the table would be the remains of a rhubarb or gooseberry tart, the fruit for which Mademoiselle Aubier had picked herself from the bushes by the kitchen garden. The tarts were usually made in the way I had persuaded Seinecé to prefer them—upside down or with crisscross pastry. Delphine was probably dreaming of balloons, drinking from a magic spring, or discontented dolls. Every now and then she'd yawn immensely, like an old hippopotamus. I yawned too. And I too gradually began to dream. I dreamed of Bergheim and the valleys of the Jagst, the Neckar, and the Rhine;

of France, too, and the flambé tarts we had at my uncles' in Weyersheim and Riquewihr; of how exciting it was when you crossed the border; of my sisters hiding their playing cards, and the six dormer windows in the slate roof that glinted in the sun, and the swings, and Pfulgriesheim, and Hingsingen, and the inns along the Zorn . . .

I grew up with four sisters. I was the last born, the darling, the scapegoat, at the center of all the chatter and ferocity. It left me with a strong taste for solitude and for meals where there aren't too many people. At teatime on Sunday I used to dress up as a priest in a black satin dress borrowed from Hiltrud, one of the chambermaids, and shortened with the aid of clothespins. In this getup I'd do the rounds of my sisters' bedrooms. In each I'd celebrate a brief mass in a vague but complicated gabble and then be invited to take tea and eat bits of cookie and lumps of sugar and slices of raw carrot. I ate, gave a blessing, and moved on to the next penitent. At six o'clock old Fräulein Jutta, our governess, would come and fetch us for the concert we were supposed to give on three half-sized violins, with Luise at the piano and me on a quarter-sized cello. This was the only time in the week when I saw my mother, on the rare occasions when she came to Bergheim. I could just make her out sitting beside Aunt Elly in the dusk, so slim and beautiful in her evening dress as she smoked a cigarette and leafed through the art catalogue that lay on her lap. I kept stealing glances at her as I rasped away. I was really scraping just for her, putting incredible, unimaginable effort into my bowing in the hope of making her notice me.

But she never looked up. And above her neither Psyche nor Eros looked either. They were looking at each other in the light of a lamp whose flame was like a sudden flash of lightning. For over the sofa on which my mother sat while we played our quintets in the salon with the bow window on the first floor, there hung a large but undistinguished nineteenth-century painting of Eros and Psyche. In the picture the maiden is seen obliquely from behind, her hand visibly trembling as she holds out the lamp and the burning drop of oil falls on the splendid though smaller body of the god. And Psyche, represented in the picture with a long white slim body, heavy round breasts outlined against the dark, her head deliberately thrown back wide-eyed, the slender mobile hands stretched out toward another body she would rather glimpse briefly by lamplight than enjoy at leisure in the dark—Psyche, whose mythical fate it was to be changed one day into a butterfly, was somehow like my mother, or indistinguishable from her. And maybe Psyche was somehow like Isabelle too.

Isabelle was incredibly beautiful, but nothing is harder to convey than an impression of beauty or youth after twenty years have gone by and another, still living body gets in the way of the image—an emotion rather than an image—surviving in or reconstructed by the memory.

The first time I really saw Isabelle was in the town of Saint-Germain at the end of April or beginning of May, a cold rainy day of low clouds with a light that belonged to autumn rather than spring. She looked supernatural as she stood there beside Seinecé, dripping with rain: tall and shining in a voluminous dark blue English raincoat that she clutched around her with both hands, her face extraordinarily rosy and transparent beneath a dark cowl-like hood that was much too big for her, her nose spattered with rain and her huge eyes made to look bigger still by the light or the reflection of the rain. Seinecé introduced us briefly.

"Charles, this is Isabelle," he said.

"Hello!" she said, and putting out her hand drew my head toward her and kissed me on both cheeks.

I was taken aback and awkward. I fiddled nervously with the brown army scarf I was wearing round my neck.

"Florent has told me so much about you. I've been quite jealous!"

Her eyes were extraordinarily bright, her nose damp and pink. The wind, cold and wet at the same time, whipped and stung our cheeks. I ran a hand that was itself damp and chill over my own wet face, as if that would help me to see her better. She chewed or sucked at the inside of her cheek—a mannerism of hers. The range of her voice was astonishingly varied; it sounded almost studied.

"Oh Florent, let's go home!" she said, smiling at me. "It's so cold! I feel like a wet blanket!"

Florent had already fondly described to me her habit of using ordinary expressions wrongly or with an unusual twist, though I don't think it was as unconscious as Seinecé claimed. Without exactly doing so on purpose, I think she'd turned an earlier tendency to get things wrong into a foible intended to charm, ridiculous though its manifestations sometimes were. I watched them go on their way huddled together against the wind, which blew her vast blue raincoat against her legs.

Isabelle had adopted the nickname Ibelle, and this was what Seinecé usually called her—and sometimes Delphine as well. She liked inventing new names for things and people, a practice that could be annoying or even hurtful. Our given names, though we didn't choose them ourselves, are a kind of skin that has grown up with us and been fed and watered by all that we are. To begin with we had no teeth, then we got milk teeth, then we lost them; and so with our hair and moustaches and beards, our nearest and dearest and our illusions. But our names always stay with us. It's said they're still used to refer to us occasionally even for a few weeks after we're dead.

"And how are my little Siberians?" she'd say to her parents when they went to see her in Prenois or when she called them on the phone from the house in Saint-Germain-en-Laye. She was making a feeble pun on the fact that they lived in Lons-le-Saunier.* At first the name "Ibelle" made me think of Lisbeth, and the resemblance gave me pain. My eldest sister Elisabeth lived in Caen, married to Yvon Bulot, one of the childhood playmates we used to meet every summer on the beach at Regnéville, near Coutances. I myself always find a lack of seriousness about names displeasing, almost cruel. When I was a child it upset me that people addressed me indiscriminately as Karl or Charles. Lisbeth usually called me Charles. Luise, Cäcilia, and Margarete, my other sisters, called me Karl or even Ka. Cäcilia called her younger sister Ma or Marga, and me "mein Ka." My mother always called me Charles. I worked out elaborate rituals for deciding when it was best to say my name was Karl and reminded myself when I did so of the advantages it might bring. But for the most part I stuck to a simple system of superstitiously avoiding both Karl and Charles.

A similar worry, which lasted a long time, derived from the fact that here were three Bergheims: one in France, near Haut-

* *Saunier* means a salt mine.

Koenigsbourg, about nine miles from Colmar, and two in Germany—one on the Erft and the other on the Jagst. This seemed to me wrong and inexplicable, all the more so because by far the smallest of the three, though perhaps not the least well known, was the one in the south. Ours.

Did my sisters suffer as much as I did from the split in their own given names? I can't say. I think Marga did. Elisabeth and Lisbeth, Louise and Luise, Cécile and Cäcilia, Marguerite and Margarete, Charles and Karl—the transition was easy for the people around us, especially as it was based on an arrangement between Mama and Papa; but it wasn't easy for us. We used to carve our names on the elms and beeches in the grounds, and sometimes even now when I see tall beeches and, more rarely, tall elms, what I think of first isn't the huge garden at Bergheim, it's our names. Not the letters carved in the bark but the sound of our names when someone else pronounced them, as if they were physically and painfully cut into our souls, materializing like breath turning into visible vapor in winter. I still feel the old unease and discomfort: it was as if one hadn't really been christened, as if it were always still to be done. Sometimes I gaze at the tall trunk of a beech or elm or oak from twenty or thirty paces away, convinced that by willpower or concentration I'm going to conjure up—what? Not one of my sisters' faces, not exactly her name, or exactly her body. But something emerging from hiding, as from behind the tree or a stone wall in our old games of hide-and-seek when you thought you had seen a shape behind a tree but there was no one there. Those old games—perhaps they are no different from these pages. You stamp your foot and shout, "You're cheating! I saw you! Come out! Come out!" Even now I think I can see Marga, Luise, Cäci, Lisbeth. I shout, "Come out! Come out!" I think I'm going to conjure up Isabelle—Ibelle—Delphine, or tiny Juliette. And why, if I stare long enough at the thickest and mossiest trunks, shouldn't I conjure up the dead as well? Mademoiselle, Seinecé, or Louise? My mother, or Dido, or Pontius Pilate?

Everything sinks into oblivion. My life, those faces, those little scenes—they all sink into oblivion if I don't write. I just bring a few colors back into the light, perhaps their brightness too. But usually there's no gleam, no smell, only shreds of sounds. Inner hummings. Musicians all suffer from this disease or at least are infected by it, and it never leaves them even in their dreams. If I concentrate all my attention and try to bring the house at Saint-Germain-en-Laye to life again, it's the sound of Mademoiselle Aubier's sewing machine that I hear, just as the clicking of cicadas resurrects the little cottage at Bormes. I owe my love of music to Luise. I could still sing by heart the complete editions of Kuhlau's and Clementi's sonatas that she used to play when she was eleven or twelve and I was three or four. I studied the piano myself until I was thirteen, as well as the cello. The piano was an Erard upright, stained saffron color, and what made me give it up was the shuddering of the copper candelabra. The four candles smelled sour and dusty too. And Luise, at fourteen, decided she was a romantic and that nocturnes and transcendental or appassionata études could only be played by candlelight. She wouldn't even use the special practice lamp. But my memory of all that is vague; I have to make an effort to recapture it. As soon as I was twelve my father started me playing the organ. And it was for my twelfth birthday that I was given my first full-sized cello; an undistinguished but sound nineteenth-century Markneukirchen. This instrument had four little screws for tuning that every so often would take on a life of their own and send me into a fury by clicking or twanging in sympathy with a neighboring string. This makes me suddenly realize a mistake I've been making all my life and that I've just made again: without a doubt I'm a direct descendant of Grimmelshausen's hero, although it was the bagpipes that Simplicius played to frighten anything that frightened him. For a long while I believed that what inspired my passion for the cello and the viola da gamba was the fine collection of them in Mersebourg and the portrait of the duke of Mersebourg himself, who bore some resemblance to Jutta. But this isn't really possible, and my sisters were always telling me that Papa "teutonically" (their word) *decreed* that I should play the cello. Lisbeth was allotted the violin, which she played badly; Luise the piano, which she played well; Cäcilia played the violin too, but so atrociously that it was tuned a fifth lower so that her squeakings wouldn't sound so loud and she could take the viola part; Marga was a remarkably good violinist and, above all, as a child had a marvelous voice; as for me, as soon as I could stand and was able to read my letters and my notes a bit, I was to be found clutching my miniature cello. I imagine that if a sixth child had ever issued from my mother's womb he, like me, would have been destined for the cello and ended his adolescence propping up a double bass. So it wasn't the noise of the candelabra that made me give up the piano at all. We are always ready to invent memories or legends in which we ourselves figure as strong-minded heroes. It was the need to have a second instrument that made me play the piano, and also the custom that decreed that the men of the family had to play the organ. And the choice of the cello, if not the gamba, which became my destiny or at least my profession, was not a decision I made for myself.

I'm very sensitive to individual dialect—to the complex aural transaction that takes place between a person and his or her family, surroundings, social class, and the languages spoken or heard in childhood. This is probably due to the fact that I spent my earliest years in a French-speaking family living in a small town in Germany. To make matters worse it was just after the war. It's probably because of this that I'm more expert than most people in the smallest nuances, more musically attentive to them. Mademoiselle Aubier's language was flowery and old-fashioned. If Delphine ate with her fingers Mademoiselle would say, "Oh Delphine, now you've gone and dirtied Father Adam's fork!"—and she would moisten her table napkin from the water jug and wipe the child's tiny fingers as if she were cleaning up a watercolor. Seinecé's language was mannered, even pedantic. He was always using unusual, rare, crude, or shocking expressions and interjecting affectedly "Can one really say that?" in order to test the other person's knowledge. Delphine's language was that of a child—astounding, marvelous. Isabelle's was uncertain, as if she scorned to be bound by it. It mingled puerility, provocation, and pride, and as she spoke she'd chew the inside of her cheek and look at us defiantly.

"Of course," she'd say on Sunday evening, furious at having to go, and perhaps jealous because we didn't seem sufficiently downcast at having to part from her, "of course, you're all right here—you live the life of pigs in a poke!"

This kind of memory is moving only to oneself. In other people such evocations are unbearably tedious. Another disadvantage is that you only have to mention them for them to come crowding in and carry you away. They're like smells, which touch you in people you've loved and which you can't stand in people to whom you're indifferent.

The expressions Ibelle would loftily throw into any argument were usually so garbled as to be meaningless. I remember her saying once, during a disagreement about the Vietnam War or some terrorist attack, "He who dies by the sword shall perish by the fire!" We both clapped our hands gleefully at this, and she was annoyed and couldn't see what we were laughing at. She was always sure she was quoting from a perfectly reliable store of proverbs known to us all, and as unaware of her own malapropisms as a person often is of the perfume he or she is wearing. Those peculiar sayings were her perfume.

She didn't wear the usual kind. The second time I saw her—it was still May, I think, or the beginning of June, a very hot day in May or June—she was walking down the street, her face and arms already covered with a light bloom from the sun. She wore a little white dress that didn't cover her knees, and faded pink sandals. She was carrying a brown radio set. Mademoiselle Aubier was holding forth to her. "I was wearing my otter-skin collar," she was saying, "and a beautiful hat in shades of mauve, covered with lovely pale flowers—anaemias, I think they were." We didn't listen. Isabelle started to talk to me about Seinecé. She even managed to mangle some of Mademoiselle Aubier's antiquated turn-of-the-century expressions. One day when Delphine kept putting off washing her hands before a meal, the old lady had said tartly, "The way of In-a-Minute and the road of Tomorrow lead to the Castle of Nothing-at-All!" Isabelle rendered this as "The way of In-a-Minute and the road of Tomorrow lead to the Castle of Liberty Hall."

Anyone who didn't experience the sixties in Saint-Germain-en-Laye has never known the joy of living, or at least the feeling of being born anew every day. In the distance we could hear Mademoiselle Aubier singing Devienne's "Spare Me the Rest . . ."

The new "kitchen"—i.e., the old ground-floor sitting room once used as a junk room and now annexed by Ibelle after slow and laborious negotiations worthy of ancient Byzantium—seemed especially warm and bright, though it was low-lying, badly lit, and hidden behind the front steps. Little Delphine used to spend hours messing around at the table. She cut her bread very slowly and carefully, then pulled the butter dish over, and spread a thick layer of butter on the resulting pieces. These "soldiers" she'd proceed to dunk in her bowl, watching the golden globules of fat cling to her spoon. Sometimes she would suddenly jump up and turn the flame out under the milk saucepan. For some reason she was terribly afraid it might boil over. Strewn about between us on the table were always countless sticky pots of jam of every color, together with apricots from the garden, yellow plums, and candies of various hues, shapes, and origins that Seinecé hadn't got around to putting away in his pockets.

Isabelle used to grumble at him. And despite her irrelevant or pointless proverbs, she could express herself very formidably and be cutting and elegant at the same time. "When I think of it all—what life with you is like . . . the dreary future that seems to lie ahead . . . and never any surprise . . . not a chance of anything surprising happening . . . only this cage, this prison of obsessions—when I think of all that, the sun of my life seems nothing but a little electric torch. We ought to invent a deodorant for the absence of smell." Seinecé would gabble an answer extolling the virtues of obsessional people—how hard they work, their seriousness, their accuracy. But Isabelle never listened. She just walked away, and if I happened to come near would say in a regal manner, "Don't listen to him—he doesn't mean what he says." Or, "He's just grousing. Let him get on with it."

On Saturday afternoon, if it was warm, she used to borrow one of Florent's long shirts and lie in the sun to get a tan. Her breasts moved up and down under the shirt as she breathed. The scrape of wooden clogs on tiled floors. Hair washed in the sink. Picnics in the forest or in a corner of the garden, all of us chatting to one another on the grass, safe from Mademoiselle's prudish glances, though not from Pontius's nose.

And in a way it was also like Bergheim in mid-August, when we came back from Coutances. We used to take cane chairs into the bushes so that we could hold our secret conclaves in comfort. Bergheim is a small town set among vineyards and fields of wheat and hops in a valley that leads into the valley of the Neckar, halfway between Bad Friedrichshall and Neuenstadt. My childhood was spent there, and with its Romanesque churches and chapels, its narrow sloping streets, its wooden calvaries, cast-iron stoves, and pink flagstones, it seemed to me, I remember, as old as Mauer's jawbone, the Venus of Willendorf, or the antelope carved on the wall of the cave at Kelheim. I've probably got some of the Swabian stolidness and love of drink in my composition. I didn't think I'd ever go back there. If anyone had suggested it I would have said it was impossible. I shared my mother's hatred of the place. In my memory the house was as old as the hills, as ancient as Lascaux, with its dormer windows in the roof and its bow windows on the first and second floors. The huge compartmented bays protruded into the grounds like the prow of a ship, with red and white blinds that could now no longer be drawn right up, if they ever could, and satin half-curtains on little copper rods that allowed grown-ups to look out over the spacious grounds with a pond in a hollow in the distance, and children to hope that one day they'd be tall enough to do the same. The pond, like the Jagst and the Neckar, was a relic of what had been lakes in the Carboniferous era.

How could one dream of ever setting foot again in such infinitely prehistoric places? And why should such an idea ever occur to me? I was having a wonderful time. My military service would soon be over; that futile, sordid, useless period would be behind me at last. It was June in the Ile-de-France. The weather was incomparably bright and mild. I was getting to know my new friends. It was the garden of Eden. And I could sleep then. I used to be able to sleep for five or six hours at a stretch—six hours without a break, without a dream.

Our eyelids are forever opening and shutting, but in between we don't see very much. One day Delphine was pushing a huge wheelbarrow about, full of heaps of grass and worm-eaten apples. It was a birthday present; Seinecé's birthday was on June 19. Throughout his childhood, he said, his grandmother used to din into him that she received the telegram announcing his birth on the same day that Japan sent France an ultimatum. He lifted his daughter up and kissed her, then built a kind of burial mound with the aid of the splendid wheelbarrow she had just given him. That done, he offered up a sacrifice to his own genius: he poured a glass of wine over the piles of grass, invoked the Lares and the Manes, and scattered sugared almonds and bits of stale macaroon. He then arranged the packages containing his presents from Mademoiselle and Ibelle around the mound, together with the three parcels that with enormous difficulty I'd had sent from Nevers—as you could see from the postmark. Seinecé was made of the same foolish, sentimental stuff as myself. Anything that lent itself to celebration he celebrated.

Delphine climbed on my lap and made herself comfortable.

"Kal!" she said—she was always asking me Sphinx-like questions—"Kal, do fish drink a lot of water?"

I was very unhappy because I didn't know the answer.

Seinecé undid his parcels with much ceremony, letting out great yelps of glee. They included some marvelous little monographs, a Second Empire lamp from Mademoiselle, and candies of various kinds, including Neguses—warm soft chocolate centers with a shiny hard toffee coating rather like the varnish on an old violin. Lastly came the Lolottes de Nevers—creamy-textured fruit jellies wearing saris of crystallized sugar—which Mademoiselle doted on.

"Oh!" she cried. "Lolottes de Nevers!"

What attracted me about them—contact with Florent was beginning to make me more and more interested in candies—was the notion of putting several layers of sugar around a center—around truth, or despair, or desire, or sin. Candies palm a kind of pill off on us, and we feel anxious unless we've identified it with our teeth or tongues. They're like sonatas, theories, religions, love, perhaps even fear—so many layers of varying degrees of sweetness or bitterness clothing naked entities themselves of varying degrees of brazenness or crudity. To tell the truth, that's why, though I'm curious about them, I don't really like candies of any kind. I like cakes: they don't conceal any secret. They never contain a pill; at most you find a lucky charm in them, and then only if the sky is clear enough to follow a star. In a way the rivalry between Seinecé and me, which also bound us together, was a contest between confectionery and pastry. He also liked fish and fishing—another kind of invisible secret, the only sign of whose presence is the strange, slight, multicolored float. I myself am very fond of game—a warm, mobile, visible, tangible prey. And so, again, it was fishing versus hunting.

There was just one exception to my scorn for candies, which belonged to the time when I was a child. It was because of the tins—not the tins that contained almonds, aniseed balls, cherries, or liqueurs hidden from view by sheaths of sugar. Licorice tins. I didn't really care for licorice, but I pretended to like it because I collected the tins from Uzès and Toulouse. Beautiful black or red tins containing licorice in various shapes and forms, and bearing various trademarks: Florent, Zan, Cachou-Lajaunie, Loretta, Millet, Athos. Marga and Luise really liked licorice. The kind they liked best—preferring it to sticks, to the cones that stuck on the tip of your tongue, and to Chinamen's heads—was in the form of twigs, which they insisted on chewing, despite all my efforts to patronize other varieties in the interests of my collection. I remember some of my friends unfurling funereal black ribbons of licorice in the playground in Bergheim. They cost a fortune in Stuttgart and were almost impossible to buy in Bergheim in those most difficult postwar years. Each velvet ribbon was coiled up like an Egyptian snake, surrounding a kind of pearly button right in the middle. The whole thing made me think of a strange curved bow in the end of which the maker had set a fragment of mother-of-pearl.

I still have that collection of tins. I keep treasures worthy of Cortés's galleons in them: paperclips, foreign stamps I save for young Vinzenz and Egbert, foreign coins left over from concerts abroad: pennies, centavos, shillings, agoros, zlotys . . .

But above all—and this was probably the great attraction—when we were children and not tall enough to see in mirrors, we used the tops of the licorice tins as looking glasses.

Isabelle was a very good cook, but only in fits and starts and usually at inconvenient hours. She'd open the door and call:

"Dinner's ready! I've roasted a knuckle of veal . . ."

"But we're having dinner with Mademoiselle tonight!" Seinecé would shout back.

Isabelle would be furious. She'd shout and weep and pound her husband on the shoulders; she'd sulk and sniffle.

"All right then. All right. I know you and Mademoiselle are as sick as thieves," she'd hiccup. And go on complaining, with other weird locutions, that she'd gone to all that trouble for nothing.

We'd try to calm her down. And before long we'd start to laugh. Florent would go and put on a shirt and tie. We didn't agree on this point. Once I'd left the army and started to wear civvies again I refused to put on a tie. But Florent was irresistibly attracted to anything that had to be done up or laced or buckled. I remember the whiteness of the light, which seemed to smell of tarragon or bay leaves. I remember the naked light bulb in that room underneath all the rest of the house, neither cellar nor kitchen. I think there's a special name for rooms behind front steps.

I went into the kitchen with Isabelle. She turned off the gas. A wisp of steam rose from the two-burner stove. There was a smell of bay leaves. I can see and smell that wisp of steam still. Our past isn't really memorable. I don't know why I like recording these scenes from it.

CHAPTER 2

The Cottage near Bormes

> *There be three things which are too wonderful for me, yea, four which I know not: The way of an eagle in the air; the way of a serpent upon a rock; the way of a ship in the midst of the sea; and the way of a man with a maid.*
>
> PROVERBS 30.18

We were released from military service in the last days of May 1964. We were overjoyed then. I'm not sure I don't feel a certain regret now. We'd just lived through sixteen months which we saw as thrown into the garbage bin, into the void. We'd met each other, but affection soon forgets the chance that presides over meetings, and if it's true affection, forgets forever the impersonal aspect of the most irreplaceable friendships. When we parted we were eager to get away from one another.

I went straight back to the cello, selling my practice instrument and buying a Bocquay gamba. Căcilia, who was living with her husband in Glendale, not far from Los Angeles, lent me some money, and I bought a secondhand green four-horsepower Citroën for twelve hundred francs. It was my dream. I made contact again with Jean, Klaus-Maria, Stanislaus Arraucourt, and Madame Clémence Véré. Madame Véré introduced me to Madame de Craupoids, head of the International Music School on Rue de Poitiers in the seventh arrondissement. There was a possibility that I might teach the different viols there when the academic year began in October, and as there weren't all that many students, cello as well. Madame de Craupoids couldn't yet let me know for sure—but this is not the place, nor have I really any inclination, to talk about my professional life, about my real passion. Though I have been staggered by it, dazed, my whole life long. I set about looking for an apartment.

At the beginning of June, wanting to show off my "Four Horses," I went to Saint-Germain. Florent had put off moving until they knew where Ibelle was posted and where he would be working. I also wanted to see Mademoiselle Aubier. In the excitement of the birthday presents and the rush of leaving, I hadn't said goodbye to her.

It was a hot June day, about eleven o'clock. Isabelle opened the door to me, still only half awake and wearing only a camisole and panties.

"Is Mademoiselle Aubier in?"

"Hi!" She offered her cheek, and I kissed it. "She's in the garden."

Mademoiselle Aubier was sitting motionless by a bed of tomatoes and giant lettuces, her eyes shut under her cloche hat. She held both my hands in hers for some time, whispering good wishes for the years to come as though they were prayers. Then she started to chatter.

"You really shouldn't go about in an open-necked shirt. Of course you'll stay to lunch. Papa used to wear pongee taffeta ties—they did suit him. Would you believe it, I mislaid my neck-ribbon yesterday—I was all in a tizzy. And do you know where it had got to? . . ."

I could see Seinecé coming and tried to disengage my hands.

"Oh, here's Monsieur Seinecé," she went on. "You'll never guess. It was tied round the little lamp on the piano. You're a musician, you'll understand—a ribbon stops the voice from climbing too far up the throat."

I showed Seinecé the Citroën. And gave him a box of Lillig bergamot candies. As he got into the car he compared it to the chariot of Hector dying at the hands of the Achaeans, to Delphine's wheelbarrow on his birthday the previous year, and to his own perambulator when he was a baby. I liked the first allusion best, though as I'm writing this I recall the two wheelbarrows at Bergheim. Marga used to pull me round the garden in one when I was small: it was made of thick, soft, worn dark wood, the wheel had a metal rim and screeched loudly, the sides were like great fences, and the bottom had holes in it and smelled of earth and dead leaves. This was a game we played until we were quite old. There were ten years between me and my eldest sister, Lisbeth. For her and Luise I was a sort of doll on whom they tried their hand at being mothers. I didn't mind. But I preferred using the wheelbarrow as a fort or a tank, or a coach in which Marga pulled me around.

Seinecé liked bergamot candies. And really they did look beautiful in the light, as Seinecé sat on the wing of the car with the lid of the tin in one hand: little bits of clear hard yellow glass, with their secret, conspiratorial, sometimes too pungent tang of pear.

"Bonbons," he said. "That means they're good twice over! Bergamots used to be called mother's kisses."

The name sounded droll and strange, like a squared circle, or a lush Norman orchard in the middle of the Libyan desert, or a green Citroën entering Troy during the siege and drawing up at the feet of King Priam.

Isabelle and Florent Seinecé left Delphine in Lons-le-Saunier with Isabelle's parents and went to Ireland. I moved into the sixth arrondissement. Stanislaus Arraucourt was going to be away from Paris for a couple of years, and I took over his three-room, third-floor apartment on Rue du Pont-de-Lodi. It was difficult to practice there because of a crazy neighbor: he liked arpeggios but couldn't stand scales; he was fond of fast tempi but banged on his radiator and threatened murder if I played anything slow or sad. He was a nice fellow, subject to terrible attacks of persecution mania, accompanied by mad howls, and his name was Laineux. In French that means woolly.

André Valasse brought me a kitten as a housewarming present: Dido. She was a little black thing, very timid and trembling. I can remember her when she was tiny, hiding under a low chair, poking her little nose through the fringe on the upholstery to peer at all the plates of food I'd put down to coax her, and then disappearing from view again. Then she took refuge behind the piano, smoothing her fur, licking her paws, and stopping thoughtfully at intervals to look at me. She took some time to decide I'd pass muster. I can understand her. It took me forever.

Isabelle and Seinecé came back in the middle of July and set off again with Delphine for a little house in Bormes belonging to Florent's mother—a two-roomed cottage with a couple of lean-tos fitted out as primitive bedrooms. I was to join them sometime in August. I was still in Paris when Ferdinand Groy phoned. Sthull's great biography of Antonio Stradivari had just been published in Bonn. Groy edited a list of books on music for Gallimard. And that was how for twenty years, on top of my real life as a musician, I came to translate musical biographies from English and German for three or four different French publishers. For doing the Sthull, Gallimard paid what seemed to me (I was twenty-one) a fantastic advance, with which I at once paid Cäcilia back the money I'd borrowed to buy the old green Citroën.

The gods were kind to me. Madame de Craupoids asked me to go and see her at the music school on Rue de Poitiers, near Rue de Verneuil. It was a grimy and dilapidated old townhouse dating from the neoclassical period. I don't know why I was so dazzled by it. If the big front gates—once the carriage entrance—were left ajar, you could look from the street right past the long dark corridor that went through the house to the little bright green rectangle of the garden beyond. Passersby glimpsing this vista would be struck by it and stop for a moment. Perhaps we all have a nostalgic longing for a garden. Seinecé used to say that although he and his family had been city dwellers for generations, he had the same feeling. It seems that a tree, or the color green, anything nonhuman, natural, anything that doesn't shrink from the sight of nakedness—concrete being a kind of enormous garment or armor—anything small or child-sized, ranging from a garden to a bunch of flowers, imparts a tiny pleasure. In the true sense of the word.

The ground floor of the house was very dark because the partitions added in the nineteenth century were built very close together and the stairs, passages, and recesses that gave onto the corridor didn't have any windows. But the higher up you went the lighter and more welcoming it became. A tall window admitted a wide and constant swathe of sunbeams onto the staircase, making its little diamonds of marble look almost yellow. The room in which the cello lessons usually took place had five windows looking out on beautiful gardens. These had been divided up by ivy-covered hurdles or fencing into separate little plots, silent, hidden, selfish, delightful, and very unusual in the heart of Paris, or at least in the seventh arrondissement. But year after year—at least during the nineteen years I spent teaching on Rue de Poitiers—the worthy citizens who owned them, afraid of the earth, the moss, the creepy crawlies, the mud, and the weeds, gradually slashed them down and graveled them over. But what surprised me most was that there was never anyone in them, even in the summer, never any sign of life, not even the murmur of a child's voice.

Whenever I went through the big gates on Rue de Poitiers, whenever I maneuvered my gamba through the wicket and myself after it and caught a glimpse of the tiny garden behind the house, a memory stirred and awakened in me: the memory of the back garden at Regnéville, near Coutances, where we used to spend the summer when we were children—among the rocks or in the salt meadows or on the huge sandy beach, going back home at last to the house at the top of the ancient village. There too you saw a sudden scrap of bright light at the end of a long central corridor. To the left were three cellars where not only the wine was kept but also painting materials, butterfly nets, and anthracite nuts. On the right was a glazed door with loose panes that rattled. When I was four or five years old I managed, after several attempts, to lift the latch, which was stiff with paint or rust: the door itself was very light, and when I pushed it open it swung back, tinkling faintly, to reveal a garden containing wild peach trees, tall grasses, and a willow. And some jasmine. The most intimate place on earth. The core of the world. Little wood strawberries and tiny yellow snails. Heat, the humming of bees, a bench with bare and swollen slats, a huge spider's web stretching from a bay tree to the ivy on the wall. I was the first of my species to set foot in this world. It was Eden.

I'm touchy, greedy, cheerful in company, incapable of confiding in anyone, and passionately fond of being alone. I like reading because it's the only kind of conversation you can cut short whenever and as abruptly as you like. I'm not very fond of sleep, an abyss that's in league with memory. I'm musical as far as playing is concerned. And I quite like reading music. But I can't bear listening to it—sitting there doing nothing, helpless, terrified at the thought that I might dissolve into sobs. I used to get pleasure out of teaching children—more than from teaching adults, to tell the truth—over and above the money it brought in. Their faces, their clumsiness, their dirty knees and calves, their little ink-stained hands whitening with effort, their big anxious eyes—all these are among the things I call beautiful. During a lesson I completely forgot about the mother or grandmother or maid sitting somewhere behind me, her face yielding to drowsiness or feigning rapture. I liked the scared look on the child's face when at the beginning of the lesson I made him or her play long and loud without tuning up. One of my first pupils was called Madeleine Guillemod: she was eleven years old, with bitten fingernails, cat scratches on her hands and cheeks, and bruises all over her thighs. At the slightest comment she'd either burst into tears or dissolve into helpless fits of giggles.

Cats are among the few creatures I'm prepared to talk to unreservedly and at length, and I expect close attention from them. I even like alley cats as long as they purr and chase flies. And I had Dido. I was happy. Stringed instruments are capable of lament, but not of the main human emotions—not groaning or yelping. I prefer the sound of an untuned string to the human voice. But I prefer a look from a cat to the sound of an untuned string because of the silence it springs from and the unremitting cruelty and solitude it evokes. Such looks used to make me excuse my own desires. But I'd still rather have a plum tartlet or a macaroon from Nancy than a look from any cat, even a Persian or a tiger.

I'm as thin as I am voracious. People used to joke about it when I was a child. I was the only boy in the family, and I was violent and tyrannical. When I sat down at table my sisters used to laugh and make fun. "Karolus Magnus!" they'd say. "Hail to the Emperor! Look, girls—Karl der Grosse feeding his face in his palace at Ingelheim!" And of course humiliation made me all the hungrier, and the more they taunted me about my appetite the more helpings of Spätzle I took.

It was extremely hot in July 1964, and sometimes on Sundays I used to drive out to Saint-Germain-en-Laye. Mademoiselle Aubier didn't have a telephone, so you couldn't warn her you were coming. She never invited me to stay the night. We missed Seinecé and Isabelle. They had been in Ireland—I can still see the two postcards they sent me, pinned up on the wall here: no message, just their names—and they had gone back a few days before, she to Prenois and he to the archives at Beaune. "Such a long way away," Mademoiselle would say. "To hell and gone!"

He didn't write, even if he did talk all the time. We were walking through the garden. Mademoiselle had tied the ribbons of her straw cloche under her chin to keep the sun off, even though we were in the shade. "Yes, Monsieur Seinecé can talk all right. Like . . . like what? Like a carrot grater!" said Mademoiselle Aubier. "Sometimes I say to myself, what's he trying to slither out of?" I said speech wasn't necessarily evasion. "How young you are, my friend!" she said. "Alas, I'm a good fifty years older than you, and I've come to the following sensible and useless conclusion: those who talk too much are shying away from something, and those who talk too little are up to no good."

We came to the steps leading up to the house. Mademoiselle Aubier used her parasol to help her climb them. I watched my feet going up the curved treads and remembered that in France architects call the worn, hollowed-out part of a step the "soul." The souls of Mademoiselle Aubier's front steps were gray, deep, and curiously narrow. The same little foot had trodden them for a century. In classical music the word "soul" has a different meaning. And the viola da gamba never has a soul in this sense, or rarely. Soul is the name given to the little wooden cylinder fitted inside stringed instruments between the sounding board and the back, level with the bridge—the focus of all the pressure on the tautened strings. The instrument maker inserts the soul with a little rod called a "soul point" and shaped like a capital S. What was my soul point? Or what fear had I put in its place?

A cello is a cumbersome transitional object. A scrap of blanket, a handkerchief, or a teddy bear are perhaps more reasonable. But it is the invention of the bow, even more than that of stringed instruments themselves, that seems to me really wild. Why should anyone ever have thought of drawing an arc across an arc? It's like the way the immortal cicadas—if they're not immortal, at least they preceded man and will survive him—scrape their wings across their resonators. Only cicadas are better than I, in that they don't make recordings. You take a horsehair arc and hit a catgut arc with it. That's what I will have spent my life doing. In baroque music, which gradually became my speciality, the bow is curved like a child's hoop and held with the player's hand turned downward; he can alter the tension of the horsehair at will with his fingers. The strings mounted on the other arc, the instrument itself, are made from the gut of a dead goat. The bow is made of hairs from the tail of a wild horse. What have you done with your life? I've scraped a horse's hair over a goat's gut.

The organ at Bergheim was a completely different matter, and I often thought I was betraying it, and betraying the fifteen or so Chenognes who had played it. But the organ has never really seemed to me to speak to men, nor quite to go with music. It is the only instrument I know that tries to swamp and blur everything, is inaudible when it is recorded, and speaks not so much to the listener as to its surroundings or God: a flood of sound that from the very first wave irresistibly and imperiously engulfs and invades everything up to the very vaults. Listening to it never seems really individual and human.

And yet we had been in charge of the undistinguished organ at Bergheim for three hundred and ten years, not counting the odd seven years here or thirty years there when a replacement was put in until a son or a nephew of the family grew up, or when a regular kappellmeister was hired. The lower church, the one that housed the organ, was very beautiful and very ugly at the same time: a hodgepodge with a thirteenth-century Poitevin nave and the remains of an ambulatory about twenty yards long, supposed to be from a Parisian workshop. The façade was nineteenth-century—in the style of Louis XVI. On the left as you went in was a large, murky yet distinctly sadistic painting of the mocking of Christ, which used to terrify me as a child. But before that there was a mannerist Bathsheba by Ignaz Günther that was staggering in its beauty and shamelessness.

My grandfather had left Bergheim in 1871 after the proclamation at Versailles whereby Alsace, Baden, Lorraine, Württemberg, and Bavaria were for the first time in their history made subject to

Prussia. My father, like me, was French. He was born in Paris and went bankrupt in the twenties in Condé, not far from Coutances and Caen. He then went to Bergheim and took over a chemical factory near Heilbronn. When the German mark crashed he left Bergheim and married my mother in Paris, swearing to her that he would never set foot in Württemberg again. He played an important part in the Resistance as a member of the Center West network. At the Liberation he went to Germany with the French army and after Potsdam returned to Bergheim. There, somehow taking advantage of the de-Nazification, though this is something I don't really know much about, he bought the family house and grounds back from Aunt Elly, though not the farm that went with them.

My aunt Elly was in dire straits. Her husband had been killed fighting the Americans in Normandy in 1944. She had three children older than us to look after. My father made a large number of highly profitable real estate deals just after the war and died suddenly of a heart attack in 1957, at fifty-five. He had been awarded a major disability pension as a result of his experiences in the Resistance. My mother spent a couple of years with us in Germany early on, but in 1947 she went back to France for good, leaving us children in Aunt Elly's charge. My parents were divorced in February 1949, and my mother remarried in March 1949. She died very young of lung cancer. She used to smoke more than two packs of English cigarettes a day. She died in 1962 at the age of forty-nine, in the Necker Hospital in Paris.

In 1945 my father was the Pharisee, the St. Vincent de Paul, and the Godfather of Bergheim all rolled into one. Our Lord wouldn't have needed to ask him what he had done with his talents. He rebuilt, he helped refugees, he dried the tears of the widows, he helped clothe the orphans, he lent money at low interest, he distributed international aid, and bought out the land of the dead and the starving. Heilbronn, Stuttgart, and Bergheim—distress and humiliation were everywhere, though shame kept people silent. By fighting against the Wehrmacht my father had been fighting against Prussia. By organizing aid and coming, nay hurrying, back to Württemberg he was trying to clear himself, to wash away the Württemberg and family blood he'd shed. But he also did it because charity is good business. And because he couldn't bear to lay down his arms and go from the Resistance to civilian life without a transitional phase that still had a dash of wartime excitement, comradeship, and freedom from restraint. Perhaps too he was trying to elude suffering by working and moving about: my sister Lisbeth still speaks of how frightened she and Luise used to be by his sudden fainting fits. He had lost part of one lung, and underwent brain surgery in 1943.

According to family legend the Chenognes had lived in Bergheim since 1675—when Turenne was dying in Grimmelshausen's arms at Reuchen. In fact the first evidence of their presence dates from February 1761, when a certain Friedr. Chenogne, musician to M. Philippe de la Guêpière, was arrested and, despite the fact that the charge was withdrawn, sentenced to a heavy fine because of a brawl in the inn at Bergheim. Philippe de la Guêpière is much better known than Frédéric Chenogne. He rode away from Stanisław Leszczyński's court in Lorraine and presented himself at the court of Württemberg. He built Monrepos. He built Ludwigsburg. He built Solitude. I can't remember how many times, perhaps chiefly in order to gratify my mother's French tastes, our parents took us on pilgrimages to contemplate the 453 or 463 rooms at Ludwigsburg, the Floralies flower show, the huge French-style garden at the palace of La Favorite, and Nicolas de Pigage's Schwetzingen, "the most beautiful French garden in the world," as it said on a gray sign, "where Mozart and Voltaire . . . ," and so on. But we still liked Monrepos best: there we were allowed to hire boats and row on the lake. The name Philippe de la Guêpière cropped up so often in my childhood that in the end it even put me off Versailles.

My father used to say, "Until the disaster at Sadowa the duchy always fought against Prussia. Württemberg belongs to France just as much as Alsace and Corsica and Lorraine do. Anything else is just an invention cooked up in the Hall of Mirrors!" My father, like all heroes, had rewritten history to make himself look heroic. (As I get older I find this not only inevitable but also quite legitimate—Mademoiselle Aubier, with her characteristic combination of compassion and cruelty, would no doubt have said that it is everyone's duty to see that his own bread is buttered.) Anyhow, my father never tired of saying that France failed in its duty in 1919, maintaining that by not taking back Alsace and Lorraine it had basely handed over the Palatinate and the Saar, Baden, Württemberg, and Bavaria to northern Germany, to which their whole history opposed them. To be quite accurate you would have to admit that their history opposed them just as much to France.

I wouldn't want to give the impression that my father's experiences in the Resistance had left him slightly unbalanced, but I'm sure that if he was one of the first to join the maquis in the west of France it was because of an old and long-cherished hatred of Prussians, Saxons, and Protestants. I think one of the reasons he fought so dauntlessly against the Nazis was a secret hope that Swabia might be avenged and become independent or neutral, incidentally plucking out of the scum and detritus of war those little stylized figurines, the lion and stag of the Württembergs.

The garden at Bergheim was large and hilly. We used to go fishing in the Jagst. In the early fifties my father bought some office space in Stuttgart, but his business was located in Heilbronn, in a big warehouse belonging to a bombed-out chemical factory. I remember the pink flagstones in the narrow street leading up to the house, the little old timbered houses, the rococo fountain. Below lay the church of the Trinity and the belfry. Higher up you had to go past the Protestant parish church, and then you came to the pink flagstones and the little gate into the grounds, and the bushes.

I consult my little diary—the first engagement book I ever had. I see that on August 2, 1964, I joined Florent and Isabelle in Provence, near Bormes, in the valley of the Dom. It was the first time I had ever seen the Mediterranean, and I was dazzled by the little cottage, primitive though it was, without gas or electricity. Yet it was only an ordinary crude little shack with lean-tos tacked on, almost hidden among Aleppo pines and enveloped in oleanders and the incessant song of cicadas. Those black cicadas with five eyes, insects specially created by God to put us off music. There was also a rather ridiculous bougainvillea trying to wind itself around the door.

There were two aloes trees in the garden, and I spent several days trying to make a potion from their leaves, but the result was undrinkable. It was a strange romantic garden with gloomy rocks speckled with mica; lentisks; mimosas; a group of parasol and Aleppo pines near the little house; and in addition to the two aloes bushes the only grapefruit tree I've ever seen.

We gorged ourselves on squash, sea bass, cuttlefish, eggplants, persimmons, octopus, and pomegranates. Delphine stuffed herself with grapes, washing each bunch beforehand at great length because she was terrified of wasps hiding inside.

We used to go down to Le Lavandou or Le Layet to swim among the flowers. A long while afterward I was told that in the seventies the little village had foolishly been renamed Bormes-les-Mimosas—rather like talking about Paris-Pigeon-Droppings or Le-Mans-Pork-Pâté. I had brought all kinds of nougat down with me and tins of aniseed balls from the abbey in Ozerain. I know the abbey of Saint-Pierre-de-Flavigny in Ozerain very well. It's just opposite the hill of Alésia, where on a clear day Seinecé would certainly have caught a distant glimpse of Vercingetorix smoking his clay pipe.

We ate apples straight off the trees. We laughed. We went into the pastry shops, the fruiterers, the port. The Citroën ferreted out pine-sheltered creeks like a dog trained to find truffles under holm oaks. We wandered about, jabbering endlessly.

On the walls were silly Beardsley engravings. In the lean-to woodshed where I slept was a fairly good engraving entitled "Dog Pretending to Chase a Blue Tit," which hung beside a terrible triple shaving mirror. The floor was covered with pink tiles. How cold tiles are to children's bare feet: however old you are the memory of it runs through you whenever you dress or undress. Tiles feel like a frosted windowpane, or a mirror, or an iceberg. Though to tell you the truth I've never come across an iceberg.

When I arrived, after driving all night, Delphine ran to meet me. She had gotten a sunburn—or at least her face had: it looked as if it was made of red Strasbourg stoneware—and she lost no time in taking possession of Dido. She had big blue eyes like her mother, and her mouth was smeared with barley sugar and bergamot candies. She was three and a half, with grubby fingers and hands covered with scratches and cuts. She put the terrified Dido down on the ground and proudly showed me a gash, or rather the scab it had left on her thigh.

Then Ibelle arrived in one of Seinecé's shirts, still only half awake and shivering with cold. "Jeeper's peepers!" she exclaimed, yawning. "You already! That car of yours must be a Talbot-Lagonda!"

I note all this at random. It seems to me I'm giving a bit of life, of my own fate, back to the general chaos. The way you give peanuts to spider monkeys and toss fish to bears.

Delphine showed me how she killed sparrows with a gun that shot rubber darts. Meanwhile Ibelle would be reading with her feet up on the garden table, her fashionable miniskirt showing her long slim young thighs burned almost black by the sun. Or else she'd be outlined against the cottage's one window, at the right of the door that was the only source of light for the kitchen.

Delphine also used to play on the sand at Le Lavandou, building ruins, sand pies that soon collapsed, ancient tombs and wrecked caravels as splendid as the drakkars in the barrows at Öseberg or in the Seine ports that King Charles—or Karl—lost to Rollo the Viking.

I remember the unbearable smell of the geranium essence Isabelle used to leave lying around in saucers on the tables to ward off mosquitoes. She also anointed Delphine with it, and the thresholds of the cottage and the two built-on bedrooms. I must have been a bit of a mosquito myself, or a lover of blood and hater of geraniums, because I couldn't stand the stench and used to smoke accordingly. As a result of my military service I smoked civilian Gauloises, which then cost one franc thirty-five centimes a pack. (I've got the retentive memory of a typical skinflint.) But Isabelle didn't only irritate me. The sun first of Ireland and then of Provence had turned her skin the color of German bass viols, dyed with Cassel clay and roucou. Seinecé was finishing a paper on some strange Medusa-struck heads that had been uncovered in a barracks in Cahors. We had long conversations while Delphine discoursed to the birds, yelling and shooting rubber-tipped arrows that never hit the target.

I seem to remember we were washing the dishes. I had my hands in an old basin, Isabelle was scouring a frying pan, and our bare arms brushed against one another. As we tried to draw away, our thighs touched, making us even more uncomfortable. I was wearing a short-sleeved shirt. Ibelle suddenly caught me by the elbow and looked at me. We stood quite still. Then she took her hand away and went out of the kitchen. My heart pounds even now as I write about it. There are some confessions one isn't really eager to pursue. I remember my sister Lisbeth giving Marga a miniature kitchen set with tin utensils which, though out of proportion with one another, were small enough to fit into a pencil box. The toy kitchen got rather dilapidated with time, but I was very jealous of it. I used to sit surrounded by Marga's saucepans and stoves and ironing boards, intrigued by the lightness, the chill, and the sound of the metal.

I remember the following scene as somehow mixed up with that of the toy kitchen. It happened after the incident over the dishes.

"Where's the jug?" I asked Delphine and Dido. Dido wouldn't come out of the lean-to that served as my bedroom. I had lost the watering can somewhere, left it in some flower bed perhaps, and had taken instead to using a battered old jug of green-and-white glazed earthenware. I had promised Seinecé to water the flowers, which we'd forgotten to do the previous evening. It was thus my job to pour the ritual libation Seinecé had invented in honor of the special gods surrounding the terrace.

When I finally found the jug it was empty, so I took it to the well on the far side of the kitchen garden, by the wall. I trod carefully as I went past the blackberry bushes as the lower canes were overgrown with nettles. Ibelle was there, again in one of Florent's shirts, spreading blackberries on a piece of bread and butter.

"Where are you going, Charles?" she asked.

"Hi," I answered.

"Don't you think it would be a good idea if I made a purée? A blackberry purée?" she said thoughtfully.

I went through the honeysuckles and along by the wall, and put the jug down on the slimy coping of the well, under the spout of the pump. When I worked the arm of the pump it produced a loud, raucous, wheezy, heartrending screech. The water was a long time coming. Its gurgles and wails stirred up dim memories of Regnéville and Bergheim. Then suddenly it arrived and gushed forth. The pump was old and the lever stiff and difficult to work. The water came in sudden icy spurts, trickling into the jug and splashing my legs. As I was working the pump I suddenly sensed a hand on my shoulder. It had been put there, close to my neck, while I was struggling with the lever. I could feel it resting on me. I don't think I wanted to understand at first and just stared at the condensation gradually forming on the metal of the pump and the chipped green surface of the jug. Her body, the sudden presence of Ibelle's body, her hand, the weight of her hand—I turned around. I took her hands. Kissed her. We kissed each other. Or at least our lips touched, our extraordinarily dry lips, so dry our mouths seemed to have been emptied of saliva, as if we were dead; our lips touched and we kissed the void. Then I drew back—or rather, with my head still stretched forward to kiss her, I pushed Ibelle's body away.

"No!" I said, and yet wanted to kiss her. She was naked under the shirt, and as I clutched at her to push her away I could see her pubic hair.

"No," I said again.

What I dreaded most was that she might look down and see how I'd been physically affected by our kisses. I wanted to run away. But the more I tried to get away from her, the more I imagined she tried to cling to me. I thrust her away more roughly and ran. I forgot about the jug.

I ran. I didn't stop till I got to the steep path that led up to Bormes. Just where the path became a narrow street an elderly man was padlocking an iron gate. He tottered slowly toward me—he must have been very old, and as he went past he yelled at the top of his voice, "Did you hear about the lads down the mine at Champagnole?"

I began to get my breath back. I told him, still panting slightly, how awful I thought the accident was. Then I said goodbye. I was calming down. I went into a café, though I didn't have any money on me, and in order to get first a brandy and then a beer I had to leave my watch as a guarantee. I remembered the pond hidden by reeds in the garden at Bergheim, beyond the coppice and at the end of a path lined with chestnut trees. The pond was full of hydra and tadpoles. Paula was fascinated by it. When she was small she was in love with me, or with the pond. My sisters used to call her Popo to annoy me: in German it's a childish euphemism for "bottom." I was quite willing to flatter myself that she liked me; she laid claim to all my drawings and was always trying to touch my hand. Standing by the pond in our gray duffle coats, we had exchanged the same dry-lipped kiss as Ibelle and I had exchanged just now. And the scared and despotic puritan in me had felt the same resentment.

To tell the truth I can't quite remember if the first of those kisses really did take place by the pond—all I'm sure of is the impending danger from Aunt Elly or Fräulein Jutta. It might have been on the towpath. Obviously I don't like dwelling too long on the scenes at Bormes, the scenes with Ibelle. Whenever we went along the towpath with Aunt Elly and she saw someone fishing, we were treated to black looks and gestures to match, urging us to keep quiet and not frighten the fish. As a result it is fishermen rather than cathedrals, churches, or temples that inspire in me a fearful silence and make me feel so guilty at the thought of breaking it that I hardly dare breathe until I've tiptoed past. For me they're like the idols in the temples at Harappu or Ur. Or the bodies of my mother and Luise in the morgue. Like the scarcely human shapes of motionless, pitiless gods ranged along by the water. Like humiliated, widowed, ruined mothers and aunts, completely Calvinist however Catholic they claim to be, staring at a cork float that stands for their nephew's or son's unforgivable sins.

"Tinten! Tinten!" Anchor, ink, color, blot, sin, mess—a stain that neither scraping nor soapy water could remove. I used to dream in German. I do so still if I've done something wrong. What wrong had I done concerning a jug and a well? It was woven into the substance of my dream: I had been dreaming around a word in German. When I dreamed of happiness—damp dreams about shady streams and banks—it all turned around the name of Bach. But if I was unhappy I dreamed of anchors. I would be jumping off a ship to rescue the anchor I had accidentally let slip. I dived into the sea, and it became the ink from a cuttlefish trying to blind me. It chased me and rang at the garden gate: "Tinten! Tinten!" The cuttlefish was clinging, alive, to my lips. The word *Tinten* means anchor and ink, and what children call bad luck. Where was I anchored? Was I German? Was I French? Mama had left us to choose between Germany and herself. What had we done wrong? I used to wake up angry. I still wake up angry—assuming I've been able to sleep. I cut the night short and dismiss the daydreams that lurk for you when you wake. I can't find a solution. I'm more likely to find pain or suffering. How little we know ourselves.

To go on with the maritime imagery, morning is a boat without oarsmen washed up on the shore of the day. And there I am. And to tell the truth, by noon it's a question of oars without a boat. In my left hand the hard wood of the fingerboard, in my right the bow for so many hours that it gets heavy. As for the evening, on the whole I prefer not to pursue the comparison.

I can't bear listening to music. My friends see this as an unseemly affectation. Music fascinates me more than anything else in the world, but it hasn't always interested the people I love. Few years have passed in which I haven't translated a musical biography or recorded or edited some baroque composer—Demachy, Muffat, William Lawes, and the like. Or even more often some unknown or unpublished composer, like Maugars, who played the viol for Richelieu: I've made three recordings of his mournful and moving music. I have the same aversion concerning language. I was brought up on German, and I can't bear either to speak or to write it. It's obvious I'm trying to side with the person who forbade us to use it. To be quite frank I don't know if my mother really hated German, but my sisters and I always clung to the belief that this was her sole, inadequate reason for leaving my father. There was another thing too, something that can never be cleared up: one of her relatives, I don't know which, died in Belsen during the war. And her younger brother François was run over by a Wehrmacht half-track. I have always believed he died in May 1943, when I was born. I think this proscription against Germany explains my paralysis when it comes to the German language, though it was the language I spoke as a child and the medium of instruction in all my lessons, including music. But I've never used German for the letters of the alphabet, and for a long time I said "*la ti do . . .*" though I've always begun with standard pitch rather than with *do*. Anyhow, the tuning string on the cello is *la*.

I've helped myself to words from both languages. My pupils—the younger ones, at least—often used to correct me. I used to say *dur* instead of *majeur*: I liked the idea of the major being *dur*, which in French means "hard," and the minor being *moll*, which is like the French word for "soft." You can't help forging links, and at least you forge so many of them in a lifetime you might hope they'll strangle you one day. But shared aversions make for the most lasting friendships, and they've stood me in good stead in bed, too.

The first time I felt our bodies being attracted to one another, felt that it was natural for them to touch and to be stirred by touching, strikes me as rather ridiculous, yet there was also something marvelous about it, down-to-earth as the circumstances were. At the corner of Rue de Beaune and Quai Voltaire there's a restaurant where the food is not particularly good. On one of the last evenings in May 1964—before we handed in our kit bags—Seinecé and Isabelle, André Valasse and Louise, Paul, Klaus-Maria, and I all met there for dinner to celebrate our "release." Nehru had just died. We talked at random. We drank a lot. I ordered profiteroles for dessert. Ibelle, sitting opposite me, ordered a magnificent Napoleon smothered in powdered sugar. She kept eyeing my plate and I hers. My passion for dolls' tea parties got the better of me, and I said, "Would you like a taste?" Her eyes shone greedily and she bent over. I took a spoonful of pastry and ice cream and held it out carefully. She leaned forward with her mouth open, and I felt rather than saw the touch of her teeth, the pressure of her lips on the spoon. I felt it right up to my shoulder—and if it wasn't absurd or romantic (but then I *am* a romantic) I'd say I even felt a little jolt in my heart. We looked at each other, sharing our pleasure in pastries, but in a communion that to tell the truth was more than merely symbolic. She in turn held a morsel of pastry and French cream out across the table. It was a delicious offering, and she had blessed it; I shrank from eating it, but when I did it melted inside me. Eating and drinking like that, it wasn't exactly the exchange of spoons and salivas via the food that aroused me—it was the shock of contact that created desire. Or rather it resembled and prefigured the resistance I felt when I was working the pump at Bormes—the stiffness of the handle, the gushes of icy water trickling into the jug—and Isabelle tried to kiss me, and I tried desperately to embrace her and push her away at the same time. The later resistance recalled the resistance of the fork offering the piece of Napoleon on Quai Voltaire, of the spoon offering the piece of profiterole. Perhaps that was really the first time that Ibelle and I made love.

The next time we met was by the grapefruit tree near the Aleppo pines. I implored her.

"All right—we won't touch one another anymore," she whispered.

"It didn't mean anything!" I begged.

"No, just a flash in the pan."

"So we're still in the frying pan."

"Right. It never happened."

"Shake hands on it!"

I held out my hand.

"Shake hands, Ibelle!" I insisted.

And she did.

We separated. I gave Delphine her tea. We sang a nursery rhyme about a greedy little girl.

I was trying to avoid Isabelle, who had gone down to the beach at Le Layet. Seinecé was still poring over his Medusa-struck heads. Delphine had chocolate all over her face and hands, and I washed her with the watering can, which I'd just found near the grapefruit tree. We sat among the lentisks and cork oaks, and I cut her nails. I told her about how Baron Münchhausen only cut his once every forty years because he used them as shovels to move whole cities and forts about.

In the evening I went out. But I dreamed of her that night. I dreamed of her most of the nights that followed. Several times her image wetted my hand and my belly.

* * *

I played with Delphine. I was trying to forget. That year there was a plague of wasps. I hunted them ruthlessly. I was trying to protect Delphine. Sometimes I killed them. I remembered how as children we used to see who could collect the most dead wasps and how we hated ants, earwigs, mosquitoes, locusts, bees, slugs, caterpillars, and beetles. We were terrified of hornets, men, and spiders. But we liked grasshoppers, earthworms, tadpoles, and flies, and felt friendly toward snails, pine cones, squirrels, frogs, minnows, and butterflies.

On August 10 Seinecé and I went back to Paris. Isabelle had been posted to Rueil-Malmaison, nine miles from the capital and just south of Saint-Germain-en-Laye. Seinecé was hoping to get a job in a Paris museum. Friends in Saint-Germain rallied round, and after much telephoning Denis Aubier and André Valasse rented a small house for the Seinecés in Chatou, not far from Mademoiselle Aubier's, with a little garden for Delphine. So we moved, or rather decanted, the contents of the salon at Saint-Germain. It was then that I had the signal honor of being allowed into Mademoiselle Aubier's bedroom. Seinecé envied me for this as long as he lived.

"You've been into Mademoiselle Aubier's bedroom," he'd say whenever he wanted to make fun of me, or to reassure me if I complained about the undistinguished future I was letting myself in for. As if that visit constituted some miraculous success. It was a big, typically nineteenth-century room, fitted out in the English fashion with pale wood paneling, beveled mirrors, and ample gray velvet curtains. The bed was in a recess hung with voluminous drapes.

Mademoiselle Aubier was lying on a brown plush chaise longue when I entered.

"Come and sit down, Monsieur Chenogne," she said, pointing to a white armchair near a large ever-blooming mimosa, the scent of which I found particularly heady after Bormes.

"Oh," she said, "how I used to love curaçao!"

But she couldn't think of anything else to say. She was really very embarrassed that I was there. There was another silence. Then she told me how she wished people still said "oilcloth" instead of "American cloth."

We had to make three or four trips in the Citroën to move all Florent's books, bookends, lamps, and stones. That summer

Mademoiselle Aubier wore white: a white serge dress and a white wide-brimmed hat tied under the chin with white tulle ribbons.

Seinecé saw Mademoiselle Aubier as a kind of mother; at least he was always comparing her character and attitudes with those of his own mother. The latter, according to him, had one intolerable defect, which seemed to get worse and more exasperating as she grew older: whenever he went to see her she would regale him with reminiscences about his childhood that had nothing to do with what had actually happened, describing mawkish scenes and deeds of derring-do that he wouldn't go into detail about. She recalled witticisms he was supposed to have uttered at the age of one or two or even in the womb, aphorisms as weighty and profound as La Rochefoucauld's *Maxims* or the Book of Amos.

Seinecé would remain polite and indifferent as long as he could, but he and his mother would soon be at it tooth and claw. The imaginary reminiscences were infuriatingly cloying and sentimental, and their "morals" irritated him. But when he tried to reinstate the truth or at least introduce a bit more objectivity, his mother got angry, as if it was he who was lying.

"You always look on the black side," she would say. And then she'd lose her temper, and her account of things would lose all its sugariness and exaggerate in the opposite direction. At this Seinecé too would get carried away and remind her of things that had such an impact on their lives at the time that she couldn't have forgotten them, but she only shrugged and wouldn't listen, swearing he was making it all up. The worst of it was, Seinecé said, that she seemed to be speaking in good faith, and so of course was he, or at least he thought so. One day he had just been talking to her on the phone. It was very hot in Marans, where she lived, and she couldn't stand the heat, but even so she'd managed to dredge up some more wonderful stories about his childhood. What was really upsetting, he said, was that the closer she got to death, the plainer it was to him that their shared past simply didn't exist. All their memories had crumbled to dust while they themselves were still alive.

Seinecé's father, unlike my own, had spent most of his time away, working abroad. So Seinecé had been tied to his mother's apron strings and even slept in a cot in her room. But the tie would often be broken, and this may have accounted for the pitiful rituals he was always indulging in. He told me there was no fear to compare with what he felt when he was very young and his mother got dressed to go out, leaving him alone in her room with a night-light, the telephone, and some candies. It's quite a common ordeal but it seems very cruel to a child: as soon as he's swallowed his tea, to be gripped by anxiety about the night and lie with his head under the blankets trying to stifle the fear of being alone and the distress that goes with it. I found it hard to imagine Seinecé as a little boy wandering around his mother's room hoping for kind gestures or caresses, the sobs gradually gathering inside him, but ashamed at the thought that he might not manage to be brave. Sometimes he couldn't hold out, couldn't wait until she'd actually left him, and would go to the bathroom, where she couldn't see him, and shed the first, hottest, saltiest, tears of the evening. Tears do lessen pain, but there's nothing comforting about the exteriorizing of pain, the horrible transports behind a closed door, the rebelliousness, the wild fantasies that try to mollify sorrow.

Fortunately it wasn't a nightly sorrow. It happened only one night out of two, like one of those syncopated tunes that jolt the heart. Terror made him jump out of the bed where she'd tucked him in. He would reach for the candies on the chair beside it. Then feel thirsty and run to the kitchen for a drink to wash away the cloying taste. Then start to cry and stamp his feet and call out at the front door until he fell asleep with exhaustion. As if he were a little brother of the doormat lying parallel outside.

Seinecé put his hand on my arm and roared with laughter when he recalled all this, saying: "Yelling and stamping your little bare feet by the door is a first-rate soporific!"

Moving the furniture into the little house at Chatou took Seinecé and me a day longer than expected. Ibelle's parents had gone to Prenois from Lons-le-Saunier in order to organize things from there, but the moving van they'd hired had some sort of delay and arrived about ten hours late. The more I found myself alone with nothing to do, the more I thought about Ibelle and Ibelle's body, and the more I suffered. I was trying to repress the beginnings of an inward rage and anguish. We didn't want to start out for the Mediterranean again during the day—it was August 15, the middle of the long summer holiday period, when crowds of people would be on the road. So we planned to leave in the evening, and that was how Mademoiselle Aubier came to have an unexpected audience. At a quarter past two, after we'd finished off lunch with some tasteless stewed pears, she rose and said we must go down to the music room. And I suddenly wished she'd die. She tapped me on the shoulder and I stood up. Once again I opened the yellow mahogany Erard. She rummaged about among the scores and brought out something pink and torn.

"Shall we have a song?" she simpered.

I would have given months of my life for the ceiling to split asunder and come crashing down on her head. I couldn't take these stilted imitations of a bygone age anymore. We gave each other the note, or rather tried to produce some sounds that wouldn't be too discordant.

Then a brownish, quivering hole opened up in her face, a shaky, quavering voice came forth, and I averted my eyes from the heavings of that ancient bosom.

By the morning of the 16th we were back at Bormes, telling Isabelle and Delphine all about the little house and garden at Chatou. Isabelle was strange and preoccupied. She kept out of the way, and I stayed in as little as possible. I took the Citroën and went bathing, or dozed and read on some beach.

The summer got hotter and hotter. Isabelle wanted us to cut our stay short and leave, to put an end to the cat-and-mouse game that was also some kind of flirtation. She was anxious, too, to see and arrange the little house at Chatou, to meet her Saint-Germain friends, and prepare for Delphine's first term at school. But Seinecé had almost finished his thesis and wanted us to stay there one more week. The Medusa heads were at last beginning to produce their effect. But on the 22nd Seinecé got a telegram to say his mother was unwell. He phoned Marans from the post office in Bormes. The weather was extremely hot, even on the Atlantic coast: it was only a little attack, his mother told him—nothing to worry about. He called her every evening. Isabelle had decided to go to Chatou on the 28th or 29th to check on how we'd arranged the furniture and so on; we hadn't been able to tell her very clearly what we'd done with things.

When Seinecé called up on the 28th the phone was answered by a nurse—a surprisingly brusque nun—who said his mother had had another stroke and couldn't speak to him. Seinecé was frightened, and it suddenly struck me that his telling me so much about his mother at Saint-Germain-en-Laye, during the move, was a kind of presentiment. He asked me if I'd mind driving him to La Rochelle, or rather to Marans, which was nearby. Isabelle asked him if he'd really like us all to go. He didn't think there was any point in Delphine coming, in being there to see him suffer and see his mother on her deathbed. So we drove Isabelle and Delphine to the station in Toulon, then shut up the house and set out for Marans.

We got there at about five in the afternoon after a long and almost silent journey. But I remember it as a beautiful drive through regions whose names I didn't even know. It was a huge old gray house. We hurried up to Madame Seinecé's bedroom on the first floor. She was lying there motionless, hollow-eyed, her face transparent, her mouth dreadfully puckered up because she hadn't got her teeth in. She didn't move when we went in—neither her head nor her hands gave any sign. Seinecé went over and clasped her fingers, thin and white, ivory white, the color of dominoes, against the white sheet. She smiled—or rather a smile flickered across her eyes. We tried to say something comforting. Seinecé said how marvelous the weather was and asked her if she'd like him to open the shutters, but she didn't answer and he stood there helpless, looking suddenly panic-stricken. The nun, who had a red face with marked features, rather like François I, came up from the kitchen, took Seinecé aside, and spoke to him in a very audible voice.

"It's very good of you to come," she said.

He whispered some reply.

"You can speak normally, she can't hear you. I don't suppose she can see you, either. But you never know. We all have a natural need for affection," she bawled, "and we probably begin and end with that small need."

"Yes, Sister."

"She eats, she urinates, and she needs affection," she repeated.

"Can't she speak anymore?" asked Florent timidly.

"No," said the nun firmly. "Do we speak when we're born? Did you speak when you were born, Monsieur? We come naked into the world, and naked we go out of it."

"Yes, Sister."

"Your mother no longer has all her faculties, but we can never say she's a vegetable. For me she's still a human being. Her sphincter muscles still work. An occasional little accident . . . But not very often."

She thought for a moment and went on more mildly.

"But even if all her reflexes had ceased to function," said the metaphysical nun with François I's rubicund countenance emerging from her wimple, "vegetables and animals are equal in the heart of Our Lord."

I went down to the kitchen. I wanted to go have a look at La Rochelle. Seinecé stayed upstairs for a while, but when the nun told him she had to give his mother an injection he came down and joined me. He told me, though not very gaily, how the nun—a very saintly woman, nonetheless—had adduced various arguments and quite convinced him that God had a place in his heart for vegetables and even for nuns. I told him I'd looked through the cupboards and the refrigerator and was going out to do some shopping.

"Mother's had her injection. I'll come with you," he said.

We went to a co-op grocery store. I have a grotesquely acute memory of it all: we bought turnips, leeks, potatoes—Seinecé had decided to make his mother some broth—sausages, and wine. When we got back I piled all the things on the kitchen table, and he went up to sit by his mother while I put some water on to boil. When he came down again I was peeling potatoes and happily gouging out the no-doubt-psychosomatic defects called "eyes." I could feel him standing behind me. He was staring into space, his mouth hanging open.

"Cry," I told him.

His lip trembled.

"Go on, cry," I said.

Then I put my arms around him. We put our arms around people who are suffering because we can't bear to look at them. He stammered out that she must have died while we were at the grocery store. He blamed himself for not being there. He practically didn't speak for two days. I saw to everything. He didn't want me to send for Ibelle and his daughter.

We know not the day nor the hour. It comes as a thief in the night. That was how God in his infinite mercy conveyed death to man, according to my missal when I was a child. On the morning of the second day Seinecé told me about a nightmare he'd had, which intrigued me because it consisted only of smells. He was walking toward a heap of dead wood and was surprised by the smell of damp and mold the logs gave off. It was the smell of delicious mushrooms, morels perhaps. He saw in a dream a morel omelette.

He also remembered the endless scenes between him and his mother, tense and tedious battles in which they'd hurled conflicting memories at one another as if they were arrows or cannonballs. He couldn't get over the terrible thought that he hadn't been able to share any kind of past with his own mother. But then he realized, and it was a considerable comfort to him, that there never was any common past, there never was any past that could be shared: the only things there were to be shared were legends. This idea descended on him like a bolt from the blue. It had a dual effect. He was appalled to realize he was so alone, alone until death, yet at the same time he was suddenly free of the notion that had nagged painfully away at him for so long—that he and his mother had spent years jealously wiping out the past so that nothing in their two versions would coincide. Now it was all quite plain. And simply, terribly, he had outlived her.

He sniffed, snorted almost, as he wept. I'd phoned Isabelle twice at Chatou. Finally, Seinecé called her himself. They talked for a long time. He told her we couldn't possibly be back until the evening of September 2nd or the morning of the 3rd. The lawyer was away on vacation all the month of August. Delphine was well, Ibelle said, and played in the garden, but she left her with Mademoiselle Aubier in the afternoons. Everyone was very helpful: Denis Aubier, Louise Valasse, Paul. She thought about us all the time.

Seinecé had another strange dream, in which the word "singultus" appeared to him written in Gothic characters on a medieval banner. He was very proud of this vision, which might have been the prophetic dream of a Roman emperor with a good opinion of himself, and went on and on about it. He thought up all sorts of interpretations of the word on the banner—such as "sole" or "sob." This got on my nerves, and I tried to outdo him. His word somehow made me think of another. It was on the tip of my tongue, but to my annoyance I couldn't pin it down. I grew even more irritated by my friend's maternal and Roman preoccupations. I hate the Greeks and the Romans. I can't read a name ending in *-us* without a feeling of loathing and a desire to bite—a desire both to bite and to swallow. I say to myself, "I ought to have a chance to get my own back!"

In Bergheim, in the year that corresponds to the seventh grade in France, my father arranged for me to be taught Latin and Greek by the Protestant minister, even though we were Catholics. My sisters were very unfairly let off the classics because they were girls. Herr Hans Nortenwall, involuntarily and unsuspected by me, added a whiff of the wars of religion and of the Franco-German War to his teaching. One wrong hiatus or elision in a Lucretian hexameter and it was as if another Protestant were being thrown out of the window on Rue de Rivoli. Aeneas in burning Troy was also the eve of St. Bartholomew and the German army in Strasbourg.

"Havergeiss!"—the word came back to me at last. There used to be an old ebony Havergeiss or Habergeiss in Bergheim. I adored it. I wasn't going to let Seinecé take it away from me even in a dream. It was a special kind of spinning top with a wide hollow body about eight inches across. You pulled on the string and it jumped around in circles, very fast, producing a humming sound, at first quite terrifying like that of a huge wasp, then settling down into something more mournful, like an owl or a cello, knocking against chairs and tables, steps and tubs of flowers.

As I remember it, my mother preferred little Meissen animals to little boys.

But I loved her. We are jealous even about the dead, even about other people's serious illnesses. The death of Florent's mother conjured up in me, almost in a spirit of competition, memories of the death of my own mother. And it was almost as if I'd never actually experienced it. I have an odd way of setting down my memories. I can never make out what links them together, and yet the pattern seems quite inevitable and self-evident. I break down fragments of the past the way I used to dismantle Easter rabbits on the kitchen table. I can still see the excitement of that particular day, and the marvelous eggs, all colors of the rainbow, that the Easter bunny laid: the sugar rabbits in their shiny wrappings that I patiently tore to pieces, my mouth watering, on the kitchen table. Luise sent me sugar or marzipan bunnies for years, accompanied by a little ageless, almost childish note. Always something like: "My dear Karl, here are the rabbit and the eggs. I wish you a happy Easter. Much love from all seven of us. Luise." She had five children. There used to be five of us. Now she's dead too.

My mother's death seemed so recent. I'd flown to Paris and gone straight out to Neuilly. "Yvonne! Yvonne!" But I can't bear to think of it. It was October 22, 1962. The day John F. Kennedy announced the blockade of Cuba, the day my mother died, the day of General de Gaulle's referendum—de Gaulle had of course been my father's great hero, duke of Württemberg or no duke of Württemberg. When I looked it up in the encyclopedia I found these things didn't really all happen on the same day, but they all merged together like a wound. They became an unforgettable mnemonic, as if all concentrated into one minute of time, somber, black, bitter.

Latin and Greek weren't the only things I hated. As Mother loathed German and wouldn't speak it, I almost stopped using it myself, and the sudden irruption of a word from my childhood—such as Habergeiss—invariably depresses me and makes me almost suicidal. Rebelliousness was the distinguishing virtue of the Württembergers, my father used to say, thus justifying the way he'd lived his own life. According to what Herr Stodt used to teach us at school in Bergheim, though I must say it sounded rather odd in the late fifties, the dukes of Württemberg claimed that the first word their subjects uttered after they came into the world, and the last word they said as they gave up the ghost, was "Nein."

I gradually came to dislike all German words, especially "Nein." I may not have been the spitting image of my mother—our passions are not really very much like us—but everything in me tried to be. I still seem to hear the noise of the heated arguments. My father maintained that all northern Germany was inhabited by savage yetis, and the German language had never produced anything spontaneously and of its own accord: he compared it to the Latin of the Roman army in Greece. "It's an imported literature!" he'd cry. My father's fixed ideas were in fact variable and confused. At one moment he might be obsessed with reviving ancient Lotharingia; at another with revising the frontiers of and restoring the duchy of Lorraine, the margraviate of Baden, or the old county of Württemberg. All this would prevent the revival of fascism, weaken Deutschland forever, and ensure peace for a hundred years. I can't remember now what my mother used to say, or rather used not to say. She either remained magnificently beautiful and obstinately silent, or answered in a brief, curt, fierce, malicious whisper. But my father never tired of telling us, "Never trust countries that haven't had a Renaissance or classical period! And Prussia's one of them!" Such apostrophes still scare me and make me tremble, even more by their tone than by their stupidity.

We thought we'd be staying in Marans for five days, but we were able to leave after three. The lawyer came back early from his vacation. We couldn't get in touch with Isabelle, but by dawn on September 1 we were on our way, through violent rainstorms after Azay-le-Rideau. Sometimes it was so bad I had to stop the car. On the outskirts of Versailles we had a flat. We didn't have an umbrella and had to change the tire in the rain. We arrived in Chatou at about three in the afternoon, though the sky was so dark it might have been the middle of the night. We dashed from the car and ran straight into the house, drenched to the skin. "I'm going to take a bath," I said to Seinecé. "Do you want to go first?" As we rushed up the stairs two at a time I tried to pull my sweater off over my head, but it was so wet I got caught in it and Seinecé went ahead and opened the bedroom door.

Suddenly I bumped into him. He was standing stockstill, a look of utter shock on his face. I looked past him to the cause.

They were crying out in their pleasure.

Florent went into the bedroom. They didn't hear him, and the sounds grew louder, the lovemaking more intense. He switched off the light. They were suddenly silent. Everything was silent. Seinecé came back to where I was standing, closed the door quietly, and walked past me. His jaw was set, his face as white as his mother's hands had been against the sheets. He went into the bathroom and locked the door.

I didn't know what to do. I was soaking wet. Suddenly the bathroom door opened and a hand came out with a towel. I took it. Florent locked himself in again. I didn't know what to do. I mechanically dried my hair and face. I saw the furtive shape of a man slink out of the bedroom, along the wall and down the stairs. I heard the front door shut. I thought it would be best for me to leave husband and wife alone; that Seinecé had indicated that he wanted to be left alone by locking himself in the bathroom; that Delphine must be at Mademoiselle Aubier's. And so on. Suddenly I cravenly started to run, and found myself out in the rain rubbing my hair with the towel. I drove over to Mademoiselle Aubier's in Saint-Germain-en-Laye.

All earthly happiness, the slightest human pleasure, awakens the jealousy of God, revives the suffering of him who was put on the cross, reopens the wound in his side. Seinecé became terrible, jealous, building up fantasies out of nothing. I listened despondently for hours to these wild imaginings. His mother's death, his wife's temporary defection—everyone was deserting him. They wanted him to die. I didn't like to interrupt, but I wished I could run away. I myself had no pride. My friend's body was a shell annexed by a parasite. I was a parasite too.

I haven't a particularly strong sense of being in the hand of God, and up till now—knock wood—haven't been visited by any transports or mystical visions. But I believe I did witness something of the sort in Seinecé's visionary suspicions. They were like the epiphanies of a god—a jealous god. They were like revelations, which made him suffer inexpressibly yet never once by any chance made him think of me. Every detail was a fang. Every remark of Isabelle's was a dart. Every time she was absent was proof of the worst.

The disappointment—a pretty ordinary one, to say the least—of not having aroused a completely exclusive passion made him feel an utter failure, like an unsatisfactory meal, a candy without any taste, a worn-out doormat. A famished pack of griefs howled inside him. More than desertion he wanted humiliation; more than sadness, grief; more than grief, anguish, self-hatred, self-contempt. He was possessed, even in his sleep. He wanted sweat, nightmares, sudden pains in the heart, yells. He used to wake Isabelle up.

I sometimes have a terrifying feeling that we invented fear and distress in order to console ourselves. Seinecé was always detecting secret messages, suspicious tones of voice, surreptitious looks, hints of embraces deferred. He had become a sort of private detective, and he was a genius at it, a monstrous owl in the night.

I believe, with good reason, in metempsychosis, the transmigration of souls. In previous existences I've been a cancerous cell, a tear, a horsefly, and an ass. I've also been an oyster, a wind, fear, a lump of butter, a sigh. But Seinecé had been transformed into a mass of tiny grubs pullulating like protozoa or octopi to fill all the space available, the way madmen's drawings fill all the paper or canvas they're given. There were sudden crescendos and passionate accelerandos in the relationship between him and his pain. Nothing escaped him. The slightest twitch of a muscle and it was, "You see!" The faintest whiff of perfume: "I knew it all along!" A caress was a wound, a sigh an insult.

I tried to see him only when he was alone. But his possession never left him, and I was the unwilling spectator of many farcical scenes. He worked like a slave, but it was no use. What with brandy and other drinks, cigarettes, coffee, and candies of all kinds, which made him drink some more, he wasn't getting any sleep. After his thesis he wrote a whole string of learned articles. But again it was useless.

The new school term had just begun. Isabelle was teaching German at Rueil. She didn't believe in her husband's sufferings.

"He's only bluffing!" she would say, shrugging her shoulders. "It's just playacting in bad taste, designed to punish other people." But I thought Seinecé was more deeply affected than she would admit. He was jealous of the past, the present, and the future; he was jealous of Isabelle's parents, of his own daughter, and of his mother who had just died; he was jealous of everyone Isabelle met, even of the tradespeople, even of her dreams, which he claimed she wouldn't tell him about.

"Is that all you have to say to me?" he'd shout. "Why don't you answer?"

Sometimes it was almost comic. "Why do I shout? I shout to make myself heard, if you must know!" The paltriness of it all was extraordinary. On second thought, perhaps not all that extraordinary. One curious phrase, heartrending and absurd, kept cropping up and leading to endless arguments.

"Careful, Ibelle! Don't make me say things I haven't said!"

There was something threatening in his tone which made this sound enigmatic and frightening. And when he'd finished he was always panting slightly. If Isabelle hurried in a little later than usual in the evening, Seinecé would go over and demand in a tense whisper, "Where've you been?" "You shouldn't have waited for me!" she'd say gaily. And the litany would start up again: "So you don't want to tell me where you were?"

And the shouting and the accusations of lying would start up again too. I left as fast as I could. I only went to Chatou if Seinecé phoned and asked for me. I lay low in my apartment and worked at my cello and my translation. At night I would wake Dido up, put her on my lap, and ask her what I ought to do. She refused to open her eyes and walked away without answering. Not even a little meow, or a glance, or little pat with her paw. She disassociated herself completely. I suspected she was jealous of Isabelle.

Everybody in this sublunary world trails a shadow around with him. These shadows are called memories, and they're very tedious. Each is made up of habits, a certain way of attracting other people, and infantile recipes for getting attention, food, and favor.

In my own case, trying to make other people like me would

involve ridiculous efforts to derive some sort of appeal from my own awkwardness or at least using it to evoke sympathy and pity. It seemed to me that if you wanted people to like you, you had to be a klutz: it couldn't fail. But that strategy's not even worthy of an infant in the cradle: it's more the role of a bulb in a pot or a tub of chrysanthemums in a graveyard.

I was very fond of the green Citroën I'd bought a few months back. At ten on a Saturday morning, after I'd already done four or five hours' work, I used to drive it out to Chatou. By eleven I'd be there, or going through Saint-Germain. I was a heap of dry leaves. I still am—the leaves are a bit dustier, a bit more crumpled now, but more red and yellow and white, and shinier after all the rain and squalls. The spark was put to the heap the very moment I arrived. Ibelle was wearing a black dress made of light silk—she was so beautiful, so tall, so relaxed.

"Oh Karl! You're too late! Delphine and Florent went off to her school party a few minutes ago, and they won't be back till half past twelve. There's a shoulder of lamb for lunch. And baked squash," she added with mock grandeur, as if this were a very rare vegetable indeed.

I kissed her on the cheek. She made us some coffee. Her silk dress clung to her limbs and followed all her movements. I didn't move. I didn't look at Ibelle's body. Just at the scrap of black silk that she was wearing. She went over to the coffee table. Moved a stone. Moved the flowers.

"I don't think," she said, as if to herself, rather grumpily, searching for the words and then rapping them out, "I don't think one really has to spend one's whole life waiting till the cows come home, only to find all of a sudden that there aren't any cows and there isn't any home."

"I know, Ibelle. And you're right."

I was dumbfounded, weary, drained. She was crouching down by the table with her back to me. Then she added, in a low, rapid, smothered voice:

"Karl! I want to take my clothes off—here, now, in front of you. I really want to."

There was a silence, and it seems to me now that it was mine. There was something trembling and anxious in her voice; her suggestion simply shattered me. She was still crouching there with her back to me. I went over, took her by the arms, raised her up, drew her close, and kissed her shoulders.

She pulled away and said again, "I want to take my clothes off."

I said "Yes" in a voice hoarse with embarrassment or desire. She looked at me with indescribable boldness and radiance, her head on one side. I watched her dress, that large scrap of black silk, falling in folds at her feet. It was still soft and warm from the curves it had been hiding. Then I looked up at Isabelle herself, and I can't express how beautiful her body was and how much I loved it.

You take a human body that is burning hot and is everything in the world. You embrace it. You yourself are now only a point in space—almost an idea. The only body in the world is the warm being in your embrace.

Our eyes stay wide open. We are so surprised. We can't believe the evidence of our senses. We never get used to our own sex. We never get used to its metamorphosis, to the attraction it exerts—it's all so amazing, so bewildering. We never tire of testing it out, year after year, age after age. And our curiosity about it is never assuaged. So we're always getting involved in absurd affairs. And each time our heart thumps and our eyes feast and we can hardly speak. And we're always infuriated by the fact that our sexual organs alone are bereft of meaning.

She reached out and switched on the Carcel lamp. It was raining again. That was after we'd made love. I was lying with my head on her thighs. She stroked me and asked, "Karl, how did you get this scar on the tip of your shoulder?"

So I told her, with some embarrassment, about that morning in 1946. I was three years old. I thought my mother was throwing a Daum vase at my face, and in trying to get out of the way I twisted around so that it hit my shoulder instead. The injury was quite serious and I had to go into the hospital, where I suffered less from my arm than from being separated from my sisters. (I didn't mind being separated from Fräulein Jutta.) My homecoming is probably the happiest thing I can remember in my whole life. I was rather proud of having been specially distinguished in this way by my mother. My return was a triumph, the occasion of a great orgy of shortcakes and cream puffs and jam and almond biscuits with glamorous names like Suvarov and visitandine.

As I was speaking I discovered something both incomprehensible and stunning. I scrutinized her face intently.

She smiled. I examined her look, her eyes. What fascinated me, though I didn't yet realize all that it implied, was the resemblance between her and my mother—both tall and slim, with something prickly and violent in their expression.

Our bodies are transfigured by love's games. People trying to please one another absorb and accumulate light. Lovers' bodies are radiant. Their movements are easy and sure. At least before they've been making love for too long, before they realize that the desire that drew them together was not so unique as they thought. Every love story ends the same way: "Sorry, I made a mistake! I thought I recognized . . . I thought you were someone whom . . . Someone who . . ."

I believed in something immense, something that could be compared to Isabelle's huge blue and gold eyes. Transparent eyes, totally disarming, infinitely profound. Wet, misted—as her nostrils often were—with a tear of anger or laughter. Her eyes, her pupils, and a glint of light on the blue. A tiny Australia on a blue globe.

I'm trying to describe Ibelle's eyes, to express the inexpressible, to articulate silence. I scribble some notes. But I can't get any further than a few scenes that keep bursting inside me like the strange bubbles on the stagnant pond in the garden at Bergheim, full of catfish, little turtles, and frogs. The sound the bubbles made as they burst used to fill me with wonder and fear. I probably record these phantom scenes because they too frighten me—perhaps not so much because of what they are as because of the unpredictable and bewildering way they return. What I'm writing strikes me as sober and necessary, and yet it's as if it were dictated by a ghost. I set down these notes because it isn't something you can tell like a story. Love isn't tellable, neither is its suffering, neither is its happiness. Neither is its light: the wondrous light that illuminates nothing. And you don't know in the end if that feeling, that halo of truth, intensity, trust, nakedness, and authenticity isn't untruth personified in the shape of a human body become a furnace, a sun—

and these images are the most dubious of all. It isn't tellable. How can you say, "Her breasts were like this . . . Her thighs were like that . . . Her buttocks were like something else . . ."? And then go on to talk about the burning bush? Or God? Or the sun? What fools we are.

But I did love her. And I loved her eyes perhaps most of all. Her wide, blue, shining, harsh, terrible eyes—the words are atrocious and tell you nothing. Her huge blue eyes, her black hair, the way she held her head. Her voice wavered, stumbled a little, rather muted, suddenly animated, not hoarse or cracked but captivating, especially in the winter, when she usually had a cold and a drip at the end of her nose, which only made her prettier. A red nose, and yes, a hoarse voice, a cracked voice—an eternal frog in the throat, or, as the French say, a "cat"—a voice that was rough and moving.

I remember September 1964 as very cold. And I recall Delphine wearing a tartan skirt and a thick green wool sweater. She was crouching on her heels—like her mother—on the small concrete terrace of the dull little garden at Chatou, holding a big bunch of grapes. Each time she sucked the pulp out of a grape she inflated the empty skin and blew it as far as she could, then ran with a piece of chalk and marked the place where the farthest ones fell.

I was drawn to the house at Chatou and to Isabelle's body. At the same time I wouldn't let myself go there, I forced myself to work in my apartment on Rue du Pont-de-Lodi. Isabelle was sullen; she wanted me to put everything into words, was more demanding than I myself had it in me to be, and perhaps more exclusive than I could have wished. I was sleeping badly. Whenever I was at Chatou I was always on the watch. I was suffering. Unlike Seinecé, who seemed jealous of everyone except me, I was growing jealous of him. I wanted to spy on the other two, though I fought against it. But whatever we try to do to flatter our vanity, our ears are always flapping. It's a wonder we don't trip over them more often. The house at Chatou was small, and the walls were thin. I slept in an attic room on the second floor.

I desired Isabelle. I never slept much, but when I was at Chatou I didn't sleep at all. I can't sleep when the world is all lit up. It's as if light made you have to see. And sometimes during the night I would think I heard them groan, and it was a light haunting the whole world. Isabelle's hoarse moan, Florent's sudden sobbing plaint, which he tried in vain to stifle—whether I imagined them or no, to me they were torture.

Sounds have boundless power over me. All love, all quarrels, all scenes that lead to divorce are mere sounds to small children who can't sleep. When we were small—Marga, Cäci, and myself—we used to hide behind the quince tree with its dark, gnarled branches and downy, ugly fruit. I didn't like the jam that was made from it, still less the sort of sweet pink cheese that was kept on a marble slab and cut up into little rectangles. We used to peer into the kitchen to see what Hiltrud or Beate or Vinzenz was doing; and later on, by the pond, we watched what Lisbeth and Luise and their friends were up to. And sometimes I'd shut my eyes and spy with my ears. I didn't do it to shut out sight altogether but rather to see more intensely by filtering my impressions.

Learning to be a musician consists in trying to get control of sounds, trying to train their violence, to soothe their ancient suffering. My friends often make fun of me for making practically unsalable recordings of the music of comparatively unknown composers, writing biographies of them and spending one day a week giving lessons; whereas I never go to the opera or to concerts, I have a very poor collection of records, and I don't listen to the radio. They don't understand that for me all the world's woe exists in the form of sound. Of course there is some happiness in the form of sound; but it's almost been lost. On holidays in Bergheim, when I heard sudden bursts of the town band playing in the distance, I used to be frantic with joy and tell myself, "That's what I call music!"—contrasting it with all the triplets of notes that the five of us vainly tried to keep in time with one another every Sunday afternoon, often ending up in either giggles or hysterics. I'd run in the direction of the sounds, sometimes misled by the wind. But I ran and ran. A hedge or a bend in a street might confront me and involve a detour, but in the end I got there, my chest swelling with the rhythm, my hair standing on end, already intoxicated, transported by an emotion that scared me so much it stopped me in my tracks. Or else I just slowed down and stood there on the pink flagstones of Bergheim. The emotion was so clearly and painfully greater than my body it seemed to me utterly boundless.

I didn't like the idea of making love to Isabelle in the little house at Chatou, so we used to meet in a poorly heated room in a small hotel halfway between Chatou and Saint-Germain that I'd already patronized during my military service. The hotel was quite near the Seine at Le Vésinet, but our room usually looked out on St. Pauline's church; and it was right underneath a zinc roof. It made a terrible noise when it rained, and even when it didn't the pigeons and sparrows either sat there fidgeting or suddenly took off like bombs. A meager electric heater clattered and clicked, producing more sound than heat. I can remember October mornings when Ibelle's nose was as cold and damp as Pontius Pilate's, and before she opened her eyes she would ask me to hold her, rub her, and kiss her to warm her up.

We looked at each other surreptitiously, like children, as we undressed. Then, either because of the cold or because we were shy, we got under the blanket, itself covered by a red eiderdown, which in turn was buried under our raincoats. Weight seemed to us to guarantee warmth—and perhaps invisibility.

I could never manage to sleep in that little room, and I caught cold after cold. And the following day I always used to swear I'd never make love again.

Life, which up to then had merely been awful, now became sad. Even the child, sitting with her chin propped on her knees, her thumb in her mouth, and her eyes full of unease, seemed to be accusing us. We racked our brains trying to keep her amused. Isabelle and I played at miniature cars with her, sitting with our legs wide apart at either end of the hall. But it seldom produced a laugh. Delphine's oft-repeated riddles, of the "Why did the chicken cross the road?" variety, always brought tears of mirth to Isabelle's eyes but made the child herself laugh less and less.

Then the weather got worse, and Mademoiselle Aubier wouldn't look after Delphine anymore.

"My dear," she said to me, "now that autumn's here I'm not fit to be touched with a pair of sugar tongs."

It wasn't so easy now for us to meet. Delphine herself chafed at going to the house in Saint-Germain, whatever presents Mademoiselle might give her—an old red lacquer pencil box, an ebony ruler with brass edges, a wooden penholder. Perhaps she sensed what was going on. I've always thought Mademoiselle Aubier guessed everything right away, from my face. She'd become sour and crotchety. We clashed about the slightest thing.

"We used to attend the concerts Monsieur Colonne conducted at Châtelet," she would say. "We went in a cab with pneumatic tires. We used to get out by the Fontaine des Palmes and cross the road on foot."

I remarked that the fountain was still there. She immediately got huffy.

"No, it isn't! It's not the same now!"

"Yes, it is."

"No, it isn't—it doesn't smell of horse dung!"

We quarreled. I avoided her. Isabelle and I stopped seeing one another for about ten days. Isabelle took a poor view of this interruption of desire. She wanted me to come on weekends, but she didn't want Seinecé to know, or me to be seen at the hotel in Le Vésinet. She didn't want us to be seen together anymore, either. She asked me to go and visit her secretly in the house at Chatou, but I refused, trembling with fear. I'd betrayed Seinecé's friendship, but I didn't want to tie myself up hand and foot, neck and crop, in the ties and laces and Gordian knots he himself was so fond of.

I went to the hotel twice in the first week in October, but Isabelle couldn't join me. Then I had to go back to the little house in Chatou on weekends. Everything was so rushed at the time, the dates are confused. All the hurry and greed of young puppies just let out after sixteen months in a gilded cage in Saint-Germain—though the gilt was artificial. At about eleven at night Seinecé would take some tablets, which, as he mixed them with alcohol, made him stagger, and he and Isabelle went up to bed. The second Saturday evening Ibelle gave me a strange look, and as she kissed me goodnight—I'd already said goodnight to Seinece—she said suddenly:

"I'll come to your room."

"No."

"Yes! I'm coming!"

She said it obstinately, and I don't know why but somehow I felt more moved than when I made love to her for the first time.

Three times we made love there, silently, ears pricked up, like animals in their lair. Isabelle used to come to my room at about one or two in the morning. I'd hear the stairs creak, and listen to her coming up them very, very slowly. Then she'd turn the cold, white, slightly clammy china doorknob. I couldn't hear her breathing. She didn't switch on the light. I couldn't hear her moving. The first thing I perceived was her smell, then a sensation of warmth, then her body. And we made love clumsily and desperately, like all who turn away from pleasure and aspire to love. We didn't breathe. We exchanged mechanical, nervous kisses, and the slightest noise would interrupt our pathetic, uninspired caresses. All we really exchanged were frantic heartbeats and perhaps a few little stifled moans.

There was an old table, once used as a washstand, near the door, where I kept my scores. Isabelle always put a vase of flowers there on Saturday morning. At 2 A.M. on November 3 she caught her foot on the cello case, and as she tried to keep her balance knocked over the vase of chrysanthemums she'd put there the previous morning. It must have made a terrific noise as it crashed to the floor, though to tell you the honest truth I can't remember. We stood rooted to the spot. But no one came. The house remained utterly silent.

We mopped up the water with the sheets from the bed. Ibelle opened the door a little way; the house was still dark and silent. She wanted to stay, and I couldn't make her change her mind. She stood with her eyes fixed on the little green clock, drinking her own tears as they trickled on to her lips. We got all worked up and spent the night swearing it couldn't go on like this. In the morning we went down together, determined to tell all and spread the pain around, probably because we didn't feel we could face it alone. But Florent wasn't in the kitchen. He'd already gone. We didn't know where to. He must have seen Ibelle wasn't in the bed. He'd probably heard the crash the vase made when it fell and broke to pieces at our feet—the big white vase full of bright yellow, egg-yolk-yellow chrysanthemums.

He phoned at ten as if nothing had happened, and said we ought to go to the market and get a bream for dinner. He'd noticed they were very good this morning, and cheap. He'd be waiting for us to join him at Mademoiselle's for lunch and the concert.

We played this sad and anxious game for one more weekend without saying anything, pretending we weren't suffering from grief and remorse. Ibelle stuck to her guns and insisted on coming to my room at night. But our eyes were riveted on the little green clock, our ears strained for the least sound on the stairs, probably in the secret hope that a step would creak and our fear would find its prey. We didn't really make love; as we went through the motions we were listening to the silence. Not a very profitable activity, I can tell you. When all four of us were together we talked as coolly and calmly as if we were just passing the time while we trimmed our nails.

"Annie said she'd drop by."

"Mademoiselle kept going on about the treaty of Vereeniging."

"I've made a mess of the béarnaise sauce."

Seinecé sat down with a good appetite and leaned over to taste the sauce—a kind of green paste he was in the process of concocting, nothing like a real béarnaise sauce. He added some pepper and fennel. We were having fish again for dinner that evening—red mullet cooked with fennel. I was cold and sneezed. Ibelle turned to me and said:

"Give me some salt. Straight out of the shaker. Unscrew it."

Suddenly Seinecé's eyes filled with tears. I was just passing Ibelle the salt. Seinecé's face was all distorted.

"What's the matter?" asked Ibelle, looking at him as if afraid.

"Oh!" he said.

"What is it?" she asked again.

He was doubled up.

"But what's the matter, Florent? What *is* the matter?" she cried, weeping now.

He pointed at me.

"You called him *tu*!" he said.

We looked at each other. I can only describe how in terms of drops of rain, those huge slow drops that fall at the beginning of a storm and make you impatient for the chaos, the catastrophe itself, the downpour you feel hanging over you in the sky.

Delphine came in, sensed the atmosphere, and babyishly asked her father to lift her onto her chair.

I remember the tablecloth. It was oilcloth, with a pattern of little electric blue violets and pale lemon daffodils—bright, shiny as lacquer, and horribly smelly. It was also clammy and sticky—worse than clammy and sticky, almost prehensile, like a yellow snail or slug that somehow gets on your hand when you're gardening. I can't remember what we had to eat, or if we actually ate anything. I think we did. But we couldn't break the silence. The strange silence. Even Delphine was affected by it and added her own unusual quiet. I can still see her carefully spreading a layer of sugar over her plate, then using her fork to separate the quarters of her clementine as if it were a bunch of red currants, and the little bits of fruit dropping slowly and silently into the sugar, glistening in the light from the lamp overhead.

So tense was the silence that when Delphine's imperturbable clumsiness resulted in a quarter of clementine dropping on the floor for the fifth time, a terrible weakness of mine assailed me and I had an irresistible desire to laugh. I didn't actually guffaw, but I couldn't repress a kind of speechless, nervous heave accompanied by little squeaks.

"I'm glad you think it's so funny!" shouted Seinecé, suddenly slamming both hands down on the table.

Glasses and plates shuddered. Delphine, having a drink of water, wept into her glass. I couldn't hold back my hysterical laughter, but each outburst was like the thrust of a bayonet inside me: a pang of remorse, a stab of unadulterated pain. Florent shouted and bawled.

CHAPTER 3

The Villa at Saint-Martin-en-Caux

My only talent is some kind of inner ear which nature has given me so that I may suffer.

WIELAND

We didn't speak. It was one of those silences of which it's strangely but aptly said that you could cut it with a knife, so strongly does it suggest blades suspended in midair and murders waiting to happen. We sat staring at our plates. Our eyes tried only to avoid one another. We seemed to be listening to the silence.

We parted that evening in silence, too. We didn't say anything; we scarcely looked at one another. The parting between Seinecé and me had something inevitable about it. The head of the red mullet cooked in fennel lolled on the edge of the dish. It was gray. I can still see that unseeing eye. We were once fish. And the wisest of us stayed there in the carboniferous lakes. Among the vertebrates who chose silence.

Delphine opened a tin and took out a fruit drop, and I saw her offer one to her father for the last time. And though as a rule I'm not very keen on that kind of sweet, in fact I rather despise them—they're really only a depressing, miserly recycling of the syrup left over from making candied fruit, retaining like a defect or a symptom the colors of the various fruits that have been steeped in them—my dislike doesn't affect this particular memory. Looking back, I see the kind of candy Delphine held out to her father's mouth in her sticky little pink fingers as delicate and translucent, like the ancient blue or pink or yellow stained-glass windows you see in an old church that you visit on a dull day, and that are suddenly lit up by a ray of sunlight. But here, instead of the contrast between the bright glass and the dark lead framing it, what I still see and admire is the beauty of the little white threads, like the marks on antique viols, which ran through the sweets and didn't disappear even when you sucked them, as you saw when Delphine, looking strangely preoccupied, took the sticky little tetrahedron out of her mouth to make it shine in the electric light.

Isabelle and Florent got divorced. I was François Ravaillac of Touvres. I was on Rue de la Ferronnerie. The wheel of the coach was muddy and high. I climbed on the axle holding a knife. François Ravaillac, murderer of Henri IV, is said to have told the judge with an air of great satisfaction: "That's one good job done, anyway!" I must have seemed like him. For three or four weeks I even felt a certain exaltation, though of the kind you try to hide and restrain. Something akin to gladness, though of the excited, agitated kind that succeeds the sudden explosion of a crisis long foreseen and long postponed. The feeling wasn't unlike the catastrophic pleasure, the sense of joy, the desire for benediction, the almost physical relief and religious satisfaction that follow the final breaking of a titanic storm.

That last dinner was like a storm. There was even a death: I can still see the unseeing eye of the fish. In the course of that extremely fraught meal I seem to remember we also ate some potatoes in béarnaise sauce—rather, in Seinecé's fennel concoction. And I see my mother again, in Bergheim, trying to teach us French and saying severely to Lisbeth: "The spots in potatoes are called eyes." It was as if she'd told us that human beings too had to be peeled and have their defects removed with the point of a knife. And indeed, by the power of her own keen or disapproving eyes she could bring out of our heads one by one the darkest defects and sins, the most deeply hidden threats and dreams of revenge.

They decided to part. I fled. Or at least I fled a quarter of an hour later. Seinecé wore a kind of fixed grin. His fingers gripped the edge of the table and a napkin ring—gripped them so tightly his knuckles were white. His face had grown ugly, petrified in the frightening grimace worn by those particularly craven men who've sworn never to cry. Ibelle told me afterward that later on, when they met to decide what was to happen about Delphine and to settle the conditions of their separation, it was all in vain—they couldn't speak. Finally Seinecé went over to her with the ironical, self-important smile he couldn't help assuming, but which was so inapt a defense for his own unhappiness. He leaned over and gently put his lips on her tearful eyes. Then he left, his back shaken by some kind of nervous tic, and making extraordinary little farmyard noises.

Subsequent discussions were more acrimonious, with Seinecé trying to get, and finally obtaining, custody of Delphine. Ibelle was uncouth and unhappy, and for hours on end would keep desperately sobbing phrases like "I must just make the shoes pinch! I must just make the shoes pinch!"

They traded accusations based on trifles, old grudges of no importance—leftovers of syrup from old candied fruit. Then they mixed all the stale sticky ingredients up in one infernal brew, one terrible long unending phrase. The final decree wasn't pronounced until the spring of 1965. I remember it as happening near the anniversary of La Belle Otéro's death, but unfortunately that isn't recorded in the little diary I'm consulting. There's no doubt that they suffered, and in a way they never quite got over it, because of those terrible pitiless interviews. But Ibelle told me she was surprised at how long the pain took to declare itself openly. She did suffer, and it nearly drove her crazy, but for some time it seemed to her that the pain she ought to be feeling wasn't there in the purely physical, total, almost lethal form that she expected.

In March 1963 we met at the barber's. In May 1964 we were free and the best of friends. In November 1964 we parted without a word—only with nervous laughter and dead mullet. At the end of November Ibelle asked if she could come and live with me. I hastened to say yes. She left Delphine behind. It had snowed. The sky was black. It was still snowing a bit. Ibelle handed me two cases, and Delphine stood by the brown iron gate in the little garden at Chatou, not crying, not even glancing in my direction, just vaguely waving goodbye. Then she went up the path until she was only a few steps from the house, threw back her head, and opened her mouth for the snowflakes to fall in. She alternately waved goodbye and drank in a few bits of snow. Then she went back indoors to Florent, licking her lips carefully.

Ibelle went on teaching at the lycée at Rueil for the rest of the school year. Sometimes, when she had an early class the next day, she slept at Louise and André Valasse's place. We went to the Alps for Christmas, to a little village called Valloire. I liked it: it wasn't too new or too spoiled. But there was no snow. Only rain. We drank. To pass the time. It was a strange passion she had for me: she was always shaken with sobs, and all she thought about was Delphine and Seinecé. How we like playing at making ourselves cry. I didn't much care for this life—the perpetual trips in the Citroën in search of only half-pleasurable pleasures, the passion without real joy or eagerness, sitting lugubriously in cafés and on beds, as if we were on the banks of the Acheron making continual descents into Hell. Ibelle slept for eleven or twelve hours; I stayed awake and kept watch. And yet nothing that really unites two people needs to be guarded or protected. I remember Dido and me spending a whole night contemplating the difficulty I was in, my painful eagerness to call the whole thing off, and considering it from every possible angle. And rugged angles they were, too; some as sharp as acacia thorns.

Dido was basically a severe and implacable cat, worse than the Jansenist God. She used to sit up straight with all four paws drawn up underneath her. I'm sure she didn't think there were any human beings among God's elect. The matter didn't admit the shadow of a doubt—at most a slight hesitation out of mere politeness. Her round cheeks, bulging with self-assurance and a passionate conviction worthy of a bishop; her double chin, like that of a monk in a particularly prosperous community or a psychoanalyst who's just made mincemeat of a fellow human being; her armless and in a way maternal bust—they all combined to make me feel in the wrong most of the time. Moreover Dido, whom I loved more than anything in the world, was, incredible as it may seem, a cat who never spoke. And by refusing to answer me now she not only told me I was wrong in particular to want to turn my life upside down and break with an excellent young woman who was as proud and haughty as she was herself and to whom she'd finally gotten used, but also that I was wrong in general to keep upsetting the order of hours, days, seasons, and the universe itself by not going to bed at night.

I didn't come to any decision. I put it off. That year I worked unremittingly with Uwe at the violoncello sostenuto and the Tourte bow, then suddenly dropped them and started to specialize in the baroque cello and the tenor and bass violas da gamba with Klaus-Maria and Stanislaus Arraucourt. I translated a biography of Forqueray and one of Jenkins. In February and early April I corrected the proofs in a dark little office in the Gallimard building on Rue Sébastien-Bottin. My cubbyhole must once have formed part of the upper regions of a magnificent room. Sometimes Ibelle came there at the end of the afternoon and brought me pastries from Constant's. The window looked out on a garden: limes and gaunt acacias. The end of winter lent a kind of beauty to the hoary earth, the tall bare trees, the damp gravel, the dark empty fountain, and the little pavilion in false perspective standing like a piece of scenery at the back of a stage. Indoors, the labyrinth of dim narrow corridors made you feel as if you were in a monastery. Voices were never raised. We whispered to each other. We were lizards in a ruined palace, fleeing the light.

I think it was that year, in Normandy—we went there at Easter during the school vacation—that I first had a close view, only three or four paces away from me on the cliff, of a brown and gray herring gull. At first it was moving about among the other gulls, then it let out a cry and took off, soaring endlessly round and round. Ibelle had the use of a very nice villa near Saint-Martin-en-Caux, looking out over the valley and the sea. As well as spending a week there at Easter we went back again in the summer. A stout Quakerish-looking woman of about fifty-five with tanned cheeks, flowered overalls, and severe transparent blue eyes looked after the house and cooked lunch and dinner. She lived in a little keeper's lodge that stood some distance from the gate; according to Ibelle, it had once been used as a bookbinding and marquetry workshop.

At first, Madame La Georgette—that's what you had to call her, absolutely not "Georgette"—terrified me with the roughness of her manner and the virulence of her opinions. But in my memory her curtness and asperity have acquired a deeper dimension. She had an extraordinary way, when she was telling you what people had said, of miming them in detail with her whole body, and, if she was telling you some story, of echoing its incidents with movements of her head and arms and hefty thighs. Hearing her account of a film produced much more terror than you would have experienced by going to see it yourself in the village hall in Saint-Martin-en-Caux. And the feeling was much more lasting too: it took her two or three hours to do justice to a film that ran for ninety minutes. She strikes me now as resembling one of those prehistoric creatures, naked, shivering, and simian—couldn't the same still be said of ourselves?—who used to change themselves into the animals they hunted by wearing their skins and heads. Their prey was more themselves than they were, and they depicted it magnificently on the walls of their caves, their eyes still impregnated with their one target, their one food, in the kind of ever-renewed chase that has since come to be called painting. But they found less food for art in themselves than in the prey that also provided them with physical nourishment, and the only self-images they left were little sexual diagrams, ridiculously puritanical.

Almost as soon as we got there—she scarcely gave us time to get our bags and even my cello out of the Citroën—Madame La Georgette told us dinner was ready, and one of the first things she said to me as she brought in a steaming tureen of soup, the kind she made herself out of dried vegetables, wine, and stale bread, was, "This won't do your asshole any harm!" I was staggered. And the fact that I could be shocked by such earthy remarks showed I was almost as puritanical as a troglodyte of the Pleistocene age myself. Another day, when she was telling me about a film she'd seen on television the night before, she gave me a real fright by leaping up, overturning her chair, pointing a kitchen knife at my cheek, and shouting, "No, Monsieur le Commissaire—you'll never take me alive!" She was saintly, pious, and arrogant, but subtle too, or at least shrewd, like a lynx or an anglerfish. Her ample frame was always enveloped in a long-sleeved, high-necked print overall with a pattern of tiny dark flowers.

In the morning I could see the sun and the mist rising in the valley, and vague shapes, still gray and clammy with sleep, slowly dispersing. The mist, seemingly made up of separate grains or tears and gradually pervaded by the sun, wrought on trees, bushes, sky, houses, and every shape in sight an astounding transformation. Sometimes it was beautiful beyond expression. Love seems to exhibit this transforming power too—though when I think of it now I can't remember which element changes the other. Love, love in its early days, is like the sun-pierced mists that change the look of the whole universe, performing miracles, taking it out of the past and out of the future. I've never really loved anyone but Ibelle. "My belle." So slim, so tall, so naked. She undressed with a modesty and a majesty I've never seen in any other woman. But she didn't take off her clothes: she gave the impression, in her confusion, in the confusion of desire, that she'd never manage to strip entirely bare. And your desire for her was aroused at once and prevented you from seeing her really naked, so eager were you to embrace and make love to her blindly.

But with her, even nakedness covered something—and this isn't merely a pun. And it still seems to me that when one desires another very much and searches their nakedness, one is looking in their body for something no statue or skeleton can ever yield. The secret we're looking for may actually be in ourselves, and yet, when we ourselves are naked—in order to take a bath or be examined by a dermatologist or enterologist or line up for a shower in the army—there's never anything to indicate or even suggest it.

Ibelle slept with her lips slightly parted and her nostrils flared, and all of a sudden she'd wave her arms around or kick out with her feet. Her flat, compact, warm breasts rose and fell like someone's cheeks when they're chewing. I always got up before dawn and pressed my lips to them and to her hair. Her body was abandoned to something other than me. And this seemed to me quite sensible. It was completely abandoned to a dream, to some old hatred or fear that assured her of her own identity. Then suddenly she would shudder. All that ample feminine body would heave an immense sigh—I was afraid I'd woken it up—but it only shifted position or turned over heavily. That whole body and its drowsy weight entrusted itself to a vision, dedicating the beauty of its muscles to some unknown universe. My fingers could feel the warmth and softness of the skin between its thighs; its breath fanned now my cheeks and now my lips. It would soon be day. I jumped out of bed and closed the various doors quietly behind me. In the kitchen it was almost light. I put some water on to boil. It was an old stove that you had to poke, with circular lead lids you had to take off with a special lever. This primitive apparatus was a pleasure fit for the Garden of Eden at first, but shoveling in coal, crumpling up newspaper, hastily putting back the lids, and so on soon became more like one of the plagues of Egypt. With a great blast the flames would leap up in the air, scorching your hands and threatening to set the whole kitchen on fire. Finally I'd put the kettle on, lay the table with butter, bread, eggs, fruit, salt, jam, and meat, and go and take a bath. I used to spend three or four hours reading scores and musical biographies. I'd contracted with two large publishing houses to translate a biography a year from English or German. This I did, dictating the work into a tape recorder, until I was forty, when my recordings brought in enough for me to give up this despised, unprofitable yet interesting task. It was tiresome, too, as it involved endless ferreting through French, German, American and English musicological reviews full of arrogant articles bristling with annoying paradoxes and intimidating slogans. At 8 or 9 A.M. I stopped work and went and cooked some Spätzle or potatoes.

Ibelle said the smell of cooking made her feel sick to her stomach that early in the morning, but she'd yield to the human being's natural voracity so far as to pick at a kipper, some steak tartare, or a piece of orange, sipping at a small glass of Tokay. She objected to my getting up at what she called "the crock of dawn"; or rather she felt that because she got up so much later than I did, when the day was already advanced and the light wasted, my timetable, due really to insomnia and the habits of childhood, was meant as a reproach to her. I've often been criticized on this score by the various women who've been kind enough to live with me. But just as I wouldn't have dreamed of blaming her for her good luck in being able to sleep—and thus die—for so long every day, so I never felt the least resentment about its practical consequences for me. Those hours of solitude have been a blessing. People in love think they're indispensable and make it a principle to cling like a leech, just as they make exclusivity an end in itself. But in fact there's nothing nicer than a few hour's leave from the person you love, and nothing wiser than having a bit of a change when you're unfortunate enough to be the victim of a passion.

For all the pleasure Ibelle gave me; for all the marks of love and abandon and daring she so generously bestowed; for all that she was natural, tough, funny, and beautiful—still we were gradually drifting apart. Astonishing as it seems even to me, the gulf seemed to get wider every time at the moment of greatest pleasure, the moment when pleasure lent her face a kind of smile, a kind of triumph. This smile detached from memory, this smile behind a smile, a mixture of lethal pity, connivance, divination, and foot-on-the-neck, is the smile fortune-tellers sometimes wear, as if forgiving you in advance for a sin you don't know you're going to commit. Similarly when she asked me for money. I had some then, not because of the Jenkins biography, which didn't start to sell for another six years, but because through Raoul Costeker—that was how I got to know him—I'd bought and then sold again a Salomon cello that had once belonged to Cupis and Duport, and which I still wish I had kept. When I gave her the money she wore the same disagreeable smile—divine, greedy, scornful, and stupid.

I've kept some of the photographs I took then. Ibelle squatting down on her heels and looking very serious, like a princess of the blood in a ruff or high collar learning to practice Zen meditation. Isabelle, her lips curving in a laugh, standing by a group of little apple trees with various scarves or shawls around her shoulders. Isabelle naked, tugging with both hands to take a boot off, like a hero in the *Iliad.* Isabelle, head bent forward, putting on a blouse. She used to undress with such swiftness, pride, and disregard for tidiness that it stunned me and made me almost ashamed of my own body. What was it she hated, that made her so impetuous in taking off her clothes and flinging them about so roughly? But she looked after her skin with an obsessive, almost irksome care, anointing it with all kinds of creams and lotions. Every day she spent nearly an hour gazing at, losing herself in, and traveling around her own reflection. As a matter of fact, she didn't all that often direct the sort of attention she lavished on herself at anyone else; but then she was so beautiful.

It's difficult to summon up the appearance of a once loved body, to describe its beauty and the desire you felt for it in the past, when it still exists, older, distracting you from the former image however indulgent you are toward it, however pleasant the remembering—or however sweet the revenge. We often tell ourselves that with a bit of effort and audacity it ought to be possible to say anything; that it's not so much a matter of the ability of the person who has the experience as of a kind of reconciliation of two or three worlds—reality, ourselves, and language. And yet there doesn't seem to be a language to describe love, the beauty of a body, the memory of the shameless, miraculous movements that are common to everyone. Or rather it's as if not only language is lacking but also oneself, and both memory and reality itself elude us.

The vocabulary that expresses the parts of the body derives little energy from slang, which is often insipid or childish. The words used by adolescent boys and girls—who constitute the majority of activists in this field—have always struck me as sugary and therefore dirty, fearful and therefore inappropriate. Nor do the words that apply to the parts of the body derive any more strength or accuracy from the vocabulary of science or from Latin, assuming the person concerned was unlucky enough to frequent the classics in his youth. Far from ennobling their objects, such words as "fellatio" and "cunnilingus" make you think straight away of lovers wearing bow ties, pince-nez, and starched cuffs. Such words aim less at designating things than covering them up. And they succeed. So anyone who wants to describe his passion often has no alternative but to blush and say nothing. Unable to give expression to the most important scenes in his life, those that have given him the most happiness, he either resigns himself to silence or else tries to get somewhere near it and achieves only coarseness.

If I try to name the appendage that can sometimes be a nuisance when you're walking or asleep or competing in a bicycle race, I soon find the words at my disposal disappointing. Rod, prick, cock, etc.—they're all either too solemn or too facetious or have the wrong associations. Penis? Mentula? The first is too scientific and prudish, the second too pedantic. The word "genitals" itself is too aseptic and almost asexual, and applying equally to two opposing mythologies is inadequate to both. "No, that's not it!" we say angrily. Our language is very unsatisfactory when it comes to naming something that isn't merely an object: things and scenes are colored by the eye of the beholder. It's easier to describe Venus being greeted by the Seasons, robed by the Hours, or discovered by the Sun in the arms of Ares; it's easier to suggest what Psyche saw of her lover's body by the light of her little lamp, or what Gyges saw of the queen from behind his curtain—it's easier far to describe all these than it is to describe the inside of the thigh that you're actually touching and that you have to admit is your own. So I whisper the word "hirsute": Ibelle's "genitals" were incredibly hirsute, and the word has come to be her nickname, at least in my memory.

But for all my arguing and thinking, I'm not so sure of myself anymore. Maybe we don't see anything. And that is why Eros disappears. That is why the queen of Lydia insists that Gyges must come out from behind the curtain and marry her. I'm so overwhelmed by and blind to what disrobes. Everything is thrown down in confusion and leads to movement, predation, suction, desire. We become millionaires in terms of perspicacity or sadness or cynicism in the presence of someone getting dressed again, but then we no longer desire. The wish to express or describe is no longer motivated by union, but by separation. The relationship of the tongue to the secret parts of the body reminds one of the sangfroid of certain sophisticated women when you run into them accidentally in the daytime: their voices are smooth, elegant, and completely forgetful of what they may have cried out during the night. And when we see them again at night they say how afraid they were that their voices might have betrayed them earlier, and we don't believe them. But we're wrong. Fear always tries to hide, and the most acute fear becomes inarticulate. So perhaps we should say that lovemaking never is and never will be graced by one scrap of language, but only by a bit of a cry, a groan, or a vague silence.

You could go along by the sea, the cliff, and the rocks to reach the town by a steep, sandy lane with a slight but pervasive smell of human excrement. Which undoubtedly has a more pervasive smell than the waste products of butterflies, wasps, or gulls. It says in the Bible that God appeared to Moses on Mount Sinai in the form of a bush that burst into flame but was not consumed. Just before the disused railway bridge—the line had been closed down—that crossed over the road to Neuville, which we took to go to Saint-Martin-en-Caux, we used to pass the "floorcloth bush." We called it that because the railway bank there gave off a horrible smell like that of a rotten old rag that's been used to mop up urine.

Even on the finest summer days I could never see the waters of the Durdent in the distance; the river was always shrouded in mist or rain down there in the valley. At low tide we used to go down a long, difficult, rocky fishermen's path to a creek where every sound echoed back and forth. The cliffs closing it in, dotted here and there with pink and gray grass, saxifrage, and thyme, looked yellow and chalky as we were going down the path, but almost black as anthracite when we looked back up at them from the beach. The sand got the sun until about two or three in the afternoon, after which we went home to lunch. The noise on the little scrap of sand was deafening when the tide came in, even when the sea was smooth as glass. There were about ten really hot days during the summer, when there were swarms of flies and mosquitoes and insects of all kinds.

Isabelle missed her daughter terribly and had quarreled with her parents, who had disapproved of the divorce. She felt she was letting everyone down. She resented the fact that it didn't occur to me to talk about marriage. Regret, deprivation, disappointment—I couldn't really say what her feelings were. One day she suddenly said she was thinking about Delphine. I thought of her too—of her little hands tousling my hair or that would have played in the sand, peeled the peaches, dug up carrots from the kitchen garden behind Madame La Georgette's house, and collected shells and seaweed. I thought how my own insomnia had started when I was a child and my mother wasn't there. I used to lie awake with my hands by my sides like a knight on a tomb, trying to slow the beat of my heart and listening to the cars and carts going by on the little street paved with rough pink flagstones that ran by the end of the garden.

On July 15 or 16 Maria Callas and Giovanbattista Meneghini were divorced, and it started to rain. I asked for a separate room to work in. Ibelle shut herself up in the room we had made love in since we got there. The room was cold, and she gazed at the empty hearth, debating for hours whether she should light a fire. On the mantelpiece stood a row of postcards from Delphine, written by Seinecé in a clumsy, touching imitation of a child's hand. There weren't any chairs. Just the bed on the right.

Delphine was due to come and spend nine or ten days with us at the end of the month. Sometimes we were very excited about it; sometimes we were very anxious at the thought of seeing her again. When I think of the state I was in at her coming and the useless guilt I felt toward her, I have some idea of the frenzy of impatience Ibelle must have been in. I remember the strange dreams I had at the time: the ferocious yells of our childhood games of hide-and-seek as, riding on one another's backs and wearing thick white woolen slippers, we flushed our prey out from behind doors and curtains, from under beds and armchairs and inside chests. There's a scene in *Baron Münchhausen*, too, that is like what I dreamed: he's lost on his sleigh in the Estonian forest and driving as fast as he can. He whips his horse fiercely. Then whips the wolf who's eaten the horse. Then whips himself, who's eaten the wolf.

We slept in a big neoclassical bed made of stained and varnished wood, with an ebony light switch hanging down over the headboard. This switch, and reaching up to use it, was one of the few things that made Ibelle perfectly, childishly happy.

At about nine or ten in the morning, if she hadn't already come down, I used to take her up some coffee. I woke her up, having already had my kippers, my Späztle, and my Tokay hours ago. We made energetic love. What she liked most then, after our bodies had parted, was to jump up naked and open the window, throwing the iron shutters back with a clatter, filling the room with light, and rushing into the bathroom, leaving me to doze for a little alone on the bed before I started practicing my cello.

She couldn't bear to think of Seinecé, but countless sweet and touching memories that we couldn't help conjuring up were always accompanied by that familiar face, kind, mobile, and handsome. She'd known it long before I had, when he talked to her about how they would be together until they died, about the dozens of places where they'd live together and where together they'd die, designing them, arranging them, altering them, imagining what they'd do, what habits they'd form, what work would occupy them, and talking about the softness of her bare skin, the sweetness of her sleep, the muted texture of her voice. But I wasn't him. I didn't dream about places or the future. I was young and timid and looking after myself. Guilt brought back my childhood: half Catholic (at home) and half Protestant (at school). It brought back endless biblical memories. I was Judas Maccabeus undoing Apollonius and stealing his magic sword. The house at Bergheim was full of old wood engravings or copies by Wende depicting biblical scenes such as Susannah bathing, Judith slaying Holophernes, and Salome, her bosom bathed in sweat after her dance, laying her hand on the charger bearing the head of John the Baptist. Mother preferred Cozens and Girtin.

But Ibelle and I loved one another. We had many delightful hours. We shared our useless anxieties, our undermining remorse, our fears. We laughed together. But what I was afraid of was the inarticulate groans and involuntary noises of the body, the smell of vomit and bile, the white or transparent mucus you slip on on the pavement, the motionless bodies that have to be washed with a flannel by someone else, all cloying and scented smells. What Ibelle feared was a beard growing in silence, nutcracker jaws, people staggering about in the street and silently collapsing.

She was shorter than I but seemed very tall to me because of the way she moved about all the time, sitting down and stretching out with astonishing ease. The stunning clearness of her eyes disguised what she was thinking. I gazed into them without ever understanding anything. Her eyelashes were magically mobile. Her sex was small, strong, warm, gentle, delicious. At the height of pleasure, the spasm, when the incoherent movements of the body sometimes make lovers' lips part from even as they seek each other, she didn't cry out but gave a sort of deep and lilting laugh.

We were young. We were still, so to speak, splashing about in the timid intimacy of youth. It's only when the body promises much less than it has learned to perform that it begins to throw off the shackles of shame and use its knowledge to procure joys it unfortunately now scarcely deserves. The body becomes a more and more unworthy sacrifice to the god to whom it would offer itself up. But truth to tell, as I get older I wonder if there's any gift at all that's not insulted by the donor.

But perhaps it wasn't only that. Our love was greater than our desire. How could we avoid making love badly? Love isn't really suited to lovemaking. Ours consisted of violent caresses, and no matter how frequent they were they were always both robust and gauche. For my part I was hampered by my very ardor, and by remorse.

At Easter I'd brought Dido with me to Saint-Martin-en-Caux, but I was careful not to make the same mistake in the summer: I never got a wink of sleep because of going out to look for her in fields and woods, lanes and orchards. I knew all I needed to know about the pains of desertion. So this time I left Dido with a rich and strange friend of Klaus-Maria's who was staying in Paris in a huge apartment on Rue d'Aguesseau and whose name was Egbert Heminghos. It's often said that he who desires another doesn't wish only for the good of the person desired. Isabelle loving me, or gratifying some of my desires, was rather like Dido eating a tinned sardine—gobbling it up with enormous eagerness and yet with fastidious care, teeth flashing, discarding the bone. Isabelle liked the violence, the semblance of hurry and hunger, better than she liked the pleasure itself. The essence of the desire that attracts us to another body longs for that body as a predator longs for its prey or grass for water. And every body that is loved suddenly removes itself and withdraws like the sea. All longing longs to be rid of the goad of longing, and confusing it with its object, tries to get rid of the object itself. And so, in an awful way, everything that soothes is a kind of little baptism, the effect of which may be rather like that of death itself.

And there's another thing about love that has always frightened and to a considerable degree inhibited me. What comes menacingly to the surface in pleasure itself is that the most certain pleasures, and the dreams we base on them, are not really proper to man. They can only be called inhuman, and we share the inhumanity of our joys with rats and crocodiles, baboons and hippopotamuses. And what comes menacingly to the surface in pleasure is all the more terrible and frightening because it is by definition supremely agreeable, supremely voluptuous, supremely superhuman—in other words, it is beyond the power of language; it is ineffable. What fills desire with anguish and imbues it with excitement and fear is the chaos that results from anything excessively agreeable. Perhaps *we* didn't tremble with fear, but *I* certainly did. We were young, clumsy, speechless, scarcely giving each other more than a furtive glance. My memories of the love that drew me to Ibelle are almost childish. At Regnéville, near Coutances, ten years earlier, under a bridge over a dried up stream—it might have been called the Drochon—I and a little girl of twelve or thirteen, slightly older than I, used to go into the damp darkness under the low arch and sniff the smell of dried mud. We pushed away bits of excrement with our feet and bashfully sat down. We spoke in whispers, leaning against one of the stout, uneven piles. We awkwardly pressed one another's hands, breasts, lips, and private parts. It was rather painful. We pinched. We loved one another intensely for nine days. But we always forgot to embrace one another's toes. We never embraced one another's toes.

"Come along, you're not going to sit there chewing your lips all day, are you?" Madame La Georgette would cry.

We used to bathe in the creek, which according to a little wooden notice was called Slipping Stone Creek. Coming out of the sea and lying down quietly on a scorching hot towel on the sand, half dreaming vague and foolish dreams, is one of life's deepest pleasures, and one that even the poorest can afford. An additional source of satisfaction is that nothing can take it away from you. The strangeness and romance of dreams forms a part of a total well-being made up also of breathlessness after a buffeting by the waves; of feeling the pulse of the blood in your temples; and of being aware of the weight of your limbs, of space and volume in general, and of the warmth of the ambient air on which a curious fate has doomed us to depend.

I loved her legs, with grains of sand and little bits of shell glittering on them when she was lying on the beach in the sun. We went to see her childhood friends—Dominique and the Amaurys. As we came up the cliff path we could see Amaury and his wife in the distance, leaning on the balcony of their villa, built solidly in a combination of southern and Gothic styles at the beginning of the century. We could see Marion's light-colored dress fluttering around the pillars of the heavy concrete balustrade. From far away they were not so much people as fortuitous little marks against the dark green background of the hill to the east. The colored dots, the scraps of fabric on the land, were gazing out at the boats, at their sails, at other scraps of colored fabric on the sea.

Delphine's visit was different from what we'd tried to anticipate. Worse. She was mulish. She hated me—or my own awkwardness made her do so. She was looking magnificent, with deep red cheeks that looked as if they had been stained and polished. Ibelle wasn't any softer or easier to deal with than her daughter. She'd seen Seinecé, and her haughtiness had intensified into silence. All she did was spit out an occasional word. I irritated both Ibelle and Delphine. For the one, I had stolen her mother. For the other, I was a mere "artist" who kept unearthly hours and was unrecognized and hard up. "Must you always flinch your pennies?" she'd say when I wouldn't take her to the movies in Saint-Martin-en-Caux or to one of the little café-restaurants in Neuville. A poor replacement for a qualified archivist with a future. Or rather one driven by unhappiness into vengeful and, as it turned out, brilliant activity. He had been producing a series of learned articles, writing prefaces to catalogues, arranging exhibits, inventing all kinds of projects. Proud, thin, and fuming, Isabelle was furious because Seinecé had offered her a box of special salty caramels called *chiques de Caen*—as if I were a *guest*, she said. He'd also had the cheek to add that they were "for you and Karl": I'd told him once how much I used to love them when my sisters and I were little and spent our vacations in the Cotentin, near Coutances. I looked at Ibelle as she refused to meet my look, repeating to myself what my sisters used to say to me when I sulked: "Just like Götz von Berlichingen sending the emperor's envoy away with his butt in his hand."

Sometimes we hired bicycles for the day and rode into the "hinterland," through shining red villages already deserted and depressing. We pedaled along either silently, smoothly, and rather sadly, or else fast and furious.

The best days were when we went to Slipping Stone Creek. Delphine liked scrambling up on the rocks and then jumping off again with a yell to land just by my head. It nearly drove me crazy. She'd go on for hours, until the tide started to come inexorably in. Then, driven by a kind of nervousness or rage, she'd rush to the water's edge and start to heap up the already wet sand, slapping it into little mountains with her hands, only for the sea to sweep in again ruthlessly and with its eternal rhythm undermine and bring them down. I could see the pyramids of Cheops, Chephren, and Mykerinos being gradually surrounded by foam, but Delphine stole a march on the sea and stamped them flat herself. And as she stamped she yelled.

When the skies grew cloudy again we made plum jam. There was a glut of red and white currants in the market, but they were of poor quality. I decided to make some currant jelly, using the method they use in Bar-le-Duc. We took Delphine with us to the farm and got some goose feathers. These we took home and sharpened, then used them to remove the seeds from the currants, which were so soft they crushed when you touched them. This economical process greatly fascinated the farmer, more Norman than the Normans, who'd come with us, but I was put off by having him as a spectator as I slowly probed each currant for its seed. Then I replaced the little flap of skin and tossed the currant into boiling syrup. It wasn't a great success. Ibelle and I only managed to de-seed one currant out of every twenty; Delphine ate the other nineteen. Another farmer sold us a wild rabbit, and to our great surprise it was quite delicious when we cooked it with de-seeded red currants.

"When I was a little girl," Ibelle used to tell her daughter at great length, "I didn't want to make jam—I wanted to skim the foam." Delphine wanted to be a fisherwoman, catching sole in a huge square net lifted streaming out of the sea by a giant crane. Ibelle told me one day that when she was a child she wanted to be a laundress, so that she could roll up her sleeves and shout like a fishwife as she thumped at other people's underwear. Then she and the other girls would sing delightful ditties in the orchard as they pegged up lines of empty skins and energetically wrung-out shrouds. These images left me at once admiring and uneasy.

It was cold now—the last days of July in Normandy. The fire in the sitting room didn't give out much heat. We felt the only way to get warm was to throw ourselves on the fire instead of logs. We piled on several sweaters each. There was a bellows, but it was broken. At least the fire diverted Ibelle, who'd squat or kneel in front of it for hours every day, rearranging the burning logs with the poker.

Sometimes Delphine would forget she was supposed to hate me and climb on my lap. There she'd lean against me, suck her thumb, and gaze at the fire and her mother crouching there prodding at the dying branches and leaping flames. Every so often she'd whisper, "Henri IV wanted to go to war." And I'd put my lips to her ear and whisper back, "But Henri III didn't."

One rainy day she and I lay on the floor, competing at drawing our dream houses. My drawing depicted what seemed to be Mademoiselle Aubier's house but was really the house at Bergheim, with the rose garden, the grounds, the pond, the big bow window with its six half-curtains, the six dormer windows, the chimneys, the beeches. But when I'd finished, and Delphine was amusing herself by spitting plum stones at her own magnificent Louis XIII château with its forty-two windows—though it must be said a curious warp made the porch and the attics come rather close together here and there—something strange happened. The house I'd drawn and colored in time with Delphine coloring her own—"Green crayon!" she'd shout. "Ready, set, go!"—the house I'd thought was like the house at Bergheim suddenly changed. As Delphine burst into a song proclaiming that we never had and probably never would see a mouse's tail hanging out of Dido's ear, my house turned into a big, blank, sad face like that of a corpse. I thought of my mother in the Necker Hospital. My stepfather was there, and I don't know why, but regardless of the fact that I was now grown-up, and suppressing the repugnance, tension, and even rebelliousness I felt at the sight of him, I rushed over and kissed him. My older sisters looked away, and Cäci whispered the familiar supreme insult in my ear: "Ass licker!" I suppose I must have looked at my mother—how can I even doubt it?—but I can't remember anything about it except that her face was all puffed up with cortisone. My cozy house was my dying mother.

As long as I have life and breath I'll remember the day she died, the cold, the smell. We'd heard Kennedy announcing the blockade of Cuba on the radio. Aunt Elly, Fräulein Jutta, Holger, my sisters, and I had been arriving one after the other every half hour at the apartment in Neuilly. Only Marga, who was carrying Markus at the time, didn't come. Then we all climbed into Holger's big van. The date was October 25, 1962. It was Luise who'd arranged—perfidiously arranged—for Mother to go to Necker, not only because that was the best place for her to be treated for cancer but also, it seemed to me, because the hospital's German-sounding name was a way of somehow repatriating her, bringing her back to the banks of the Neckar. Luise hadn't spoken a word of French for years, and her five children were never allowed to learn it.

I looked at my drawing in dismay. I didn't like to crumple it up: it would be not merely as if I'd resurrected someone but also as if I'd committed a murder. I picked up Delphine's drawing and slipped mine underneath it as I argued with her. I had a lump in my throat. We didn't vote on which of us had won. I don't know why, but the pictures she drew and colored were always the best.

The butterflies were marvelous that year. First at Easter, and then during our longer visit in July and August. I'd never been so far north in Normandy before. I explored, I walked, I cycled. I picked bunches of thistles and valerian, and some almost white wild carnations with a faint, slow, distant scent—the result of rain and sea and dew, and perhaps of the ancient tears of the gods.

Isabelle spoke less and less. She just kept up the fire in the sitting room, her lips slightly pursed and sulky. We could scarcely believe that only four days ago it had been so hot and we had gone swimming in the creek under the cliff. We would leave our bag, towels, clothes, and watches on flat projecting rocks up above, like the misericords dotted about among the stalls in ancient churches for elderly preachers and priests to perch on.

I didn't know what to do. I practiced for nearly six hours a day. At Easter I needed mittens like the ones the Chenognes and all the other organists in Bergheim had worn for centuries in the winter. The tips of the fingers on my left hand were so calloused they were deformed and almost devoid of feeling. To warm myself up, to fill the empty hours, and to break Ibelle's silence, I brought in wood from the pile Madame La Georgette had clipped and pruned and stacked on the lawn. It was a very tedious task.

The house was always full of the smell of damp, smoking wood, which gave us not so much a permanent headache as one that advanced and retreated like the sea, but so slowly and imperceptibly that I never had the pleasure of realizing that it was going or gone. I occasionally felt as if I were wearing a musketeer's cap jammed down over my eyes, or an Army Service Corps beret, as at Saint-Germain-en-Laye.

The wool sweaters we were obliged to wear had a mixed and eventually nauseating smell of fires made of oozing wet wood; of damp, slippery grass; and of earthworms. At the beginning of August we still went swimming, though the horizon was always a curtain of rain that looked only a couple of yards away. The world seemed to be without depth, the sea without extension. We swam not so much in the sea as in great floating masses of brown seaweed torn by storms from their moorings. You swam through all this with the energy of disgust. If you turned on your back it was like swimming through vegetable peelings or dead animals.

In order to keep warm, so she said, Isabelle went climbing, as she used to do as a child in Lons-le-Saunier. She clambered over the rocks, clinging and groping for holds with her hands and feet. This involved scraping her fingers, thighs, and knees, which didn't detract from their charms though it didn't always add to them either. This made me envy the gracefulness of cats, and the genius of snails and slugs for slithering up tree trunks, walls, and cliffs. Though of course I have the typical musician's smug, narcissistic, namby-pamby fear of damaging my fingers.

Particularly annoying for such a sensitive plant as myself was the crude way Madame La Georgette used to lay into me. For instance, if, having made love to Isabelle when she woke up, I came down to the kitchen with her in my pajama bottoms—not even the largest pair could, after the usual miraculous shrinkings, protect quite all of me from the cold—not only would Isabelle remark on how they fitted me like a pimple on a haystack, but Madame La Georgette would have to go one better and say they looked like a ruff round Jesus Christ's neck. Since there is nothing like repeated pleasantries to keep you warm, Isabelle spent the whole day making these flattering comparisons. My undershorts suited me as a wig would have suited Julius Caesar. The corduroy trousers I wore to shield myself from the August heat on the Normandy coast looked as appropriate as a pair of pince-nez on Attila the Hun. In the sea, my swimming trunks made me look like an American among the ruins of Nineveh. And when I was naked—this was no doubt a charitable view, though I myself could only imagine the effect so described—I was like an inhabitant of Nineveh in the caves at Lascaux.

It got colder and colder. I bought bottles of liqueurs and the old-fashioned aperitifs that Ibelle loved. And the sponge fingers called "boudoirs" that she and Madame La Georgette dunked in their glasses after lunch or dinner like a couple of old women.

And that was how love became as tedious as the wisdom of Solomon or the aggressive darts Madame La Georgette used to aim at me when she came in at ten or eleven in the morning to cook lunch. We'd gradually stopped believing that love meant throwing ourselves on one another with gritted teeth and nerves at breaking point. We'd gradually given up clutching one another so tight we ended up crushed and bruised.

If Isabelle ever offered herself now it was as if she wasn't completely there. Her appearance was there, enveloping her, but inside it she drew back into herself. All I ever touched was a scrap of soft, warm, pink skin, a smooth nail, a little strand of hair, the glint of ivory teeth shown by a small carnivorous animal that is suddenly a little more humble and affectionate than usual. But this wasn't what I used to call "Ibelle," and I couldn't always manage to desire her. And yet it was she, accompanied by that body, that I loved.

As we didn't moan together anymore, Ibelle liked to crouch or sit on the floor, and I used to feel both shame and self-satisfaction at being able to look over her head from where I sat on a chair or the bed. Even our discussions were different now. Instead of "Do you remember when I first saw you?" we asked, "What shall we do?" Instead of "The first time I realized that you . . ." it was "Promise me that in 1966 we'll . . ."

We avoided mentioning Florent's name as if the very sound had power to wound us. Every time it emerged from the oblivion to which we tried to consign it—and that was often—it was as if something was torn inside us, as if we were losing blood. Only Delphine prattled on about what her father was doing, his fantastic virtues, and how lucky she was—she said this lightly, as if in passing—that he'd been given custody of her. And she'd crouch down to suck or stroke the bits of blue and green glass she'd picked up on the beach, fragments of broken bottles rubbed smooth by the sea.

Veules, Saint-Martin, Sotteville, Yport—they're not exactly memories. More like one little fairy-tale picture of a secluded hamlet at the foot of a cliff. We were so high up. You couldn't tell the washing on the line from the seagulls. And the gray church tower and steeple mingled with the masts of the fishing boats.

Halfway down the hill you came to a little garden—a few flower beds, a mossy gravel path, and pools of light. You went through the gate, walked across the grass, and came face to face with a bush that sobbed. It made you think of a Middle Eastern god: the cloud from which he'd issued had probably strayed out and dispersed forever over the Atlantic. (There are plenty of these lost gods in this part of the world; people don't pray or bow their heads anymore.) When you put your hand in among the glossy leaves you found a child looking at you openmouthed. You reached out, drew her to you, kissed her. On her cheek was something of the dawn.

It seemed to me that even Madame La Georgette was different, though I think now I was mistaken. She seemed to have become aggressive and hateful, a moralizing old witch—demoralizing, surly, brusque, sour, and shrewish. She was always quoting "Our Lord Jesus Christ" and followed up every noble sentiment, theory, consolation, or argument exchanged between Ibelle and me with, "So, Ibelle, would you kindly tell me what that means?" And she'd turn on Delphine and tell her to "eat your fist if you're hungry!" if she got under her feet. (The phrase she used was "in her skirts," though her skirts took the form of a voluminous pair of shiny old brown jersey trousers.)

Under the window by the kitchen sink there were several pairs of brown rubber galoshes which Madame La Georgette made us put on whenever it rained or the ground was muddy. We used to go through great contortions trying to drag them on over our shoes, but when we got back they were comparatively easy to peel off, and even before we took off our oilskins we put them back on the kitchen floor, wet and muddy and covered with shiny little yellow leaves.

"You're nice ones," Madame La Georgette would complain, "making a pond in my nice clean kitchen! Soaked to the marrow, you are!"

We changed our clothes and lit a fire, which Ibelle would tend like a gardener growing a rare plant and helping it with stakes and constant watching. We burned old apple tree stumps. Delphine had gradually become tame and, probably following her mother's example, sat in front of the fire with a lapful of green pine cones that she had collected, singing and chuckling as she picked them up in her little hands and threw them on the flames.

One morning when I'd gone down to the harbor in my freezing yellow oilskins to buy some fish, I ran into Raoul Costeker and Sylvette Miot.

"Oh, Karl!" she said, "you've been crying inside!"

I went over to the fish stall. There were some little sea bream. As I tried to make up my mind whether to buy one, Costeker took me by the arm, shook it vigorously, and kissed me on both cheeks.

"Go back to Paris!" he said. "Normandy isn't good for you. It isn't good for anything but ponds and grass. You must go back to Paris!"

"I'll have a little piece of steak or shoulder of beef," I said.

The fishmonger made me say it again and looked at me wide-eyed. My hand was shaking. Costeker kept on urging me to go back to Paris.

I refused. It's like a Bach chorale. We grope as if in the dark. We stagger as if we're drunk. In German, Bach means stream. And it was in the form of a stream that he appeared to me in my dreams. I've had a recurrent nightmare ever since I was four or five years old. A huge, completely hollow tree, a kind of eucalyptus, is swarming with earwigs. A saucepan full of boiling eucalyptus leaves stands on a big dark tiled or iron stove. There's a strong smell in the room.

The pan has boiled dry, but it's still left on the stove. It has become red-hot, and the eucalyptus leaves turn into earwigs. The bottom of the pan is really a great bloody ear swarming with earwigs. I was the ear. The earwigs were eating my brain.

I've often had that nightmare. The ear, the stove, the half-open door, and sometimes salamanders instead of earwigs. A stove that's not the one at Bergheim—which was tiled, as a matter of fact—I don't know where it belongs, but I'm not supposed to touch it. I can see its little door now. The little brass handle tempts me, tempts my fingers because it's so forbidden. On the little door there's a scene from the Bible, though I don't know either whom it depicts or what it means. Not that knowing names necessarily helps you to understand what they mean. A woman with pointed, milky breasts is bringing a billhook close to the hair of a huge man asleep with his head in her lap. In the distance another giant with fetters on his neck and hands is going around a millstone. I remember I confused the face of the woman with a sort of fairy cow in doubtful taste that excreted sand into people's eyes at night.

This is my earliest memory of the nightmare. I was four or five years old and I'd hurt myself. I'd climbed the plum tree and a branch had given way. A week or two later my mother returned from Caen—not Neuilly—and came into my room. I was in bed, but she didn't come over to me.

"What have you done to your arm?" she said.

"I broke it," I answered.

"Just your luck!" she said, and went on into Lisbeth's room without kissing me. That lack of a kiss—but how can you talk about a kiss that doesn't exist, about the almost voluble effects of its absence?—still burns my cheek. Or, to use another image, it opened up what feels like a great almost incurable wound inside me and gave me a continual desire to scribble words and scrape strings.

The gray tower in the harbor at Saint-Martin-en-Caux made me think both of the Tour Guillaume at Regnéville and of the tower built of blue stones at Bad Wimpfen. There's a famous Christ with movable joints at Bad Wimpfen, and that too pervaded my dreams and terrorized my childhood. It had real hair. So did my mother.

I was in the grip of a strange sadness that was never actually painful but never ceased. It naturally affected my love for Ibelle. I felt myself gradually being drained of the emotion that's usually aroused all the time by the presence of a beloved body. People's affections can be measured in sounds and smells. They are yokes on the shoulders and bonds on the hands and feet. But to feel them pressing on your neck or fingers or ankles, or in your nostrils or the lobe of your ear, is already a kind of betrayal. To hear them is already to bid a tiny farewell to the person you've loved.

Our bodies were no longer transfigured. We had gradually lost the ability to spend hours on each other's bodies without ever getting bored, contemplating the beauty of the light falling on them and the marvelous fragility of curves, of belly, finger, ankle, ear, or thigh. Everything had become humiliated and raw.

In my view it's difficult to contemplate at length organs that are not terribly unusual—which in fact are extremely common—and to entertain sentiments, which are extremely common too. Of course, we do admire at length, and with great and marvelous expressiveness, the genital organs of plants, which we call flowers. We're always giving them to people. "I've brought you a nice little genital organ!" If I talked to Isabelle about the alternations of light and shade inside us she only shrugged and said derisively, "Solly, Cholly!"—a harmless pleasantry that nonetheless gave me a lot of pain when I was a child. She didn't believe that familiarity, though it may strengthen the understanding between two bodies by gradually doing away with clumsiness, shyness, and embarrassment, can also erode their amity. She didn't believe that proximity can separate people or that affection is a rather tedious sentiment, by its very nature bound to be tinged to some degree with boredom, soppiness, and somnolence. Every shadow is cast by some body. And the body in whose shadow we now lived and which darkened everything was Seinecé's.

We didn't want to acknowledge that name. We were displeased with ourselves, and the reproaches we started addressing to one another, all the time and over trifles, we would have been better off making to ourselves. We ate together, dressed together, spoke to one another, watched one another, clashed with one another wearily but persistently. But we fell silent more and more often, and the silence was more complex, more charged, heavier with unshared thoughts and dreams and resentments than the occasional hackneyed shafts with which we halfheartedly tried to wound one another.

"I'm happy as a shark," Ibelle would say, with a pathetic attempt at sarcasm.

"I can't stand this life either," I'd reply.

"I can't stand it, you can't stand it, we can't stand it . . ." she'd shout, claiming she'd abandoned everything for me and giving me little punches with her fist which might have been affectionate but might also have been meant to assuage a certain amount of hatred.

We had increasingly heated and unpleasant arguments. Isabelle had to take Delphine back to Florent at Chatou, and decided, by way of getting at me, to spend three days with her parents afterward at Lons-le-Saunier. So I was alone in the house at Saint-Martin-en-Caux. It rained. I went and shut the big heavy rickety shutters. When I came in I lit a few lamps to make the place, and myself, brighter and more alive. I spread a newspaper over the kitchen table and fetched a dozen wrinkled, speckled apples from the garden. I was going to stew them.

Madame La Georgette came in only during the day, so I was alone. Nights are a trial to me because I sleep badly and the time goes so slowly. I dislike sleeping alone. The claws of the field mice clicking across the attic in sudden rushes, the very fact that the little brutes were there, seemed horrible and outrageous. My hand hung out over the side of the bed, and I put it under the sheet so it wouldn't get gnawed.

I couldn't get to sleep. Bright moonlight came through the diamond-shaped hole in the shutter. I gently pushed the sheet aside.

Certain memories, certain chance happenings stay in the memory as almost unbelievably perfect. When I awoke it was one of those rare days of dazzling sunshine. Perhaps, there on the Normandy coast, the miraculousness lay in the rarity. I worked for a few hours, then hurried down to the creek. But I could see from the path that someone had gotten there before me: three bathers were lying on the sand. I hesitated for a moment about going on. From the cliff I could see the Slipping Stone itself standing out black as ink against the sea. Sky and sea were both a lovely, milky, Meissen blue. I decided to go on down. I went past the little oratory and the bush of the unseen floorcloth. I went on down, wanting to get into the sun. I began undressing as I passed the three bathers, a man and two women, lying face down and obviously asleep. I spread a towel out by the water's edge, went in and swam for a few seconds, then shook myself partly dry and came and lay down in the ten o'clock sun at the water's edge.

It's mostly been as I've lain in the sun, like a plant absorbing energy through its chlorophyll, that I've felt something eternal welling up in me: forgetfulness, gratitude, and an intense feeling of being alive. I fell asleep.

The incoming tide wetted my feet and awoke me from my dream. I stood up and spread my towel out again further up the beach, not far from the other three bathers. Then I lay down and started drifting off again, but whenever I opened my eyes for a second I could see one of the women—the darker and more southern-looking of the two—watching me. I smiled at her and she smiled back.

Desire is a strange thing. All of a sudden we find ourselves on the same wavelength as someone else, seem to have a secret understanding with them. We looked at one another with pleasure, almost friendliness. After a while she got up and waded slowly into the sea. She was very large, with well-defined curves and a certain stiffness in her bearing; but that slight resemblance to an idol, that athletic yet hieratic back, is a type that has always impressed me. We swam and chatted and laughed.

When we came out of the water we lay down near one another, and she told me about her vacation. She was Greek. She had come from Paris and was going to Bordeaux with her friends, then on to join her husband and daughter in Provence on the way back to Greece. My name was Karl Chenogne. Hers was Photini Gaglinou. Her husband's name was Stephanos Gaglinos. She didn't say any more about him. Her skin, beaded with salty sweat, gave off with every movement smells that were increasingly heady and desirable. Smell is intoxicating. I was invaded by desire as a neglected garden is invaded by grass. I covertly watched the hesitant yet rash beads of perspiration gradually creep down between her breasts. I stroked her hand. She held mine. We lay there for a while like that: like a couple of five-year-olds in little gray smocks lined up in the playground before marching off into the cold classroom under their teacher's eye. Then we moved our bodies closer and joined our lips.

"Can we go to your place?" she whispered in my ear.

I was afraid of Madame La Georgette, who would be preparing lunch by now, and I preferred to go to a hotel. The hotel stood in the middle of the curve of the harbor, and the only room free was a little one on the second floor with sham mahogany furniture, 1950s style. We made love joyfully and without sentiment, but with indescribable hunger and pleasure. I took her to lunch at a farm restaurant at Ouville-l'Abbaye, near Yvetot, and we came back and had dinner in Fécamp.

I feel like Baron Münchhausen, telling endless stories about his hunting prowess, each more incredible and boastful than the last. I'm building up a flattering picture of myself as a successful seducer. But I must correct this impression: I can count the bodies I've desired, not violently but long, on a mere two fingers of one hand. I've probably been attracted by five or six women altogether. I've attracted even fewer of them. Of the eight women I lived among in my childhood, only Marga and Luise—and to a lesser degree Hiltrud—paid any attention to me. Seinecé was the first person to give me, in addition to friendship, a little disinterested affection—something that seemed to me an attribute of Homer's heroes, but certainly not of the gods, or Jesus' disciples. Since then, out of the five women who have lived with me for a while, three have left me. I suppose I must want it to happen, and that it's partly this possibility in them that attracts me, from the very first twinge of desire.

Photini was extraordinarily beautiful—muscular, massive, radiant, athletic, outgoing. Beauty is never internal. That would be a contradiction in terms. It's revealed to us by a kind of reflection, a reflection that in itself is pure appearance. She never spoke a single word of love—but I've never seen anyone else so open and wholesome and cheerful. She spoke very good French, as far as I could judge, lapsing into English if she couldn't think of a word. But we didn't talk much. It was only in passing I learned that her husband was an industrialist, and why he happened to be in Nice with her daughter. I've forgotten the reason now. Ever since the most ancient songs—not about birds or dolphins but human beings; ever since the invention of the bow as a weapon (I think I have the right—all musicologists have the right—to speak with confidence of things of which no trace remains); ever since earliest times, love has been compared to a single, sudden, unexpected, terrible arrow. You say to yourself, "My soul has been dealt a great wound that is growing bigger all the time!" And every time it's a revelation. And every time, unable to recognize what it is that the revelation reveals, you can't get over it.

We loved each other for about forty hours. On the second day it rained again and we stayed in the room, going out for breakfast, lunch, tea, dinner, and *medianoche*. Her body had a beauty that was strong, dense, earthy, greedy, sublime. Those parts that usually seem rather ill-smelling, that are usually kept out of sight, that never are really altogether clean—why is it that the thought of licking them makes one's heart beat faster? That day, that double day, was an unending joy. And it seems to me I still feel some desire for that body.

Photini and her friends left Saint-Martin-en-Caux to go first to Mont-Saint-Michel and then to Provence. Our goodbyes were short and shy and perhaps moving. We didn't even try to exchange addresses. We never saw one another again. But I remember that strange name: Photini Gaglinou, with its curious demeaning genitive. Belonging to Gaglinos, it meant, and it applied to our few hours together. I waited for Isabelle to come back: she'd never been altogether "Seineçou." Unfortunately I've never been able to make convincing, amusing puns. The rain had come back, and it poured down tirelessly.

Rainy evenings when it drizzles down all the time are awful, nerve-racking. There's nothing I loathe more than the sound of rain dripping on concrete or stone steps, or the sight of it leaking in and streaming down the walls. It makes me feel as if something inside me were oozing furtively away, not daring to stream, gnawing. On the other hand, a real storm, with the rain beating at the window, makes me feel excited and happy.

Isabelle came back morose, with a sore throat, a cough, and a husky voice. And I realize it's only sounds that come back to me, not colors or materials—the sounds of coughing, of someone suddenly losing her voice, of a nose sniffling. Ibelle's return from Lons-le-Saunier, the noise of the rain on concrete or steps, the sound—the hoarse panting—of love; they all bring back to me the wheezing plaint of a pump over a tank and the spurting of water into a bowl or bucket. It was the tank at Bormes and the beginning of my love for Ibelle that they brought back then. And there again it was a matter of sounds. The plaint of the pump over the well had almost become the sound of my own body, the sound stamping my body with Ibelle's name, the sound that bore witness to the first time my body hardened because of her, drawn toward her and at the same time rejecting her desire. And now I had turned away from her. One evening I stopped loving her, though I didn't know it. I don't really remember which evening it was, but an evening came when we knocked our teeth together. For a moment we lay as if dead. The sound of our teeth, the enamel of our teeth clashing together, was extraordinarily loud, dull, disagreeable, and real. Again it was a matter of a sound, an acoustical warning—or perhaps of a musical score more profound than that at the mercy of the tongue; a delusive and perverse shoot growing up out of a network of sound deeper still. A passion had been diluted, had become mixed with the drizzle and the rain and the sound of the rain. Everything seemed terribly fragile, tedious, temporary, transitory. We were in transit. We are in transit. Our feet were frozen, are frozen, our noses dripping, vapor coming out of our mouths. And we huddled together again in the corner. We huddle still.

We are in transit. That also means we move toward the past. We move totally, entirely, toward a total past. About twenty-five miles away, on the banks of the Seine near Notre-Dame-de-Gravenchon, were some large circles of sand that an old man had told us were quicksand. Your feet soon sank into them, and the more you tried to struggle free the deeper you sank. Our love was sinking deeper and deeper too. And gradually, like water growing smooth again after being disturbed, the surface closed over faces and bodies now become invisible. Our love itself had grown strangely invisible to me. The past, death—they are the quicksand that swallows us up. Sand itself is only mountains broken down into grains. Like memories. And alas, like all I am and all I do and all I write. If we pick a handful of sand up on the beach and open our fingers a little, what sifts through them is a mountain. And the sound we hear as it falls is the whisper of a cliff.

At four or five in the morning I carried the heavy, smelly, black rubber garbage can out onto the road. At about eleven I went and bought some bread in Neuville's main street, and beer, wine, vinegar, and cookies from the grocery store. Then, since Ibelle wouldn't, I started cooking lunch. For some reason I don't remember, Madame La Georgette no longer cooked for us at noon, and Ibelle had lost interest in that kind of thing. Love had its etiquette, and it would have been wrong for unhappiness to dirty its hands or think about groceries. I used to whisk a broom or a duster vaguely around the house in the evening, provided Ibelle didn't see me. I quoted Klaus-Maria, who was keen on cross-legged meditation: "Buddha is just as present in the broom that sweeps the toilets as he is in a temple." Ibelle replied that as I wasn't likely to live in a temple I might as well resign myself to the alternative. It's true no religious precept, including those of India, has ever been of any use to me. I was careful not to touch Ibelle's clothes, which lay scattered all around the bedroom.

All the women I've met in my life—and who have undoubtedly lit it up, mainly in its sunniest hours—have been so remarkable and had so high and accurate an idea of their own value that they never did anything that might have lowered themselves in their own eyes; they never did anything very concrete beyond just possessing a body. They felt no great enthusiasm for what nourished them or for the setting they lived in, for places, colors, thoughts, and sounds. Nor did they care for the things that can create complex and varied bonds and bind people together deeply and long, though I myself find discussions about ideas extremely appealing because they're reminiscent of the refrains we sang over and over again in our childhood, and of the pleasure, the deep and amazing pleasure, that empty clatter gave us. Yet women excel at that clatter. But at what do they not?

It was nine o'clock. I had stopped translating. The sun was back and flooded the room where I'd been working. I went down into the garden and sat down on the highest part of the lawn. I set out two cane chairs to show Ibelle I'd be glad for her company. The morning sun was almost scorching again. I could see the smooth, dark green sea in the distance, beyond the oaks and the parasol pines. I remember I was reading and preparing some Sebastian Lee and Goltermann scores and I was rather bored. Then I had a sudden sense of upheaval, as if a long-awaited decision had been made without my knowledge. This is what it was: I didn't like that kind of music, I liked seventeenth- and early-eighteenth-century music, I was leaving Ibelle and going back to Paris, I cared only about baroque music now, I was getting to be a great cellist, Arraucourt was taking me on, everyone made way for me. "Who is he?" people asked as I went by. Others whispered back respectfully: "That's the new Sainte Colombe—don't you recognize him? He's the new Marin Marais, the new Cupis!" I decided to leave, to go back to Paris, to start a new life. I was beginning to hate Normandy. It was like the oilcloth with little pink nuts and apple-green ferns that Madame La Georgette cleaned—if you could call it that—with a greasy damp rag after meals. There, under the light hanging from the middle of the kitchen ceiling, it was as bright and shiny as a waterlogged meadow, as smooth and sticky as a dying passion.

For whatever reason, all that grass, that rain, that sea, that woman had become a source of loathing: the rocks, the limpets on the rocks, the broken cockleshells that cut your feet, the slippery seaweed, the beds of mussels, the shoals of swimmers, the vulgarity of everyone, the suburban relationship one had to the town, the holiday relationship one had to life in general, as if one were living in a suburb in time, a blind alley in time and space and in the heart. There was also the ceaseless sensuality: it was like always milking the cows at a fixed time, or like a festering wound that you felt would heal if only you left it alone for a day or two. Then there was the distress, the constant distress, that made the lawn wet and sitting in the garden so revolting. And all the wasps and bees and flies that year. The jellyfish on the beach, the mosquitoes at night.

I grabbed an old novel full of melodrama—the sadistic death of a carpenter's son, beautiful women showing men their naked charms and then murdering them, or so hungry they ate their newborn babies, together with the umbilical cord and even the placenta—and passionately squashed mosquitoes with it. Whenever I killed one I said to myself, "Good! So the Bible serves some purpose!" By August 6 I was back in Paris. On August 8 I was reestablishing an old privilege; I was back in Saint-Germain-en-Laye kissing Mademoiselle Aubier on the cheek.

When I drove up in my four-horsepower Citroën—the quadriga was drawn by a team of four horses in Roman triumphs—Mademoiselle Aubier was just stepping cautiously out of the house carrying a green Empire card case under her arm. I drew up sharply and opened the door of the car.

"Good gracious!" she said. "Is it really you, Monsieur Chenogne? This *is* a pleasant surprise!"

I parked the car. She walked with me to the gate. I renewed my acquaintance with Pontius, Mademoiselle Aubier's dog, and we shook hands and rubbed noses.

"Here's the key to the house," said Mademoiselle Aubier. "Denis is in Iowa for a couple of months."

She pronounced it "ay-oh-wah!," like an anguished little cry addressed to Pontius.

"I've got an errand to do, but I'll be home before you've had time to get back to the Pont-Neuf!"

Mademoiselle Aubier had aged. She was wearing a gray crêpe dress and a magnificent hat trimmed with gray mauve-spotted butterflies and a gray tulle veil. Her hair was arranged in a low, untidy bun. She was seventy-nine years old now, but she still had a kind of gentle, crumpled, shriveled beauty. After she got back and we were having tea, almond cookies, and éclairs, I told her about my love for Ibelle.

"Tell me the old, old story!" she said. I was hurt by her obvious scorn. She put her handkerchief to her lips, scrupulously wiping away a crumb or an imaginary drop of tea or saliva.

I didn't conceal the difficulties we'd been having.

"You know," she said, "I didn't get to my age without learning something about human emotions. You think you love Isabelle. But I suspect it's more like the rows young children take so seriously and yet enjoy so much in the playground. And I know a cure for it, the only one that hasn't been refuted by experience. What you have to do is spray the bedclothes lightly every morning with essence of wild thyme. In moderation, of course. But you must agree the whole thing is pretty optimistic, and pretty pointless. Tell me frankly, Charles, have two bodies ever merged into one? If you ask me, it's just something dreamed up by people who were dropped on their hats when they were young."

And Mademoiselle Aubier, cynical one moment, prudish and strait laced the next, told me how she'd never allowed any idle caresses—except once. The person concerned was a friend of the great Stéphane-Raoul Pugno. She herself was very young at the time. Nineteen. It was in 1905.

"I think it must have been 1905," she said, "because it was the year we had to move from Rue du Quatre-Septembre—they were building the métro, and the noise and dust were unbearable. But Papa liked to go and work in the National Library."

She paused.

"Shall we have a little something to wet our whistles now to restore us after all this deep conversation?"

I realized we'd been using this expression for two years. So had Seinecé. Mademoiselle Aubier thought it very vulgar to talk about apéritifs.

"Can I say a rude word?" she'd simper every time the tiny Directoire clock struck noon, putting her hand in front of her mouth like a little girl giggling or pretending to giggle. "What do you say to wetting our whistles?"

She poured me some fortified wine, filled a glass to the brim for herself, and went on, wandering from the subject to talk about music and her mother.

"Mama was a friend of Jane de Théza, and in January 1899 she sang in public for the first and last time in her life, at the Philharmonic Society in La Rochelle. She came before Mademoiselle Menjaud, who gave a brilliant performance of Fauré's 'Cradles.' But Mama was a great success too, even though with her usual modesty she wouldn't admit it. She sang Guiraud's 'Do You Remember?' Would you like to hear it?"

I didn't want to refuse, so we went into the house, though I'd have preferred to stay in the garden. We were sitting by the willow tree, near the front steps. I had brought out the chaise longues as soon as I arrived, and Mademoiselle Aubier had sipped her tea and wine and eaten her coffee éclair in the shade of her parasol.

She leaned on my arm as we made our way slowly to the damp music room behind the steps.

I had to sit at the piano and accompany her as in the old days. Mademoiselle sang her mother's piece, "Do You Remember?," first, then we finished with "Sweet Tree That Brings Back Memories," and then went to sit down under the willow. When we were stretched out on our chaise longues once more she reverted to our previous conversation.

"On the one hand I say to myself, Charles Chenogne is down in the dumps—it's as plain as the nose on your face—and I ought to try to cheer him up. But on the other hand I say to myself, this sort of thing can't really be patched up, and anyway it's more of a lark than a tragedy, and it stirs the blood. I promise you, old age is quite another kettle of fish. No fun at all. And it doesn't stir up anything . . .

"You know," she suddenly burst out more loudly, "I find it extremely unpleasant to think that our consciousness of the world and the people in it should cease when we die."

"But highly probable, just the same!" I replied with the self-assurance and arrogance of my age at the time.

"You'll think I'm a bit nuts," she said, lowering her voice to utter this "modern" expression, to which she descended in order to be on my level. "But I'd have loved to see what happens after I'm dead. And I might actually have liked to survive for a while too . . ."

She stood up, leaning on her parasol, and thought for a while. "Just for a few years," she whispered.

I left Mademoiselle when she suggested I should stay and she would cook dinner for us both. But I agreed to share the rest of the macaroons and almond cookies—there were no more eclairs—that she'd bought when she was out shopping, after I arrived. I ate two macaroons.

"Monsieur Chenogne," she said, "this is such a pleasure. Of course you're a kind of giant. For years I thought the height of human experience was to have a prune tart in Rumpelmayer's on Rue de Rivoli."

"And *isn't* it the height of human experience?" I asked, suddenly anxious.

"No," she said. "It isn't the height of human experience. But it *is* the height of wisdom."

When I left her and turned round to see that little gray silhouette outlined in the distance against the dark boxwood trees, I realized how lonely her life was. She lived in an absolute solitude, out of time if not out of space, and in a way already out of this world. Denis wouldn't be back from America till September.

Back in the car, hunched over the steering wheel, I dreamed aloud. I was still a child. Isabelle said she never missed her childhood in the least. She said she hated family life and grandfather clocks, homemade rolls that were only half-cooked, and horrible things like nettles, flies, wasps, hornets, and hens. I wasn't sure, myself, that you ever left behind the age when you're terrified by strange sounds, when you can't get to sleep, when nobody loves you, when you discover the piano, when you first pluck the strings of a miniature cello—the age when you measure yourself against the still enormous and all-powerful stature of adults. For the first time I felt an aversion for my own excessive height and resentment at my lack of age. I would have liked to be as old as Mademoiselle Aubier, and as diminutive. I was knee high to a grasshopper and at the same time nearly six feet tall. And as thin as a rusty nail.

I went back to Saint-Martin-en-Caux on August 9. All that made me go was anxiety, the desire to get it over, remorse, the beginnings of pity for Ibelle, and a weakening of my own mendacity. I brought Isabelle a present of a low chair, a delightful little thing—or at least I thought so—made of imitation ebony with a seat of red and blue straw. How pointless these memories are. I see this book, or perhaps I should say these pages, like the little flypapers that used to hang from the lights and the beams. They were yellow, and a fly would crash into them, stick by its wings to their yellow glue, and die very, very slowly, making a noise quite disproportionate to its size, while other flies danced around it. Flypaper too is now a thing of the past. When I was a child and held a fly prisoner in my hand, its dry, tickling, noisy buzz soon made me open my fingers and let it go. That image of the fly with its dry, terrified wings, that titillating presence, is for me the image of desire. But desire had vanished now. Ibelle put the black, red, and blue chair down, and her lips and hands came close. But she saw I was sheepish and embarrassed, and the lights in her eyes went out.

"You don't love me anymore," she said brusquely.

I had already experienced as a child these desertions of desire, these panic longings to go away or die. Fat little Gudrun had captivated me. I was fascinated by her breasts underneath her sweater and intrigued for a long while by the way they bounced when she walked fast. I took her to the remotest part of the grounds at Bergheim—a most unattractive spot, no doubt because it couldn't be seen from the house. There was a line of washing hung out to dry between two trees. The discussion we had was highly academic, thanks to me: shame, desire, and the place combined to make me surly. I gazed at the water dripping from a pair of white underpants belonging to one of my sisters. "They're falling in dactyls!" I thought. Then I looked at Gudrun, pushed her aside, and went away. The clothes out to dry, the chubby body, the Latin all shocked me: desire had disappeared from the face of the earth. I just got up and ran away. Gudrun had no idea why.

The same thing happened the night I got back to Saint-Martin. Ibelle's body had become more distant and slightly repulsive. I was invaded by memories—as I have been whenever I've slipped and stumbled into a kind of depression; I've even had to cancel concerts sometimes—and the memories cut me off from the world, or rather from the people around me. I'm familiar now with the sequence in which it happens. I saw Heinsheim again, and Bergheim, and us fishing for perch and pike from the banks of the Jagst and the

Neckar, and heard lieder being sung by Fräulein Jutta and Schwarzkopf:

> I shall come back in the form of a pike,
> As shiny as and as cruel . . .

I hated those memories, coming back like raspings of pain, like blinkers, like smothering cloaks or rough balaclava helmets. I heard Elisabeth Schwarzkopf sing in Bad Wimpfen when I was young. But however much I try to think of it in terms of Schwarzkopf, Bad Wimpfen for me is the terrible jointed Christ with human hair. I still want to shriek when I think of it. Real hair—the hair of a human victim. And the arms ready to clutch you.

I waited for Isabelle to come home. I dreaded it when she was there. I didn't want to meet her eyes anymore, or see her body, hear her voice. I didn't want any more to do with her, not even her memory or the memory of her name. I'd decided to break with her, but I couldn't. I went to Paris, where I saw Raoul Costeker, who finally talked to me as Mademoiselle had done—"Bream don't hunt in the ocean." And on the way back I kept repeating to myself one of the sayings of Buddha that Raoul was always either quoting or inventing: "He who follows the road is lost." (I didn't know how right I was.)

I didn't want to see her, and yet I spied on her out of the window. Cäci used to call that "playing Jehovah" because the Bible says, and it's used in one of the finest of the chorales, "For at the window of my house I looked through my casement." I mutter the words. It was my room at Bergheim, and I looked out of the window at my father waiting for my mother or yelling at her on the lawn. I couldn't hear anything. I just looked, as a child, through a windowpane with a bubble of air in the glass. I loved that bubble. I looked through the bulge that both sealed off and warped the bird I was looking at; that bent the cloud gilded by the dying sun and twisted the little gravel path winding over the lawn, down to the pond and the wall. The bubble calls to mind drops of syrup drying on a tiled floor, drops of fresh sperm on a hand or thigh before it becomes diluted and transparent, drops of wax creeping slowly down the side of a candle before they solidify. Things not sticky, and only fleetingly transparent or opaque, according to the quality of the wax or the age of the semen.

So there was I, distorted by the old air bubble—it's said such bubbles are altered by the rays of the moon—watching out for the strange, haughty, arched, silent, inscrutable body of the beautiful woman whose return I so much dreaded. I feared her look, the dreadful tension that filled the rooms, and the fascination of those huge eyes, which accused me—rightly—and terrified me.

Bereavement can be torture. But perhaps remorse is worse, and as far as I'm concerned—no doubt I'm not so splendid as my fellow creatures—the two have always gone together. And perhaps jealousy is worse than remorse, though it's there in bereavement, desertion, remorse itself, and betrayal. We are guilty. That probably underlies all our feelings. When we think about it carefully we see that we are guilty. That we've envied someone else's job, been jealous, cherished a desire to kill and devour. And it's our desire to bite and tear others to pieces that recoils upon ourselves in remorse.

I maintain that sentences written in the past conditional tense are the worst there are. They're like crabs' claws walking sideways, or the pincers of Dublin Bay prawns, which tear though they don't cut. "She would have liked . . . ," "He might have said . . . ," "If only I . . ." Such claws grip more painfully than those of the simple past.

Anyhow, perhaps what terrifies you and awakens you sweating and shouting out of a nightmare is not so much the bite itself as what goes before—the gaping jaws and bare teeth; the curled lips which are inevitably and forever recalled by anything curled; the grave and pleasant laugh of a predator about to swallow its prey. But it's a laugh seen only in a carnivore, which leaps on, kills, and tears up its food with its teeth. Laughter is an attribute of lions and hyenas and men: of all animals that know there's a delicious morsel in store when they see their prey stumble. Look how we enjoy ourselves when other people trip.

When she cried, or just before, her upper lip used to pucker and twitch. She was leaning against the mantelpiece with her chin in her hands. I was trying to talk to her, but whatever I said she wouldn't answer. It was like a dream or a story: One spring day in the garden I hear someone ring the bell on the wooden gate that you have to push open because it's overgrown with ivy. I open the gate and stand aside for whomever it is to come in. But there isn't anyone. I'm standing aside for nobody.

"I'm as miserable as a fish in water," she said in a fury.

"You mean a fish on vacation on the coast of Normandy."

I made her come out in the drizzle. For the last time we went past the floorcloth bush, invisible in the rain like one of the little goblins hidden among the branches in puzzle drawings for children. Some organisms lack the kind of chlorophyll that fixes happiness, includes it in the synthesis of age, memory, body, and circumstance. As a matter of fact all men probably lack this chlorophyll, which is why we're so white or yellow or black. Whereas clearly we would have looked marvelous in apple green. With a flowered hat.

I plucked up the courage to tell her I didn't know anymore if I loved her.

"I know! It's Florent you love!" she said. "You made a mistake, coming away with me. Go back to him."

We wept. Sniffling, I suggested we go on a farewell excursion to Yvetot and make some blackberry jam. The brambles that grew on the ledge halfway down the cliff were smothered with fruit. We went, and came back with a milk can full. We sniffled all the time and held hands.

I hadn't been able to make love to Ibelle properly the last few days. I had resorted to other measures, and perhaps they gave her pleasure. It's said that the cry uttered in orgasm—and by means of which it can always be feigned—corresponds to the wail we utter at birth, of which we seem not to have particularly pleasant recollections. Ibelle's cries of pleasure were violent, angry, nervous, and aggressive. Listening to them you might have said that the cry uttered in orgasm is, anachronism apart, a vague and bitter echo of the death rattle.

I dreamed of Photini Gaglinou. But I no longer felt the hunger that might have let me extinguish my desire for her body in that of Isabelle. It wasn't that desire had left me, like a snake sloughing off its old skin. What deprived me not so much of desire as of the ability to bring it to a conclusion—which may be pretentious and certainly overlooks the powers of virility—was the terrible, childish feeling that I was back in the salon at Bergheim, clutching and scraping. There scraping away as I used to as a child, back in the days of short trousers and universal indifference—but what had I done to break that wise ice?—perched uncomfortably on my chair, my bare knees gripping the sides of the cello, my nails white with effort, producing a series of screeches. Though of course I never actually saw myself playing a miniature cello as a child. And yet I saw myself as if I had. I see myself through my mother's eyes. During her rare visits. But she doesn't look up from her catalogue on Meissen china or her cigarette holder. And there's no sound.

It was morning. The wind had dropped, but it was still cold and there was a dense, clammy fog. I shivered as I took the garbage out—the truck would go by just before seven. Not far from the gate, near the boxwood trees, I caught a glimpse of a shape in the mist. I went toward it, calling out "Who goes there?"—a throwback to hungry, gloomy nights on sentry duty in Saint-Germain-en-Laye. Then I saw it was Isabelle. Barefoot on the wet grass, in her nightgown, holding in both hands a bowl of coffee steaming in the cold.

"You must be crazy!" I cried.

"Leave me alone, please," she answered curtly.

It was absolutely silent everywhere. The fog was heavy and oppressive. The atmosphere somber.

"Come on, let's go inside!"

She pushed my arm away. I went in, drenched in dew, the moisture condensing on my hair and pullover. I went into the kitchen and heated some water and milk. I like to drink a cup of milk and chicory in the morning, then a cup of chicory by itself, then a cup of coffee. Ibelle came in sneezing.

But I was the one who fell sick. I couldn't bear Ibelle anymore, but it was on Madame La Georgette that my hatred was cravenly deflected.

"I want to be on my own! Go away! No, wait! While you're at it, you can take all this away! The toast's burnt to a cinder, the butter's awful—it tastes like margarine—and as for this cup of wet hay! It's more like cow's urine! It's disease in liquid form! Please take it away and then *leave me alone*!"

I turned back to the window, sweating. A door slammed. The sea smelled of dead fish, of decomposition. I could see the little boats from the harbors along the coast. I was cold and perspiring at the same time. I wanted to dress and go to the station and take a train to Paris.

I was delirious for three days. I was in Normandy trying to catch a train, but I couldn't because it was a pedal boat. There was a house like ours, but closer to the ocean. It was drizzling. The train whistled out at sea. The drizzle mingled with the mist. A dense low mist. It was a little house built of granite rubble, with a carved lintel and a shiny slate roof. The slates were tears. The sea moaned. There was only one window, oval in shape with a light shining in it, for although all this was taking place in the daytime it was nearly as dark as night. Isabelle opened the iron gate into the garden. It creaked. I suddenly thought, "They made love to one another here. They came here often. They had pleasure here. They were happy. They came here to make love. They rushed from the station. And through the iron gate into the garden. They . . ." But I couldn't get in. My heart was in my mouth, even though it was dry. I stayed there bent in half, clutching the iron bars.

"Seinecé!" I said. "Seinecé!"

I remember hearing ships' sirens and train whistles out at sea. I got on a train that drew a pedal boat along behind it. It was an odd train altogether. The carriage had walls more than a yard thick, like a blockhouse, and I buried my head in the sand on the floor. The ticket collector was a little girl three or four years old with a terrible saber scar across her face. She wore a ticket collector's cap and held a shiny wooden darning egg in one hand, probably a present from Mademoiselle Aubier, with which she tapped me on the head. I quaked with fear.

"Good morning, Mademoiselle Aubier!" I said.

I find it very disagreeable, even after more than twenty-five years, to record the memory of those nightmares, obsessions, and hallucinations. Memories used to mingle with my dreams. I know only one other man with a repertory and power of recall equal to mine, and that's Claudio Arrau, in his salon in Douglaston. The memory involved in this case was a very simple one: we used to go by train every summer to Regnéville-sur-Mer, with its carefully tended, almost Japanese garden surrounded by massive walls six feet high and nearly two feet thick. We went there twelve or fifteen years running, but everything was merged and concentrated in my feverish dreams. I can see them still, and they still frighten me. First came the arrival at Coutances station with the steeples of the cathedral sublime against the sky, then the dark banks of the river Soulle, the stream known as the Bulsart, and along by the Sienne and Highway D49 (I can still see those figures). We never went there by sea. I can still see the marvelous houses dating from the time of Queen Mathilde rising straight out of the sea: for me their cold, severe perfection, the style of all the typical dark gray houses thereabouts, represents an ideal, an austere dream of an absolute way of living. You entered Regnéville from within, so to speak—an image of our own fate.

The very name of the place presented a problem to the five children from Bergheim, children with two languages, doomed to have four ears and two loves—in other words, no language and no love. The sound of the words "Regnéville-sur-Mer" suggested the notions both of reigning and renouncing, *régner* and *renier*, together with an echo of the word for "mother" and the idea of something floating on the sea, and so in danger of sinking. All five of us, in childhood and adolescence, using the name of the village where we spent our vacation every year, rang the changes on the terrible conflict between that which reigned and that which renounced or denied, and on the connection between the sea and our mother's desertion. The nearby estuary of the Sienne was another element in the puzzle, as "sienne" in French means "hers."

I play with the words as I used to play with them as a child, but if I examine them closely what I seem to see deep down, yet again, is Seinecé's face and the marvelous, ceaseless wordplay of his conversation: St. Peter's tears when he denied Christ, and the cock crowing, and how authors used to seek its feathers for writing their masterpieces, and the brazier in the courtyard of Annas the high priest, Caiaphas's father-in-law.

In those days the elm trees were still alive. They grew around the severe, white-shuttered house and lined the massive, flat-stoned garden walls. *Ormes* is the word for "elms" in French; *hommes* the word for "men." *Ormes*, *hommes*, and Bormes all interchanged with one another in my feeble delirium. I had already left Ibelle.

It was at Regnéville that my sister Lisbeth met Yvon Bulot. Our mother's name was Yvonne. *Bulot* was also the French name for the rubbery whelks we ate all the time at Regnéville, where they were endlessly served as a first course. The church there, with its steeple dating from the Romanesque period or even earlier, now seemed to me like the oldest church in the world, going back to the days when Darmstadt man went to mass with his wife, the Venus of Lespugue.

The floor sometimes creaks. The wardrobe too. A chair spring replies. A cello string relaxes. A bed frame calls. All the houses in the world, especially in summer when they're dry and resonant, are slowly, slowly collapsing, sapped by a nonhuman destruction. My bedroom got gloomier and gloomier. The ceiling, low to begin with, came lower and lower and would eventually crush me. The wall opposite the bay window, near the cello, grew shrouded and dim in a kind of brown mist or shadow. Ever since I was a child I've been able to tell when it's going to rain by the quality of the light. But I never went near the windows. I didn't press my nose to the glass to see if the clouds were getting nearer or darker, or the size of the raindrops, or whether the gusts were blowing them to the left or the right. I turned away from the windows and plunged into the half light that was their antithesis. I sought out a corner or a chair near a lamp. Whether I read or only dreamed, I tried to forget the sky and the world outside, the wind's violence, and the darkness, as of night, that goes with it, and the distraction, amazement, and anguish that violence aroused in me. I switched on the light and huddled inside its halo, its armor.

Several times a day Ibelle, visibly irritated, came in to see how I was and whether my temperature had fallen and the congestion in my chest improved. I had managed to persuade myself that she was jealous of my illness. She would stand there for a while, somber and skeptical, then turn on her heel and go. There was only one bathroom in the house at Saint-Martin-en-Caux; it had a big green old-fashioned iron tub with short legs and lion's claws, rather like the two creamy yellow tubs at Bergheim except that the brass taps there weren't tarnished and partly rusted away.

The old doctor in Saint-Martin-en-Caux, practically retired by then, had advised Ibelle and Madame La Georgette to give me warm baths to bring my temperature down. They used to undress me and take me downstairs—the bathroom was on the ground floor near the kitchen—then watch over me as I sat in the bath rambling. I felt as if they were standing guard over me; as if what they were most afraid of was that I might manage to escape. I was a great hypochondriac—in the course of time this passion has been displaced onto my musical instruments, and instead of surrounding myself with doctors I badger the makers of cellos and bows wherever I go—and I'd gotten it into my head that I had been injured and that was why I felt so ill. But sitting there naked in the bath with lion's feet, I couldn't find any wound, however carefully I examined myself. My body was completely intact. So why was I sick? I looked and looked again. No trace of any injury. Ibelle regarded her patient with the utmost contempt, making fun of me, treating me like a baby, and talking twaddle: "Izzums misewable then? Where's our smile? Are we feeling hungwy this evening?" This made me furious.

But I gradually got better. One day I opened the window, and the air seemed to smell like a bucket of garbage. I felt better, though my temperature hadn't fallen much. I wanted to consult a couple of doctors in Paris. Or so I said. I really wanted to see my sister Margarete. She'd hinted on the phone that the results of Luise's recent physical hadn't been so great. But I didn't feel strong enough to drive. I said I'd come back to fetch the Citroën as soon as my temperature was below ninety-nine degrees. But I was just making excuses, like a child getting notes to take to school.

The day of my departure arrived. Ibelle couldn't take me to Dieppe or Le Havre because she couldn't drive, but she said she'd walk with me to the little station in Saint-Martin-en-Caux. The hill was shrouded in mist that morning. It clung to some oak and apple branches and was torn by others, but seemed to avoid houses, shrinking away from their warmth.

It was cold out in the garden, but although there was no sunshine you could feel that the sky would soon be light. The colors were lovely—Isabelle's green blouse, the brick pink of her face, the dark gleaming countryside. It was six o'clock—she'd gotten up earlier than usual. We hadn't kissed.

"Bye!" she said suddenly, giving me a kind of slap on the arm. Her voice was slightly husky. Or perhaps I imagined it.

Then she turned away and went back into the house.

We left for the station between eight and nine. The mist had dispersed, succeeded by a tiny, almost invisible drizzle shot through every now and then with sunshine. In Saint-Martin, by the little bookshop, it started to rain, and we sheltered in a doorway. We didn't speak or touch one another. A ray of sunlight suddenly lit up the street like a miracle—even the spinach-green paint of the bookshop. We emerged from our doorway, shaking off the rain, and walked on past the covered market in the middle of the main square. It was then I noticed that Isabelle's face was covered in a kind of damp film. She looked placid, her eyes were shining, but she seemed to be wearing a sort of mask frozen in surprise; her mouth was open, as if soundlessly crying out. I noticed that the light seemed somehow to be coming up from the ground and falling on her neck, nostrils, and eyes rather than on her hair or forehead or the bridge of her nose. Then it slowly dawned on me that this effect was due to the reflection of the light coming up from the damp pavement and intensifying the impression of pain.

She took my arm. I was sweating. I heard the doorbell of the pharmacy jangle a few yards away: a fourth, a true, lively, shrill fourth.

I remember a scene from my childhood. It was at Coutances. The sky was dark. I was marching away from Villa Marthe, carefully repeating to myself, "Good morning, Monsieur. I've come to collect the tersinol and linseed meal that my mother ordered this morning." I was walking first on gravel, then on flagstones. The street was dark and steep and narrow, and I walked faster and faster. I entered the pharmacy with great determination. A man in a white smock, with a scrawny gray beard and pince-nez that almost hid his nose, turned to me and said, "Good morning, Monsieur."

"Good morning, Monsieur," I answered. "I've come to collect the tersinol and linseed meal that my mother ordered this morning."

The pharmacist ceremoniously invited me to take a seat on a shiny round chair made of some black wood or other that felt cold to my thighs. Every so often I cast a furtive glance at the tall shelves lining the walls, but most of the time I just contemplated my own bare knees.

Then suddenly I heard a voice saying, "Monsieur Chenogne!"

I blushed and stood up. The pharmacist closed a box the color of green blotting paper and held it out to me. He also gave me a gumdrop.

We went around the market and down a little alley called Devil's Wind. Ibelle's lip quivered. She squeezed my arm, and it seemed to me she wanted to make me stay. But I so longed to go. I foolishly set my heart on not giving way, on not showing any emotion. "I'm not nice," I said to myself. "I must be like a pharmacist and just say, 'Here you are, Ibelle—here's the tersinol and the linseed meal.' "

A paperboy must have gone by just then, and it must have started, or tried, to rain again. Because I can still hear the flat, broad, unmistakable sound of drops falling on newspaper. We got to the station. I can't remember whether it was gray and modern and made of concrete and plate glass, or one of those little nineteenth-century chapels with Gothic features picked out in brick. But I do remember, as clearly as if I were still rooted to the spot, the green of her blouse. And then all of a sudden it goes hazy. As if the green of her blouse and the blue of her skirt were still blurred together in my tears.

CHAPTER 4

The Hunting Box on the Banks of the Loire

Thou shalt not examine thy dreams.

LEVITICUS

I didn't wipe away my tears—at least, when I look back I still feel they're there. They rolled down my cheeks. The green of her satin blouse, the blue of her eyes, the blue of her straight skirt, the shape of her high breasts, her hands, her face—they all seemed to blur. I didn't put my handkerchief to my eyes for fear of blotting out those colors, that flesh, if I dried the tears through which I saw them. My embarrassment, or was it pain, may have found a kind of pleasure in dismantling that body, trying one last time to merge into it, even at the risk of annihilating form altogether.

For seven or eight days I forgot everything. I went back to my publishers', to the music school on Rue de Poitiers. I renewed contact with Costeker, Egbert Heminghos, Ferdinand Groy, Uwe, Jean, and Klaus-Maria, who was leaving for the United States. Madame de Craupoids told me I could go on teaching the baroque cello and viola da gamba classes more or less for life. I left Rue du Pont-de-Lodi. I missed my Citroën, but put off replacing it. Thanks to one of Raoul Costeker's numerous boyfriends I rented a tiny, rather ugly one-story house on Quai de la Tournelle; ugly or not, it was marvelous. It had four very small rooms, two on the ground floor and two on the first, with a narrow, inconvenient staircase. But it had the priceless advantage of being on a street that was nearly always deserted, and having two rooms so isolated that no one would be disturbed by the sound of the cello or the piano. So I could work whenever I wanted to, early or late.

Once again I managed to sell a gamba for Raoul Costeker. It was a fine instrument, beautifully strung and with a rare and terrifying Medusa's head in carved cherry wood, though the sound it made was very impure and dull. With the commission on the sale I bought an exercise viola da gamba and a cheap replica of a Hemsch clavichord. I was filled with a kind of intoxication. At last I was living right by the Seine.

When everything was ready and habitable, at least as far as I was concerned, I spent three days with my sister Marga in my other sister Luise's studio in Stuttgart, overlooking the trees in the Schlossgarten. I saw Luise there too, and her son Vinzenz; she didn't seem too worried. Then Marga brought me back to France, to Pfulgriesheim, where her husband had bought a little country cottage. Then suddenly, I don't know why, I decided to go and see Bergheim again. I wanted—I don't know—to mark the occasion; make a new beginning, a pilgrimage; seek a blessing from a place connected with my childhood. And when, having set out alone from Heilbronn, I stepped onto the platform at Bergheim at five in the afternoon, it was like stepping into a very old, very flat, very familiar picture postcard that had been lying bright and shiny in my memory. I hadn't been back there for eight years. In 1962, after the burial service for my mother in Neuilly, I'd refused to go in the little black bus that was bringing her body to Bergheim. The evening light gilded even the white lines on the road and the chromium fittings on the cars. Perhaps the color of the sky was duller than it used to be—or I was more unhappy. But how could I be unhappier than as a child? "Well," I said to myself, "perhaps the blue of the sky was newer then."

For thousands of years the sky has been undergoing great changes in the eyes of men, as they've contemplated it and grown older. I suppose it was originally a purplish blue, almost black, the color of a shark, closer to indigo or Sèvres than to cobalt or periwinkle. Then time went by and the sky faded. I remember that was the year—1965—when they closed the cave at Lascaux.

I recognized the typical Bergheim smell, sickly and sweet; a faint, vague odor of hot liquid manure fermenting. I went and had a drink at Florjan's, a little inn near the station. German, the hated language, came back to me bit by bit, in little gusts. I gradually became attuned to the conversations going on around me, and to their rhythms, through a series of almost chemical, almost tangible impressions, though some of the words and a complete understanding of their meaning still escaped me. Eight years had gone by, but it was as if the past were even farther away than that, and I another person. I went to the church in the lower part of the town, but it was shut. I went and asked for the key from Herr Geschich, the organ blower; he didn't recognize me. I had grown up a bit: I'd been thirteen when I was sent away to school, and now I was twenty-two. He had aged a great deal, but I recognized him from his expression. Herr Gustav Geschich had much of the white beard and a little of the beauty of Caliph Haroun al-Raschid in the *Arabian Nights* engravings. Aunt Elly, Fräulein Jutta, and my sisters claimed he emptied whole casks of wine in the manner of the Princess Palatine, who was said to swig them off in gulps of two quarts at a time. He had a violent temper. Mademoiselle Aubier would have said he worshiped St. Paunch and St. Puke. And he was so Lutheran he forgave himself everything. "We are all sinners," he cried—and drank and beat his wife. "I am humble before my wrongdoing," he wept—and drank some more and beat his wife harder. But for all that he was the best of men. The only mystery was that such an admirer of Martin Luther should have been organ blower cum sexton in a Catholic church. Admittedly mass was no longer celebrated there.

The Württembergers are a southern people, and he flung his arms around me with tears of joy and a series of little sighs and murmurs. I told him I wouldn't be going up to the house. The first thing I wanted to do was pay my respects to my father, and perhaps to all the others whose name I bore. He took this very seriously and came with me. I went up into the organ loft. It was an old organ with two manuals and sixteen stops, each with a mixture stop. Originally made in Italy, it had been restored by Gottfried Silbermann in the 1720s and renovated with varying degrees of success several times since. It had a winged case, and the rococo look of a sugar-covered pastry. The electrification of the foot bellows, begun during the war, had never been completed, so there had to be not only an official organist but also an official blower. I used to have to go get Herr Geschich to come and blow for me, and he would walk very, very slowly behind me to the church like a huge Haroun al-Raschid caught in a quicksand.

The console (the organ is an instrument that suffers from delusions of grandeur, and the word "console" is a provocation in itself) had been patched up at the end of the last century. It was complicated, but I knew it by heart. I amused myself pulling out the stops to play permutations and combinations of themes from Bach—conjuring up a whole universe with my feet and hands. But the results arrive only after a delay that can never be recovered, a kind of counterpoint in which the sound echoes back from the body of the church leaving the organist forever unsatisfied. I was glad that the keys weren't black and white but made of little squares of rosewood and rectangles of limewood. I pulled out the bärkpfeife, the sordun, and the schalmei stops. The flue-pipes and reeds were more than out of tune—they were openly at war with one another. But it didn't matter. I was happy.

After three or four quarters of an hour of music—and daze—we left. I made Herr Geschich come with me to the grocery store, where I bought a few bottles for him, and then to the square, where I bought a cake for Frau Geschich. We arranged for me to stay the night at his house, and he went home. I went for a walk. I saw Kurt and dropped in on Anna.

Evening came, and I went back to Herr Geschich's place. Behind the little house was a field of carrots and some trees on which sour apples grew. Frau Geschich had made me up a bed in their daughter's room—she'd gotten a job as a secretary in Mannheim, so I stayed for a couple of days.

We dined in the kitchen by a pink and blue fireplace. Herr Geschich told me our house had been put up for sale twice and then withdrawn.

"I don't have any money," I said with a pang. I believe that kind of pain is not uncommon. He got drunk in my honor and told me the ancient family stories about how his great-grandfather used to blow the organ for mine. When Frau Geschich had learned that I was coming to dinner she'd hastily cooked some carnival puffs, and these she'd arranged around the cake. They used to be my greatest delight when I was a child.

I finished off the puffs the next morning, after getting up just before dawn. The village was wrapped in mist, but not the kind of mist I'd seen a few months before at Saint-Martin in Normandy. It was thicker here, like sheets, torn sheets. Shrouds. You couldn't see the fountain in the middle of the square. I left the village and climbed up beyond the Schehe to the little graveyard. The sun rose, a tiny little sun whose feeble rays just tipped the gravestones and the acacias. I stopped and read the names, but not aloud.

The gate creaked as I left the cemetery, and I found myself back in the little wood outside. The clouds parted, the sun shone through, and I could see Bergheim: meadows lying in the sunlight and dotted with bright little houses like toys. A Chinese legend says that old Li Po just smiled and said nothing when asked why he'd gone to live in the blue mountains.

Frau Geschich drew up the chairs, rummaged in the sideboard for some crystal glasses, opened a bottle of Tokay, and held out a plate of cookies.

"Now tell us why you went away," said Herr Geschich impatiently, drumming on the table with his fingers. They listened, wagging their heads and rolling their eyes, raising their eyebrows and frowning. Ludwig Erhard had just been reelected Chancellor. I tried to change the subject. They wouldn't hear of it.

As I came down from the cemetery, past the blackthorns, I saw Aunt Elly halfway down the hill, going past the roadside calvary back to the house. She drew her shawl more tightly around her. Pretended not to see me. Turned her back on me.

I realized that what I was looking for was something that couldn't be found. I realized I didn't like finding myself in a place located not in itself but in time. I had overestimated my strength and deluded myself about what I wanted. To this day I still dislike the emotion aroused in me by my return visits, my brief twenty-four-hour return visits, to Bergheim: the magnetic attraction I feel before I arrive at Echterdingen station or airport, the taxi to Stuttgart, the boat on the Neckar, friends' cars. The unreal image in my mind of the place, and its sound, and its light, and even its size, attracts but at the same time wounds me. I get off the plane or the train. I leave the station or the airport and stand there paralyzed at the sight of something too well known, a kind of ultravisible reality. Sounds and smells jostle one another to reach me, and trample one another to death before I have time to embrace them. Going up the hill, it's: "You're thyme, you're mint, you're Frau Minge's lime tree. You're Florjan's syringa. You're the smell of Frau Geschich's soup; here comes Pauli's bakery and next Leonhard's anvil. Then the Kirstens' dogs, the bells, the carpenter's saw, the garage owner and his aura of oil and tar and paraffin. Here at the bottom of the street is the sour smell of curdled milk, and here's the dusty smell of the market-place, there the smell of Fräulein Jutta's face powder, the post office smell of wax, the stationer's smell of new leather, and the scent of old Frau Hageschard's soap!"

I'm a dog in his world of smells, weeping at the memory of flesh and places and shapes, commemorating different kinds of food. As a dog I find myself suddenly rising higher up the scale of being, though I haven't yet soared to the dignity of being able to bark. Or to be silent.

The woods and copses in the Neckar and Jagst valleys, and the light that shines in them, have an inexhaustible fascination for me. It was among those little trees that I spent my childhood. The light in them is secret and sporadic, the skies changeable and rarely clear; there are vines on the steep hillsides, thickets full of strawberries, wrinkled and yellow old hands picking blueberries off their stems. I spent the afternoon wandering about. For me cities are always unnatural, lumps of porphyry marble heaved into a pond, pretentious liveries in which mud and purple are mingled. Ponds and oceans may reflect the sky and the clouds, the setting sun, the whole universe. But I prefer the boughs of a tree. Foliage doesn't reflect the universe, it doesn't reflect anything, and that makes it more ancient and more vast. And it goes on rustling forever amid the incomprehensible leaves, the incomprehensible whims of the breeze, and the incomprehensible existence of birds and fruit.

At the end of the day I took the boat back to Stuttgart. I thought about the waters of the Seine, about Quai de la Tournelle, about Paris, Ibelle, and the waters of the Durdent. I said to myself: "Let the tide rise and fall. Go and buy vegetables and meat. Phone Marga and tell her to come home early. Run a bath." And as Dante led Virgil through the Inferno, children played by the rail and lovers stood close and touched one another's breasts. A loud and sinister-looking Prussian lectured his wife about how to hold her purse so as not to have it stolen.

I caught the bus, and in Stuttgart I bought some Allgäu, a few portions of leek tart, a bottle or two of Tauber, and some pastries from a shop in the Königstrasse.

Luise wasn't there, so Marga and I had dinner by ourselves. I was leaving the next day. Marga was amusing. "If it's a storm you're looking out for," she said, "you won't know about it till you're struck by lightning!" This made her laugh.

We may have been drinking rather a lot. We laughed a good deal. We talked about the old days, and I secretly thought we were both cheating a little, trying to steal ourselves a morsel of happiness. We none of us ever think for a moment that any disappointment, discouragement, or misfortune that comes our way is really ours, is really meant for us. But if one fine day, by some incredible chance, a dewdrop, a tear, of something resembling heaven or happiness falls upon us, we immediately think we've somehow annexed it for ourselves, though it probably wasn't meant for us at all.

It was time to go to bed. I'd soon open up a convertible sofa for myself beside little Markus, aged two, who slept on a narrow mattress on the floor. In the old days, under the iron rule and inflexible orders of Hiltrud or Aunt Elly, we used to have to go through the kitchen first when we went to bed. And there, waiting for us on a table in a little pantry, stood a regiment of Pigeon lamps officered by a group of oil lamps. The five of us would trail up the stairs one after the other like little old men, carefully holding up our Pigeon lamps and throwing on the walls more shadow than light.

I was frightened and didn't look about me. Head bent and teeth set, I concentrated on the lacy brass collar around the little glass globe I was carrying. Then, after stamping on the floor first to scare away the monsters, I would bury myself as fast as I could in the icy sheets. And in intermittent nightmares and a terrified listening for strange sounds.

When I got back to Paris it was as if I'd returned to what priests and pastors used to call the world and the devil. They didn't call it a pack of hounds trying to eat its prey alive. Or the place where a single desire unites all in the attempt to abduct one mythical Helen. They didn't see everyone as children, or gold diggers, or in terms of manly attributes or symbols. Unable to see it as hell, I saw it as a school playground, the place where you size one another up. And it didn't appeal to me much. You eye one another, kill one another with fierce looks, cruelty, honor. One glance was enough for us to judge the quality of a pair of flannel shorts, and whether they had been made by a tailor or by their owner's mother. If the latter, we used to point at our victim and choke with laughter.

But I got back to Dido too. Every evening when I opened the door on Quai de la Tournelle I'd find her sitting on the mat on the little table in the hall. She'd inspect me for a fraction of a second as I went by, then jump down and come with me into the kitchen. We were both too careful of our dignity to show any eagerness, however ravenous we felt.

We used to spend hours talking to one another. Was I unhappy? I don't know. I was doing the best I could to stifle something sad and yet vague. I worked harder than I'd ever worked before. I was starting to make recordings and to play regularly abroad. I slept for five hours every night and spent six hours a day practicing the gamba. I was the Emperor Leopold tapping his foot impatiently all day long in hopes of being left a little time at his spinet. I was working chiefly on the baroque bow and the weight of the body over it. At that time the old rule that every note had to die away was just beginning to be revived. I was very good at those old tricks. Perhaps it was the biographies I translated to occupy myself at night, and all the reading I did around them, that taught me old notions that had been lost when romantic music took over, together with the Napoleonic methods and institutions that derived from it. For the first time I made some recordings—Loeillet sonatas—with Nicolaïevna on the pardessus and George Shire on the violone. We were criticized for our "rococo" ornamentation of the adagios. Our upbowing was supposed to be too emphatic. People objected to our recording in a studio and using acoustic and editing techniques. All the criticisms were justified, really, except the last. I don't think every age has necessarily had at its disposal the instruments best suited to the music it produced. Instruments are merely accessories; it's the music itself that is the marvel. And music doesn't reside in the sounds or the instruments or the scores or the performers. It is a dream for the ear. Every composition calls for an instrument that doesn't exist. You can't re-create anything as it was in the past.

Later on I recorded earlier works, and in the course of radio interviews and television broadcasts often came up against very narrow musicians from the Concertgebouw or the Concentus Musicus. I shocked a lot of people by recording two of Sainte Colombe's nine *Suites lugubres* on the cello.

But this isn't the place to talk shop. Sometimes it seems to me there is a whole area of my life, its essence, that is not accessible to words. All I want to do here is pay tribute to the memory of a man I loved. And to whom I never really showed it, except in the most elliptical, confused, and awkward way possible.

The International Music School opened again on October 1, and I went to Rue de Poitiers every Tuesday. From January 1, 1966, on, I also worked more regularly—twice a week—at the publisher's. I was filling in for six months for Ferdinand Groy, who was spending a semester in the United States.

Unexpected emotions sometimes reveal to us fears we didn't know we had, or suddenly penetrate the secret of one of our nightmares. One day toward the end of the winter when I was working in Ferdinand Groy's office, the telephone rang. I recognized the voice, and my face was suddenly damp. My pulse leaped: the voice was Isabelle's. But I was wrong: Isabelle's was merely the voice I wanted to hear. It was really Nicolaïevna, inviting me to dinner.

Sometimes Mademoiselle Aubier called me too. Very occasionally she would ask me out to Saint-Germain on a Sunday. Or else she would ring to thank me for a translation or record I'd sent her: "Monsieur Chenogne, I've dipped into your last book and I must say I'm licking my lips at the thought of reading it." Or again, although she never allowed herself to complain about Denis Aubier's absences, she would talk about her insomnia and how she hadn't slept a wink the night before. "But still, Monsieur Chenogne," she'd say, with a spirit I always found admirable, "as Mama used to say, as long as you're tossing and turning in bed, at least you still haven't passed over into another world!" And a particularly frail and sad little laugh would sound in the earphone.

My office window at the publisher's framed a little rectangle of garden, cold and covered with snow. My numb and weary gaze moved from the empty old fountain—the water had been cut off because of the cold spell that had started in January—to the leafless trees, whose motionless white branches reached at innumerable angles toward a low and somber sky.

Confessions have a great appeal in a highly civilized society—the admissions we hesitate to make because they're difficult to utter, because they wound our pride, and, more pettily, because they undermine the image of ourselves that we would like to project (even though every image is so meager and inexpressive, as flat as a pancake, as fine as a baby's hair, as utterly harmless as everything that's lifeless). And confession became almost irresistible at the end of a winter's day, when it was getting dark and I was tired, in the little office where Costeker, Klaus-Maria, or Egbert Heminghos would come to pick me up or just to sit and dream aloud. The mere fact that you're lowering yourself a little in someone else's eyes, that you're gently opening some small wound that you and your friend may have in common, can often make you believe—wrongly—that by the courage and dangerous precision of your avowal you're actually increasing the esteem you're pretending to forfeit. But more profound still is the feeling that we're communing with what is basic in ourselves, confessing to belonging to something that forgives us our belonging. We feel we're all animals—rather low, pretty fierce but also extremely rare animals. We feel relief, almost gratitude at the thought that we resemble one another through the lowest common denominator. And as it's so rare an occurrence, we take pleasure, just this once, in not trying to be different from one another.

I experienced this bond and pleasure again with Raoul Costeker. I still do: his shop is still there under the arcades on Rue de Rivoli. Inside were low showcases of books scattered pleasingly around. There are not so many places like that now. In those days there was no window display. The walls were lined with carved wooden shelves. A few very old and a few very modern paintings were always there on the floor or hanging from little brass rods. Raoul always looks like a very cold person. He was then about fifty, and dressed like a fashion plate. He likes men, at least for the moment of pleasure, but immediately afterward dreads the thought of ever seeing them again. A creature of immeasurable solitude, subtlety, and distress. The bookshop dates from 1820, and there's nowhere I find more pleasant or soothing in the evening, until he closes up and we go have dinner at his place. The shop is usually empty: potential customers are frightened off by its size and austerity, the armchairs around the showcases, the absence of any window display, and the formidable prices of the instruments, manuscripts, and books that are for sale. I sit down in a corner of the room and think about almost nothing as I watch the play of light on the beautiful old Bapaume and Avielhar bindings. Or look at an autograph manuscript by Haydn or Rameau, or contemplate a lute made by Pierray or a big gamba made by Antoine Veron suddenly caught in the halo of a lamp that either Raoul or a customer has switched on. And I dream of the days of the Revolution, when the old instruments died with the Old Regime and Koliker sold viols off in lots of eight for seventy-five centimes.

What strange shadow was it that sat down to work at four o'clock in the morning? Who was it inside me that was so assiduous? Oddly enough the constant dripping, drop by drop, day after day, never wore away the stone. Work never made my head spin. I've never been able to understand what need of pain and suffering it could have been that made me fill all day and every day with so much toil. What real face lay behind this Spartan appearance?

Sometimes I thought of a little rhyme my sisters Lisbeth and Luise used to sing to one another when they were skipping:

Chop chop chop the wood,
Chop the wood for mother . . .

I look at all the words I'm writing, and I can't really justify them, except by a keen desire for confession and the hope that it may bring me a kind of peace. But unfortunately I don't quite feel the peace, the warmth, the soft nostalgic light that confession hopes to achieve; as though the voice were a sort of password giving access to something very different from the voice itself, something more than forgiveness—a kind of caress, with your head buried in the bosom of a being who never could bestow a caress.

And the embarrassment I seem always to have suffered from—the unease, distress, and feeling of being in a false position—that too must have had something to do with the sense of guilt I had when I spoke German in my mother's presence, and with the shame I was made to feel about French by my schoolmates, pointing at me as if I were a thief, a withholder of food, a member of an occupying army. All Ithacas are out of bounds to me. I can't make landfall either on the banks of the Jagst or on the banks of the Seine. I work as hard as I do in order to earn forgiveness for not being where I ought to be—forever passing through, trimming, compromising, moving on, translating from German into French, or English into French, like a smuggler, like a traitor trying to justify himself by methods that only make him seem more treacherous. I must have translated about twenty biographies, working on them only in the mornings from 3 or 4 to 7 A.M.: lives of Caccini, Fux, Couperin, Galileo the Elder, and Archangelo Corelli among others. The royalties weren't much to begin with, but eventually they added up to a useful supplementary income. But I didn't drop any of my activities: the teaching on Rue de Poitiers, concert tours, recordings—I kept them all on and was becoming quite well-off.

I have a typical Swabian appetite, worthy of Pantagruel, and stick scrupulously to the Swabian habit of eating four meals a day. And at night, when I first sit up in bed and then get up, I'm nearly always hungry, my appetite no doubt whetted by some dream. Perhaps a shade holding a bowl, a sorcerer stirring a soup with Spätzle in it and cutting up mushrooms into little cubes and slices, making the frying pan splutter with a few drops of vinegar, little scraps of marinated beef or Bachsteiner, bits of cheese and liver and noodles. And in spite of all that, I'm as thin as Grimmelshausen's hero in the hermit's cottage. A few years later, in 1969, I was standing naked with a frying pan in my hand when I got an urgent phone call asking me to do a life of Gesualdo. It was very light and romantic, but it suddenly started selling like hot cakes, and the next year, 1970, I was able to buy a little old house at Oudon on the banks of the Loire. A *muette* or hunting box, they said it was, and that word, with its connotation of muteness or silence, may have been what attracted me. The lawyer explained that *muettes* used to be little buildings in the forest where falcons were kept during the molting season or *mue*, and stags when they shed their antlers. Then the word was applied to small houses used as meeting places during the hunt, rather like the aristocratic little bowers known as *gloriettes*.

The times I spent on vacation at Oudon were my molting seasons. Because of its name, *muette*, that old hunter's or fisherman's cottage stood for change and silence, change in silence. I liked to call it not only my *muette* but also my *havre*, or haven: a little river called the Havre flowed into the Loire just there. It was about six miles from Liré and Ancenis, and for five years I spent the summer there, pottering about and trying as far as I could to live like another Simplicissimus. Kohlrabi, beans, peas, lentils, berries, pears, apples, cherries, birds, snails, frogs, mullet, eels, an axe, an iron pot, the river, the sun, a spade, a knife, a net, some birdlime—those seemed to me the things and creatures necessary to happiness.

Mademoiselle Aubier aged rapidly in 1966. When I got back from London at the beginning of July that year, she'd given up singing. She couldn't have accompanied herself anymore on the piano, anyway—her hands shook too much. I tried to tell her about the trip I'd made to Ramsgate in a Hovercraft, but she didn't take much interest in things now.

It's a long time ago now since I used to arrive at Saint-Germain-en-Laye in my "Four Horses," drive to the edge of the forest, then turn and park by the gray railings. Pontius Pilate would bark and jump up and down and fling himself on the car, and as soon as I opened the door he'd get hold of my arm—not biting, but gripping me firmly—and drag me, crouching down, to the steps leading up to the house, and then round behind them to what came to be called "Ibelle's kitchen."

Now Mademoiselle Aubier found she couldn't get down the six or seven steps anymore on her own. Denis used to help her downstairs from her room. She wore a yellow scarf over her head, a loose robe of pink and yellow voile—her night attire—and an expression that was usually dazed rather than welcoming. Her cheeks had gone blotchy. It was as if she had turned into a little unbaked, leaky clay pot swathed in scarves. "A little unbaked, leaky clay pot wrapped in scarves," I said to myself. You could see the level of the water sinking. A few months earlier she was still saying proudly, "I went for my first ride in a motor car in 1897"; now she was silent. Her trembling hands were held out in front of her like a squirrel's paws.

She stooped like a hunchback. Her nose almost touched her embroidery hoop, but she couldn't embroider anymore. A wisp of gray hair had escaped from her bun and quivered in the light. She listened without speaking. Then suddenly, without looking up, she put her needlework frame down on the table and said,

"That's life—all that."

Later on she could no longer pretend to hold a needle. She just sat still doing nothing. I couldn't understand what she said. I found these visits painful and began to shrink from them.

One of the last times I went to see her at Saint-Germain-en-Laye it seemed to me—she'd given up wearing her dentures—that she was talking about how she kept falling asleep and then waking up again. It was August. We were in her bedroom. She'd just sung, forgetting most of the words, a song she used to be very fond of and dinned into our ears constantly a few years earlier.

> Little girls of Augans, give us back our breeches,
> Give us back our pants and our fine linen jackets!

Pluck up your courage, now,
And give us back our drawers!

She was saying—at least that was what I thought, or rather hoped, she was saying—that people who are sleeping ought to be awakened to make them realize how happy they are when they're asleep. We ourselves had had to be born in order to find out how lucky we'd have been if we'd never been born at all. She seemed to be sucking or chewing her lips, as if they were pastries or acid drops.

Mademoiselle Aubier was gradually melting into the dusk. I hastily switched on the central light and all the reading lamps. Her invisibility made me fear she might pass over into death itself.

She fell silent. Then, her head bent, her disintegrating bun suffused with light, she went on, or at least such is the sense I managed to extract from that extreme of decrepitude:

"You know, Monsieur Chenogne, one really oughtn't to die at my age!"

Then again she fell silent. And put her cold, dry, shivering fingers on mine. I felt that never before had anyone brought me so close to the abyss.

The autumn and winter of 1966 were very difficult. In just a few weeks Mademoiselle Aubier's faculties declined rapidly. She went into the hospital at the beginning of October, and to tell the truth I loathed going to see her there. I hoped she'd soon die.

I would take the elevator and walk past the nurses feeling very uncomfortable. The corridors always seemed empty. It was the third door. I tapped on it loudly with one finger—Mademoiselle Aubier was now practically deaf as well as more or less dumb—though trying not to sound rough or impatient. Of course I wasn't expecting even the faintest or most quavery "Come in!" But I did go in, bashfully—or rather some inferior actor did. I was no longer conscious of the smell of ether; I no longer saw the cadaverous, gradually degenerating shape on the bed.

"Mademoiselle!" I cried, putting on an amazed expression. "I don't think I've ever seen you look so rested!"

She didn't look at her visitor, of course. There was just a faint grimace of a smile on her lips which you could if you liked pretend was for you.

"I've remembered your favorite flowers and your favorite color, Mademoiselle," I said.

And I'd hold out to the sightless eyes or empty walls a bunch of horrible freesias. Then I threw away the old freesias in the vase on the bedside table, changed the water and arranged the new ones, talking all the time.

"Freesias—aren't they lovely!" I cried ecstatically.

I've often thought since that we both hated freesias really. They're rather like bean flowers but not so sturdy, more plaintive. But they were the only fairly fresh flowers to be found in the buckets on display at the little yellow florist's shop on the corner by the hospital. The only ones willing to last a little while in the artificial, ether-laden, overheated atmosphere of the room in which Mademoiselle Aubier's life was running out. The dwarf head on the white pillow was almost unrecognizable—a waxy, yellow, wizened puppet's head, like an apple that's fallen behind the refrigerator or the gas stove that you find a few months later shriveled and shrunken to three-quarters of its proper size.

I found myself a green and white woven plastic chair and sat down by Mademoiselle Aubier, going on with my pointless maunderings.

"You'll never guess what happened as I came out of the pastry shop . . . By the way, here's an éclair and a cream puff . . ."

But it was only I who ate them. I burbled on. Mademoiselle Aubier tried to move her head to and fro, but it was very difficult, and she looked terribly unhappy, giving a polite little smile while I could see her eyes were red and bloodshot with pain and tearlessness and lack of sleep. I realized she couldn't move her head around anymore, as even tiny babies can when they're hungry or feeling the lack of some more or less loving body. I stood up and took my chair round to the other side of the bed so that she could see me, or at least so that her face would be turned toward mine, toward the only words I could find to say, my endless rigmaroles:

"Madame Filonge—do you remember Madame Filonge?—is dead."

The smell of urine was much stronger on that side of the bed. As it's not a very pleasant sensation and even filled me with a certain disgust, I sought forgiveness by laying my hand on Mademoiselle's. For the last three weeks she hadn't spoken distinctly; perhaps she didn't understand anything one said to her anymore either. But she suddenly frowned as if to convey something.

"The other day," I went on, "I took the train to Versailles . . ."

Her brow puckered even more painfully. I rang the bell. A nurse came and looked at her, went away, and returned with a hypodermic syringe. Meanwhile I said to her (the memory of the whole scene is so unpleasant it's still almost alive, and it's at the same time both painful and easy to recall):

"I'll have to be going now, Mademoiselle. I have to check in on Rue de Rivoli and then go on to the Conservatory. Madame de Craupoids asked me to collect the set pieces for the February exam and take them to Rue de Poitiers. And then unfortunately I have an appointment at the dentist's."

The furrows on her forehead deepened. Her eyes wept a kind of thick white pus.

"Goodbye, Mademoiselle," I said. "I'll be back as soon as I have a moment . . ."

But Mademoiselle wasn't looking at me. She seemed to be looking at the hypodermic with a kind of hunger or hope.

I put my hand on hers again and pressed it a little. Then I went away, feeling horribly base, guilty, vile, and unhappy, and assailed by terrible thoughts. We are always forsaking people. We are so much like the gods. What is love? What is medicine? Alas for all those places that smell, where sounds have little to do with language, where eyes are always on the watch!

I made a wreath out of fir branches. It was December 6. Always on the lookout for occasions for festivity, I was celebrating St. Nicholas and Hans Muff, and had made up my mind to celebrate alone. I was just trying to fix the wreath to the ceiling when the doorbell rang. A postman handed me a telegram: "Aunt Clothilde dead. Come at once. Denis Aubier." But I didn't go. I immediately called Denis. I was too afraid of seeing Seinecé. I was too afraid of seeing Isabelle. I was too afraid of seeing Delphine. I told him so, and asked him to forgive me.

He was good enough to say it didn't matter. An elderly cousin, whom he knew only through the birthday cards she'd sent him when he was a child, had come to live in the house in Saint-Germain. We arranged to have dinner together in a few days' time.

To be quite frank, Mademoiselle Aubier's death didn't affect me. I was even rather relieved. "Clothilde, daughter of Clovis, wife of Amalaric, queen of the Visigoths!" I kept repeating to myself like a lesson as I finished off the wreath. Surprisingly enough, I believe I first found out what Mademoiselle Aubier's given name was from Denis's telegram announcing her death. "Clothilde, daughter of Clovis, wife of Amalaric, queen of the Visigoths," I muttered over and over for about ten days. I couldn't cry. It took several years for me to be able to do so. It was in Japan, at Kyoto, after a concert, when someone was giving me a bunch of pink and yellow tulips—probably sent by plane from Rotterdam—that I wanted to weep. As I touched the velvety pink and gold petals I saw Mademoiselle Aubier's face—her real face, not the dying one. The face of Mademoiselle Aubier alive, talking, sucking Lolottes de Nevers, and singing eighteenth-century songs. And then I really suffered. And then Mademoiselle really died, because it seemed to me as if long ago, when I kissed her cheeks, they were of the same velvety softness as the great tulip petals.

A few days later Denis Aubier came to pick me up at Quai de la Tournelle. It was cold. I remember I still had a horrible green loden coat that I hated but couldn't get around to throwing out. No one had gone to the funeral. Neither Seinecé nor Isabelle nor Delphine. I recall that Denis and I had a heated discussion about the agreement between the Communist Party and the socialists. Denis had brought me a green moroccan leather toilet case as a memento of Mademoiselle. It had little imitation tortoiseshell boxes inside and little imitation cut crystal bottles with silver-plated stoppers.

"We don't amount to much," I thought bitterly. "In the heart of another you're a toilet case, and with imitation fittings at that!"

Delphine had taken Pontius, the dog, and didn't want anything else. Denis was leaving for Brussels and couldn't keep him. I remembered Mademoiselle Aubier sitting on the stool near Delphine's little mattress laid out on the floor, and singing to her softly:

Kaiser Bill, did you have a good lunch?
Yes, thanks, Poincaré—I had some grenades.

Or singing the same song as she danced Delphine up and down on her knees, each tiny hand holding tight to a finger so as not to tip over.

What strange dreams our memories are. And what strange rivers our forgettings, and our lives. Out of all our moments only a few strange fragments remain afloat. And we can't see what necessity presides over the cutting, the breaking, the fraying, the shipwreck. And books are strange wreckers. Mademoiselle's body soon sank into the waves. Whole sections of what she was were engulfed, and among them undoubtedly the most essential parts. Only her cheeks survive. More than twenty years have gone by, and what remains of her for me is certainly not a green moroccan leather toilet case. But I can't understand why her cheeks were chosen. They were all that came back after her death, and this irritated me. The memory haunted and still haunts me like a ghost. Like warm cherry plums, amber globes speckled with red. Or sometimes they were like the clay marbles that we flipped or flicked in childhood. Or Seinecé's and Delphine's fruit drops in the electric light. Another strange thing, in addition to the way I discovered that her name was Clothilde, was the way a superstition Mademoiselle had told Delphine about kept coming back to me in the form of an enigmatic daydream, an absurd vision. "Between midnight and one o'clock on Christmas Day," she'd said authoritatively, "the cows in the byre all go down on their knees."

Finally I thought of her affection for flowers, which she passed on to me. And perhaps it's to her I owe a predilection for tulips, too. Ever since the time when I really reacted to her death, I've always brought bunches of flowers home with me every two or three days. Apart from anything else they're also tokens of friendship, and it's probably wise to rely on ourselves for adequate supplies. They're gifts we make to ourselves to maintain mutual respect—and this requires great perseverance and some skill in sleight of hand. I loved and still do love buying old-fashioned vases of uncertain if not downright weird taste, which I take in out of pity. Unlike animals, plants—if you'll pardon the platitude—don't have nervous systems. That makes them superior to us in the scale of being. Some men of a very melancholy disposition can't look at plants without weeping.

I don't know why, but Mademoiselle Aubier's death coincided with the darkest period of my life. Everything got me down. I avoided my most wordy and worldly friends. I even stopped seeing my sister Elisabeth (she used to come up to Paris from Caen every couple of months and stay in a very luxurious two-roomed apartment she owned on Rue Saint-Dominique—a very different affair from the studio in Stuttgart that belonged to all five of us): she would make long speeches about beauty, science, society, education, psychoanalysis, politics, God, civilization, love and the whole bag of tricks.

An evil god—are there any good ones?—who looked for all the world like a gladiator, and I've always loathed the Romans, suddenly caught me in his net but didn't bother to stick his trident through my throat. He just dragged me around the arena for a few months. I was his victim—in other words I'd lost in advance, trammeled in my armor, my shields, and my visored helmet. I occasionally saw Katharina Ubmann again when she was in Paris. I suffered to the point of deficiency. Men have a tiny cape hanging on a kind of rudimentary peg on the lower part of their abdomen, blowing about like a garment hanging on a nail, and swelling up in the draft if anyone leaves a door or a window open.

I was scarcely twenty-four years old. I was still a child. And children and adolescents can't guess that suffering doesn't last—at least if you don't take pleasure in feeding it. My sister Lisbeth wanted to take me to a urologist, a neurologist, a Zen monk. And I certainly wasn't very well. I kept on working, but racked with anxiety, dazed with medication, and filled with an almost unqualified desire to die. I was Job, on the borders of Arabia and Edom. "Why were there two knees to receive me, two breasts for me to suck?" But I hadn't been suckled. Had I been received? If all *my* griefs could have been laid in the balances together, all the pains I suffered in various parts of my body, they too would have been heavier than the sand of the sea.

Katharina, like Lisbeth, kept telling me I ought to look after myself. Ought to occupy myself with practical things.

"Karl, perhaps you ought to strip the wallpaper in the bedroom and repaint everything. You ought to clean up the hall. You ought to . . ."

I didn't feel like doing anything. I was so anxious for her to leave I actually suggested it. I couldn't sleep a wink, so much did I long to sleep, to die. They say, and it's very likely true, that the memory of an act that hasn't been fully accomplished tries to find peace and release in a kind of death. Anyhow, an old desire does seek to appease the drive that still haunts and torments it. All night and every night for months I used to lie with my eyes wide open, waiting for the long beams cast on the ceiling by the headlights going past on the quai. That was my main occupation—the only thing that faintly interested me. The yellow shafts came in through the top of the blinds, over the wooden rail from which the yellow velvet curtains hung, and moved slowly over the ceiling like the rod of a huge metronome. The room was dark and each beam so brief that it didn't light things up distinctly; but it lasted long enough for its disappearance to blot everything out and plunge it into a sort of death.

In fact, after cudgeling my brains to round up these memories, I realize it wasn't really Mademoiselle Aubier's death that was to blame for the state that I was in and that I now find so little pleasure in recalling. It was Dido's death, three months later. She was two years old. It was the last thing I expected to happen, and it took me aback. There was a bitter smell in the kitchen. She lay hidden behind the refrigerator in a little fetid puddle. It was March 12, 1967. The date will be engraved inside me as long as consciousness lasts. And it was *her* death I was forgetting just now, or refusing to revive. God!—when I put my hand under Dido's slack belly! The little cat that I loved. And the only creature in the world that loved me.

* * *

So it was only after Dido died that I had what my doctor called a nervous breakdown. Admittedly Stan Laurel and Joseph Buster Keaton had just died, and while that might have nothing to do with breakdowns it had everything to do with the abyss. But the abyss wasn't nervous: it was a state of complete apathy.

I loved Dido. Whom had I ever loved more? Whom would I ever love more? Several dead people had come back to me in her. If I had to be more precise I'd say five percent of her was my mother—the better part of my mother, the implacable eye and total absence of solicitude. Twelve percent was a young Swabian girl from Waldenbach, sturdy, funny, mischievous, and warm, who surrounded my childhood with her laughter. Fifteen percent was Marga as a child, collecting all the kittens on the hillside in her bedroom. Twenty percent was Ibelle—Ibelle's pride and way of moving. Ten percent was André Valasse, who had given Dido to me, and five percent was Louise, his wife, the Chenil bakery, and the room I was allowed to rent for over a year in Saint-Germain-en-Laye. But thirty percent was Aeneas's lover, whose name she bore, who hated the light and chose to stop collaborating with the universe rather than do without the presence of a certain male body. Dido herself—her true, alien, unpredictable, cat self—made up three percent of the whole.

I swaddled her up in one of my pullovers, absurdly choosing the one I liked best, a big, thick, soft, shapeless sweater of Venetian green angora. Then I put the trembling, almost warm mummy into a Pugno carrier bag. I shrink from admitting that I went and looked several times to make sure Dido's beautiful body was really dead and not still twitching. I kissed her, then went downstairs and put the cold little black heap in the garbage bin. I loved her. A cat is a warm, breathing weight that jumps on your body unexpectedly, weighs on it, and shows you you're still there when you've forgotten and been thinking you weren't. Who would ever do that for me now? And who would put *me* in the garbage bin?

I can't express the grief I felt at her death. One of the many disturbing symptoms that went with my breakdown was that my right hand started to tingle whenever I thought of her. This was very inconvenient when I was playing the cello or the viola da gamba, even though my bow hand wasn't affected. My hand still tingles as I'm writing this page, as if it still felt, even after they've ceased to exist, a certain skin and its warmth and the vertebrae beneath it. As if, beyond all reason, it still hoped to feel that contact again, still longed in vain for a demonstration of love.

Between the sudden shafts of light, awaited wide-eyed with passion and languor, which at any moment a passing car was sure to throw on the ceiling, I was visited by the oldest of my nightmares (sleeplessness is never so absolute or merciful as to abolish them completely). Again I saw the big, bulbous tree, fragile and completely hollow and swarming with earwigs. This nightmare reflected a destiny: not because a musician was pursued by earwigs, cries, and pantings, divinities he tried in vain to appease, but because a dreamer pursued by earwigs had decided to become a musician. This dream of an ear full of sounds it perceived as strident sometimes went with another little nightmare more peculiarly appropriate to a cellist, in which my left hand was crushed and didn't have any bones. I kept having visions of the jointed iron hand of Götz von Berlichingen in the museum in Schöntal.

Then in the morning, before trying in the thin, dim light of dawn to see what the coming day would be like, what the time would be spent on, what person or desire or substitute for desire, I'd be visited by the shreds of my dreams. Shreds of recurrent fears, scraps of tunes that heralded what the mood of the day would be, its slow sadness or anguished rage, its pure distress or fussy, verbose hypochondria, my belly taut as the horsehair on a bow, my skull persecuted by a sporadic clicking like that of the screws used for tuning. I would get up out of duty—I can't remember what duty. I've never known what duty was. I'd chew a piece of bread, not knowing on which side it was buttered, and out of a feeling of obligation—I can't remember what obligation. I remembered Hiltrud. How I'd loved her, and how she frightened me. I did as she told me without a word. I was like a slave at her feet. Like Baruch at the feet of Nebuchadnezzar, the shade of Nebuchadnezzar. I washed and shaved and showered in accordance with the terms, the dictates of an invisible contract prescribing that I shouldn't be perceived or noticed. That I should be invisible. I couldn't read biographies of musicians anymore, but I did go on translating them and practicing my scales. I kept on endlessly playing Feuillard's *Tägliche Übingen* by heart, and Bach's six suites and the exercises by the brothers Duport—because it was the lesson, because I might be tested, because I didn't want to be kept in, didn't want to have to kneel down on the wooden dais in front of everyone or stand by the blackboard with my hands behind my back reciting the names of the dukes of Württemberg in chronological order. Because I didn't want to have to go without lunch; because I was afraid of being caught out, and afraid of my tutor or, as the French say, my *répétiteur.* Unfortunately I wasn't afraid of repetition.

Time came and time went, and by fits and starts the sun regained a bit of its brightness and imparted a little of the warmth it had lavished in the past. I tried to get out of the forest that had no trees or animals or coppices. But however much I stuffed myself with tranquilizers, coffee, and alcohol, it was very difficult to leave the vast waterless sea, the vast endless shore, the vast unmoving desert of illness.

Costeker surrounded me with affection on Rue de Rivoli. He liked paradoxes as long as they were uttered quietly and with complete gravity. He tried to reassure me, saying that most of the people who exuded guilt from every pore had nothing to reproach themselves with. "It's an almost infallible sign of blamelessness," he said.

I was always humming snatches of tunes I couldn't remember in their entirety and couldn't even identify. I anxiously, manically, got out my old anthology of folk poetry, *Des Knaben Wunderhorn*—The Youth's Magic Horn—and went through it like some old scholar to try to find out where my fragments came from. Unhappiness is like desire; or, at any rate, extreme depression involves an immunity to pain comparable to the strange anesthesia produced by the imminence of pleasure. But such indifference to the world, nature, time, and people is in some ways a proof of strength and rude health. Like Seinecé at Chatou after Isabelle left him, I worked unceasingly. But my thoughts were utterly chaotic. I was haunted by scraps of ridiculous scenes from childhood; or senseless ones with Mademoiselle Aubier or Fräulein Jutta; or more amusing and brazen ones with Hiltrud, Isabelle, or Gudrun. I spurred myself on as best I could. I'd have liked to be set challenges or given tasks. Bach walked all the way to Lübeck to hear Buxtehude.

The Bible says God is not in the great and strong wind, or in the earthquake or the fire, but in the still small voice or breeze that foretells destruction. My acquaintance, familiarity, and finally friendship with ever more hours of anguish had made me something of an expert on that breeze. It is indeed more terrifying than the thunder, the earthquake, or the fire. When anguish comes it comes on the wings of a dove, raising a tiny wind that can devastate the mildest, warmest, loveliest landscape as thoroughly as an icy tornado. It's the breeze that faintly stirs the acacia leaves in the graveyard at Bergheim. The breeze that must have stirred them when my sisters brought my mother's body back there from Paris because my father had made them promise to do all they could to see that she was buried in the family vault. And it was this breeze that without a sign unleashed all the shadows and all the whirlwinds. For terrible as it is, it is invisible. It wouldn't bend the silvery head of a dandelion.

In the room where I lurked like a parasite, a cuckoo in a sparrows' nest, there would come a sudden gust like the one before a storm, after which the leaves are still again in dull, unbearable expectation. It was death. The almost imperceptible little gust in the heart, or on the back of the neck or in the eyes, that whips up a motionless swell and plunges our whole soul and all its organs into a sense, a certainty, a fervent conviction of disaster, either commemorating or heralding it, without producing the slightest tremor in the net curtain.

One day in November 1967 it was raining as I came out of the music school on Rue de Poitiers, having said goodbye to Madame de Craupoids and Mademoiselle Lésour with a courtesy that was infinitely elaborate, infinitely sad, infinitely slow and polite. Then I went into a bar on Rue de l'Université and bought some cigarettes. I felt like smoking. I felt like having a drink. I ordered a glass of burgundy.

"Münchhausen," I said to myself, "you've got to snap out of it!"

I realized I was alone. I tried to think of someone I could ask for advice. The ancient Egyptians consulted Apis the bull. In the past I had consulted Pontius the dog or Dido the cat, and their oracles had always been reliable, though inclined to be rather indulgent. I used to have Mademoiselle Aubier. I used to have Seinecé. And I didn't have them anymore. But hadn't I always been alone? And wasn't it very pleasant? Costeker liked men, works of art, unsentimentality, and violent, secret, silent pleasures; and he was even more solitary than I. Egbert Heminghos shrieked with terror in his huge apartment on Rue d'Aguesseau. Should I buy myself another cat? In my study on the first floor on Quai de la Tournelle, among some Cozens and Girtin engravings that had once belonged to my mother, there was Heinsius's portrait of Wieland, or rather an engraving of it. It was like a father to me. I'd learned German from Lichtenberg's *Münchhausen* and from Wieland. And Bergheim meant Biberach. I could hear it calling. I had to go and see Luise among the trees on the second floor on Konrad-Adenauer-Strasse. In fact it was Marga I met a few months later, in April 1968, after four months in the United States, and we drove through the rain in her magnificent white Mercedes to Biberach, everything dripping, to the presbytery at Oberholzheim, everything dripping there too. And for the first time I saw the garden of the presbytery where Wieland, getting up before the sun rose and going to bed after it set, worked among the great tall limes. They were drenched that day, but by a miraculous piece of good luck the sun came out and shone on them before the rain stopped. Then we went, Marga and I, into a village pastry shop as hot as an oven, with walls that looked as if they were made of French cream.

I came back to Paris on April 24, 1968. The fact that I've kept my diaries gives me a pleasure I could never have imagined: as I turn the pages of these little dark red, almost episcopal notebooks bound in grained leather, I feel as if I were pulling a miraculous catch of fishes out of the sea in nets or scales—or hanging, still wriggling, from different kinds of hooks. Admittedly, people who go in for reminiscences—most of them mere drivelers—also go in for revelations that would make one blush. And as I turn the pages and contemplate the entry relating to May 3, 1968, the blood actually does rush to my cheeks. You might say I've hooked a boiled crayfish.

I was leaving Madame de Craupoids's place, where I had been having dinner with Madame Clémence Véré, Benoît, Nadejda Lev, and Mademoiselle Lésour. Madame de Craupoids lived on Rue de Verneuil, a stone's throw from the International Music School. I've never been much of a lady's man. However hard I tried, my sisters always beat me at the game of double almonds. As I tried not to fall asleep so I could be the first up, I'd just be gently dropping off when they jumped on my bed yelling "Vielliebchen!" I've always lost at that game.

I'd been getting bored, and at about eleven o'clock I stood up and said I had to be going. I muttered that I had to be up early in the morning—an excuse with which Madame de Craupoids was familiar. I shook hands all round. Nadejda Lev, a singer who was already famous but very chilling, hadn't opened her lips the whole evening. She spent her time checking her appearance in the various mirrors. But she took advantage of my departure to leave too. So we said our goodbyes together, and when we got to the elevator she haughtily held out her hand to be kissed, still without honoring me with a glance. I chose to take the stairs. When I reached the courtyard I saw her going through the gateway into the street. I lingered a little, then opened the gate myself and stepped out onto Rue de Verneuil. As I turned to pull the heavy door shut behind me, I sensed someone nearby. A hand touched or rather gripped my arm. And Nadejda Lev said in a loud voice, with what can only be called her international—that is, utterly affected—accent:

"I'm going with you, my friend."

"With the greatest of pleasure," said I.

We looked in silence for the Volkswagen van I'd bought to transport my cellos and gambas more easily and unobtrusively. She came to my place. It was a strange love affair. Nadejda Lev was beautiful, with a peculiar kind of beauty: her body looked slim and handsome, but her round Slavic face had something of the terrible chubby blandness of Genghis Khan.

Inordinately fond of herself, she had wonderful talents that have since been revealed more fully; and to these she added enormous pride and haughtiness. But to my great surprise I found that the Genghis Khan face concealed a plump little girl of twelve, shy and gauche and affectionate—whose sensual side, though she tried to give the impression that she was indulging in a great and ardent passion, was low-powered, slow, coquettish, and timid. Pleasure didn't wrest loud cries from us, I remember. Maybe she was anxious about her voice; maybe I was trying to weep like Dido. At any rate we only meowed. We literally meowed with satisfaction.

Nadejda Lev cried easily, and I too tried to seem given to tears and despair. We all cherish the illusion that somewhere about our bodies there's a vestige of childhood. A scrap of skin. A specially sensitive place, hidden from view and ordinary light, where the skin is softer and tenderness is preserved. A square inch where something still survives of the skin of newborn infants, their cheeks, the palms of their hands. Hidden in some fold of the body, usually a soft area near the groin, close to the sexual parts of whatever sex, and only recognizable by the lips that kiss it. That is all that's left to us of the home of our childhood. A privileged place.

"Oh, I didn't dare hope for you!" I said aloud, probably addressing Nadejda's body, but also some unknown person, the pleasure itself, the emotion itself, the voice. She lived in Stockholm. She wouldn't stay the whole night and left at about three or four, my usual time for getting up. I took a shower and to her amazement prepared a copious breakfast. She saw it as a token of love and was moved by it. The joy of living returned to my muscles, seeped back slowly into my soul, and came into my eyes again. I squeezed an orange. We made love to one another again from time to time.

We usually met for dinner at her hotel. During the meal she remained on duty—curt, stiff, with downturned lips, and tough with the waiters. But up in her suite she became a little girl again. We undressed, faced each other, and kissed without impatience, perhaps even without any extreme pleasure. We made love carefully and conscientiously: we were solemn and serious—puritanical, modest, rather slow and boring. Noble and very conventional. Yet deep down inside us, no matter how perfect and narcissistic and irreproachable we might be, I think there was a definite desire to love, as unassuageable in reality as it was shy in appearance: a kind of heart huddled away inside us, pumping away inside us, which

I've never felt again in making love to anyone else and because of which, when we both happen to be giving a concert in the same place, we still sometimes make love to one another.

The charm was so sweet and so kind to our two egos—quite apart from the physical pleasure and the way I'd been cured of my previous impotence and general helplessness—that I thought of marrying Nadejda Lev. One evening I whispered as much. She reacted swiftly; she refused. She had a little boy of eight whom she called up and talked about all the time. I think she even saw him for a few weeks every year.

They say neuroses proliferate like broken veins. I'd had a temporary depression that lasted nine or ten months. I'd been "enchanted" or "bewitched," as I was told the French used to say, meaning unhappy. I find it hard to understand the term "mother tongue," unless the adjective is intended to mean disagreeable, impenetrable, and severe. But mothers are not the only ones who are tortuous, disagreeable, and inaccessible. Languages too are inscrutable; they're always distant, intimidating, inflexible, and exacting. And nothing ever "disenchants" us enough or restores us sufficiently to reality and the simple light of day, and the simple satisfaction of our desires.

Several years went by. I was doing well. Unhappiness and illness still merged into one another like water in water, but in a way that was more incidental now than obsessive. The days between April and June 1968, in Paris with Nadejda Lev and the bonfires, were very thrilling. I went to Stockholm in July. Then I had some regrets about myself. I was sorry to have become what I had become—obsessional, ceaselessly playing the gamba, rather well known among the neighbors, mildly famous in the record shops, a hack. Nadejda's fame came between us. We only met at odd times. We had been reduced to money and contracts. I remember the seventies as a series of exams and crammings for exams. Deep down I still hankered after May and June 1968, the discovery of Nadejda's cozy body, and the ability to enter into a popular, festive atmosphere such as I'd known in Bergheim as a child—the procession, the pounding heart, the drums, people getting drunk, the shouting, the polkas, the Schuhplattler's swift and terrible bounds, the black velvet frock coats lined with pink and blue and yellow satin.

I spent April 1972 with Marga and her son in the mountains. I was tired. We were staying in northern Switzerland, on the other side of the Rhône. I remember the balcony, facing southwest rather than south, where I spent my time muffled up in an anorak, blankets, and rugs, sitting in a deck chair lined with a blanket to keep the wind from getting to my back. That year I'd dreamed up a touch of tuberculosis, though the doctors I saw didn't seem very convinced. There I sat looking at the snow, the pines, and the larches, and the squirrel running along, stopping suddenly and sitting up on its hind legs, holding its hands up to its face just like a hominid, then bounding from tree to tree again as if it were playing. And at last lifting its face up in the warm sun and looking toward the slopes, the mountain tops, the sky.

I was like a consumptive. I read like a consumptive. I spat blood too—real blood; a success, you might call it—which convinced me almost enough to give me a scare, a kind of self-importance, and a shivering intimation of death. But I was cheerful and glad to survive. You love yourself the best you can, and to me sporadic illness had become a reliable companion, warm and tender and demonstrative; and all the more reliable because it was completely imaginary. It was a poison that heredity, chance, and childhood had injected into my veins. They vied with one another in whipping up attacks of anxiety and various other maladies, though they never stopped me from practicing my scales, reading books about music, giving concerts, or making recordings. But even though I was in a way the maker of those fantasies, I wasn't by any means their master.

All in all, that time in Switzerland was a happy one. I didn't then, at the end of the winter, show any special enthusiasm for life. I was even sure I was dying—a prophecy that costs little and is bound to come true in the end—and I did all I could to add to my chances of being right. I had a nephew near at hand—Markus was nine or ten—I had near at hand almost a son, who came back from the slopes with cheeks as red as Chinese lacquer, sparkling eyes, and a body that never kept still. The joy that rippled constantly over his face was like a tiny stream washing against a rock, making it sparkle in the light.

Markus's joy had few limits. We even had great, in some ways universal, discussions. When the weather was at its best we used to make our way down and then up to the lakes at Thoune and Brienz. I limped along behind, wiping a little blood from my lips. I dabbed at my mouth as Mademoiselle Aubier used to dab at hers many years ago.

One lovely sunny day at Thoune, kneeling by the lake, young Markus—whose age acted as a kind of anniversary of my mother's death—asked Marga: "Mama, what *is* death exactly?"

"Right," I thought to myself, "this is it," and coughed a little more into my handkerchief.

"Whatever it is, it's exactly the opposite of Karl!" Marga answered curtly. "Collect up the flattest and roundest stones you can find, and we'll skip them!"

They gathered some little shiny gray stones from the water's edge, and polished them carefully. "Watch this one, Markus!" she said, crouching down and sending the flat pebble flying over the surface of the water.

It ricocheted about ten times, then disappeared into the lake.

"Now you do it," she told her son.

And he did.

"That's death," she said—and I found myself coughing again. "So long as it keeps on bouncing it's life. When it disappears and you can't see anything anymore, when you don't even know it's existed, when there aren't even any rings on the water—that's what people call death."

Young Markus got the hang of the thing very well, and shouted as he skipped. I thought about my life. Desire hadn't granted me very many bounces. I didn't care for the comparison. There was something both horrifying and tedious about it: nothing but repetition, with everything depending on the angle at which the stone first hit the water.

Anyhow, one or two days later I managed to break my left leg. It was on a slope where there weren't very many skiers. I suddenly smelled a familiar smell as I lay alone in the snow, before help arrived. It was the handful of dusty, crackly eucalyptus leaves they used to put in a saucepan on the dark blue porcelain stove when I was ill. The potion bubbled noisily in the pan, sending up clouds of reeking steam that became associated in my mind with delirium and a streaming forehead. That probably accounts for my fierce though, alas, intermittent hatred of Virginia tobacco.

In order to be able to get up early myself and take advantage on the second floor of the most expansive phase of the daylight, it was my habit to turn over the ground-floor salon to the women with whom I lived from time to time. It was a large room with a floor of red and black tiles. A big square mattress on a much larger frame occupied all one end of the room. Odd armchairs of all kinds were scattered about, three windows overlooked the street by the river, and the kitchen was opposite.

I used a north-facing room on the second floor as my study, with a little desk facing east, not only to get as much light as possible but also so that my collection of baroque cellos and violas da gamba couldn't be seen from the street. The little bathroom window over the kitchen looked out onto Rue de Pontoise. At around ten o'clock the sun, or at least some of its rays, poured into the bedroom, reflecting off the red and black tiles and making them look white.

It was one day in April 1972, after I'd gotten back from the Bernese Alps, that I caught a glimpse of Peruvian gold. It was a sunny day and I was in a bad and gloomy temper when I got up, my left leg still in a cast. I was living alone at the time. It must have been about 5 A.M. I felt guilty and ashamed, as if I'd been idling and wasting my time; as if I'd missed out on an important ricochet on the lake at Thoune. I've always had—stuck in my throat like the bit of apple Eve gave Adam, which he couldn't get down and which ever since Eden we pitifully commemorate every time we swallow, especially when we're suffering from anguish or a sore throat—I've always had the childish belief that you lose the world when you can't see it, and that what enables us to see it, what makes it visible, is the god himself, the sun, the god of Sonntag. Would I be willing to make human sacrifices to my god, as they did in the Aztec empire? I think I could be persuaded: when I come to think of it, there are some of my friends I wouldn't mind offering up. To see them broiling naked in a paella dish over a roaring fire would be a not altogether unpleasing spectacle.

Well, it was on that bright, idle, gloomy day that I received an incredible phone call. I was up on the second floor, so I must have had to use my crutch to hobble down the stairs to the salon. As I held the black receiver in my hand I felt as if I were being offered gold on a silver salver. But I concealed my delight and pretended to hesitate in order to raise the bidding. Whatever the offer was or became, for the first time in my life I was rich. A few years before—though I don't want to talk about music here, don't want to talk about that voiceless, speechless and yet audible heart—I'd found, in the gray cupboards of the council chamber in the town hall at Neauphle-sur-Mouldre, the Inspired, Lugubrious, Dreadful yet Human Suites of Monsieur de Sainte Colombe.

"This is the Eastern Section of the Neauphle-sur-Mouldre archives!" the schoolmaster had said, smiling, as he showed me the two metal cupboards, searching his bunch of keys carefully for the right one. I'd published the suites in a Schimm's Library edition in New York and played a few of them without any particular success.

And now a voice from the other side of the Atlantic was coming out of the black receiver and asking me to record all Sainte Colombe's works for the viola da gamba—there were practically no others. Also to write a biography, compile the illustrations for an album that was to be heavily promoted, write a catalogue for an exhibition, and prepare a treatment for a film on his life. The production was to be financed by two American foundations and a university in California. The film was going to be made by a famous director. It was as if the whole world suddenly woke up to Sainte Colombe's existence. I thought about the village in Normandy where I used to walk to buy tobacco: it wasn't far from Ibelle's house at Saint-Martin-en-Caux; it was the place nearest Neuville, and it was called Sainte-Colombe. I saw the creek again, smelled the floorcloth again, the black rock. Sainte Colombe worked in a little house in the branches of a mulberry tree. He was the greatest of all the gamba players in the reigns of Louis XIII and XIV. Marin Marais, his pupil, said Sainte Colombe dismissed him because his talents threatened ultimately to eclipse those of his master. Sainte Colombe retired to a house he owned in what is now the seventh arrondissement of Paris. It was surrounded by a lovely garden in which he'd had the tree house built as a convenient place in which to play, and Marin Marais, who wanted to complete his studies on the gamba, used to slip into the garden at dawn and lurk for hours under the mulberry tree, waiting to hear the master at work. But one day Sainte Colombe heard him sneeze and had one of his footmen chase him out with a cudgel.

And now Sainte Colombe, or his ghost, was to revisit this world in triumph. And for me it would bring, if not glory, at least some measure of ease. I hung up the telephone. I'd finally accepted—finally, with apparent reluctance, allowed myself to be persuaded to accept. Now I could give vent to my joy. I was also very glad I'd had the nerve to hold out for a better bargain. I sat down. And suddenly, that morning, as I sat daydreaming and looking at a ray of the long since risen sun faltering by the window frame and hesitating whether to flood into the room, I felt something that didn't exist though it had existed greatly once, and that all at once sprang up and settled comfortably on my knees, burrowing a hole for itself between my thighs and over my sex—fidgeting, grunting, stretching, warming me, yet disregarding me completely as it made a hollow for itself and went to sleep. And as I felt that life had come back to me; that the blinkers of depression were falling away and the storm of emptiness passing over; as I was already sobbing tearlessly—I realized that thanks to a trans-Atlantic telephone call and a ray of sunlight, the memory of Dido had jumped onto my lap.

I record this feeling because it struck me not so much as a still rather frail and pretentious sign of a return to life, but as a milestone marking the farthest limit of a dark empire. With that phone call—transformed into the ghost of a beloved cat jumping onto my knee, coming back to me mingled with a ray of sunshine, transformed also into an unprecedented longing to work—everything came together, found its measure, its rapid tempo, its speciality, its fate. I went on one tour after another. I always tried to avoid Germany, but I liked going to Sweden, where I met Nadejda, and to Japan and England. I bought the little house on Quai de la Tournelle, rented a studio in New York as soon as the new project took shape, and often went to California and Texas. I saw Cäci and John again in Glendale, though with less pleasure than I'd expected. I translated biographies of Corelli, Telemann, and Biagio Marini. My hypochondria took on a new form. Wherever I went it wasn't I who felt ill at the slightest shower or the smallest pimple, but the two or three instruments I took around with me whenever I could in my Volkswagen van. The stretcher of the E-string made a noise. There was a distant and disturbing vibration. Was the peg cracked? Or the bridge? Or the soundpost? Something was wrong, anyhow. My obsessional anxiety about my body, like that of a child being followed by a wasp, had been transferred to my instruments. Instead of consulting cardiologists, dermatologists, spasmologists, and astrologists, I now sought the help of all the instrument makers I could find. That's how I made a whole circle of marvelous and discriminating friends. They can sandpaper a fingerboard, fix a soundboard, or adjust a bridge in no time. And as a toothache often fades or even disappears completely in the dentist's waiting room, so they have only to bring their eye or hand close to the anchor of a tailpiece for it to stop vibrating. Such ministrations are eternal—ministrations that in the past, in all other civilizations, were called maternal. I love instrument makers' workshops. I love the smell of new instrument bodies drying, and the beauty of the wooden screws with their round heads. Every year I celebrate the rites of St. Cecilia more fervently. Every year in one case and every five years in the other, I keep free of all engagements in order to go to the instrument-making competitions in Poznan and Cremona. I go and I judge, suspicious as a rat confronted by a trap, with bent brow and wrinkled nose like a dog hunting among holm oaks for truffles.

Caix d'Hervelois's collection, in the eighteenth century, consisted of thirty violas da gamba. When *I* got rich I bought a small baroque organ and a cello made by Pierre-François Saint-Paul in 1739. I also bought a gamba that was stranger still; the maker was unknown and the back was poplar wood. To all intents and purposes it had no sound, only a kind of unexpressed sadness, a soft, sublimely veiled, sublimely distant voice. Unfortunately I could never play it in public or even to make recordings. It was a short instrument, dyed with campeachy. In order to be heard you would have had to play it in an empty room no more than about fifty or sixty feet square, with the ceiling, the floor and all four walls covered in marble. Yet of all the instruments I had, that was undoubtedly the one I most loved to play. But the body got broken in 1982 and I had to part with it. It had been made in the early eighteenth century, but was of no particular value.

I made the house at Oudon more comfortable and had the garden leading down to the river rearranged. And with all the money flowing in, I suddenly wanted to buy the house and grounds where I'd spent my childhood. Aunt Elly was dead. I went back to Bergheim and talked about it at length to Luise. But my sister, and especially my brother-in-law, didn't see eye to eye with me, so I fell back on enlarging Oudon, which I'd bought after the devaluation of the franc in August 1969.

So it was at Easter 1973 that I saw Bergheim again. Years had gone by, and I was another man. My body felt bigger as I got out of the bus and looked up at the hillside and the pink towers. From the main street you can't really see the house—the house I now hankered after. I felt I was there as a traitor rather than out of filial or family piety. I was full of a secret desire for revenge, and this bothered me. I felt as though I were going against some decree of fate. Why did I want to see all this again? Why did I want to own it? And at the same time I was overwhelmed with happiness. As before, in 1965, I was driven by the strange, crazy curiosity you feel about something or someone you love. I call it strange and crazy because everything I saw I already knew by heart. I went up the hill. The slope was as steep as ever. On I went. Halfway up a bicycle sped by me. Then I heard the screech of brakes.

"Karl!"

I turned around and saw the vinous countenance of Leonhard Minge. It was as if Johann Sebastian Bach had fallen into a tub of madder.

I went through the church square and knocked at Frau Geschich's door. She told me her husband was dead—Haroun al-Raschid, the drunken, violent, marvelous, Swabian, biblical Caliph, was dead. Then I rang at Frau Hageschard's for the key—she was the one who used to smell so strongly of eau de cologne.

Once again I went up the little paved alley. The smell of liquid manure gave way to the smell of moss and fungus and slugs. I reached the garden gate. It had recently been repainted. I put the key in the lock and turned it, lifting an ancient latch with a little click. The gate creaked open and I was inside. Under the elms. My feet sank into the damp, muddy earth. If I may be forgiven the ambitious comparison, I was Orpheus. In the Underworld. Greeted by shades. Going along by the Styx. Entering the cavern of Taenarus.

I walked up through the "grounds"—it was really just a big sloping garden, a kind of small wood, then the pond surrounded by hedges. All the things I saw were like spirits of the dead. Then I came out onto the lawn and saw the house up above, the big tall house. Eurydice. It was like my mother's face, the face I'd once drawn, playing with Delphine, in the house at Saint-Martin-en-Caux. I felt neither huge nor tiny. I didn't feel any size at all. A dog ran up to me, barking, and I froze like a frightened child. Luise was there for the weekend.

"How did you get in?" she asked as she kissed me.

"I got the key from Frau Hageschard."

Going into the house—into the terrible face from the past—after seventeen or eighteen years, I had a curious feeling I couldn't decipher. I sat down in one of the Voltaire chairs in the downstairs salon. The upholstery was much the worse for wear. My feeling now was similar to the one I'd had a little while before when I got off the bus. Not guilt or sacrilege, but as if I'd made a mistake, an error of calculation. In the lower left corner of the maps hung on the blackboard at school in Bergheim was a key showing, among other things, the scale. The map was the house, but the scale was me, and I'd grown larger quite independently. It wasn't that I didn't feel small enough for the house. It was rather as if I were looking down on it. Then, passing from the notion of scorn and humility to that of physical size, I realized the reason for my discomfort: a smaller body, a child's body inside me was calling out, asking for me to be smaller. It wanted the old measurements back—the height of a child less than four feet tall, not the six feet that had since fallen to my lot, though time has slowly reduced them. The childish body within me wanted to have back the vastness of door when I first saw it, the unattainable, ungraspable doorknob, the impossible fastenings on the windows, the ceiling lights like eagles' nests, the armchairs like statues, the fireplace like a cathedral.

This return wasn't sacrilege or lèse-majesté: it was a kind of lèse-size. I had the right to grow bigger. But I didn't have the right to belittle the universe, to make it grow smaller. It had grown in me—it ought to have grown in reality. It's the same when you see your mother after a number of years, on a bier or a hospital bed—always assuming you have an eye lynxlike enough to tell the difference between the two—and you realize your idol was really this frail body, those terrible eyes were these little pupils the lids can't now quite cover, and you begin to feel sorry for yourself and kick against the pricks and weep because we have to be born nine or ten times smaller than the bodies that suckle us. The bodies that, even with that distance between us, mark us so strongly and exclusively that they never leave us, even if they forsake us. The bodies of those whose desertion never deserts us.

I sat there. Luise, who'd gotten terribly thin, went to fetch some wine. And I sat as if I'd been there for weeks, unconsciously pushing into place the footrest with "lion's head" legs that I used to have to sit on as a child when the salon was crowded with guests. All my memories are of Württemberg. Strangely enough, I don't remember the slightest thing about the first two years of my life, at the end of the war, in Paris. Except perhaps one thing, though I can't be sure I wasn't merely told about it: the little white domes on the buses powered by burning wood. I can see them now. I'm supposed to have thought they looked as tempting as "floating islands," the dessert made of whipped egg whites.

I couldn't bring Luise round to my way of thinking. She was even downright disagreeable. She'd grown gaunt and old, pale and sour. She was thinking of her five children—or rather of her husband, Holger, more than of her children: of Klemens for example, who now spent all his time with Cäci in California. I didn't stay; as there was no one to work the bellows I couldn't go play the organ. I called back to see Frau Geschich, and before leaving for Stuttgart-Echterdingen and Paris I went up to the Schlehe and the little graveyard. As I walked along, patches of sunshine fell on the village below and on the fields and the river. After the wood I went through the creaking gate, up the path, and turned to the right. Then I came to the grave and stopped. I didn't say anything. I looked at the tall stone and read just one name, which seemed to express something more real than all the rest of the universe. I stood there without moving. Then I murmured,

"What is hell like? Is it as unpleasant as I imagine? Is it as terrible as what you inflicted on me?"

Because of my money, my age, my celebrity, and the fact that I was getting older, the seventies—at least up to August 1976—were the time of my life when I had most to do with women, though so intermittently it's nothing to boast about. I like to think they couldn't put up with the inflexible timetable to which I'd irrevocably committed myself. But I'm only flattering myself if I think what they didn't like was my putting the early hours of the morning before them. I'm not as worthy as all that of being loved; and I myself don't love enough. Those who really love will overlook anything—but to tell the truth they burn for only a few moments, then yawn and shout and clear out. I have little inclination for marriage. I don't care for domestic women, housekeepers, or headmistresses. Most of the women I've known who didn't work had a "nanny for adults" side to them that terrified me. I'm not at all keen on keeping a teacher or nurse or cook or maid. I'm too passionately fond of arranging my own things, cooking, getting up when I feel like it, doing a bit of dusting when I'm tired of sitting down too long, going and choosing my own fruit, running my own bath, and packing my own bag. Above all I hate the little cakes most women in love think they're supposed to bake as evidence of their affection. To have to smile as you swallow plaster, gazed at by tender, self-satisfied eyes proud of having managed to make something fall which ought to rise, to have scraped off the black from what should have been brown, to have invented some concoction you're supposed to praise to the skies as it nearly chokes you to death . . .

But apparently it tends to strike the women you love as a bad sign if you scorn their company and leave their beds before dawn. What woman doesn't see herself as irresistible in the warm, curled up disorder of her last sleep, the sweetness of her final scraps of dream? And to compound their grievances, getting up in the small hours leads one to yawn comparatively early in the evening and lend an inattentive ear to the words and grand ideologies that proliferate after dinner in the flush of wine and the tenderness of approaching night.

Four meals a day: I don't know why, but all the women I've known have found the intake involved in this old Swabian custom excessive. Personally I've always dreamed of having a paunch. I had an uncle in Pfulgriesheim whose belly—though not, I admit, his moustache—was Buddha-like in its mildness and serenity. But my desire is so strong and the happiness would be so great that my wish will probably never be granted.

Insomnia makes me break my fast at 3 or 4 A.M., and the meal I eat at 8 or 9 is a substantial one. In the early days, those who are good enough to share my life like this additional repast. Then, with something I'm tempted to call ingratitude, they suddenly turn against what they used to love and start blazing away against the kipper fillets poached slowly in milk, the fried eggs with just a drop of vinegar, the Spätzle with meatballs or fish. While going out to the bakery to buy one or two fresh baguettes restores *me* to a confidence in reality that reading or work may have dimmed and reassures me as to the solidness of the earth, the sound of my own voice and the profound, unconscious, ardent greed of shopkeepers, the very warmth of the bread is accused by the women of spoiling their figures and lessening their attractions.

And there's another bone of contention directly related to Swabian custom. I eat meat with sections of orange or grapefruit that have been tossed for a second in the frying pan. I like mixing tomatoes with apricots in early summer. Sweet and savory go together. But the Swabian way of life, for which in some respects my admiration is extreme to the point of complacency, has the further disadvantage of making me need to use the kitchen, together with all its utensils and techniques. And although the women I've known have been very ready to complain if the kitchen was left to them, they've never seemed very pleased at being dispossessed.

But I guess it's their last grievance that really does it for me. I find it hard to make others understand my lack of enthusiasm for the hotels and inns where I spend most of my time when I'm abroad. I consider it unhealthy and immoral to go into noisy, crowded, overheated places reeking of prey you don't want to hunt; where it's impossible to relax or feel safe; and where you're served bad, stereotyped, insufficient food by starchy and eccentric attendants who do their best to drive you away from your table—usually too small, anyway—and give it to someone else as soon as possible. Someone who's been visibly waiting for you to warm the chair for him and is as likely as not your sworn enemy. I believe they call these places restaurants. They're ruinously expensive, to boot.

In July 1976, for the first time in my life, I granted myself eleven weeks' vacation. I went to stay at the hunting box near Oudon. I felt as if I'd had enough of abroad, of London and Glendale, and of Quai de la Tournelle. I wanted to hear the cry of the teal again over the Loire. The river, when I saw it, looked immense, more beautiful than the Seine or the Tiber: a kind of huge Ganges bathed in its own strange light. A vast river, a vast, grainy, marvelously golden light. And dazzling too: an enormous dome that in the preceding winter had been tethered to the ground by the sand quarries and the little riverside willows. And in the mist of the morning I saw the children running off with rods over their shoulders to fish off the little jetties projecting into the water.

I'd gone back to living the life of a bachelor. I stayed for three months in the "molting" house I'd bought a few years before and had enlarged and completely done over in 1972. But it still looked like an old peasant's or fisherman's house, standing damply with its roof of moss-covered flat tiles amid the wild rose bushes and a couple of elder trees. Above the front door was what I believe is called a "marquise," a little fan-shaped glass canopy shaped like a scallop shell, or like one of the cookies they used to serve with ices in Bergheim.

People used to say, "The light in Thuringia, or Carinthia, or the Erzgebirge, is the loveliest in the world." But we always like to give our favorite sayings the lie. The light in Coutances in the Cotentin, and the light in Oudon, Ancenis and Liré, was pure gold. Coutances was a veritable mine of light.

I didn't work much in Oudon—only from seven to eight in the morning. There was all the rest of the day waiting, with the song of the redstarts and warblers, the silence of the running river, the leap of a bream, the swish of a chub, the moths, the toads, and the mayflies. I settled in. I had breakfast on the white balcony in the library. I went and sat under the old blue cedar.

I'm sorry I sold the little house at Oudon, on the riverbank, close to the stream called the Havre. When the sun left the earth, I would stay on alone by the river in the dark. I'd think of an expression I'd heard a maid from the Limousin use, in Coutances, when I was a child. She never switched on the light in her room to knit. "I'm used to going by the sound of my fingers," she said. "I only need to feel what I'm doing!" I spent the afternoons wandering about, taking a swim. After dark I just sat at the end of the garden by the river, doing nothing: drinking, smoking, listening to the fish talking to one another, dreaming, "going by the sound of my fingers" to sing a song that wasn't very audible but that beat within me like a heart.

I was happy. For I have been happy. I hate images—they always take the happiness away. All comparison is unhappy. I didn't need anyone else's eyes or ears to communicate my happiness to, or to feel it to the full. I just sat by the Loire on the soft sand bordering the river.

CHAPTER 5

Quai de la Tournelle

Der du von Göttern abstammst, von Goten und vom Kote . . .

(You who were born of the Gods, the Gods and the mud . . .)

HERDER, *On Goethe's name*

Everything bleeds on Good Friday. Easter 1977 is the heart and center of my life. Two days—in February and April 1977—were the most important days in my life. Then—at Bergheim, in the April rain—they covered even the face of God with a purple cloth.

I hadn't been back to Bergheim for three years. I'd spent the previous Christmas at Pfulsgriesheim with Marga. When I got back from Glendale in September 1976 I'd had a frantic phone call from Marga saying Luise's condition had gotten worse and there was cause for serious alarm. Luise had been taken from Heilbronn to Stuttgart. I made the trip there and back and didn't go to Bergheim. Her body had shrunk. As she sat in the hospital room on a woven plastic chair I felt I was looking at a caricature of what she'd been like as a child, when she played Kuhlau and Clementi sonatas by the light of her precious yellow candles, which smoked, wavered, and flared in a rhythm independent of the tempo of the pieces she performed so well. I could still see her short fair locks wreathed in that living light. I had a horrible feeling that death had caught her by the hair. In the fifties, after my mother had gone away, my father liked to tell the story of the duke's old mistress, la Grävenitz, loved, dismissed, grown older, then ten years later returning from Schaffhausen to Ludwigsburg and La Favorite—the places where she had desired and aroused desire—and dying almost at once of fatigue on the way from Stuttgart.

Luise is the only one of my sisters who married a German. She hated everything French, everything that reminded her of Mother—and yet the cancer that had killed Mother had now caught up with her. I must admit I didn't get on with her husband, Holger—Herr Holger Diktamm. He was an industrialist involved in the stock market, pompous, ruthless in business, bursting with religion and morality. Of Luise's five children I liked Klemens the best. He liked pottery and working in glass and had gone to live in Glendale with Cäci and John. After being appalled at my sister's thinness and by her face, I caught a plane back. Holger had wanted us to have dinner. I refused. I shouldn't have done that.

When I was a child I used to like playing with Luise. She wasn't the most forward of my sisters—Cäci was that by far—but she was the most anxious, the most inquisitive about everything to do with sex. Or, to be more exact, she was endowed with the true spirit of inquiry, the sensational powers of deduction of a genuine expert on anatomy. We'd both hide behind the glass-paneled door to the storeroom, where you could see without being seen, watching Gudrun and Egbert—a divine pleasure, one that all the gods and all the prophets in the Bible allowed themselves. Annegret was Bathsheba. Or else Luise would take me to the laundry adjoining the caretakers' house: a gloomy place, with scrubbing brushes, wire brushes, a wooden crate of soap, and two or three washboards and clotheshorses always scattered around the boiler. The little window high up in the wall had a yellow cloth over it. My sisters said that when Beate was doing the washing in her petticoat you could see she didn't wear any underwear. They used to take me there whenever Beate did some laundry. And on the emptiest and most unconvincing pretexts they'd push me forward and pull me back, giggling and asking me if I'd had a glimpse of what they were preventing me from seeing.

When I got back to Paris at the end of September there was the inevitable autumn dinner at Madame de Craupoids's place on Rue de Verneuil, not so much to negotiate the new schedule as to listen to her eternal exhortations about teaching. After dinner, as I was trying to get away on the excuse that I had to be at the airport early next morning, Madame de Craupoids kept hold of my hand as I bent to kiss it, and asked:

"By the way, are you going to the christening of Madeleine's new baby?"

"Madeleine?"

I must have looked rather stupid. I couldn't think who Madeleine was. Madame de Craupoids kindly refreshed my memory: Madeleine was one of my earliest pupils, and because her fingers weren't strong enough for the cello I'd advised her to change to the viola, at which she'd done brilliantly, winning two first prizes. Gradually a vague recollection came back to me of a little girl of twelve with cat scratches all over her face and hands, thighs covered with bruises, and fingernails bitten to the quick.

"No," I said. "I haven't been invited. I didn't even know she was married."

"How strange she didn't let you know! The letter must have gone astray. But you can come with me! I'm sure she'd be delighted. Would you like me to ring up and ask?"

And she signed to Thérèse, who acted as her companion and maid, to fetch the invitation from her desk.

"Here we are," she said, taking off the pink horn-rimmed spectacles she used for long distance and nagging at Thérèse to find her reading glasses. Meanwhile she tried in vain to make out what was written on the card. I went over and read out the name Juliette. Then I saw mention of the church of Saint-Sulpice and Rue Guynemer, and suddenly I froze. I felt like one of those men whose shapes you see imprinted in plaster at Herculaneum and Pompeii. I'd just read aloud, from the middle of the invitation card: "Madeleine and Florent Seinecé request. . . ." I uttered the words without realizing I was speaking, and as I heard them I was engulfed and immobilized in a kind of lava. I felt as if I could hear a diamond being slowly scraped over a windowpane.

Madame de Craupoids waxed sentimental. "What a wonderful child she was," she sighed. "She was a pupil at the school for sixteen years."

And that was how I heard that Juliette Seinecé was born—but

above all it was how I found out that Florent Seinecé and Madeleine Guillemod were married. That was how the light of day changed color before my very eyes; and it also changed character. The world was the same as before, but I was afraid. And I couldn't have been more surprised if I'd suddenly become left-handed.

We can lack something for a long time without being aware of it. How could it be otherwise? How could we know about something of which we don't feel the need? I experienced recklessness again, and the gnawing of passion. My mind was in a turmoil. To put it less picturesquely, I worked myself up. I imagined Seinecé putting pressure on Madeleine to prevent her from sending me an invitation. I took a sudden dislike to the music school and to Madame de Craupoids, Nadejda Lev, Madame Clémence Véré. When I called Stuttgart for news, the news was terrible. Luise had left the hospital at the end of September, but she hadn't gone back to Heilbronn, nor, of course, to Bergheim; she'd gone to live in the studio on Konrad-Adenauer-Strasse. In November 1976 she had to go into the hospital again. Moreover, Holger had had to close Bergheim and was tempted to sell the farm. He'd gone back to Heilbronn, and according to Marga his business wasn't going well. I caught a plane to Stuttgart again—to Stutengarten. We called it "Garten." The name really meant the Garden of the Mares, and perhaps it was the simple word "Garten" that patiently fed the love that drew me to gardens throughout my childhood and has kept growing stronger ever since. Mother died when she was forty-nine. Of cancer. Now my sister—the second, not the oldest one—was dying of the same disease and at practically the same age. Forty-five. And smoking the same English cigarettes. I've sometimes wondered if the hatred she always felt for our mother—she stayed in Germany, refused to speak French as a child and an adolescent, and never referred to her—didn't make her embrace her corporeally, didn't make her come so close to her that she embodied the cause of her death and almost celebrated her desertion in the supreme desertion of death. Just as I'd renounced German (from the age of two I strained every muscle not to learn it) so Luise (strangely enough when compared with Lisbeth, living in Caen and married to Yves Bulot) having gone to Bergheim at the age of six, gradually banished French.

I went back to the same hospital as before and took over from Marga, who as I arrived got up and left to do some shopping or go to the movies. It was plain Luise couldn't sit up on her own. I helped her. The nurse put two pillows behind her as I held her up. She stretched out her arm toward the drawer in the metal bedside table. But she couldn't manage it. Big drops of sweat ran down her forehead, then her cheek and nose, like tears.

I took her hand and helped her. Later on, as I was leaving, I tried to be funny—but I have to admit I'm not usually very good at it. "Arrege harrige," I said, repeating the old game she had taught me.

"Ich hab's vergessen!" she answered in German. I've forgotten!

"Serega Sirige," I went on.

She didn't answer. She looked at me in terror.

"Ripeti Pipeti," I continued imperturbably.

She had difficulty speaking. Her eyes were misty with tears.

"Knoll!" she said at last, and smiled.

Everything was shattered at Orly airport when I got back from Stuttgart. They say our dreams fulfill our desires. I don't know. But I believe our daily actions tend rather to echo the punishments that used to put down those desires. We weep when we're asleep yet at the same time have an erection. In the daytime we joke, our bodies contracted, invisible, hidden. We spend our lives remembering moments we didn't fully live. Moments we lived incompletely because then as now we were too busy remembering other moments we'd lived incompletely. And the fact that I'm engaged, my heart still thumping, in writing down and reliving old emotions is an almost irresistible proof of what I say. I rebuke myself: "Stop making your heart thud over and over again about old heartaches! Give the whole thing up!" But I rebuke myself in vain. However much I'd like to give it all up, it all still survives and is reborn. Time scarcely passes at all. I may say to myself, "What's the good of remembering? The print of a shoe isn't the shoe itself, and it's no use at all for walking!" But I still go back to the print and am fascinated, hypnotized anew by shadows.

I saw them. In two months a double coincidence—it seemed miraculous, crazy. It was at Orly airport. I'd just come back from Stuttgart. I was on the escalator going up to customs. And above me, on the one heading down to the boarding gates, talking to one another, immense, I recognized them. It wasn't Madeleine Guillemod that I recognized first. It was Seinecé. He was radiant. They were going down. I was going up. We were going to pass one another. I wanted to hide. I fiddled with my face. Tried to hold my ticket in front of it. I clutched the handrail and huddled over to the right. I made an effort to look detached but couldn't pretend to look elsewhere: I was fascinated. It was magnetic. It was what the sun is to fire, what the sea is to rivers, what death is to men. It was the fascination a rat or a man feels, faced with an anaconda.

Suddenly, no doubt attracted by my looking at him, Seinecé saw me. His face went white. He slowly straightened up, looking more immense than ever. Madeleine looked at him, puzzled, then at me. I let my hand, with my ticket in it, fall. How shall I put it? I didn't look at them: I contemplated them. I contemplated them in fear, in a kind of intoxication due to fear, which might have looked like provocation, like something aggressive or insolent.

He said a word to me as he passed, or rather as we passed one another. "Ah!" or "Ka!"—or "Karl!" or "Charles!" or "Arles!" I don't know. I myself said nothing. I imagine I must have stood there with my mouth open, looking stunned. Like someone coming out of Raoul Costeker's bookshop on Rue de Rivoli, finding himself face to face with Assurbanipal in his chariot and trying to raise his hat to him.

When I reached the top of the escalator—God, how I hate these pseudo-Latin words!—I felt like going and sitting down on one of the semicircle of gray plastic chairs. My legs were like jelly. I felt like Baron Münchhausen when he sees his enemy riding a cannonball. My heart was a kind of muscle shaken by spasms, like a kitten when it squirms to get out of your hands. But I didn't sit down. Passionately curious, I swiftly but cautiously retraced my steps, trying to see them again without their seeing me. Not to meet them. Just to see them, follow them.

I got on the escalator they'd been on. Perhaps I was on the very step they'd stood on when their being there made my heart thump. It was thumping still. I couldn't see them in the departure lounge. I went over to the window. Suddenly I saw them near a bus. In the distance, Florent Seinecé was going away. "Seinecé!" I murmured. "Seinecé!" He was very tall. Madeleine looked shorter. But when I saw them again later I found this wasn't so.

I stood with my forehead pressed to the window. My heart was throbbing. They didn't get on the little bus. A few people got off. The whole group then made for a plane standing not far away. Seinecé walked slowly, the top part of his body bent forward. I would have liked him to turn around and feel my gaze weighing on him, imploring him, calling him. To turn around, look me in the eye, confront me, explode with wrath, kill me. Make some sign.

When they were near the plane the heat rising from the ground made their outlines shimmer, and I couldn't see them clearly. It was as if they'd disappeared, as if I'd been dreaming. I strained my eyes to see them as if I'd lost the most precious of objects.

I tasted blood in my mouth again and thought I must have relapsed to the state I was in when I went to stay with Margarete and Markus in the Bernese Alps. I couldn't have looked well either, because a middle-aged lady—she told me she was from Reykjavik—helped me sit down, patted me on the shoulder, and said in English:

"It's nothing, it's nothing. It'll pass . . ."

And I felt so ill that even though I hate the language I found myself answering in German:

"*Gewiss, gewiss. Ganz gewiss.*" Of course, of course. Certainly.

Then she said goodbye, twiddling her fingers in front of her face and giving an exaggerated smile. I bowed and thanked her.

"It'll pass, it'll pass!" I said to myself. "Of course, *gewiss*—the world and its mysteries, *Mensche*, colors, and sounds, and the *sics* and the *donecs* and the *transeams*!"

All the direst languages came back to me. Like the blood I could feel in my mouth again.

* * *

No point in trying to describe how upset I was. I'm the sort of person who's haunted by everything he's ever experienced. I went through a period of terrible nights, but gradually they gave up and became more peaceful. Little by little my metamorphoses grew less megalomaniac, less frightening. Eventually I turned into a little fly caught at dusk on a sticky chestnut bud. It was April. But some people can't endure the thought of being at peace with themselves. We protect ourselves better against happiness than we do against real danger—such as a leak in the ceiling, a broken beam, or a family party. I was quite willing to accept this broad moral truth, but scold myself as I might, I couldn't quell the mental and physical spasms the scene at the airport had produced in me.

For the whole of that winter I imagined I saw them everywhere. I went to a cinema on Rue Hautefeuille, and there they were, sitting in the row in front of me. At the Musée Carnavalet, one of my favorite haunts, I saw their figures in the mirrors made to look like doors. In the Duc de Biron's garden—the fact that you have to pay to go in only adds to the charm, but unfortunately it's manured with sculptures by Auguste Rodin—they were in the bushes and avenues of chestnut trees, hiding behind the statues and lurking in the flower beds. All this was sheer obsession, sheer madness. Their faces mingled not only with those of passersby but also with my memories. My mother and Isabelle merged into one. Mother gave Jane Eyre–Ibelle a stroller with a Daum vase in it, wrapped up like a baby. Then again: Mother opens the door; I'm in the main salon at Bergheim; she walks toward me; the light suddenly comes on; she strides to the middle of the room, and her shadow all at once shrinks almost to nothing at her feet; she weeps. And I wake up screaming, the sweat running down my back.

A log crackling in the hearth and lighting up the room is said in French to "snore" or purr on the now almost white embers that kindled it into flame. I usually have no patience with snoring. But I myself seem to be snoring in no uncertain manner on these embers of memory and remorse. I might almost call them voices—voices that I don't exactly hear but anticipate, as mothers anticipate their children's wishes in English and American novels.

In January 1977 my sister Luise Diktamm died in the hospital in Stuttgart. Once again I flew to Stuttgart-Echterdingen—looking carefully in every corner. Marie Ruppel, with whom I was living then, wanted to come with me, wanted to see Bergheim and the valleys of the Jagst and the Neckar. But I absolutely refused. I met a number of nephews and nieces for the first time and saw my sisters again. Lisbeth—an enormous Willendorf Venus—was bitter and complained that the rest of us hadn't been to Coutances or Caen for more than twelve years. Cäci, tanned and muscular, with apple green spectacles and Mickey Mouse earrings, was delightful and funny. Marga was shattered. Two hours later I was discussing things with Holger, who was really up against it now. I repeated that I was willing to buy Luise's share in Bergheim—the house, the grounds, the farm, and the vineyards. Holger himself wanted to buy out all the shares in the property, but for ridiculously small sums. I asked my sisters to reject his offers, and they attacked me furiously for talking about money and thinking about buying Bergheim with Luise not yet cold in her coffin. The fact was that Luise's death had driven all four of us off the rails. We quarreled over trifles. We were really reliving Mother's death. There, in the Necker Hospital, we hadn't seen only a still body. We'd been present for the first time at someone's deathbed, and witnessed the suffering involved, and the grief and stifled sobs of friends and relations. We were all extremely nervous—my sisters and myself and our stepbrothers. For after she married again, Mother had two more children, whom we'd never met. My sisters were angry too, now, because on the very evening of Luise's funeral I went to dinner with the president of the state of Baden-Württemberg in his private apartment. I couldn't really get out of it: Egbert Heminghos and Klaus-Maria were friends of his, and he was a great patron of the arts, especially the art of making beer. The modest fame of the cellist was beginning to make a breakthrough, to arouse a certain amount of jealousy, and to reach as far as Glendale, Caen, and Pfulgriesheim. During my three-day stay in Stuttgart for fruitless discussions with Holger, I went for walks in the cold and the snow through the familiar gardens of the Altes Schloss and revisited for the umpteenth time the Swabian museum of prehistory nearby. I tried to remember the beautiful litany for the dead that Buddhist monks chant; Raoul Costeker often recited it for a joke, in a more poetic, more rhythmical English translation: "Who then has a mother? Who has a father? What man has a friend? What man has parents? What man has a wife? What woman has a son? Bones burn like a bundle of wood. Hair flames like straw. All is dead and consumed by the void. Why anoint one's body with perfume and sandalwood? Why chew betel? A silent sound goes on echoing."

And I looked at the bare earth and the snow. The sky was white. But I experience everything in terms of sound. Death was like iron in a forge. I went and devoured pastries in the teashops in the Königstrasse and the Charlottenplatz. Iron cries out when it's being tempered. Its cry still echoes in my ears. The forge was opposite the cottage where Reginbert lived. He and I used to sit on the steps leading into the little front garden, holding on to the bars of the gate: we felt as if they protected us. I used to look at the enormous wooden stall into which the blacksmith backed the horses to keep them quiet while he shod them. They would kick. Droppings fell on the ground. Our nostrils were filled with the smell of scorched horn. One day a heavy white plough horse vomited grass and green bile. With loud, desperate cries.

And as I review those January days of 1977, as I write this page, I realize how old I've grown. It's incredible how much the sound of my memories has faded with the passage of time, and how much the smells that once affected me have gradually become part of the atmosphere. I've decided, once I've finished this account, never to hold a pen again. I can feel suddenly dying within me the echo of a name I once loved to utter.

I went to Bergheim with Holger and saw that the place was indeed leaking and dilapidated. But I was again strangely drawn by something in those walls, those shadows. Holger and I failed to come to any agreement—always assuming we ever intended to. Before we left we had dinner in a restaurant in the Bahnhofsplatz. Marga told us she'd read in the *Bildzeitung* that there were still two villages of French émigrés in Brandenburg where everyone, after three hundred years, still spoke French. "For three centuries people have been speaking French right in the middle of Brandenburg!" she said, scandalized that we hadn't done as much in our own few years in the big "house with half curtains." That was what she always called Bergheim. The people who lived in the villages she was talking about were Huguenot émigrés who fled from France after the revocation of the Edict of Nantes.

We no longer live in the palm of any god's hand; no longer does any divine hand warm us, shelter us from death, or bear us up in the void. I would be alone when I went back to Bergheim. But I wanted it. And one day I would have it. I thought of my father, of my dead sister, of Dido, of Ibelle, of Mademoiselle Aubier, of my mother. My tears mingled with the half-melted snow falling slowly out of the sky.

"I *will* have Bergheim!" I told myself. And I swore great oaths to myself, as I did when I was a child. "I must be there in time for the first daffodils!" I told myself.

The job of a really good teacher is to root out two-thirds of the wheat and let the chaff flourish. The best teacher is one who never stops talking and makes his presence felt. I'm a cello teacher. There's something excessive about such a description. Too high pitched. And I'm only a record with a scratch on it.

I find some consolation in the fact that, judging by my friends, everyone is the same. And we're all playing someone else's theme, someone else's obsession, ambition, or defeat. They say the least scratchy records, those that sound clear and almost perfect, are creative people, but I don't know any. For my part, I've never created, never composed anything. I play, read, and translate. And the player in me judges the composers' works as I interpret them, horrified at how much they repeat themselves, though the best of them do prevent their characteristic scratch from interrupting the song. The scratch is what connoisseurs and critics, who like to indulge in witticisms, call style. And like day and night, winter and summer, mother and child, everything seems to say ad nauseam, "You'll be back."

And scratchy records repeat themselves from one family to another. My father used to say, "There are very few German musicians. You can count the really great ones on the fingers of one hand:

Heinrich Schütz, Dietrich Buxtehude—Handel's English from head to foot. Beethoven's pure Viennese, like Haydn and Mozart and Schubert and . . ." I had to listen to this tedious fallacy over and over again throughout my childhood. Yet whenever I hear anyone say the Germans are a musical people my father's voice rises up again compulsively inside me, the desire to speak winds up a kind of spring in my throat, and my father takes possession of my body.

The idea of possession mingled with that of getting my own back. I wanted to own Bergheim again as a child wants a second helping of dessert. "Dibs on the lovely red banisters!" I thought. My mind was orientated toward Bergheim as Muslims are orientated toward the Kaaba in Mecca. But really this obsession was trying to obliterate a memory, a body glimpsed on an escalator in an airport. My mind was scratched, almost cracked. Although we had been living together for two years, I broke up with Marie Ruppel for no reason. I can't help being stunned at the speed and deviousness with which I managed it. I couldn't sleep. Marie never set foot in the law school where she'd enrolled and was supposed to be studying. She buried herself in the little house on the quai, typing theses and learned articles, going out once or twice a day to the Pontoise swimming pool a stone's throw away, and occasionally wandering around Boulevard Saint-Germain, Rue Bonaparte, and Rue du Dragon looking for a sweater or a skirt. She was quite pretty, very well-built, dark and petite, but while she took trouble to make herself physically attractive she declined all physical pleasures. Quite simply, we'd lost interest in one another.

One evening she made a few suggestions. Perhaps we ought to have separate bedrooms. Perhaps we could turn the dining room into a bedroom for her. If I may decently recall what she said, she needed a room of her own in order to put stones in her pockets and jump in the river. She wanted to be independent, creative; to turn the world upside down and begin a new life. I quite understood. What use to us was a dining room? She didn't eat. She hated entertaining. I could quite see what she meant about a room of her own. I couldn't have borne not to be able to shut myself away in a separate and if possible relatively remote place to read and rehearse. I can still feel the somewhat cruel and craven excitement that seized me. I quite agreed with her. The best thing might be for her to find a little one-room apartment. Though it could be irksome, living in just one room like a bear in a cage. Perhaps a two-room apartment near the Luxembourg Gardens or overlooking a square—she was so fond of trees.

"But Karl, I like it here."

"Of course, Marie. So do I."

"I don't earn very much money."

I tried to persuade her she ought to accept the freedom she so rightly claimed. I told her how grateful I was to her. Thanks to her I'd come to like cooking. To like putting my hands in greasy hot water and drying plates and forks and bowls. Thanks to her I'd come to dote on dusters and vacuum cleaners. Best of all I liked doing the shopping. I still didn't much care for doing the washing, but I had to admit that sometimes, in the evening, it helped me to vent my rage or at least to turn frustrated desire into rage and the rage into fatigue. In her company I'd learned to live alone.

"Karl, how much money will you give me?" she said.

Then she told me how humiliated she felt asking me for money. How well I saw her point of view! How afraid I was of humiliating her! The conversation wandered from the point, skidded, overturned. She realized this but strangely enough went on making it worse. I can remember my lungs, my whole body, being filled with growing jubilation. Marie seemed not to understand what had caused this mood and tried uneasily to take advantage of my sudden magnanimity.

I went into the kitchen, rubbing my hands with glee and excitement. I poured myself a glass of stout, came back, and pointed out that really all her difficulties arose from the fact that we were living together. We slowly went into the details. She agreed to everything but for some reason started to cry. She kept saying she didn't earn enough money to live on. I pitied her with all my heart but edged her apologetically toward the door.

"I'm sorry, Marie," I said, "but I must go down to the grocery store on the corner. I have to get dinner . . ."

I had to mend the cuff of my pants before I left for Stockholm the next day. I had my bag to pack, two shirts to iron. I had to phone the recording studio. I had to go and see a girlfriend for some physical relaxation. I shut the door on Marie Ruppel, pale and sniffling.

I was radiant. I opened another bottle of stout but didn't get to sleep as easily as I'd expected. Marie phoned the next morning at about four o'clock. She hadn't been able to sleep either.

"Can I come back?" she asked.

"I'd rather you didn't," I answered.

She offered concessions: she wouldn't do the cooking, but she would set the table; she wouldn't do the washing, but she would do the ironing; she wouldn't do the housework, but she would sew; she wouldn't do the shopping, but she would sleep with me—on condition that I guaranteed her the independence of a room to herself. I said one should never compromise or make concessions about even the least of one's demands. She was afraid she wouldn't have enough money. I sent her some money.

I didn't have a very high opinion of myself when the taxi dropped me at Orly airport. But I wasn't really unhappy. If anyone looked around him, I thought, he'd be amazed at how many people are fond of him. But if he looked into his own heart he'd be puzzled. Some mollusks live as parasites in shells. But from time to time they desert them. Perhaps I was more of a parasite than Marie. I got on the plane. I was alone again. I put my cello, in its brown canvas cover, on the next seat. Cellists and gamba players go broke paying for two plane tickets every time they go on tour. "To think," I said to myself, "that the only human shape that's always with me is a wooden box!" And when we took off I clung as always, my lips parted and my throat dry, to the leather handle of my cello case.

When I got back Marie badgered and implored. February was freezing. I maintain that altruism, like caramel rice pudding, is a very bad thing. However hard I tried I was in such a state I couldn't bear to be with her. For one thing, you always dislike anyone you've gratuitously insulted. For another, it's unpleasant to find out that our desire never corresponds to the person who awakens it. It's our desire itself that made someone who happened to be at hand suddenly seem desirable. And we found that person desirable just insofar as we merely dreamed him or her. As that someone dreamed us.

Marie was beautiful, curious, up-to-the-minute about everything—the weather, fabrics, objects, perfumes, film actors. She was a feminist. She could ski. She looked at me in amazement.

"How can anyone be such a ninny?" she asked.

She had politically correct ideas. She was strongly against war and in favor of freedom and justice. "She's very middle class," I told myself, and was obliged to add, "but so am I, even if I do show traces of the League of Augsburg!"

She had the soul of a suburbanite. "Where can I shop?"—that, according to her, was the question raised by the human condition.

She was in the living room, attempting a final scene. I looked at her and was astonished at my own reactions. I scarcely had any. "I don't feel any pain," I thought. "Only a bit of self-disgust. About the size of a mite." She looked at me wide-eyed, stretching out her arms.

"But I love you," she sniffled, clasping me to her. And the more she sniffled the tighter she held me.

"We love each other," she went on. "We love each other so much. We're going to have the bathroom fitted with apple-green wall-to-wall carpet. You . . ."

"I don't do as I'm told anymore," I said. "I don't know why, but I don't."

She took her pleated flannel skirt in both hands and lifted it. She was naked up to the waist. She brought her stomach close to the lamp.

"That'll do," I said quietly. "Clear out."

She stood there without moving, her stomach bare.

"Clear out!" I yelled.

Still without saying a word she suddenly dropped her flannel skirt. Her lips quivered. She left.

These base, dreary, pointless, painful scenes overlapped with other scenes that occurred at the same time at the music school on Rue de Poitiers. I remember that February as like a tangled skein of wool. Marie Ruppel was just a handy victim, made to pay for a twelve-year-old crime. I was driving everyone away from me.

February was freezing. Cold enough for ducks to be caught frozen in the ice and break their wings. One Monday that month while I was teaching, Mademoiselle Viorne came into the room and said Madame de Craupoids wanted to see me.

I went through the secretary's office into what was called the "waiting room": before you went into the large, well-preserved seventeenth-century salon that served as Madame de Craupoids's office, you had to pause in a little dark antechamber like a kind of escape lock. There, on a long low set of black wooden bookshelves, stood a small heavy metal gong suspended by a thick yellow cord inside a circular metal frame. A stick of pale wood hung down beside it, and every time I had to wait for Madame de Craupoids to open her massive door and summon me in, my fingers itched to get hold of the stick, thump the gong as loud as I could, and startle her into letting me in at once.

She opened the door. I went in.

"Sit down, Monsieur Chenogne," she said. "I want to ask you a favor. By the way, I've read your biography of Richelieu's cellist. It's very good. And very long. Very lively too. But rather suggestive, wouldn't you say?"

"You're very kind," I answered.

"What was his name, now? How silly—it quite escapes me."

"Maugars."

"That said, I must tell you just between us that I don't much care for homosexuals," she said in a low voice.

"You have very good taste," I answered.

"I know you're making fun of me. To be quite honest, I don't care for the human race in general."

"That shows the most exquisite discrimination."

"I hate animals too . . . ," she said musingly.

"Do seas and mountains escape your reprobation?"

"I'm really not quite sure . . . ," she went on, sounding more and more perplexed. She was holding a typed letter with a bold letterhead in her hand and seemed to be thinking. She laid the letter down on a big yellow cardboard file and continued more loudly, putting on her spectacles and frowning anxiously,

"Now this is why I asked to see you. This building is going to be listed. Please regard the information as confidential. The music school may be allowed to go on functioning here. We're not sure yet. The ministry and the city council are fighting each other over the premises, but—don't worry—not over the school itself. A member of the committee is due to come here on March 3."

"I didn't know . . ."

"I should hope not. Unfortunately, Monsieur Chenogne, I have to undergo a minor operation on March 1, and I'm supposed to go into the hospital a day early. On the 28th of this month."

"I hope it's nothing serious . . . ?"

"Thank you. It's not at all serious, but it means I can't be here to meet the man from the ministry. I thought you might see him. You're quite somebody now, and . . ."

"Thank you."

"Don't interrupt. And you've been here such a long time. You can show him around the twenty music rooms and the little theater. Don't take him to the music theory room or the lute and guitar rooms, whatever you do. You'll be able to plead our cause."

"Of course. I'll try."

"I shall count on you. I'm relieved that it's you. Clémence is too emotional. And Catherine's too blunt—she'd ruin the whole thing. It has to be a man. A man will do it better. The ministry representative is a man . . . Monsieur Seinecé."

I suddenly felt ill.

"And he's predisposed in our favor. He's Madeleine's husband, as you know. He's just been appointed a curator at the Louvre. I put his name forward to the Board. And Monsieur Massé's on our side—that makes two. But to make absolutely sure . . . Aren't you well, Monsieur Chenogne?"

I had stood up, but I had to sit down again.

"It's all right. I'll feel better in a minute."

"Don't you want to see Monsieur Seinecé? Do you know him?"

"No. That is, I haven't seen him for more than eleven or twelve years. That's a long time ago. I'm sure he doesn't remember me. We were in the army together."

"Oh well, that's perfect! Wonderful! It'll be a reunion! So I shall rely on you. Thursday the third, at ten o'clock. I'll ask Madeleine to come too. She used to be so fond of you."

"Oh no, please don't do that, Madame! To be quite frank, I might not be the best person. . . ."

"Don't you want to help me save the school?"

"Of course I do, but . . ."

"So it's settled, then."

"I'm sorry, Madame. I must go."

"I'll leave you alone for a bit. You're quite pale. Pull yourself together. Here, I'll get you a glass of sherry!"

She stood up, got a bottle of Harvey's sherry out of a drawer by the door, and put a drink on the desk between the windows.

"I'll tell them you won't be giving your classes today," she said as she went toward the door.

I stayed there alone. I didn't think about anything. I didn't feel time go by. I was like a dead tree stump in the bed of a river, washed over by the water but obstinately numb and unmoved. When Madame de Craupoids came back I was still sitting there, crouched over with my hands on my heart, and it seemed as if she'd only just left me.

"Well?" she asked. "Are you feeling better?"

I looked up at her.

"I can't see Florent Seinecé," I said faintly.

"Of course you can!"

"But he certainly doesn't want to see me!"

"Listen, Monsieur Chenogne—he actually asked to see you. Not only that, but he asked me not to be there."

This took my breath away. I felt such a fierce and tortured pang in my heart that I couldn't help letting out a cry. I had to stand up, and in doing so knocked against the desk—which Madame de Craupoids always referred to as "the Tronchin table" and which she always left open and covered with scores—and balanced myself against an old square piano. It was never used but was carefully preserved for its marquetry and because Giacomo Meyerbeer had played on it.

"But why did he ask that?" I croaked.

"Because Madeleine Guillemod—Madame Seinecé—was a pupil here for sixteen years. And her mother before her. And her grandmother, in my own mother's day. . . ."

"I still don't see . . ."

"She saw you. Passed you somewhere. At an airport, I believe . . ."

"But how does she know?" I cried. But I checked myself. "And you?" I said faintly. "Do you know?"

"Madeleine did mention something that had upset her husband in the past . . ."

"And what's your opinion? What do you think?"

"I don't think anything. It didn't sound so very unusual to me. At my age, in fact, I find it rather touching. I may not be good for much, but I'm not dead yet."

I left without saying any more. I wanted to say goodbye to Madame de Craupoids, but my mouth was so dry I couldn't speak. My throat was like a desert. I hadn't any blood left, any tears, any saliva—and I'd never know blood or tears or saliva again. I remembered having my throat painted as a child and retching. I *was* that retching now, and Madame de Craupoids was the brush. So I fled without saying goodbye. I rushed down the stairs and out through the door, then down Rue de Verneuil and along the quai. I didn't slow down until I got to Rue Saint-André-des-Arts. I'd read that Queen Ultrogotha used to like walking there, along the ancient path between the hawthorn hedges. I wanted to die.

Impatience is the strongest proof that time exists. "At once! At once!" we pant, and nothing happens. The interview with Florent was due to take place in another ten days. But I would have given anything to have it behind me. Sometimes I felt like killing myself to avoid seeing him; I couldn't bear the thought of it, though there was really no reason why I should be so agitated. It's in such situations that the slowness of time, the refusal of the present to go by, seems worse—stronger and more unyielding—than the muscles of a living adversary pitted against you.

One of time's most subtle and sadistic properties—one that is exciting as well as depressing, and allows us some curiosity about the future, always supposing the end of all ends isn't a foregone conclusion and what happens in a normal lifetime is capable of arousing any enthusiasm—consists in its unpredictability. As well as opening up gulfs in unimaginable places, it mixes unexpected haloes, pleasing mists, sudden laughter, and success with the direst occasions.

When I got home—after several hours spent wandering about, drinking, and dropping in to Raoul's bookshop on Rue de Rivoli—I found an almost incredible offer waiting for me on my answering machine. It was from Egbert Heminghos, whom I'd seen a month earlier in Stuttgart when I dined with the president of Baden-Württemberg on the night of Luise's funeral. I'd known Egbert for years—Klaus-Maria had introduced us. He used to look after Dido for me when I was abroad or staying with Ibelle in the house at Saint-Martin-en-Caux. He was very strange and extremely rich: of Prussian origin, a devotee of art, superstitious, half crazy, a homosexual with some rather disconcerting traits, such as claiming to sleep only with partners who smelled bad. He was always saying, of someone who had something wrong with his face or a crippled arm or leg, or who was rather malodorous: "A god must indeed go there, to quote the heroes of Homer!" I saw him often—I found him frightening but fascinating—and had introduced him to Raoul Costeker. I saw a lot of him in connection with this new commission, until he died a couple of years ago: his body was found in the toilets of a Citroën garage in the western suburbs of Paris.

He was a strange person to have for a friend. Not a day went by that I didn't discover some new fad or obsession, each more intriguing than the last. Take the procedure he claimed to follow whenever he had to make an important decision, especially about approaching a new lover. He called it the "Patras ritual." In his five- or six-room pied-à-terre on Rue d'Aguesseau he had a library containing nothing but Greek texts, and in the middle of the room was a little two-faced figure of Hermes on a glass table. Heminghos used to leave the door to the apartment open and the library door ajar, then draw the inside shutters and light the sixteen little blue atrocious-smelling candles that stood around the statuette, carefully linked together with fuse wire. He then placed a gold louis on the Lorraine glass table, quickly poured his hopes or perplexities into the ear of the god, then clapped his hands over his own ears and rushed out of the library and the apartment, down the stairs, and into the street. Still with his hands over his ears he would walk to Place de la Concorde, risk his life by crossing through the traffic to the central island, then take his hands away. And the first voice he heard after that was supposed to convey the answer of the god.

There was seldom anyone else on the island, which meant it was usually the sound of car wheels that had to be interpreted. He hoped to capture some voice or airy whisper from outside himself, in which he might read what he himself didn't dare to say, or hear what he really desired to desire.

One day when he was anxious to know what suburb he should seek his pleasures in, a man called out to his dog not to bite ("*Mords pas!*"), and Heminghos went out to the new town of Maurepas, near Versailles. Things were always determined by idiotic puns, jests, or answers occurring just by chance. And it might have been a man who was cross with his dog, or a maid grumbling at a little boy on the way home from school, or an angry driver, who had made Egbert think of me for the job. He offered me an unimaginable sum in cash—German marks—to organize and record some private concerts of a very special nature.

He was constantly awakened by nightmares that upset him so much he couldn't hope to get to sleep again. He paid a young Vietnamese called Iô handsomely to sleep in his room with a piece of string around his wrist so that he could be wakened as soon as his employer got worried. If Heminghos felt like wandering around the apartment during the night he'd rouse his "night watchman" and take him along while he had a drink of water, washed his face, or looked out of the window to see how black and slow and implacable the darkness is.

Or else he would sit down in one chair while Iô slumped down and went back to sleep in another, and spend the rest of the night dreaming of sleep and trying to shake off his nightmares.

Iô told me later that Heminghos had heaps of pillows of various sizes for his arms and legs to rest on. And though he dragged Iô from window to window and talked to him, stretched out on thirty or forty cushions, Iô usually went back to sleep. Heminghos said he couldn't bear that: the silence seemed to descend through the dark like a waterfall or a river, a kind of Amazon about to swallow him up.

And that was why Egbert Heminghos asked me first of all to draw up a program of music for him to listen to every night. Iô would see to carrying it out. Second, he wanted me to appraise his collection of ancient instruments, then buy additional items at international sales and have them perfectly restored. Third, I was to put together a musical library comparable to his extensive Greek one. He was particularly interested in first editions of scores, autograph manuscripts, and biographies.

The interview with Seinecé was in ten days' time. I must have been in the same state of mind as David when he looked down into the valley of the Terebinth, getting ready to confront the giant frame of Goliath. One of my favorite and most carefully observed habits in the winter, when the weather is cold, is to breathe in as deeply as I can—and I must thank heaven for granting me such a supernatural gift, in some ways just as good as a little slingshot—then to breathe out as hard as I can through my nostrils, in the hope of sounding like an ox. I was no longer David. I was an ox. An ass. Fräulein Jutta used to say that it was with the vapor of their breath that the ox and the ass warmed the infant Jesus. A kind of megalomania made me enjoy warming an infant Jesus who was nestling deep inside me—but who had hidden himself so well that he'd disappeared.

But that wasn't the worst of my obsessions. I was going quite crazy. Seinecé kept appearing to me in a dream, like a shaman, coming into the little room where I practiced on my cellos like Egbert Heminghos waking from a nightmare. He strode around breaking everything, eyes blazing, wearing a striped coat. Seinecé wasn't like a tiger, he was one. Then he stopped being a tiger and just looked at me with an expression of infinite reproach. After which he mounted his caparisoned earwig and slowly rode away into the Blue Mountains.

I'd driven everyone away—though I have to admit that didn't take much doing. I even turned down invitations from Raoul Costeker. I stuffed myself with tranquilizers. I drank. I wandered about. One cold evening I was leaning on the parapet of Pont de la Tournelle. The stone was freezing. I looked down into the water—wanting to fall, to be engulfed, swallowed up, to be nothing but a few bubbles bursting as they came to the surface, with silence above me and the water flowing on over me, flowing on forever and ever.

I saw him everywhere: one day I had a hallucination by the telephone switchboard at my publisher's office. I had guilty dreams.

Seinecé called me to account over Mademoiselle Aubier's death: he said it was I who'd killed her. I was innocent but could never manage to prove it. Then Florent turned into Savonarola, thin and malevolent, and I gave him an account of Mademoiselle's end, getting bogged down in details and generalizations about what an easy death it was and how the desire to live faded as the body grew weaker. I floundered about amid comforting images. Seinecé was a god—as if I'd ever had any doubt on the subject. A god took a jar to the riverbank, filled it with water, closed it up, and set it down on the bed of the river. Time went by, and the jar, knocked to and fro by the water and nosed at by a pike, broke. "Water has mixed with water—that is the name of death, Monsieur Chenogne," said Charon the ferryman. And Clothilde Aubier, Florent Seinecé, and Charles Chenogne were the names on the labels on the jars. I could hear Mademoiselle Aubier lamenting about death in the distance, far away past thickets and palm trees: "Where's the bread, the wine, the pleasure, the singing?" And in the lament of Mademoiselle Aubier's soul, as it floated through the air, I could hear the sewing machine, the hum of the sewing machine, and the sigh that Lachesis or Clothos heaves as the so finite hem passes under its foot.

I was filled with a mad desire for confession. I longed irresistibly to see him again, terrified though I was by the thought of our meeting. I wanted to see him again and find peace in confession, in boundless, endless words. Did I want to be absolved? Punished? Cursed? Blessed? What *did* I want? I wanted all that, and the opposite of all that: the sweetness of seawater and its bitterness; calm and storm. I've always had a very clear recollection of the fifteen or twenty confessions I made as a child in church at Bergheim—or rather in the chapel at the top of the hill. For during the winter the priest didn't hold services in the Catholic church, and I made my confession in the chapel of St. Paula. I went there at dusk after school, and the hands I clasped under my nose still smelled of rubber from the mat in the gym, or chalk and erasers and pencil shavings. As soon as I'd gone through the porch I wished I could suddenly divest myself of these smells, like a shy child undressing so fast he gets all tangled up and falls over. I didn't want to profane the clinging odor of incense, the traces of divine aura into which I was entering. Then I entered the silence, the damp, the cold. And the emptiness of my own heart. There were about twenty straw-bottomed chairs. I sat on one and it creaked. I meditated. The straw pricked my bare thighs.

When my turn came I crept softly and solemnly over, stooping, wringing my hands or scratching my nose, to the confessional, a sort of box made of light oak stained pale brown. It wasn't just oak, though—it was a Mirecourt violin. I knelt down cautiously on a cold wooden step, uncomfortable, sticky, and hard. I had a lump in my throat. I could just hear the murmur coming from the other side of the confessional and hastily went over in my mind the hallowed phrases I was about to use, the monstrous sins I thought it honorable, perhaps even courageous, to accuse myself of. I could just make out the distant whisper of someone else's confession—one of the rare sounds I didn't have to try desperately to understand or imagine. The darkness, the smell of incense, the shame of my awful sins (much more awful than reprehensible), together with dread at having to open my mouth and speak German and to force myself to speak it distinctly, as well as the peace that I expected would ensue—all this made me jump at the sight and sound of the little shutter being clicked aside by the priest. Beyond the boxwood lattice I was aware of a dark shape, the gold of his stole, and the warm rotten smell of his breath. I couldn't get the words out. Anxious at having to try to tell all, afraid of being a nuisance or of not being forgiven, I'd set off a race between sin and time. But that was life. I'd been taught when I learned my catechism that the holy patroness of the chapel was lucky enough to die not only in the arms of St. Jerome but also amid terrible death rattles. And St. Jerome said the death rattle was the only hymn recognized by God and pleasant to his ear. So much so that he'd even enjoyed hearing it on the lips of his own son.

After the act of contrition—though I must say, now, that sorrow and sadness and contrition are much more certain than the relief they're supposed to bring, and if there's anything more comforting than a repentant face it's a death rattle—and after penance pronounced on one's knees on the marble step in front of the altar, there came a delightful feeling of liberation, of freedom in the lungs, turning the sensation of inner hollowness into hunger, transforming the fear of confession into a desire to eat. My body took on a kind of lightness that seemed to make it float back home. Then, having given voice to certain misdeeds, I felt as if I'd gotten rid of conscience altogether, dispatched my nagging guardian angel back to his own heavenly sphere, banished the sharp teeth of remorse and the smile of mother, hyena, boa constrictor, Mona Lisa, and stingray. But that's all a long time ago. Thirty years. The zoo has settled in now, and nothing can reduce unbearable memories to dust anymore.

Except sometimes, when I'm startled by hearing the phone ring upstairs while I'm deep in puzzling out some music, or reading, or annotating a score and I can't get there in time. I let it ring in the distance, feeling uncomfortable at not making the effort. And once more I hear the priest swiftly sliding the shutter and smell the distancing boxwood lattice and the fetid breath of sanctity.

And so for ten days and nights I did nothing but wait my turn, felt nothing but that impatience to tell all. "Tell Seinecé everything"—that was the slogan that haunted me. And what did I have to tell him? Nothing. It's said that St. Florent, bishop of Strasbourg, was counselor to King Dagobert and so much beloved of God that when he approached the royal throne he would hang his cloak on a sunbeam shining in through a window or loophole. I also remembered how glad I'd been one evening when on my way home I'd had a bloody fight with one of the older boys. I emerged with my mouth, one eyelid, and one thigh the worse for wear. How I hated those of my schoolmates who wouldn't accept the fact that I was French, or my accent, or my father's wealth, or my English flannel trousers, fine cotton shirts, and nice warm cashmere socks. They just waited for me to trip in the mud or on the pavement, then basely humiliated me with insults about my mother having gone away to Caen—or, as they said, Paris. Then they kicked me triumphantly all over—stomach, knees, face, and hands.

I can still hear them shouting, pronouncing my name in the German fashion: "Quenogner! Quenogner! Quenogner!"—cries full of the hatred and hostility that made them fall on me in a pack as soon as I collapsed and stopped defending myself, whether in the playground or on the pink flagstones of the narrow street.

But in the midst of that Passion there arrived Joseph of Arimathea in the form of Klaus-Maria. He came to my defense, and I started to fight back again. The violence of my enemies revived too, while my own blows rained down madly in all directions to frenzied cries of encouragement from the group of schoolboys looking on, whom I absurdly called SS but who had now turned their coats and changed their hero. Soon, as I'd given up trying to protect my face and stomach, I was delighted to feel the blood running down my face and see it dripping on my hands. I plunged into victory with a great display of histrionics, deriving a kind of pride from not having avoided trouble and bloodshed. I bashed away, I danced. Klaus-Maria held my victim's feet while I beat him up.

Every second that went by added to the triumph. My face was wreathed in blood. There's a certain kind of security in touching bottom. The shouts were in my favor now. I'd crossed the border of fear and was beyond death. In reality it was the first concert I ever gave—and the only one.

When we find ourselves confronted with a moment of decision, a fateful, crucial moment that must be seized, a moment when we feel we have to risk life itself, we sometimes surprise ourselves by taking stands that reveal a side of our nature we never hitherto suspected. My sister Margarete had been calling me for several days: Holger, my brother-in-law, had changed his mind, perhaps as a ruse. He didn't want anything now—didn't want to buy our shares in the family property. Everything was back to the real price, the estimated price. The Bergheim town council was interested, and so was Hans. Marga said she didn't think it was just a businessman's trick: Holger's firm really was going downhill. I suddenly decided to buy. I sold the house at Oudon. I don't know what I was trying to do: whether to destroy or to balance the economy governing my life. All the money I got from Egbert was swallowed up in this venture. I spent two days with my ear burning hot from being glued to the telephone: calling my bank, the lawyers, the record shops, the publishers. I telephoned Glendale, Caen, and Pfulgriesheim. I added up my advances. I bought Luise's and Marga's shares one by one. Cäci wanted a couple of days to think it over, then agreed. Lisbeth was deafer to my calls and had to be persuaded. I'd never known my eldest sister very well. I was still at boarding school when she got married and went to live in Caen—

unfortunately not in the center of the town. The part she lived in was extremely dreary. A new dock had been opened at the end of the Ouistreham canal, and what had once been a middle class resort had become like the banks of the Acheron, only more anachronistic, more industrial, and almost more deadly boring than death itself.

Lisbeth had married a childhood playmate whom I used to be afraid of and with whom she used to shut herself up in the bathing huts or disappear among the rocks. We used to play volleyball with him by the Sienne or on the beach at Regnéville in the school vacations. We flew kites together and played badminton or bowled in the shade of Duke William's rickety old tower.

I asked Marga to come with me to see Lisbeth, and she jumped at the idea, torn between fear and pleasure at the thought of confronting her oldest sister but excited at the prospect of seeing Caen again. We found Lisbeth had become a hypochondriac, the image of Papa, only older, duller, and more bitter. She was always complaining about her stomach. She never talked about anything else but it and her digestion, so that Margarete, for a laugh and to lighten the atmosphere, nudged me and told her she had "*tripes à la mode de Caen*," a somewhat unfortunate joke but typical of a Württemberger. I made it worse by guffawing like a schoolboy and referring to "*gras double*," another delicacy concocted from animals' innards. As we chortled like a couple of children, Elisabeth, pale in the face and jowls quivering, rose from the table and hurled the fruit dish to the floor.

Lisbeth and Yvon were very fond of antiques, or rather rustic pine furniture, dark and sinister Norman pewter, marvelous church statues of dubious provenance, and splendid medieval armor made before the First World War or even 1870. She insisted on having two of Mother's Cozens engravings and all the Girtin reproductions. I also had to buy a tapestry, reputedly terribly old and certainly very dilapidated. It was so faded it looked like some dim and creamy abstract, though if you went right up to it you could just make out the shapes of trees, knights in armor, and hounds. Lisbeth put on her glasses, pulled in her stomach, and went into ecstasies over it.

In a day and a half the bargain was concluded. Strangely enough, even Marga's spirits were dimmed. It was hard to imagine anything more depressing than Caen at the end of February. Lisbeth's huge old house—she and Marga both claimed it was like Bergheim—stood amid a vast expanse of treeless, neglected grounds full of rusty arbors. The garden came to an abrupt end up against the new dock, opposite a group of colossal and hellish black cranes. Under the low gray sky, with terrible creakings and groanings, they hoisted the cargo out of the white and yellow boats from Ouistreham. Cargoes of coffins. Luise's, Mother's.

I went once to Stuttgart and once to Heilbronn. I bought Bergheim, but I didn't set foot there. For some strange reason I immediately bequeathed the place to Florent Seinecé, as if by way of revenge. In a sense, that is what it was. "He won't know about it," I thought. "He won't be able to complain. I'll die, and then he'll find out I've left everything to him. Then it'll be his turn to feel remorse." All these rational and profitable transactions were in fact carried out in a state of frenzy. I was completely delirious.

It was Thursday, March 3, 1977. I was completely unable to sleep. I got up at 2 A.M. and took a bath. My throat was tight with longing not to keep the appointment, and with shame. Would we have a fight? I shaved. In my left hand I held a shaving brush, in my right a razor, and as I daubed my face with white foam I was a Sioux Indian getting ready for battle. My eyes were red and staring. Would we kill one another? I dressed. It was very cold. There were icicles on the gate and along the quai. I walked for an hour. I had a few drinks, I took some pills and smoked some cigarettes. We were supposed to meet at Rue de Poitiers at ten. From five to seven I practiced scales and arpeggios. Then walked some more. I got to Rue de Poitiers three quarters of an hour early. I stood in the porch of the music school, frozen, white as a sheet and wet. I was so full of tranquilizers I could hardly keep my eyes open. I had the impression my hands were shaking, though they weren't. It was my eyes, looking at them. The snow had frozen on the cobbles in the courtyard. Monsieur Lopez, the viola teacher, went by, his head muffled up in a balaclava helmet and a Tyrolean hat without a feather. A black Citroën drew up outside, and just as the driver was about to open the door for him, Seinecé got out without waiting. He was wearing a dark suit—I couldn't say what color—but no overcoat. I thought he looked very handsome. It was terribly cold.

I took my courage in both hands and decided to go over to him but suddenly realized I was drawing away instead. He didn't move. I could only see his eyes. Then he came toward me, and I slowly drew back. I could feel the cobbles of the courtyard under my feet.

He was standing right in front of me. We avoided one another's gaze. He held his hand out, but I couldn't take it—it was as if it were a trap. Then we looked at one another. His voice was somber.

"Karl!" he said. He breathed out a little cloud of white mist.

I had a horrible feeling that something extraordinary was happening—that my name was being pronounced for the first time ever, or that it was being taken away from me. That either I was being baptized or I was dead. I looked up and tried to speak his first name too, but I couldn't. It was his surname that came to my lips, but my "Seinecé!" was so low, my mouth was so dry, that it must have been inaudible.

He put his hand on my arm. I gave a start. He took his hand away, but not wanting to let him think I couldn't bear him to touch me I stammered, "No, no!," seized his arm and propelled him toward the porch and the dark corridor.

We hurried along in silence, hearing the children playing the piano, going up the stairs, passing the violin class. We went through the little escape hatch with the gong. Finally I opened the door into the large salon that served as Madame de Craupoids's office. He knocked against the Tronchin table as we went in. We sat down at once, as if exhausted. It was very hot. We didn't speak. I looked at my hands. Florent bent down and nervously retied the bows in one of his shoelaces. The embarrassment was intense.

"Not very warm weather," I managed to observe perspicaciously.

"I asked to come here," he said in a low voice.

He paused for a while, then resumed a little louder.

"I wanted to see you. I wanted to see where you work."

"You're an important person now," I said. "You've got a driver. I'm very glad."

And I burst into tears.

Seinecé gave a brief snort of laughter, stood up, and patted me on the arm. Then he held his hand out toward a thin ray of sunlight slanting in through the window, and without his realizing it his hand entered right into the beam, so that his fingers seemed transparent, pink, dazzling. I stood up too, fascinated.

"The pink salon!" I said.

I looked at my own fingers: white, calloused, clutching the edge of the Tronchin table in front of the fourth window, where I was pretending to arrange the piles of scores Madame de Craupoids left there. But suddenly I was sure Mademoiselle Aubier's salon had never been pink. "Things are not as rosy as we think!" I said to myself, and found the thought comforting.

"What color was your room at Saint-Germain-en-Laye?" I asked.

"Pink."

He sat down again and told me—like a child reciting a lesson—that he saw Isabelle two or three times a year. She had made a wealthy marriage, her third. She had four children. Little Delphine was about to graduate from high school. I listened quite calmly to all this. I was Bedr-ed-Din in *The Arabian Nights*: ten years in Damascus had gone by like a dream, and Bedr-ed-Din found himself once again in his underwear in his beautiful bride's bed. But I wasn't feeling the same sort of emotion he did. To be quite honest, I wasn't feeling anything. It was strange. Although he talked about the Louvre and his books and his travels, and although he was good enough to mention some of my records and concerts and biographies, twelve years had gone by and yet they hadn't.

He told me he'd married one of my former pupils, Madeleine Guillemod, and had two children by her—a little girl called Juliette, who was still a baby, and a little boy of two.

"What's his name?" I asked.

"Charles," he answered hesitantly, and my lip quivered. I could feel emotion coming back to me, flowing back drop by drop as if from far away, from the other side of the world. I huddled up smaller. I was more silent than ever.

"Ssh!" he said suddenly, though we were both doing our utmost to say nothing.

"What's the matter?"

"A wasp! Look!"

"In February?"

He pointed at something invisible buzzing in the corner by the Meyerbeer piano. His right hand clutched at the arm of his chair. He was still afraid of flies and wasps. I'd found him again.

A silkworm produces its thread from springtime until it dies. A candle's tears flow until the flame is consumed. We parted in silence, slightly embarrassed. We'd promised to meet again. But I was sure we wouldn't. Was I relieved? Not even that.

There's a pleasure to be found in solitude. One that finds sustenance even in longing for past love. One summer at Coutances when I was a child, Mother made me learn some verses by La Fontaine in which the poet claimed one might take pleasure even in anguish: melancholy was a somber pleasure, certainly, but it was still a pleasure. Some people are very clever. But I declined to waste time on those kinds of pleasure—they don't interest me; I don't find them convincing. I moved my things out of the lovely house at Oudon. I shall always miss the little stream, the Havre, the sand pits and the willows, the little village of Liré, my white balcony over the water, the redstarts and the warblers, the singing of the toads and the swishing of the chub, and the dusty, sandy banks of the river in the evening.

The comings and goings took up nearly three weeks. Bergheim turned out to be a rather doubtful bargain. I had to sell the little house on Quai de la Tournelle. For the time being I rented a studio overlooking the garden of the Rodin Museum on Rue de Varenne. It was on the sixth floor of a modern building. When I got out of the elevator and opened the door into my little flat I said to myself, "Well, this is what they call a housing unit! With connecting areas, sleeping areas, and areas for cooking and storing and drying clothes!" I loathed the clean little modern functional place and tried unsuccessfully to see the funny side of it. The refrigerator, vacuum cleaner, washing machine were all built-in. "Traces of metal!" I thought. "And here's the cesspit. The bidet's like a tiny warm spring. The dishes are made of terra-cotta, the garbage chutes are disguised as cupboards!"

Modern apartments are more like funeral vaults than the kind of houses human beings have lived in for centuries. It was much worse than the prostitutes' district in Pompeii or the village of Wijster. "As for the thickness of the stratum," I said to console myself, "it's less than seven feet!" There was a book I'd translated lying on a table. "Item 107," I said, "from Layer 215 of Site 8." For another two weeks I dug holes and threw up little embankments. Then I went to Bergheim.

Sometimes a thaw is accompanied by a depressing kind of slackness, a damp trickle, when everything is wet and dirty—rivulets, tears, the slow patches of slime on the road. It's possible to resent the birth of a new season, to lose heart at the thought that life is beginning again.

March went by. I recorded Heminghos's night music and asked for a few thousand more marks. No music has ever been so close to language as baroque music—after the Renaissance and before the Revolution. That's probably the explanation and secret spring of my passion for it. It's an imitation of language that involves neither language nor meaning, that doesn't oblige you to choose between a mother and a father tongue. It's a sentence without sentences, an Arcadia where Bergheim and Coutances, the riverbanks and vineyards of the Loire, the Neckar, and the Jagst all merge with the salt meadows by the sea.

I was still trying to imitate Monsieur de Sainte Colombe. In the garden at Bergheim there was a dilapidated little pavilion that had never attracted me as a child, but I had now decided to turn it into a little music arbor where I could play the viola da gamba in the summer. I set about clearing the snow away from it with a shovel, but stuck the blade of the shovel into my foot trying to scrape the snow off my boots and had to be taken to the hospital in Heilbronn.

I stayed in bed for ten days when I got home. I hadn't remembered Bergheim was so cold in the spring. When I was a child, asleep in my icy bed, I used to twine my fingers in the loosely knitted hot water bottle cover—the "bottle" was a French shell case from the war of 1870 or 1914—stretching out my hands to feel something warm. I've never lost the foolish habit of stretching out my hands and hoping for the company of a warm skin.

Bergheim echoed with the shouts of painters and builders. I'd bought the place as if I were looking for love, some special love. I'd have liked to meet a woman and offer her peace, happiness, pleasure, the delights of the table, money—but not a gram of passion. We'd have washed our hands and eyes in Luise's magic bowl, which would ward off passion forever. Luise had told me about it when she was twelve or thirteen: if you had real warts on your hands or some purely symbolical defect, you waited for a full moon and left a big bowl out all night, empty except for the silvery light from the sky. As night was ending but before the dawn began, you washed your hands in the bowl's airy contents, then threw them at the moon, after which the warts and other defects disappeared. The effectiveness of this practice was disconcerting: Luise had once had to stay in the hospital for a fortnight to have the warts removed from the soles of her feet. Some mornings, rising before the sun, I think of Luise, standing on one foot in her nightgown in the cold April morning and trying to dip her toes into the bowl of moonlight. And there at Bergheim, still, I and a warm, selfish, lively but loveless woman would have thrown the childish, chimerical contents of the bowl at the moon, and the awful knots and scratchy old tunes of the passions would have been smoothed out and poured back into the empty night. But the empty night is death.

After several days' hesitation I decided to knock down the two long awnings with corrugated iron roofs in the kitchen garden, where my sisters used to jerk off their young lovers and pet and make love. They were open lean-tos attached to the garden wall. The roofs were rusted. Privacy was ensured on one side by a carpet hung between two beams, and on the other—more or less—by a couple of green boards that must once have been part of a Ping-Pong table. I didn't like the place, not only because I was afraid my sisters might see me, but also because of the disappointment and shame I felt at seeing that my four sisters, all older than I, were subject to desires similar to mine. Lastly, I disliked this part of the garden because it was there that for the first time, standing without my pants on and my back pressed against the Ping-Pong table, I'd been sucked off by Eberhard, the hardware dealer's son. I wouldn't have been seen like that for anything in the world, partly no doubt because I'd experienced such pleasure.

Sometimes we wish we had an external skeleton, like the crayfish's beautiful carapace. More often we actually have one but don't like it. By the end of April I was back in Paris, exhausted, glad I'd bought Bergheim but discontented with the minute Magdalenian cave that was my studio on Rue de Varenne. But deep down I did feel happy: I had come to the rescue of my childhood. I hadn't sold, even though I'd once hated it. I was gradually coming to speak German again, after a fashion, and to dream in German. But this peace didn't last.

One morning in May my heart started to pound again. I had been walking around Paris at six in the morning, then taken the train that runs along the river. After that I'd gone up Rue de Bourgogne, bought some bread, and collected my mail. I was startled by a letter written in light blue ink and recognized Seinecé's writing. My heart thumped wildly. I held the letter in my hand. I was tired. I didn't feel like opening it. I was dirty. Its mere presence was upsetting. This small piece of warm white paper was as heavy and hot as lead. I had to calm down. What could he be writing about? Theories jostled one another and shot off in all directions. I undressed and took a shower. He was asking me to meet him at our old army headquarters in Saint-Germain. He was ordering me to leave the country. I was surrounded by the old guard, I was fingering my ear, I was saying farewell at Fontainebleau. . . .

I put the letter on the glass shelf over the washbasin and shaved. I dressed with the envelope in one hand. Still holding the envelope I went into the kitchen. I put it on top of the refrigerator and got my nine o'clock breakfast ready. The kitchen was silent. My cheeks were burning.

I used to dream of imaginary letters. "My dear Karl, I forgive you. Florent." Or "My dear Karl, I dreamed about Mademoiselle Aubier last night, and she gave you her cloche hat and blessed you." I banished as best I could these foolish and annoying notions, which flashed through my mind like lightning, as irresistible as tiny thunderbolts hurled down by some internal Zeus. I propped the letter against my glass. I ate the remains of some veal stew and carrot purée. Next I went and got the speckled green-and-yellow penknife Hiltrud had given me for my eighth birthday out of my jacket pocket, finished my breakfast, and then, so as not to damage the envelope of what would inevitably become a relic, went and sat in the low armchair in the main room, lit a cigarette, and, the edge taken off my curiosity at the same time as my appetite, slowly slipped the knife under the flap of the envelope, took out the letter, and unfolded it.

> My dear Karl,
> Can you come and have a drink at the Pont on Monday evening, the 9th, at seven?
> Love
> Florent Seinecé.

I was overjoyed. A tear or two welled up in my eye. It strikes me that I cry pretty often in these pages. My life is like a novel written in the reign of George II. But tears are so pleasant. If you'll forgive the expression, I see them as a superior kind of sperm.

Baron Münchhausen punched himself in the eye and saw a thousand stars, which enabled him to fire his gun and kill five brace of duck. He collected some kindling and logs, then punched himself in the eye again, and with this thousand stars lit a fire to roast the ducks by. I was full of a joy I couldn't feel—it was as if I no longer possessed the necessary faculties. I felt as if I were three years old and about to fit a special nib into the metal neck of my dark-red wooden pen. About to attempt the impossible: to write the word "happiness" neatly, without making any blots, between the lines of my copybook. That's how I saw the simple act of picking up the phone and saying yes. I went for a stroll along Quai Anatole-France and from the Pont-Royal contemplated the Louvre, where he worked. The stone was cool. It was a cool clear May. A barge was coming up the river. Then I looked at the water—at something in it that was much older and quieter than the sounds around me, something that reduced cities and human beings to nothingness.

And as I gazed at the eternally flowing water of the river, so I contemplated the love I'd felt for this man, although there was no desire involved in it, or none that I was aware of. I thought of the shy, reserved love, at once greedy and restive that drew me to the bodies of women and accounted for their intermittent presence—for my feverish longing for their presence when they weren't there and my impatience with it when they were. In the depths of it all there trembled a creature that wasn't even maternal, a creature without sex or with a sexuality impossible to express; it was older than myself, I was interchangeable with it, and it was in a way forbidden. I thought of Pastor Hans Nortenwall and of Vergil's *Fourth Eclogue*, which we had to learn by heart and recite with our hands held out in front of us, in Latin pronounced in the German manner. Herr Pfarrer heard our recitation with a little cane like a conductor's baton in his hand, and whenever anyone made a mistake or got stuck he would strike. *Incipe, parve puer, risu cognoscere matrem . . .*

> He on whom his mother's lips never smiled
> Will not sit at the table of the god,
> Nor will he share the goddess's bed.

I went back to Rue de Varenne. I telephoned. I went to the Pont. I saw him again, often. I used to meet him in Place du Louvre in the evening when he finished work, or sometimes he met me in Costeker's shop on Rue de Rivoli.

I went to dinner with them on May 27. At great expense and with much difficulty—it took me two days—I managed to get the children a snail, a golden hen, a Santa Claus, and a smiling pig made of Dijon gingerbread. Delphine used to love Dijon gingerbread when she lived in Prenois. The biggest problem was getting hold of a bell made of real gingerbread, gingerbread made with rye, the kind that comes from Rheims and that my father, out of some old royalist reflex, used to prize above God Almighty. I also took a pot of Bar-le-Duc red currant jelly and a little jar of cranberry jam from

Lalouvese. I knew Seinecé at least would be pleased. I myself hate either giving or receiving—and, to be honest, the second even more than the first. It's one of my most profoundly disagreeable characteristics. I believe it's one of the worst and most significant flaws anyone can have. I always wait for the Gift Bearer to depart, and when the gift-bearing angel or Father Christmas or Santa Claus has gone I open the door, go and look at the table, and flee in despair.

I arrived at Rue Guynemer in a fluster. As I was crossing the road a car whizzed by and made me trip over the curb. Hoping the pots containing the jam were as strong as they should be, I rang at the door.

The apartment was beautiful beyond description, and so luxurious it filled me with envy. It was the sort of place that's so delightful it can turn envy into insatiable hate. Don't forget, I'd just come from my Magdalenian grotto. There was a huge oval salon with six windows overlooking Rue Guynemer and the Luxembourg Gardens, and a smaller salon full of extraordinary paintings and drawings. Fortunately there was also a very ugly stucco and marble fireplace that enabled me to pity them a bit.

Seinecé let me in, and Madeleine rather self-consciously came to meet me in the hall. The little girl of thirteen with bitten nails and thighs covered with bruises was unrecognizable. She was tall now, fair and brusque, and she didn't look at me.

She said good evening looking at my feet or the doormat and calling me "Monsieur."

I kissed her cheek.

"Do you remember me?" she asked.

She still wasn't looking at me. Little Charles, aged three, was clinging to her hands. I kissed him too.

"Would you like to have a drink before dinner? To wet your whistle?"

She still didn't look at me. She seemed rather feverish.

"Just as you like, Madeleine."

At last her eyes met mine.

"Have you forgotten?" she asked reproachfully.

Ever since she was a baby she'd been called Meine, and she'd always insisted that everyone should use the nickname. I felt as if I'd made a false step, as if I'd met this ploy before, and as if I was tired of it. A baby started crying somewhere, and Madeleine and her son seized the opportunity to hurry off. As she went down the hall and through the two salons, her son trotting behind her, she looked like a figure in a Christmas crèche. I was the ass, or a mote in an observer's eye. A mote whose beam is this book.

"Come this way," she said to me later, when the butler had gone up to bed and she'd offered to make a cup of coffee. She let me glimpse the huge kitchen, or at least she stood there in the doorway. Then she turned and looked calmly and steadily into my eyes. Her own were black and impenetrable. She was very serious.

"You can't imagine the bitterness Florent felt toward you for years and years," she said. "A hatred, an anger, a longing to destroy you that drove him forward in his career. Every one of your successes filled him with pain and jealousy. And then he collapsed."

"What do you mean?"

"I didn't know him. He went into analysis—I don't really know if it helped him or if it only deepened his silence and distress. But he changed."

"Yes, he's changed."

"It took him four years to make up his mind to marry me, and since then he's stopped talking about you."

"He has stopped talking about me."

"But his life is still infected."

"Isn't it rather difficult to tell?"

"He still seeks refuge in his work. Tries to anesthetize himself with it. But he's getting more and more bored with it . . ."

"He needs to work harder."

"But the other day, when he saw you were just like anyone else . . ."

"Very good of him if he ever thought otherwise. That's what I call friendship."

"It did him so much good."

"Did it? It did me good, too, to tell you the truth. But frankly, Meine, what do you want me to do?"

"Nothing."

It was miraculous to find that reality was a shore so easily reached. We went back into the salon. I helped Meine with the tray.

Florent came back from the ritual of contemplating the children asleep in their rooms. Meine complained that he never stopped working, took less and less leave every year, and tried to get out of going abroad.

"Not true," said Florent quietly as he sat down. "How deeply children sleep! And how they love traveling!"

It struck me that as he got older Seinecé had gradually come to look like Claudio Monteverdi. I told him so.

"Isn't that what traveling really is? I adore traveling," he went on, laughing, "and I'm only sorry I do it so seldom. The places the travel agents suggest don't appeal to me, though, so I don't go. But I'd love to visit places like Harappa, Ur, Mohenjo-Daro, and Troy in their heyday!"

It was true that Seinecé had aged. He didn't look like a man of thirty-seven: fifteen or twenty years seemed to have left their mark on his face. His eyes were still bright and youthful, but his forehead and nose and the corners of his mouth showed wrinkles like those of Rameau or Voltaire. And his face had the touching puffiness of those who have wept. Age, smoking, toil, and drink had taken their toll. And my face—what was it like?

But Seinecé's learned ramblings and endless recitations were the same as ever. Although the warmth in his voice couldn't smooth away the wrinkles, he still seemed to radiate childhood in its purest form, despite the gray hairs to be seen among the few that remained. We talked. We drank. We smoked. Darkness invaded the huge salon. Seinecé drank more than he used to. He drank brandy as if it were water. I tried to understand why I was so attracted to him. We were together again, but we were so strangely silent. We weren't happy, and we weren't unhappy. People say it can help if you understand where your unhappiness comes from. But on the one hand knowledge, though it may be of use in making you more aware, can never remove the ill it describes or tries to reflect. And on the other hand it's very difficult really to understand why you're unhappy.

The meal had been highly symbolic—we were really consuming reminders of the past, significant words, painful allusions. (I thought how I loathed the nods and winks with which prima donnas and elderly actresses embellish every foolish remark.) Factually, the great reunion dinner consisted of a haunch of wild boar—from the Black Forest—together with various kinds of cherries prepared in different ways: *griottes* from Strasbourg, made of cherries from Colmar; *guignes* direct from Bordeaux, made of cherries picked near Montaigne; and *guignolettes* from Clermont-Ferrand. I can't recall the name of the place where the *guignolettes* were grown, though I usually have a memory like an elephant or a Chinese tortoise.

For once I was able to show off my erudition, pointing out that it was because of my patron saint and master, Baron Münchhausen, that it was customary to serve game with cherries. Out of natural goodness and gratitude to St. Hubert, the Baron made a little cherry tree grow between the antlers of an Estonian stag, so that the flesh and the fruit should learn to go together.

But the boar wasn't quite up to scratch, and we didn't talk about it too much. We spoke of little Juliette, of their life, of Charles, and of me. After dinner I asked Madeleine to play, but she refused. She said she'd given up the viola long ago. I reacted a little too emphatically, saying she'd betrayed an unusual talent. After Seinecé had been to gaze at the sleeping children and she had spoken to me in the kitchen, and as he was offering me some crystallized violets from Toulouse, which I vehemently refused—the nasty little things look as if they'd fallen in the ink, smell horribly like lilac, and usually adorn revolting, fattening, dry-as-dust chocolate cakes—he suddenly mentioned Mademoiselle.

"Do you remember that old woman at Saint-Germain I used to live with, and who used to say "*Nom de Dieppe! Nom de Dieppe!*" when she lost her temper?"

"Mademoiselle Aubier?"

"Are you sure that was the name?"

"Yes."

"When you went to her funeral . . ."

"No. I'm afraid I didn't go."

"And there I was, half-dead with fear that you'd be there."

But I no longer knew, or thought I knew, who I was talking to. Mademoiselle Aubier had never said "*Nom de Dieppe!*" I tried to forget what he'd just said; for some reason it infuriated me.

"She had an old Merovingian first name. What was it, now? Fredegonde? Adelaide?"

"Clothilde."

"Was that it?"

Meine handed me a cup of coffee. I was in for a sleepless night, but then I hadn't expected anything else. I would go back to my little Neolithic pied-à-terre, take a long bath, shave, dress, work, and dream as if it were dawn. Already I was listening less carefully to what Seinecé said. He was lying. We were all lying. I looked at the magnificent salon, a Grien wood engraving and the huge red fireplace in dubious taste.

"Do you remember when Mademoiselle Aubier-Rosier sang . . ."

"Mademoiselle Aubier," I said very clearly. I was irritated.

". . . when she sang 'Colin Do Not Wonder That I'm Fond of the Arbor'? How did it go? 'Zon, zonzon, Lisette, my Lisette . . .' "

But Mademoiselle Aubier had never sung "Colin" to my knowledge. It all seemed quite unreal. And I wasn't sure Seinecé's efforts weren't making things worse rather than better.

We were talking quietly. Madeleine sat facing me, smoking, already half asleep. Everything was wreathed in a kind of fog. I thought of the light as it once was, the light of the past. I saw again in my mind's eye the Palm Sunday in 1963 when I saw Mademoiselle for the first time—the extraordinary, almost liquid light of spring, the glint on the little gold pruning shears she was holding, the glossy leaves of the boxwood she was taking into the house, the sound of her voice under the big cloche hat of Manila straw. And not only the sound of her voice in the air, but also the clinking of the charms, watches, lockets, and keys that emerged from her blouse at skirt level and hung against her stomach. A kind of nameless rage was being wound up like a spring inside me. The light in someone's eyes exists neither in their eyes nor in the world. I don't know where it comes from. And more than the blade of the shears or a green boxwood leaf or a watch, there was that flood of strange light. Light like the dew on the tip of a pine needle in Württemberg, like the sun on the sea at Regnéville, or the sudden gleam on the parted lips of a woman you desire, or on her breast revealed for the first time. All these, flashing throughout the universe, emanate from a single radiance, dark and more distant than time. More distant than the fragmentation of a star, which like a wounded animal, like Dido when she was hurt, like a little meow, only sheds its light when it has exploded forever and been transformed into time, into light-years, after it has lapsed back into the void and ceased to exist anywhere in the cosmos.

It seemed terrible to me that we should be exchanging recollections without really having any memories in common. We were the very opposite of the heroes of the English novels that Cäci doted on in her youth, in which people telling ghost stories around the fire conjured up authors not only dead but practically buried under heaps of learned notes and comments.

I wanted to get up and leave Seinecé and his wife. It seemed to me then, and it seems to me still, that what is most important to us are things that don't really concern us. They gravitate around an axis to which we accord, when you come to think of it, no more than a superstitious belief. If something that interests us becomes associated with ourselves we reject it at once. Or else we're so completely transformed into what interests us that we're quite unable to grasp it. And it was of this neglect of our own passions and secrets, this sinuous and hypersensitive allergy to them, that our lives and our friendship were made up. Our friendship united only our desire for friendship, but that desire reached out for something other than friendship—and reached out so eagerly that it repelled friendship itself.

Seinecé tapped his pipe out in the ashtray. I woke with a start. Madeleine just managed to hide a big yawn with her hand.

How many whistles had my sisters made me, tapping away at lilac or willow twigs with a penknife, a transparent green plastic penknife with gold specks?

"And do you remember . . . ?" said Seinecé.

But instead of listening I went on with my reverie. Sometimes it's as if we spent our days digging up bits of our lives we didn't live to the full. The tapping of the penknife was like someone knocking impatiently at a door and waiting for a voice to answer from within. And so, endlessly, every memory awaits the echo that will reveal it to itself. Our lives are ruled by strange symmetries—like that of a fish's fins or of our own eyes and arms and ears. I held the green penknife in my hand. I could see the willows by the Jagst. And the little house on Quai de la Tournelle. And the blue cedar by the Loire. I have so loved the silence and the vast infinite light on the banks of rivers.

Every river says, "I'm the Ganges" or "I'm the Jordan," and you're moved and plunged into silence and wonder at the sight of it. The singing of the water; the old anglers wearing dark clothes to conceal themselves from their victims, and there partly to get away from their families, partly to get away from words, and partly to merge into nature like a tree trunk or a stone or a blade of grass. Certainly not in order to find themselves, as they often try to make out in order to excuse their passion. There isn't anything to find.

The bright colors of fishermen's floats shining in the light . . . The green handle of the penknife, like the wretched purplish blue of lilacs and Florent's pipe knocking against the crystal ashtray—all sounds or acts or circumstances that summon up a memory are like those little cork shapes bobbing in the water and not directly resembling their prey below. A sudden wave of anguish is a jolt that indicates a bite; that shows the past is about to attack.

Sometimes the fish are dreadful indeed. Tench dating from the reign of Louis XIII: the icy bedroom in the hotel in Le Vésinet overlooking the church of St. Pauline, where Ibelle and I met in the cold, but above all in the harsh, disturbing sound of the pigeons landing on or taking off from the zinc roof. Little minnows only two days old: the name Juliette, Argan lamps, Quinquet lamps. Carp: the nun at Marans with a red face like François I's under her wimple, talking metaphysics about vegetables; and dead mothers as silent and speechless as carp, yet suddenly vast and tall and shattering and making you as speechless as themselves. Other memories drown. Stretch out their arms. Shout. Sink. They'll all disappear, die. And of ourselves, nothing will remain afloat and survive.

Someone was singing.

"Do you remember that?" Seinecé was asking. "Mademoiselle used to sing all Laurent Durand's old songs: 'Do not stroke my hand or I'll swoon away!' "

He sang very deliberately, and when he got to the song addressed to the deaf unfeeling rocks I couldn't bear it any longer—I was dying to go home. But he sang well, showing more knowledge of music than he used to have, as if he'd been taking lessons specially to please me.

Laurent Durand's songs were marvelous, he said. But they were neglected marvels. You only needed to read them to see. I stood up. Madeleine glimpsed a ray of hope. But Florent made me sit down again and gave me another brandy. He told me about a book he was writing, about virgins who suckled babies in the fourteenth century.

"Did you ever write that book about the terra-cotta Gorgons' heads they found in a fire station near Beaune or Cahors or somewhere?"

"It wasn't a fire station, it was a barracks. Of course I finished it. It came out in 1970. Haven't you got a copy?"

"No."

I realized I'd never even tried to get to know Seinecé properly—never ferreted about in libraries or bought the catalogues he'd written or the periodicals in which his articles on art and archeology appeared. He had most of my recordings, and my biography of Schütz delicately graced the coffee table. I'd never been drawn by the announcements in the papers about the exhibits he'd organized: they'd only made me dig up memories that threw me back on myself and served as pretexts for griping. He suddenly stood up and handed me a frightful volume that looked as if it had been photocopied.

"My latest," he said.

I thanked him profusely, as they say, blushing with gratitude. The book in question was called *Carolingian Cruciferous Keys.*

"What are you working on at the moment?" I asked.

"Mostly on the masters of the red figure in ancient Greek ceramics—the ascetic style."

Madeleine yawned so widely it brought tears to her eyes. I got up.

"I must go," I said. "Madeleine's asleep on her feet. I've stayed too late already."

Seinecé saw me through the long hall to the door. He opened it, and we went on chatting for a while. He pointed to a big yellow doormat with a red or mauve border, and said, "Do you remember how Mademoiselle used to say, no doubt to bolster us up, that at least our feet were among those worthy of the doormat!"

Mademoiselle Aubier would never have made such an idiotic remark. Everything, including Laurent Durand's old songs, was invented. Either that, or I had invented my own memories of Saint-Germain-en-Laye, Bormes, Caen, Coutances, the world, my life. It was frightening. I thanked him warmly, hastily said goodbye, and left.

CHAPTER 6

The Road to Les Grandes Alpes

Cursed be the man that trusteth in man, and maketh flesh his arm . . .

JEREMIAH 17.5

We adapted our memories to one another. Or at least we tried. It seemed to me he knew me by heart. And I knew in advance everything he was going to say. Yet every time I was glad to hear it. And he seemed pleased that I was so unexciting and invariable.

I discovered a whole new world. His study on Rue Guynemer was almost the equal of the Hallwylska Museet in Stockholm. It was a huge room kept in immaculate order, with three big tables and plain hard chairs of solid wood, white walls, pink or pale wood display cases and lots of objets d'art—the opposite of my old study on Quai de la Tournelle, to me as dilapidated as Stonehenge and as sacred. It had no desk, not even a small table, just a few armchairs arranged in a circle amid tall piles of books, revolving bookcases, smaller piles of manuscripts, periodicals, and musical theses. The walls were lined with books and little red wooden boxes containing hundreds of small sheaves of paper of various sizes. But really it's my own sun worship that makes me think of Stonehenge: the circle of chairs and piles of books that I've unconsciously reconstructed here in Bergheim, in the old music room, is more like the toothless jaw of a giant fossil, the remains of an unidentified species of brontosaurus. The piles are bits of molar. In a jaw shaped like three quarters of a circle.

I envied Seinecé's study. My own at that time, in the studio on Rue de Varenne, was small, rickety, overcrowded, and untidy, and looked rather like the great temple at Angkor Wat (though it didn't contain a royal lingam as far as I know), with its piles of records, books, and scores overgrown by brambles in the form of ties and sweaters, creepers in the form of music stands and bows, broken tree trunks alias bass viols left lying on the floor, and the great limp corpses of their canvas or plastic covers.

The latter, those huge half-human, half-inhuman garments, are like the hides of huge flayed beasts. And it may be that the impulse that made me transform the music room here on the second floor at Bergheim into a study—the place where I'm writing this—belongs to a similar secret nakedness, a similar ancient energy, covered up and protected. It was in the music room—where no one ever ventured except when we children had to go there for lessons in musical theory and singing, for musical dictation tests, and to practice Hanon and Czerny—it was there, between the shiny dark wooden music stand of so-called Van Dyck brown and the grand piano, in the frail shelter of some sort of papyrus plant (I'll never know its real name) that for the first time I saw in the palm of my hand the traces of desire: bitter drops produced in fear, with the awkward suddenness typical of my age, which gradually turned white and gave off a smell. And which were accompanied by a tiny little sob like the origin of music, a poor little groan like that of a mouse that you step on by accident as you go to fetch coals of anthracite from the cellar, and whose bloody remains, when you see them afterward, make your heart pound with a kind of hysterical disgust.

I regarded myself as abnormal, happy, sinful, and ill—gradually falling to pieces, my hair dropping out like water from the hem of a sheet hung out to dry, my arms and legs suddenly falling like tulip petals on a table, lifting up my hand like Götz, and my head like St. Martin. I was very worried. I could see myself rushing out to buy guayaco wood, like Albrecht Dürer with syphilis.

I developed a passion for little Charles, aged three. He had a charming fat baby face still, with cheeks like those of a hamster storing up sunflower seeds for the winter. He was often called Chalacot. Little Juliette wasn't toddling yet, but she babbled away volubly in her own particular jargon. They were growing old. I watched them. Tiny Juliette was probably the most beautiful woman I ever knew. Even compared with the most famous women ever celebrated by man. Excluding, of course, Dido. Young Charles took years to lose his baby cheeks. Even though he grew up and went from chalk to ink, from slate to exercise book, from ruled lines to blank pages, he still kept those squirrel cheeks. I used to sit little Juliette on my lap and blow into her hair and suck her ears.

"God keep you," I used to whisper, adding silently: "For my sake and for the happiness of the whole world."

I also discovered a surprising thing about Meine. She liked needlework, even though it was an occupation belonging to another age. And as she sewed she used to whistle military marches through her teeth: "Sambre-et-Meuse," "Going through Lorraine," and of course "La Madelon." Also "The Star-Spangled Banner" and "The Dragoons of Louvois." I realized later that she usually chose requiems when she was cheerful and marches when in a somber mood.

Florent tried, as he said, to patch things up with Delphine, but Delphine wouldn't go along and refused to see me. But Ibelle, rich now, living on Avenue La Bourdonnais and occasionally doing a bit of acting, wanted to see me again, and Seinecé, worried about her almost exclusive passion for drink, urged me to see her. I hung back.

I didn't see Delphine again until May 1979, when she married Luc in Saint-Martin-en-Caux. Isabelle looked down on her future son-in-law and wouldn't come: she was traveling in Yugoslavia and on the west coast of the Peloponnese. I declined to sleep in the house at Saint-Martin. Madame La Georgette was dead. So I spent one night in Dieppe, and then stayed a few miles from Saint-Martin itself in an old Gothic style English villa. I had a little bunk in the upstairs salon or drawing room, where the bow window looked as if it was actually sticking out into the sea. The weather was autumnal, with low gray clouds and yellow waves.

Delphine was still reserved, brusque, and unkind. She went out of her way to explain that she'd only invited me because her husband thought I might impress some of his friends. She did deign to introduce me to Pontius Pilate's grandson, Pontius Peter, son of Pilotis and sister of Pali-Poileau. I think it was at Saint-Martin-en-Caux that I saw her give presents to Charles and Juliette, her young half-brother and -sister—an ebony penholder and a thick pink glass inkwell for Charles, and for the sublime Juliette a mother-of-pearl pendant in the shape of an egg to put sweets in. These things had all once belonged to Mademoiselle Aubier. Then she turned to me. She called me "Monsieur," which felt very unpleasant and painful. She said she had something for me too; she'd had it for years. But she had forgotten to bring it.

During the summer of 1977 I went to stay with Seinecé in a country place Madeleine had in Brittany, near Préfailles on the bay of Bourgneuf. It was a sort of low-built, luxurious farmhouse. The general effect was strangely Japanese. In front of the house, instead of grass, there was a big yard like a primary school playground. It was planted with rushes and alders and bamboo and surrounded by thick gray walls that reminded me irresistibly of the garden at Regnéville. In the eastern corner was a heap of old white sand for the children to play in. The house was built of red shale, with a slate roof that turned quite blue in the rain. The rear garden was smaller, grassy and unwalled, opening onto a rock-strewn field. Higher up, beyond a few more slate and galvanized iron roofs and the smoke rising over them—it was August, but cold—stretched a large pond, almost a small lake. It was gray, in places nearly yellow, and its still, silent surface usually showed the reflections of the blue pines planted at regular intervals around it, exchanging a steady scrutiny with, almost looking daggers at, their originals.

It wasn't exactly the enchanted forest of legend, but rather a quintessence, a mysterious elixir. The almost Japanese farm; the calm and totally silent reflection of the pines (would I have been surprised if they'd started to speak or play the drum?); a flight of tern with blood-red beaks and feet on their way back to Africa. That part of France is so cold and strange. It was the end of summer. A gentle rain was falling. Seinecé got the better of the rain by driving for miles in search of *craquelins*, crunchy biscuits from Coutances and Saint-Malo that I'd told him about, as well as the prouder megaliths that may stand in the same relation to time as a whole as *craquelins* do to my memory. He didn't find any.

One morning Madeleine took us (Karl and Charles—Juliette was fast asleep, occasionally making lengthy speeches) for a walk by the sea. She pointed out a black and green cormorant standing on a rock, spreading its wings and flapping them feebly to dry its feathers. It was the first time I'd ever seen a cormorant, though Charles seemed quite used to it. She also showed us a flock of immaculate gannet in the distance, diving and falling like bombs. Meine said they caught the fish on their flight up out of the sea. I don't know if this account is correct—diving first and only catching hold of the little herring on the upward sweep—but if so, every memory is a herring. Pure time is a *craquelin* that can't be found. And as I remember those summers, those days, I am and have always been a gannet.

I didn't stay. I was cold. I left after four days. The beach made me feel unhappy and empty. The last day was hot, but I was still impatient to go. The people who'd rented houses and apartments by the sea for the vacation were emerging from the winter and the rain and descending in swarms upon the beach. Sea air numbs people. Summer by the sea fills me with delight for a couple of days, with confusion after four days, and with profound stupidity after a week. What does it consist of? Eating, sleeping, excreting and urinating, playing, keeping your hands and legs occupied, lying in the sun, washing, swimming, getting dry, everlastingly concentrating on the body of the spider monkey that is yourself, or on those of the little marmosets that are your neighbors. Delousing one another. Screwing your eyes up against the light, smelling things to the *n*th degree (everything by the sea smells sickeningly and obsessively of childhood, and there it smelled of Coutances—damp socks, rotten shrimp, old jellyfish, and human filth). Trying to breathe so as to escape from the regressive smell, forever pointlessly dreaming, being afraid it will rain, wrapping up against the cold, sheltering from the wind. And, to a very minor degree, talking, dressing, loving, reading, standing, and thinking.

Others were dazed animals in whom I saw myself so clearly I couldn't feel sorry for them. So I fled. I went back to Bergheim and busied myself with practical things. I had the furniture removed, and acted as gadfly—and alas, as supernumerary—to the various workmen. And one day, on the hill, I was afraid. I wasn't feeling as happy as I'd expected. I wanted to preserve everything, pile it all up. I accumulated friends like so much dust. I did the house over as best I could with odds and ends. I ransacked all the attics and derived a certain amount of pleasure from creating this haven or souvenir dump, this ark or funeral boat floating up a little eternal Nile that belonged to us all: the rooms full of old chairs, ancient divans and rickety tables, the walls covered with watercolors and engravings and academic paintings. Unfortunately the Cozens and Girtin engravings were gone; Elisabeth had insisted on having them. But in the attics I found trunks full of eighteenth- and nineteenth-century engravings that my mother had collected along with the Nymphenbourg Empire vases and Meissen china that she'd taken with her after her divorce in February 1949. I extracted the oldest, anonymous, mostly biblical etchings, with magniloquent titles in German: *David Sees Uriah the Hittite's Wife Bathing, The King of Babylon Addressing the Prophet Jeremiah, Isaiah Loosing the Sackcloth from His Loins in Obedience to the Lord's Commandment.*

I also had a Victorian drawing room suite brought down: it was made of bright red mahogany and rosewood, and I'd never seen it before. But a vague feeling of malaise still persisted. As soon as the caretaker's house had been renovated Frau Geschich moved in, and I was able to leave her in charge of the property and the work that still had to be done. I went off on various pilgrimages. I went to Offenburg, the Ullenburg, and Reuchen, where Grimmelshausen wrote all his books, and where he was mayor—a French mayor appointed by the Fürstenbergs of Strasbourg. I went as often as I could to the Liederhalle in Stuttgart. I visited the castle of Solitude twice—it was only ten minutes away from the studio in Stuttgart. The real castle of Solitude is only a second away from my heart. I wanted to go back to Biberach, but suddenly I couldn't. I left Frau Geschich to look after the house. I wanted to see Nadejda Lev again. I called her up in Stockholm.

I'm popular in Sweden, and I decided I'd take advantage of a studio recording I was doing for Swedish television to spend ten days with Nadejda on Lake Mälar or the Baltic. On the pretext that I was taking a phosphorus cure, I spent the crowns I earned in royal fashion, if you'll forgive the pun, eating fish at Ulriksdals Wardhus. Nadejda left after a couple of days. We'd become indifferent to one another: affectionate but silent, less sensual, more demanding.

My life changed. I spent half my time on tour. I saw Chicago for the first time, and Toronto, Lake Ontario, Ottawa, Seattle, and Vancouver. I made my first trip to Australia and played in Sydney and Canberra. The viola da gamba seems to fascinate the Japanese. I went to Tokyo four times, and to Kyoto and Kobe. I myself was fascinated by their grace and their fear. Listening to them listening to me, I began to learn the rudiments of music.

The terms I insisted on were strict and forbidding, reflecting a mixture of obsessiveness, greed, and vanity. I probably asked high fees to ensure that I was listened to attentively. I wouldn't stay in hotels to rehearse before a concert: I had to have two rooms at my disposal on the spot in some private house—not an apartment. I allowed no recordings or broadcasts to be made except my own, and they had to be made in the studio under acoustical conditions minutely and even pathologically prescribed.

One evening in May 1978, coming out of the music school, I passed Jeanne on Rue de Verneuil. She was an old friend with whom I'd made some recordings eight years before, and she was just coming back from giving a violin lesson. I hadn't seen her for several years. We kissed hello. She'd aged marvelously. She was wearing a long woolen coat and carrying a roll of music. She looked like a Cranach or, with her sorrowful face and convulsive look, like Van der Weyden's Mary Magdalen—that narrow waist, those large, tightly bound breasts, those tragic blue eyes. But she had black hair.

I asked her how she was and if she was happy. She lived on Rue du Marché-Saint-Honoré. She seemed in a hurry. I was on my way to see Costeker, so we were both going in the same direction and strode along together, crossing the river and walking through the Tuileries Gardens. The sky was dark and cloudy, but river and garden and sky and evening all were beautiful, and I began to walk more slowly, apologizing because I knew she was in a hurry and then going faster again so as not to make her late. She said she was indeed in a hurry, though no one was waiting for her. I must have looked surprised—she'd been married when I knew her before, with a little boy called François.

"Isn't your son . . . ?"

"It's a lovely evening, isn't it?" she answered quickly. "Even if it is cloudy."

She shivered.

"Have you been back to Germany?" she asked.

"Württemberg isn't Germany," I muttered.

And I was struck by how much I sounded like my father, even down to my intonation.

We arrived at her place.

"Here we are," she said, putting her hand on my arm.

I told her how glad I was to see her again, and it was true.

"Would you like to come up?" she asked.

I was surprised and stammered that I thought she was in a hurry and didn't want to take up any more of her time.

"It's just that I'm hungry," she laughed. "I haven't had anything to eat since this morning."

"Oh, Jeanne!" I cried. "I adore anything in the shape of food!"

I bought us some Napoleons at the Saint-Honoré market.

We ate some leftover sweetbreads and carrot purée. My sisters have always joked about my peculiar, almost freakish memory for what I've eaten. I can give a date to the most distant childhood feast and say what sort of a day it was and what the menu consisted of. Cäci said scornfully that mine was the memory of a stomach. But I don't think she was right: it was the memory of eyes, jaws, nose, and ears. And so we sat on stools in the kitchen and ate sweetbreads, Napoleons, and éclairs. She gave herself to me with a violence and boldness that dazzled me. She told me about her husband's sudden departure to California, and how he had ranted over the telephone demanding a divorce within days, agreeing to any conditions so that he could marry a healthy young heiress. And how her son had come and sat on her bed and told her he wanted to go and live with his father. I told her about my sister Cäcilia who lived in Glendale in the suburbs of Los Angeles; she might be able to see him. Cäci had a daughter of eleven or twelve, the same age as François—perhaps she could get him to write.

Jeanne lay on her stomach, moved closer, propped her chin in her hands and put her lips near mine.

"Now that you know my body and my life and this place," she said, waving her arm to include the little living room, the imitation fire in the fireplace, and the bedrooms beyond, "and that I've more or less chucked the violin, and how alone I am, and with how few prospects, haven't you had rather enough?"

"I don't like questions like that," I said. "In fact I hate them. Premature anxieties always look a bit like wishes."

"Don't keep twisting what people say to you," she said, snuggling up to me. "Be quite frank, Karl. I'm like children—I want to understand, I like to know where I am."

"You don't want to understand—you want to believe."

"I suppose so."

"Well, you know the answer perfectly well, and unfortunately I know it as well as you do. Sometimes things last and sometimes they don't. It'll last as long as we both believe it lasts."

"That's no answer."

"You've taken my measure so fast that you think I must have taken yours. We've both been booby-trapped so often we're permanently gun-shy."

The phone rang, and she went to answer it. It was dusk by now. Dark. I looked around the room: a dozen or so violin cases propped against the wall, the grand piano she used for teaching, the walls covered with postcards and pictures of musicians in narrow colored frames, the hideous white glass gilt-legged coffee table with a shiny black metal teapot on it. And I realized the pattern governing my life. We are forever going over the same old paths, driven by the same wild desire and implacable destiny that makes the salmon try all seas and rivers and choose at last the fresh water where they were born, where they will with a sudden jolt reproduce themselves and die. And as I pushed the cold teapot aside I felt a desire for heavy, bitter beer arise in me, beer bitterer than the blackest, coldest tea, and covered with shiny, coppery flecks. I'm always drawn to bitterness.

Jeanne came back and stood in front of me.

"Might as well speak out, Karl. What about living together?"

I spent the night at her place, and we lived together as far as it was possible.

Jeanne merely turned her head and looked at me. I got up and went over to her. She stretched her face toward me. I put my lips on hers and shivered. She drew me to her, and I felt the warmth of her breasts and the beating of her heart. You only love once. And that one time you're unaware of it because it's happening for the first time. That one time is when you're a very young child and not capable of much. And if that one time is unhappy, then so will all the other times be unhappy. But there's still pleasure. That makes up for it a bit.

Despite her age—the same as mine—Jeanne's body was wiry, thin, and sensual; avid and tortured, and with long breasts. In 1972 I gave a concert in Dorchester Abbey—to an audience of about two dozen people—that contains the famous Holcombe effigy of a knight who died in the Third Crusade, showing him trying to unsheathe his sword. Hers was the same body, tense with desire.

For many weeks I lived in a state of felicity, sweetness, excitement, acceptance, and luminosity that I'd never experienced before for so long. I came to have a great affection for that old apartment on Rue du Marché-Saint-Honoré, and for that part of Paris as a whole. Even the ridiculous imitation fire in the living room, with its sham mica coals, didn't displease me: it shed a pink glow on her body. Cranach, Van der Weyden—I didn't mean their names to suggest faces, but rather a color. Age might have left its mark on her skin and slightly withered her neck and breasts, but it had cleared and enhanced her light pink glow, as of very fine transparent porcelain. But my imagination may always have endowed bodies with a sensuality they don't really possess, a violence and boldness that nevertheless remain puritanical. That thin body, walking toward me in the living room, its ribs showing, seemed to say, "This pinkness is my lingerie!" And I'd think of the pink salon in the house at Saint-Germain-en-Laye and feel a kind of unease.

* * *

One evening Jeanne insisted on taking me to a Rimbaud evening at the church of Saint-Louis-en-l'Ile, where one of her friends—a violinist called Amiens—was supplying the background music and playing between the readings. And yet he didn't seem to be hard up. People are so mysterious. I've seen them use Vermeer to advertise a brand of Camembert. Jeanne loved Rimbaud. The church was incredibly cold. It was the end of September. They hadn't thought to turn the heating on. In a wan light we took our seats—uncomfortable narrow straw-bottomed chairs—beside the minister of culture. Amiens was playing a Bach sarabande in the distance. A female shape was moving about on a kind of platform that creaked out of time with the music. I suppressed the beginnings of helpless giggles. The shape—wrapped in the gown of a don of Oxford University—rose up with slow and tragical gestures. Silence fell. A ray of light was trained on the lady reciter and gradually intensified. Her voice was raucous and emphatic; it sounded scratched. I felt ill. A kind of sweat broke out on my stomach and forehead, although the church was cold enough to freeze ducks in a pond. Yet in the faintness creeping over me I could feel something very close to me, something I'd lost, something far away and yet very "warm," as children say when they're playing hide-and-seek. Then suddenly the voice became more natural and more plaintive, and the fashionable actress dressed as an Oxford don bit her upper lip: it was Isabelle.

She had a red nose. It was incredible. Her voice kept breaking. Her face had gotten fatter, but she was still as tall and straight and haughty as ever. I grabbed Jeanne's arm and whispered, my mouth dry:

"I don't feel well. I don't feel well at all!"

The light had gone out. Amiens was playing the violin again.

"I think I'm going to faint," I said, trying to stand up and struggle out of the row. But I fell to the floor.

Someone was slapping my face. I opened my eyes: it was Jeanne. Isabelle was bending over me.

"Isabelle!"

I wanted to get up.

"It's the gamba player!" someone told the minister, who looked suitably sympathetic. Ibelle blinked, smiled at me, and fled. I found out afterward that as I fell I'd taken with me a whole row of chairs joined together by a wooden bar and disconnected the sound system. There'd been a short circuit, and as they couldn't go on with their performances, Amiens and Isabelle had hurried over to see what was happening.

We didn't see one another again right away: I was leaving for a concert tour lasting a couple of months. When I got back in January 1979, it was through Amiens that we met. We arranged to meet very early one morning in the Café Dragon.

As soon as I went in I was nauseated by the smell of grilled Gruyère. Then in the distance, facing the door, I saw a fawn English raincoat waving its arms about. It was a man's Burberry, an old one, with the sleeves turned up. My heart practically stopped. It was very strange. She was forty or fifty yards away, and I scarcely recognized her. But that was neither here nor there: what shattered me was an inexpressible sense of familiarity, of a look that was closer to me than anything else in the world. And the attraction, the intimacy, the body or rather the face drawing me toward it, were so strong and compelling I couldn't go over to her until I'd overcome a wild desire to run away as fast as my legs would carry me.

She was sitting on the leather bench, her hands around a glass of whiskey. I sat down on a chair opposite, and looked at her. She was pale. We didn't say anything. It was only when we became aware again of the noise in the café that we spoke. What she'd been doing and how she was, what I'd been doing and how I was.

She grew paler and paler. She'd had three whiskies.

"Can't we get out of here?" she asked suddenly.

We stood up, and she walked out quickly as I paid for the coffee, the three whiskies, and the piece of pineapple tart I'd ordered—I don't know how I'd had the presence of mind to notice the home-made pineapple tart on the counter as I came in—but hadn't touched.

"You've aged terribly!" she said when I joined her on Boulevard Saint-Germain. "Gray hairs, wrinkles, receding hairline—the lot!"

She seemed pleased by this. It was a warm, autumnlike January.

The sun was shining faintly. I suggested we go and sit in the dreary little square on the corner of Rue de l'Abbaye.

"I didn't think I'd ever see you again," she said, "and that didn't make me happy!"

I took her arm and we crossed the street. We sat down on a bench in the square.

"I'm too hot," she said. "I'm going to faint."

It must have been about fifty degrees out.

"Come with me," I said, and took her into the church of Saint-Germain. I'd already proved to myself that the tomb of the Merovingian kings made my blood pressure fall by two or three degrees.

It was cold inside the church. I'd forgotten she only came up to my chest. She leaned her head back, stretched out her hand, and stroked my hair.

"You're old, Karl," she said again. I didn't find it particularly tactful.

But I was very moved. There was a smell of dust, and a divine, sickly odor of incense. And there was desire in her gestures. Her fingers and eyes still desired me, or rather I still desired them, changed and altered though they were.

"You're old too," I whispered in her ear, laughing. "Sort of ravaged."

And I pressed her to me.

"Bastard," she said.

"Slut," I replied.

We laughed. And laughed again. We embraced for a while in the dark. I couldn't have denied my desire even if I'd wanted to.

"Come," she said.

And we went to her place. She was divorced from Jean and owned a beautiful apartment on Avenue La Bourdonnais. Her third divorce had left her with a veritable fortune, in exchange for which she'd had to let Jean have custody of their two children. She was unhappy about this. She'd had five children altogether, and yet she lived alone. And Seinecé had been right: she drank heavily. She'd already had three or four glasses of whiskey and it was only nine in the morning. Her breath reeked of alcohol. But she was still beautiful, still as rigid and upright as ever, only a little fatter. Her eyes had kept all their old violence.

"I can't bear being dependent on a man's ups-and-downs-and-outs," she said in a slurred voice. "Men always have such comical ends in view."

I agreed, and was ready to admit that women always had admirable ends in view—so long as you didn't ask me what they were.

We made love nicely, though to tell the honest truth I couldn't get rid of a kind of unease, which may have been due to the time of day, to the smell of whiskey, or to memory. From time to time Isabelle too seemed to feel the latter's almost imperceptible censure. We'd never been able to make love. We'd always been stuck facing one another like adolescents made clumsy by desire, fear, and ignorance. And while age lends a kind of depth, gravity, and patina to wood, stones, monuments, paintings, and gambas, adding to mere conservation a fascinating and constantly increasing beauty and value, the trace it leaves on human bodies is hideous, the very opposite of conservation. No one can be attracted by the slow, broad, profuse progress of decay, and everything conspires to remind us of its irreversibility and fatal outcome. Desire finds it harder to address a face that is being gnawed at, hollowed out by nothingness to a yearning distress. What you are holding in your arms is something that is being swallowed up in its own death. Caresses are still possible, but not really desire. The immodesty and knowledge conferred by age and habit sometimes make it possible to make up for the lack of desire, but you can't always take yourself to task and make yourself see death as an attraction.

But still there were her eyes—the incredible childlike obstinacy and fierceness of her eyes. Those huge eyes, not grown smaller yet, if not grown larger, framed in tiny, living, moving, jaunty wrinkles that made them seem larger. Heavy eyelids. Fuller, downy cheeks. Husky voice, perhaps made huskier by drink. A cat in the throat, the French call it: Ibelle's cat was an alley cat, a witch's cat.

Her eyes shone in the dark. We didn't make love; we exchanged caresses. My lips were on her hair. She drummed on my back with her fists.

"Dear old Karl! My dear old Karl! My dear old Karl from the old days!"

It seemed to me she could have been more merciful.

I felt like a child back in the school infirmary in Bergheim, undergoing the regular check-up. She thought I was taller; but it was just that I didn't stoop. My hair had gone gray, I'd put on weight, and I did my best to draw myself up to my full six feet. I'd have liked to be nice and wise and paternal—the father of one of her children, seeing she'd had five of them. There was still something juvenile about her. I don't know how to put it; I don't want to be disagreeable. Perhaps it was in her posture: the way she sat down, kicking off her shoes and tucking one leg under her; the way she never stopped smoking.

I spoke about Mademoiselle Aubier's death. She hadn't known before that none of us had gone to the funeral for fear one of the others might be there. Isabelle had never seen Denis again. Only Seinecé and Delphine had done so; Delphine still saw him. It was he who had given her Pontius, and she would never forget him. Only three people had been there to follow Mademoiselle Aubier's coffin, as if she hadn't meant anything to any of those who knew her. Just Denis Aubier, with an elderly female cousin and Louise Valasse. Ibelle told me she'd been in love with André Valasse and had been his lover before being mine. Dido's beauty didn't wane in my memory, but my memory itself suddenly seemed to recede about a hundred miles into the distance.

Ibelle told me she'd always had an "insatiable curiosity."

She put on her dress again.

"I'm always trying to attract people. I keep on and on. My curiosity's never satisfied because I never find anything new—I'm forever ploughing through sauerkraut."

I could taste the disagreeable tartness of sauerkraut again. Was I any different from Ibelle? When you came right down to it, our lives were as alike as two peas. I felt my stomach shrivel.

And was it surprising, she went on, if she never found anything new in bodies of either sex? They've been the same since time immemorial—absurd, hairy and smooth in exactly the same way.

"And yet every so often, Karl," she said, "I feel sure that behind such and such a look, beneath such and such a piece of material, something new is waiting for me."

I got dressed myself. We had a drink. She recalled the little cottage at Bormes, Saint-Martin-en-Caux, the cliff, the Durdent, the creek, Madame La Georgette. And Madame La Georgette's death—falling down between two rows of seats at the cinema in Saint-Martin's village hall. Her best memory of me, Ibelle said, was in the country near Prenois early in spring. I've never been to Prenois, or to Dijon. It was late one afternoon by the little stream, the damp and ancient washing place on a tiny tributary of the Ouche. We'd made love standing up, in the cold. Not undressing any more than we had to. I picked her a bunch of daffodils and gave them to her then and there in the cold, and suddenly both my face and the bunch of flowers shone in the sun.

"Is it really my face that you see?" I asked.

She was slightly tipsy, and took it as an insult. She started to raise her voice. But I wasn't even hurt by the fact that her best memory of me wasn't of me at all. I felt as if I'd always known it. She went on. We'd walked by the stream and across the fields. Suddenly there was a shot, and a turtledove fell slowly down onto the ploughed furrows beside her. She picked it up, her fingers sticking to its damp feathers. She could feel the warmth of its blood. She could still hear the sound of children's voices that she heard then in the distance. A drop of blood fell on her skirt, and in order to scrub it off she had to hand the bunch of daffodils back to me.

"How strange memories are!" I thought. "It's not merely that they don't square with one another—they're completely insubstantial. We don't live together. We don't live through the same things as one another, or in the same time, or in the same world."

I didn't try to see Ibelle again. And I kept away from Jeanne for a while, though I didn't feel like going back to Bergheim. I dreaded the place, the winter, and the work that was going on there.

I often experience sudden summonses to solitude, like the calls of a gentle and loving mother—though that simile is perhaps like talking about a black sun or a river without any water. But one of the delightful things about a life with a certain amount of society and love in it is the way it produces these sudden panic desires to be alone. The longing to find yourself again, to be by yourself, to be able to do things without any witnesses to see. To let your features relax. To take your face off.

But really it's just the wish to have a bath, to eat a snack when you feel like it, to cut your nails. To wash your heart in silence. Wash off your weariness. People who withdrew from the world and lived alone in the desert off nuts and the leaves of thistles used to be called hermits. But I call a bath a hermitage. Or the empty head of a man alone at last, gloating silently over his idleness as he soaps himself and indulges in the tiny pleasures of an elderly baby.

During the first few months I thought about marrying Jeanne. Inclination satisfied without anguish, lust fulfilled without hindrance—these are sweeter than the sweetest honey, even if spread on a thistle leaf. But the mouth grew too accustomed.

Costeker urged me to get married.

"Take pity on yourself!" he said. "Take pity on yourself!"

It was like some incurable malady. Perhaps we're never cured of the idea of happiness, or of love. But everything in me took fright and rebelled at the thought of letting myself in for such dependence. It was as if I had to preserve some imaginary but permanent region of renunciation encircling me.

I enjoyed having love affairs in the course of trips and concerts. What is it that arouses us? The sight of blood? Fear? Filth? Happiness? Mystery? That which is different from ourselves? A body? The void that separates us from it? I think I'd go for the latter.

"Saccus ster-cor-is!" as the Bible said—or rather as Hans Nortenwall used to rap it out. The old book with gilded pages and torn leather binding—"Biblia Sacra" in letters of gold—from which I was supposed to learn the rudiments of Latin. I could still see the pastor's face. We long to embrace a sack of excrement. That is our whole treasure.

Strange how you forget most of the details of love. You remember so little of all the thousands of times, and the things you do remember survive by chance and are not particularly remarkable. So why doesn't pleasure leave behind more traces? A few words, though rarely; occasionally an attitude; more often an unflattering detail; a color. Not so much as a vestige of exaltation. Pleasure and satisfaction are mute, stupid, sated. Success, communication, sweetness, trust are perhaps the soonest forgotten. And since one forgets voices and eyes, almost nothing remains of Jeanne—the woman I loved the longest: her foot, distorted by time and shoes, and the unskillfulness of her mouth.

And that's why I am writing this book. Like a child, I've always liked looking at statues in museums—statues of satyrs, of Priapus, of gods seized with desire. They and their unimaginably enormous penises are usually hidden away in a corner. Seinecé told me of similar statues found in the country, crude and exaggerated and usually clumsily carved in wood by some wretched peasant or gardener hoping thus to increase his fertility. (And perhaps the rustic artist is no clumsier than the god, the surely rather tipsy god, who fashioned our own private parts.) Tucked away in vineyard or kitchen garden, they receive few offerings: perhaps a handful of tough old figs, some bits of fishing net, worn-out vaginas, the odd lobster shell. Or even lesser offerings, such as the verses of poets.

Strange god of fig tree and ass, of anus and rural transmogrification of the male sex organ. An organ suddenly bare, quivering in the air, and slave to a desire with nothing in the whole of space to assuage itself in. And perhaps nothing in the whole of time to appease it and make it more moderate again; more modest, more harmonious, and more childlike.

Love based on shared pleasure doesn't long survive it—which is a blessing. But the memory of it, though unable to return in its original strength and emotion, may sometimes survive in a calmer form, one containing an element of respect and humanity never generated by love itself. And its heart beats with a feeling few kinds of human behavior end up in—a feeling of gratitude. Perhaps pleasure is possible only for people old enough for their own sins to have softened them into indulgence or even tenderness toward the sins, weaknesses, and absurdities of others. Perhaps experience produces a compassion that forgives others because deep down it forgives itself.

"Ka!" Jeanne used to say.

A certain way of pronouncing our name—the little symbolic signal, which those who bring us into being cast over that being even before we exist separately from them—can open our bodies like a sudden key. It's an Open Sesame that can make its way into the forty thieves' cave, set Ali Baba free, and imprison Kassim until he dies or the wealthy robbers return. A certain way of rebaptizing us in a murmur, as if by magic, will suddenly undo us in the darkness, in our nakedness, in the battle for pleasure, in the blind yet watchful quest, silent, panting, caressing, grim, that tenses all the muscles to hold back orgasm, and then collapses into abandonment to oneself and nothingness.

I used to contemplate the beauty of this woman of forty, closer to Cranach or Quentin Metsys than to the Olympic athletes. It was a form of beauty that didn't leave room for much bitterness against the time that had diminished it—or rather the bitterness was mixed with gratitude for the fact that age or time had surrounded it with ease and skill and elegance. The pink porcelain was merely more translucent. Her lips parted.

Jeanne liked the yellow wing chair in the living room. She would take off her shoes and sit with one leg tucked up under her. She would settle, sigh, and sink back. Her career as a violinist had been intermittent and sporadic. She was disorganized, nervous, and indefatigable.

When I think of the years I spent with Jeanne, it seems to me that the feeling imparted not so much by love as by desire is the only one that is really worthwhile, fleeting as it is, disappointing and forgetful as it seems. Pleasure is a star very far away in space, but though in comparison with the whole of the sky it is minute, it gives off a dazzling light that governs the whole of life.

I saw Seinecé, Juliette, Meine, and Charles whenever I was in Paris. The day I introduced them to Jeanne, Florent and Meine were kneeling beside an armchair bursting at the seams when we arrived at Rue Guynemer. Florent, armed with a needle, said he was trying to stitch up the wounds, while Meine held the material in place, briskly whistling the "In Paradisum" that ends Fauré's "Requiem." I'd brought some marzipan candies called *calissons d'Aix*. Jeanne, under orders, had brought some buns called "canonesses of Remiremont." *Calissons d'Aix* are one of the candies I like best, because they're almost pastries and because they're light in the hand, soft to the teeth, subtle to the taste, and shaped like mandorlas, the almond-shaped auras in which Christ appears in representations of the Last Judgment. Also because in them the tragic apple, the female apple, the apple of Eden, gradually gives way to the almond; because they've retained some of the smell of green cypresses and Mont Sainte-Victoire; because their whiteness reminds me more of the color of human skin than milk, canine teeth, or innocence; because they're a kind of diabolical host, like little bits of consecrated bread enclosed in the unleavened bread of the host, like a gangster's face covered with a woman's silk stocking.

Another evening, a particularly lethargic one—the Seinecés now ate nothing but fish, with wonderful names like coley with herbs, paupiettes of sole, fricassée of dogfish, shad cooked with sorrel: all a mere excuse to drink the Alsatian or Swabian white wines I had delivered every two or three months as if trying vainly to wipe out the reckoning on an old slate—Seinecé sang a little nonsense song:

> Pimme Pomme golden apple on a spool,
> Pimme Pomme throw the apple out.

For the umpteenth time, while Charles listened open-eyed and Juliette slept on Meine's lap, he told the story of how old Mother Afchain gave "*bêtises*" (a kind of aniseed humbug with little yellow or, better still, green stripes) their name. Boring drivel on the part of Seinecé, but I still find it moving to set it down. Emile Afchain, an apprentice confectioner in Cambrai, rushed into his grandmother's drawing room and asked her to taste the result of a new recipe he'd spoiled—air bubbles had gotten into the mixture—but which he didn't think was too bad. Grandma Afchain tasted, shrugged, and said, "My dear Emile, these are sheer *bêtises*!"—that is, foolishness. We used to have the most idiotic conversations, even more foolish than the ones we had when we were twenty.

"Do you remember when Mademoiselle Aubier sang 'You're Crumpling My Furbelows'?"

"No—Mademoiselle Aubier never sang 'You're Crumpling My Furbelows.' "

Even our quarrels had become rituals. Not that our disagreements were entirely formal—my irritation, at least, was genuine—but basically our arguments were really agreements. But Seinecé's emotion wasn't feigned, either.

"Yes, she did!" he would cry, his voice cracking a little. "I remember it very well. You'd gone away with Isabelle. All my friends thought I was done for."

His voice became more vehement and harsh. " 'Upon my vesture they cast lots.' I was in the room downstairs. Denis was there. Mademoiselle was trying to cheer me up. Then, because of Delphine—thank heaven for children!—I threw myself into my work. I couldn't bear the sight of Mademoiselle, and the memories, the west side of the river, the western suburbs, the traces still plainly visible in Boulogne and Neuilly! That was when I did the thesis on the Gorgons' heads in Cahors!"

He wasn't crying, but there was a sob in his voice.

"So I was at a loss. I wrote, I wanted to die. And she sent for me. 'Monsieur Seinecé,' she said, 'we must lighten the atmosphere. So I'm going to sing you 'You're Crumpling My Furbelows!' "

And he rushed out of the room.

1981. April or May. Jeanne was in Belgium for a week: three concerts in five days, one in Ghent and two in Bruges. She'd sworn to bring me back a Flemish *koek* from Dinant, a biscuit in the shape of a heart. My Neolithic apartment was in such a mess it got me down. Jeanne's was even worse, for the same reason. Not that Jeanne liked disorder. She arranged everything carefully in heaps: heaps of scores on the refrigerator, heaps of washing waiting to be ironed on the television set, heaps of magazines on the 1920s armchair, heaps of travel brochures—especially on winter sports—piled up on the piano, heaps of newspaper clippings neatly arranged on the make-up table in the bathroom, heaps of dirty linen in the hall, heaps of beauty products. Lucas Cranach forbade the use of the latter six hundred years ago, but looking at Jeanne's skin I gradually came to think less about him than about the beautiful coloring of candied fruit—something like that of Dresden china—in particular figs, cherries, and, the height of delicacy, bergamot pears. (I don't actually speak their names—I see them in my mind's eye.) Every fruit used to be glazed with a brush, and they were even lovelier to look at than to taste. I don't think there have ever been any greater painters since Cranach, Bosch, Baldung Grien, and Van der Weyden than the confectioners of Apt, with their sugar brushes. Jeanne used to stow away little pots of beauty cream and make-up in a violin case left open on the divan—the instrument itself was laid beside its black carapace. She'd accumulated a heap of multi-colored panty hose on the table that held the telephone and the answering machine. A heap of scarves and shawls, perched on top of an ancient roughly rectangular cello case, looked like an eight- or ninefold wig.

I used to put off going home, either to Rue du Marché-Saint-Honoré or Rue de Varenne. Like every man coming back from work, I seized on any friend, any job, any errand, as an excuse. My shoulders slumped as I went through the door of the apartment; my heart shrank and curled up in my chest, exaggerated as that image may seem. In whichever of the two apartments I had to enter, everything now seemed to say loudly, "I, Jeanne, exist!" And although of course I was polite enough to be grateful, at the same time I felt like going down on all fours and peering under the bed or the sofa like someone looking for something that's been mislaid, and saying, "But where am *I*?"

It's true that whenever a woman had been living with me for any length of time I did my best to lose her. Yet as soon as I'd lost her my whole body cried out for a woman's body again. And the desire that suddenly overcame me then for the missing bodies would transform the whole universe—the mud, the trees, the riverbank, automobiles, fields, sky (or at least airplanes). This applied even to that week in spring when she was away. Just as the rising sun mists over and colors everything, so what I felt, without always realizing why, bathed everything in a sense of concealment, dissatisfaction, a feeling of wanting to undress and embrace. I think that when we attract someone else, our appeal isn't anything peculiar to ourselves of which we may be proud, but the beauty and radiance of something eager within us that makes our eyes shine and in which another avidity recognizes itself. Just as when your mouth waters it enhances the food you're about to put in it.

One of those May evenings when I got home at six o'clock,

wearied by what amounted to a siege lasting more than three years, I sat down on a pile of magazines, disentangled the phone from the heap of panty hose with their bright, warm, cheerful colors, and called up Yvaine and asked her to have dinner with me. She was a young harpsichordist just beginning to enjoy a well-deserved success. I'd met her at Egbert Heminghos's place on Rue d'Aguesseau. She was beautiful, though she had a speech defect and a love of social life that were sometimes exasperating. Her stammer had something affected about it that tended to lessen one's sympathy.

"I'd love to," she said, "but I'm just going out. I have to go to Hervé-Marie's wedding in Enghien. It'll be quite w-wild! But it'll only take me a couple of hours. What about meeting at nine-thirty here on Avenue de Breteuil?"

"You're marvelous!"

I hung up and moved the heap of scarves off the cello case to uncover the eighteenth-century engraving of Wieland that used to hang in the hall in Quai de la Tournelle; I'd always kept it with me since Bergheim, even when I was away at boarding school. Just as I was folding the scarves up carefully and putting them piously away in a cupboard obviously meant to hold groceries, violin scores, and electric light bulbs, the phone rang. It was Yvaine calling back.

"It will be so boring at Enghien—couldn't you come with me?"

I grumbled but agreed, and she came to pick me up in a magnificent purple front-wheel drive. We got rather lost in Saint-Gratien but found our destination thanks to a mass of cars parked chaotically all over the place. It was a splendid villa on the shore of the lake. Two gray-and-white striped tents had been put up on the far side of the grounds and near the road, so that guests would have a view of the lake in the distance. We made for the buffet. It wasn't very warm out of doors, but inside the tents it was stifling. A strange smell of warm grass—thick grass that had been trampled on and crushed, almost fermented—reminded me at first of a gym in Heilbronn, then suddenly summoned up a painful memory of a campsite in the forest at Saint-Germain-en-Laye, where Seinecé and I got drunk to keep out the cold and lay under our blankets with our naked legs and stomachs wrapped in newspaper.

Yvaine greeted her friends, who talked to her about a Froberger recording she had just made and asked me conventional questions.

I felt old and tried to get away on my own. Something about the smell of mown grass, the cold, and the memory of drinking too much fifteen years ago put me off drinking anything now. Yvaine pressed me to try the lobster soup.

"Karl! Hervé-Marie!" she shrieked. "The soup's t-terrific!"

She hurt my feelings by praising Soloure, a young viol player she'd worked with. I was wounded because she hadn't asked me, though I'd have refused if she had: I didn't play in public anymore, at least not in concert. I wasn't even sure if Yvaine had ever heard me play. I hated Soloure, an ingratiating performer of ancient music who used his bow like a ladle and his instrument like a soup tureen. And he kept fidgeting about. In short, I rather admired him.

I walked over to the lake and dipped my hand in the water, the cold water, among the swarms of midges hoping for a storm. I could almost see the water spiders with their feet scarcely touching the water, like Christ on the Sea of Galilee, and the mossy rocks, the old rowing boats, the river Neckar.

Yvaine appeared beside me.

"Let's go, Karl. Were you dreaming?"

"Of course."

"And sulking?"

"Of course."

"These shoes are killing me. Let's leave, pronto!"

We drove back through the Ile Saint-Denis, less depressing than usual in the softening light of the setting sun. Yvaine asked how she'd upset me. I told her about the viol, my pride, and my jealousy of Soloure.

"But I'd never have dared to ask *you*!"

"Easily said. Don't try to kid me."

"I've just bought a little upright h-harpsichord from Verona—the sound's rather weak but interesting and pure. Let's drop in at my place and I'll show it to you—I can change into some other shoes at the same time. You're in for a t-treat!"

We stopped off on Avenue de Breteuil. She had a two-room apartment on the ground floor, with four square yards of garden. She played some Couperin on her sour little harpsichord. I helped myself to a drink.

Dusk fell, invading the garden and darkening the room. She

went on playing; I switched on the lamp. She crouched over the keyboard, her thin face and frizzy fair hair suddenly lit up inside a golden halo.

I went over and laid my hand on her shoulder. Her hands halted on the keys. Then suddenly, without saying anything, she turned and put her arms around me.

We made love on the floor, between the harpsichords. Then we went out to dinner. I returned to Rue de Varenne alone. Nothing human lasts forever. Poets have repeated this lament ever since they started to write their verses down, and though the admission isn't eternal either, it's the most interesting one human beings have ever made. Man's skin isn't eternal, neither is his work, his home, his flesh, or his bones. A memory or a name is no more eternal than a smell or the sound of a voice. Perhaps teeth are an exception. The last remains of the devouring passion—consuming, vital, mortal, lethal—which also devours us. Kills us.

I tried to read but couldn't, so I went out onto Boulevard des Invalides. But I needed to sit down, so I propped myself against a windowsill. And all at once I identified my pain—the poignant pain of being in love again. The yearning to see a certain body again, to see it at once and give oneself to it; the eager, morbid desire to depend on another; the hungry longing to be in another's presence, to submit to her and have her submit to you.

The realization that I was in love took me completely aback. I stood up despondently.

"I'm going to be under someone else's thumb yet again!"

I was happy, and yet I was in great distress. I couldn't feel my legs; my heart was thumping spasmodically. I sat down again. I hailed shapes and faces in the distance and within me. I was overcome.

I wanted to see Yvaine again. I had to see her again; we had to sleep together. It was two in the morning. I went back to Avenue de Breteuil, but when I got to the door I couldn't even talk to her because I didn't know the secret of the interphone code. Of what code *do* I know the secret? I looked through the railings at the dark garden.

* * *

Yvaine's stammer was at the same time slight and absolute. Whether it was an affliction or an attempt at distinction I was never bold or treacherous enough to ask. Anyhow, she'd managed to make it seem deliberate, almost affected. "A very important p-period of my life," she'd say, using the slight defect as a kind of aural italics, allowing her to emphasize words in a way that gave the impression of modesty rather than pretentiousness.

"This album," she would say, showing me her most recent recording, "has been a b-big h-hit!"

As a crumb of earth in the mouth of a worm knows, or a worm wriggling in the mouth of a fish, or a fish being crunched in the mouth of a cat, or a cat seized alive in the maw of a snake—it isn't easy to escape. Jeanne and I came to terms. We agreed on a wise and dignified parting. The agreement lasted a couple of hours.

The tears you cause someone else to shed are extremely irritating. They make you furious with yourself—or with the person whose weeping reminds you what sort of a person you are. They provoke further cruelty. Jeanne left Rue de Varenne in tears—and empty-handed.

Two more hours went by. I called Rue du Marché-Saint-Honoré, in vain. At last she rang me. I went round right away. She was sitting in front of the mirror, bare to the waist, wringing out her hair, which she'd just washed. Her breasts were long and drooping. She was still wet and shook herself. She'd just gotten out of the bath. There were still flecks of foam in her black hair, which she was drying and trying to put up in a bun. I desired her. But we didn't make love. All of a sudden I was shocked by her unself-conscious habit of going about naked. It struck me that it might be her lack of modesty that had gradually made me get bored with looking at her.

My love for Yvaine and hers for me was of unparalleled fervor and unique brevity. It was complicated and uncertain and lasted seven weeks. It ended when Yvaine made a speech about the importance and appeal of what she called "c-culture." It isn't always possible to suppress a yawn. I was exhausted, and yawned without realizing what I was doing. The result was a sudden, stammering split.

Seinecé had met Yvaine, I remember—I'd invited him specially. He now offered somewhat foolish comfort. A woman who was friendly with the minister of culture, who religiously insisted on a "little g-glass of v-vino" before dinner and who served tea with "sugar t-tongs," couldn't be really sound.

Jeanne wouldn't see me. Seinecé was a great help. I spent hours shouting and bawling and complaining to Madame de Craupoids. I quit my job at the music school and arranged to go teach viola da gamba for a semester in San Francisco. I didn't see much of Cäci there, though; I'd thought Glendale would be much closer. I was rather bored in San Francisco. I came back at the end of January 1982 with three recordings. I let Florent hear them first, because for the first time he'd shown me the proofs of a catalogue he'd written for an exhibit of Roman wax paintings he was organizing at the Louvre. I was surprised by the spareness and the tragic erudition of his introduction and comments. And he talked to me about one of the preliminary tapes I'd brought back from San Francisco, on which five of us played a selection of very moving seventeenth-century English pieces for the viol. He seemed quite shattered. But the great thing was that for the first time we told each other what we felt. We admitted it. It was the last few days of January. We didn't meet so often now—perhaps once a month. I don't know if we were less fond of one another. But we admired one another. And it seems to me this little feeling of trust generates more warmth than the most demonstrative of passions.

During the night of February 8 to 9, 1982, I had a phone call from Madeleine in Grenoble saying Seinecé had been taken to the hospital the previous morning. They were probably going to transfer him to Paris. There wasn't much hope: the effects of the cold, added to those of the accident. . . . Five hours had elapsed before the car was found on the old road to Les Grandes Alpes, near the Telegraphe pass, before Saint-Michel-de-Maurienne. It was the February school vacation. Charles was six and already an enthusiastic skier. Juliette still wavered between sledding and skiing. Seinecé had driven all three of them to Valloire, where Madeleine had a chalet, on Friday evening. He'd left Valloire on Sunday evening at about eleven, and his car hadn't been found until the next morning, by a bus that ran to and from the station at Saint-Jean-de-Maurienne. Seinecé was still in a coma. They'd be in Paris by ten o'clock, and Meine asked me to look after things for a day, until her mother could come to Valloire to take care of the children.

I hung up the phone. Everything was so silent. I thought of one of the thousand and one stories in the *Arabian Nights*. Like its hero I thought, or rather felt the words being said inside me: "The silent music begins to sound on the guitar."

I saw him on Tuesday, February 9. A gray porcelain statue. Claudio Monteverdi in gray porcelain, bound hand and foot and kept alive with tubes and pipes and wires. I dealt with the various papers amid a smell of ether and disinfectant. I made telephone calls. Madeleine was there by Wednesday morning. I called up Jeanne and talked to her about Seinecé and me. She refused to see me again. Asked for more time. It might be a time for pity, she said, but it wasn't a time for love. I admired these admirable words. I was alone. There was nothing for me to do. I was seized by a sudden fever, a sudden void, by an anguish I simply couldn't express. Even Madeleine was jealous of her own sorrow. All my telephoning got on her nerves. I could feel it. I took a plane right away to Stuttgart. My mother was dying. Louise was dying. Dido was dying. Seinecé was dying.

It was cold when I got back to Bergheim. We always yearn for one stable. Time doesn't pass. We are old decrepit fish who can't leap up the cascades and waterfalls and get back to the source, the little drop of water where our mothers spawned. We keep going through the same pains, the same illusions. Our bodies are always being revisited by the same sensuality, the same hunger. And the same appeasement: death. I didn't dare call Meine, so I called the hospital. I wandered around the grounds. I ate. I wandered around Heilbronn, Gundelsheim, Bad Rappenau. Wanting, eating, slaying, drinking—the needs keep returning, plunging us back among the same faces, under the same sun, amid the same air and sounds and tears and colors. We keep on endlessly falling, diving like frogs back into the waters of the Tiber, the Eure, the Neckar.

At last I was able to cry. As a child I used to count the seconds between the lightning and the thunder, to see how long it would be before the terrible storm would come and annihilate us all. Sounds, music always arrive later than that which is carried by light. As a child I was certain the terrible storm would come, and one day I was likely to be right. I used to be filled with a mixture of impatience and fear, but there was also an element of pure excitement. And now again I count the seconds between each lightning flash and the deep and terrifying clap of thunder, to measure the approach of death. But I'm not impatient anymore.

Next day my sisters and I wandered among the ruins, among the ravaged flowers, the petals dashed into the earth, the puddles reflecting the sky with its clouds and its fixed or wandering stars; among the twigs, the broken nests, the broken branches, and the wrinkled paths.

CHAPTER 7

Bergheim

Though I speak, my grief is not assuaged: and though I forbear, what am I eased?

JOB 16.6

Whatever grass I chew, whatever memory I revive, everything tastes of silence and death. The sight of Seinecé's body, incredibly kept alive in a hospital room that looked like something in a science-fiction film; the uncertainty about whether he would live or die; the way he looked like a mere image of himself; even the feeble pun that would keep occurring to me, based on the fact that "coma" is a musical as well as a medical term—it's used of very small and delicate intervals, especially in untempered baroque music—all these things made us almost want to be relieved of hope, almost want death to come as quickly as possible, so that we might be left at last to the sadness of death and the black sorrow of mourning someone we loved. Tubes didn't connect us with him so much as with the fact that he was leaving us.

During the weekend of February 13, 1982, I had to go to a festival of ancient music in Rome. But the cold and the loneliness in Bergheim were too much: I didn't have the heart to go back there. By noon on the 15th I was back at Rue de Varenne. I called Meine, though I was afraid, with reason, that I might be bothering her. I called in at Rue de Poitiers. Madame de Craupoids once more lamented my leaving. I stood up. I wasn't listening. I walked away from the Tronchin table and over to the windows looking out on the neighboring gardens and courtyards. The small hoary gardens looked like tombs under the low sky. The trees were bare, the earth colorless, the concrete starred with frost. Every so often a ray of sunshine seemed to transform everything, to wash the whole world in light, to give it back a kind of purity, to lend even the ravages of time and the distance of things a sort of immanent, cruel, and eternal gaiety. No sooner had such rays appeared than they faded and vanished; while the light and hope that had filled the world and gilded Madame de Craupoids's profile as she sat at her desk and babbled on to me or to herself faded much more slowly than they had come. But eventually all had gone.

As I looked out over the gardens I remembered the time when one of my pupils—she was rather like Madeleine when she was twelve or thirteen and I was teaching her the rudiments of the cello—had hysterics because she said she couldn't control the fingers of her left hand. She sniveled and howled and sobbed, saying she knew what she was supposed to do but couldn't make her fingers obey. Absurdly enough, her age or the faint desire I felt for her prevented me from going over and calming her down as she yelled and stamped her feet on the diamond-shaped tiles of yellow marble. The memory made me think of myself, or Meine, or Ibelle, or Yvaine, or Jeanne, or anyone face-to-face with fear or desire or death—which we should like to make obey us. How we long to master and control it.

In one of the frosty courtyards I could see a youth in a yellow sheepskin jacket mending an old moped, hammering away with a transistor radio beside him. I couldn't hear if it was switched on or not. This scene was the only sign that the world was still alive and violent. Within myself I could find no trace of life, nor even of rebellion. It was in this room, on a similar winter's day, that I'd been reunited with Florent Seinecé. I debated with myself, wondering if I'd have the nerve to call Meine up tomorrow evening.

It was she who called me, late on the afternoon of Thursday, February 18, 1982.

"Karl, they've brought the body home here. Would you like to come?"

Night was beginning to fall when I arrived. I remember the stairs as being quite dark, like a human throat. I probably hadn't thought to switch on the lights. The maid opened the door, told me Madeleine was in Juliette's room, and took me there. It was getting dark. If you looked outside you could scarcely make out the leafless branches of the chestnut trees in the Luxembourg Gardens.

She was sitting on a little armchair near the window, sewing rapidly and drawing out the thread as far as it would go. Without realizing it she was quietly whistling "Sambre-et-Meuse," and I think she mixed in the song of the Foreign Legion too—an equally brisk march but possibly with more complex and interesting words. Her face was calm. From the window a few vague gleams of light fell on her skin, a few petals of light on her blue dress.

Perhaps the maid had shown me in too quietly. Madeleine had turned toward the window and was trying, head bent forward, to rethread the needle, when suddenly she started. She looked at me. Stiffened.

"We're all going away," she said.

"Why should I be going away?" I asked in astonishment.

"I mean Charles and Juliette and me," she said. "He's dead."

I didn't understand why she spoke so curtly. I expected her to say something more. To tell the truth, I don't know what I expected. But at the sound of her voice and the words she uttered, something vast seemed to come apart—as if someone inside me were trying to climb the stairs of the larynx or the trachea but had missed a step and was falling silently into an infinite void. I just stood there. I didn't move. She looked up; her lips quivered.

"Do you want to see him?" she said.

I went to see him. I'll never be able to express what I felt. Afterward I rushed to the bathroom and washed my face. Then went quickly back to Madeleine. She was still sitting there, nervously humming her uncouth military marches and sewing. I heard her introduce a new phrase in which Sambre was mixed up with sorrow. I went over to her and she stood up.

"Are the children at your mother's?" I asked.

She nodded.

"Come along, Madeleine, let's go out to dinner."

"I'm not hungry."

"I'll go down to the Italian shop, then, and come back and make you some pasta. . . ."

She went over to the door and spoke louder and more coldly.

"Please go, Karl."

When I went to see him—but it's hard for me to put into words what I felt when I entered the room, when I saw the bed, and his body on it, and the ugly, sinister little orange Gallé lamp on the bedside table.

When you visit some feudal castle on the Rhine and stand there in the cold and the dark looking up at the sky through a loophole, the little patch of blue seems unreal, like a piece of china. His face was no longer gray exactly; there was something maternal about it, something that had been in his mother's face in Marans nearly twenty years before, when a strange nun philosophized about the glorious life that went on inside the humblest vegetables and the smallest flowers in another Eden. His skin was very pale yellow, like the flesh of lemons.

They say death takes away from men's faces the grave and tragic look they try to wear when they're alive—when they're trying to be taken seriously. They also say there's a moment, after a man has satisfied his physical desire with a woman, when his face wears an incomprehensible look of serenity, though he will never remember it because he's never conscious of it at the time. A face like that of a child or an infant. But that's all rubbish. Seinecé's face was tragic. I'll never be able to describe what I felt when I looked at it—the features full of pain, the open mouth, the tightly screwed up eyes. His body had contorted as it stiffened; his limbs looked huge. He was lying on the big bed in their room. I'd never been in there before. It looked out onto Rue Guynemer. My thoughts went back to when I'd stayed with them in their house in Brittany, in the bay of Bourgneuf. Or to ten years ago, when I'd stayed with Margarete and her son in the Bernese Alps. I seemed to see a little Swiss lake, a little lake at Thoune or Brienz, its gray and yellow surface unruffled by any breeze, with a tiny fisherman and his boat as if pinned onto it. Yet nothing in that image had anything to do with the huge body, the too large suit, and the dreadful open mouth—except the distance, the infinite distance, what I'd have liked to be the infinite distance that separated him from me. In other words, the fear, my fear, that set him far apart. And yet I felt, when I touched him—and I touched his hand, just as he had touched his mother's in that second-floor room in Marans long ago—how only a finite, a terribly and extremely finite distance separates us from the dead. And the other world isn't other at all,

On the bedside table, by the little Gallé lamp, stood a pink mother-of-pearl candy box. I imagined it full of little *Quinquins* and *cassissines* and Magnificat caramels. His insignia. Like the sword they used to put in the hand of effigies of the Crusaders.

When Baron Münchhausen arrives in Ceylon he finds himself suddenly surrounded by a lion, a crocodile, a river, and an abyss. Everyone has a scene or a person inside him that belongs to the other side of time, where there's no such thing as place, no future, no yesterday, and no today. And that which is no longer governed by time, that which no longer belongs to place, is suddenly before our very eyes. The lake at Thoune and the lake at Brienz were really huge and invisible. Death is not the same after us as it was before us, even though it often seems as if each of us can remember it. We are only what we are—and not quite all of us, and not even all the time. We don't see things against a background either of a before-life or of an after-death. There was something unbearable about the body lying there, in the very appearance of its frozen sorrow and its bent-up knees—but there was also something ridiculous.

Time itself is only a little high-water mark, a little edge bordering on the absence of time. I felt that something inside us called for a background against which to die, some past on which to get a foothold, a pool in which to break surface and in which to sink again at once and forever. To rise, streaming, and then drown. So many things in us claim to be profound, yet really all they do is vaguely float as best they can.

We don't know where we come from. We don't know where we're going. We don't know who we are. What is the place we're in? the day? the world? the age?

I touched his hand. I looked at the pink candy box. I remembered life in those imaginary countries where snow was white and cold to the touch. In those countries, strange as it might seem, the place where you were existed even after you ceased to be there. Feathers were light. Stones fell. Trees grew up toward the stars.

And it was while I was on my knees, while I was holding his hand—no, I didn't dare hold his hand—that a nonsense rhyme came back to me that I must have learned as a child. It was French—I must have learned it from my mother—and it was just as silly and trivial as the marches Meine whistled to displace and wear out her grief. But it came to me like a visitation: it had existed before Seinecé did, before he existed for me, before we met in Saint-Germain-en-Laye—and perhaps it had called out then and hailed him:

Sancta Femina Godasse
Cacacaramaribo
Major towns Cayenne
And Pamaribo.

I didn't see Madeleine anymore. She got married again last year to a minister of something or other to do with the environment—by which people seem to mean trees, flowers, fish, animals, and clouds. But man is the real environment. The environment, the rubbish dump, the suburbs. It's everything that isn't man that is the center of the world.

The day of Seinecé's funeral—I was in San Francisco again—I plucked up the courage to phone her, and the day passed like any other. I never held little Juliette in my arms again. I didn't teach Charles any more birds' names.

Seinecé's death crept up on me slowly—like a mouse, slower than a wagtail. A year later, one day in the spring of 1983, I was visiting some friends in Normandy, north of Deauville, and as we were going down through the orchard toward the sea—the weather was somber, dark green, and lugubrious—I saw a bird fly past.

"A wagtail!" I cried. "A wagtail!"

I was overjoyed. It was Bergheim calling to me. It was migration, transmigration. The soul of one of the dead had come to speak to me in the guise of a little wagtail. I didn't even feel I had to go home straight away. I'd seen the wagtail. I'd seen the black rough sea. I'd learned something.

"My father died twenty-six years ago," I thought. "It's been twenty-one years since my mother passed away—she died one winter day in the Necker Hospital, just a vowel away from Neckar! It's been six years since Luise died. The family property belongs to me, and I never go there!"

I realized I had to leave the meager, overcrowded, untidy apartment in Rue de Varenne. But I wasn't going to "go back" to Bergheim—I was already there. I felt there was nothing left to keep me in Paris.

"Seinecé's dead, and Paris with him," I thought. "Mademoiselle will soon have been dead for twenty years, and Saint-Germain went with her, just as the ugly but charming house on Quai de la Tournelle departed with Dido. All that's left to me is this name from my childhood. France is nothing but the memory of my mother's dreams. Oudon, with its cedar and its silent transformation, was sold seven years ago. The valleys of the Loire, the Seine, the Durdent, the Soulle, the Havre, and the Bulsart—all things of the past. My hopes of overcoming what I really am, of fighting against the sounds of my childhood, were in vain!"

My friends were surprised that despite the small reputation I'd acquired I went on teaching, even if it was in an American university near San Francisco. I was asked to do some private teaching for much more money, but this irked me for some reason or another and I refused. But Bergheim was a big place to keep up. I could start a kind of summer school. I didn't have any children, and it would mean I wouldn't be all alone there with old Frau Geschich. I would brush up my own language—I can't bear to use the phrase "mother tongue." It fills me with dread. My mother never bent over my pillow. I've almost no idea what her voice sounded like. And yet I've written these pages in French—more or less. Her language. There's a cry inside me in that accent, and probably writing in French is a way of addressing that cry to her. But why do I use a language that failed so completely to catch the attention of the woman who spoke no other—that failed so completely to keep her with me? It was unfair of me to hate German, unreasonable of me to reject it. Instead of translating so many biographies all those years from German into French, I should have done what I did as a child in 1945 and gone from France to Germany.

* * *

Whenever I go back to Bergheim I feel as if I'm returning to the oldest place in the world. It was childhood; it was the prehistoric jaw of Heidelberg. It was a signpost made of redwood, the oldest woman in the world, the ravine at Neanderthal, the dolmens at Mecklenburg, the cave at Schuhrloch.

They say that clocks and watches sound at Candlemas. Thousands of years ago a Homeric hero believed the song of the sirens led to death. For me the sign is the blows of the hammer on the anvil, mingled with the fetid smell of liquid manure. But beyond that smell, the blows of iron on iron, the shriek of iron plunged in water, what I look for every time I go past the blacksmith's in the new square is the odor of burning, sizzling horn.

"Oh Mutti, Mutti!" I feel like crying, as through the clang of the hammer I try to catch that wonderful, exciting, living hiss.

Everything within me quivers. Beings call out through things. In silences, names creep noiselessly closer. Everything transfigures something else, just as every language transfigures every world, and it is as if an older world had thrown its net over everything—objects, people, the elements.

For more than a year I couldn't make up my mind whether or not to settle in Bergheim for good. I had the organ there electrified at my own expense. I started by spending a week there every month. One day I went down to the Jagst and knelt and drank a mouthful of river water, disregarding the muddiness of the bank. "Different from the water of the Seine!" I thought. I bent forward again and looked at my reflection in the water: I didn't find myself appealing. I drank another mouthful. "It's the Ganges!" I said to myself. I drank again. "It's the water that was in my mother's womb! Everything will finally flow into the Panthalassa!" And I hurried away to buy myself a bottle of Rhine wine.

That was how I celebrated my fortieth birthday. On my own. With a drink of ancestral, muddy water. My mind was full once more of Wieland-like dreams—dreams of placidity, gentleness, independence; of a private life, and of removing all traces of everything public, authoritarian, political, civic, religious, or connected with the family. I even went so far as to take the crocheted antimacassars off the chairs in the main salon. I hated them; they looked like bibs for old men. How many times did I make the pilgrimage to the house where Wieland was born, the presbytery at Oberholzheim? The garden there, where he worked morning and evening, getting up before daybreak, was shaded by enormous lime trees. I even felt like buying a fishing rod—that strange instrument, a cross between a baroque bow and a whip—to whisk a trout out of the water, one of the river trout that my father for some unknown reason called "farios."

When I stood up again after drinking from the yellowish waters of the Jagst, my eye lit on a cornflower. What a birthday present! I stood and looked at it. There wasn't any wind, and the cornflower, motionless in its backwater, somehow made me think of a crocodile's bulging eye, placid but watchful. It seemed terrible and incomparably strong. It had existed thousands of years before me, and would go on existing thousands of years after me. May 1983. I was forty. I could scarcely believe I was so old.

I looked at the cornflower respectfully, as a minnow gives way to a pike and yields it the privilege of the bait; as a fly circles patiently around a piece of bread on a path, subordinating its hunger to the haste of the pigeons and sparrows. Finally I wasn't altogether dissatisfied: a gamba player who hasn't been too idle may rate less than cornflowers, but inwardly I reckoned I ranked above gooseberries, or at least, as sure as the Tigris flows through Assur, above their rough and hairy leaves.

Marga was against my going to live in Bergheim permanently, though she didn't really explain why she was so angry at the thought of my being near her.

"You mean to say you want to go back and live in Württemberg, hundreds of miles from anywhere! Don't you remember what Father used to say?"

"I don't remember anything," I said. "Rather strange, that."

"He always said one ought to beware of tribes who've never had a classical period in their history—neither in antiquity, nor in the thirteenth or the seventeenth or the eighteenth century."

"He was just being a stick-in-the-mud! And even if it were true . . . Didn't he go back to Württemberg himself?"

Marga scowled at me. Screwing up her mouth made her look older.

"He lost Mother in the process," she said.

"But I've never had anything I haven't lost! And you yourself keep going back and forth between Pfulgreisheim and Stuttgart! And between Strasbourg and Baden!"

"But I don't live there. And I don't play the viola da gamba. In any case, I don't go to Bergheim. And what about Jeanne? Is it being a stick-in-the-mud to think about her?"

"You're getting upset over a word that's charming, not offensive."

"I'm not getting upset. Anyhow, I've had Walther to think of. And Markus. And I'm stupid. All women are stupid—they just repeat what their mothers did before them. So they're all stick-in-the-muds too. And men repeat what their fathers did, so they're always shouting the odds and gobbling like turkeycocks!"

"So everyone's stuck."

"Up to their eyes in the mud."

"And everyone chokes to death."

She'd been thumping on my arm as she spoke, and acting out what she said. I started to laugh. Soon we were both splitting our sides. We were children again, little Württemberger children speculating and holding forth about the universe.

Jesus walked on the water. I drank four drops of water from the Jagst and in a way I drowned. I was inclined to think, and perhaps took pleasure in thinking, that I must be a man of little faith. I sorted out the old wood engravings and had them framed in Heilbronn. Once again Jesus walked on the water. Zachariah had visions of lamps. Jonah sat under a castor-oil tree in Nineveh.

I was working, but usually in the afternoon I just sat in a chair, my head resting against the memory of a lace antimacassar, putting aside the half curtain with one finger and gazing out at the garden. Sometimes I thought: "In a dreary great cemetery just outside Paris there's someone who no longer breathes the same air as I do. He doesn't feel heat or cold any more. For him, light no longer illuminates the world. For him there isn't any more world, and for him I no longer exist." The obvious fact was coming home to me physically that we too die in the bodies of our dead friends. I can't breathe for two, or help him to experience sounds and colors. He's gone.

But once there had been someone in whose eyes I existed, who was good enough to put up with me, in whose eyes I was perhaps just about good enough to put up with.

I went on sorting the engravings I'd had framed on the big round coffee table in the salon at Bergheim. I'd planned on too large a scale; there were too many. I wasn't sure I still wanted to hang up Lot's wife looking back at the burning city of Sodom and slowly and irresistibly turning into a pillar of salt. I'd already turned into a pillar of salt myself. And I put aside Alexander the Great weeping over his horse Bucephalus. There was no comparison between Bucephalus and Dido. But—with the typical bad taste of burghers descended from ancient Schwabians, whose walls might be covered with as many as forty or fifty old daubs, together with ridiculous objects mounted on velvet, and nineteenth-century engravings such as illustrations for Jules Verne—I admired and hastened to hang up the prophet Jeremiah contemplating an almond branch in flower. Perhaps these activities of mine were an attempt to parallel the passion for old children's songs and rhymes that Seinecé had as a young man. I remembered one marvelous counting rhyme:

Brown bread,
White bread,
Silver candle,
You're dead.

For it to move me so, that beautiful and mysterious song must have had something in it that I couldn't put a name to. So I probed the brown and white dough, and with the aid of the silver candle lit up the dead body—dead, or reeling with pleasure and only seeming dead—which the anonymous childish rhyme confusedly anticipated. But probably what moved me wasn't so much the meaning of the rhyme as the mere fact that it came back to me—as if sent to me from beyond the grave by Florent Seinecé, who'd collected such things all his life. Then I remembered, and felt tears well up and run burning down my cheeks, our meeting in 1963. Perhaps "Regina Godeau," in the very first song I sang to him, had been a name for death, as was Harrige, Queen of Hell, in a song I sang him soon after. I saw him again, kneeling on the wooden floor of the barbershop and untying his shoes, the little black plastic-coated shoes issued to us by the army.

As I walked about the grounds at Bergheim I sang those old tunes to myself. I dawdled by the rushes and in the copses. I lifted up the dampest leaves under the trees. I looked for mushrooms. I inspected gnawed chestnuts, the work of a squirrel. And thinking about myself I was amazed that so many people had attached a scrap of value to me.

Those walks in the garden at Bergheim were varied. Sometimes I thought about myself, and how I more and more disliked the idea of playing in public. I thought about Jeanne, and remembering the engravings I'd had framed in Heilbronn, tried to imagine how she would have liked to see me. As Mordecai in his sackcloth, or naked and covered with ashes? Or crowned with the great diadem of Assyria and wearing an ephod of fine linen? And how would I like to see myself? I had rare moments of exaltation followed by periods that grew increasingly futile and tedious. As my plane approached Stuttgart I used to whisper "Bergheim! Bergheim!" and it seemed to me that even if the world were created all over again I would still love this place, this light, this smell, and these sounds. I'd brought practically everything there was in the Neolithic studio or in storage in Rue de Babylone. All I'd left behind in Rue de Varenne, apart from a practice viol, was the reproduction of a little Swabian landscape by Carl Gustav Carus that I'd always taken with me wherever I went. I've kept that reproduction. It's in the hall now, placed so that you can't see it when you open the door, and perhaps also so that it can protect my threshold as it used to protect my nights.

At other times I was overwhelmed with emptiness, distress, and incurable loneliness. Desire for a woman couldn't cure it—it only made it worse.

Then, as I walked about the grounds and past the rusty railings, it was Alexander the Great or Karl der Grosse wandering among the tangled, spindly rose trees, the fallen yellow leaves of the quinces, the crushed chrysanthemums, the warped, swollen, and broken chairs and tables, the scattered bits of wood, the stone pots, the old tools, the rakes, the old locks. I thought, "By the time you have plenty of bread you've lost all your teeth." I thought, "Karl der Grosse is a bachelor!" and I was sorry I hadn't had any sons or daughters to share the empire that for some reason or other I'd reclaimed. I turned out my pockets in vain: "Where are you, Louis the Meek?" My universe was as broken down, rickety, haunted, and crazy as the place, the benches, the tables, the tools.

And that's where I am now, where I'm growing old, where I'm writing. And I still regret I don't know anyone anymore who could come to Bergheim with me. Who could sit in one of these chairs. Whom I could talk to. Whom can I tell about these names, these lights, these games, and the joys connected with them? The people engulfed by time? I speak their names, but they no longer turn around when they're called. Death has dissolved those wraiths.

I feel sorry for myself. I wander. I felt sorry for myself. I wandered. I resented the fact that Frau Geschich and Radek, each of whom I'd given a little patch of kitchen garden, spent more time on them than on looking after the grounds or cleaning out the pond. I got cross with Heinrich for being too heavy-handed with the pruning or forgetting to remove the pots of dead fuchsias from in front of the house. And for having the music room repainted in too bright a yellow. I increasingly disliked appearing in public—even if it was only in a television studio. I grew more and more anxious. My heart hurt, and I sometimes had spasms. After the cornflowers I took to contemplating the dead fuchsias. "Look!" I told myself. "These pots represent winter. And winter, and age, are stealing up on *me*!" But I felt sorry for the broken flowers, violently sorry. Winter gave plants and flowers a kind of respite. But no age or death came to deliver them.

It was in September 1983, at Raoul Costeker's on Rue de Rivoli, that I saw Jeanne again. Raoul had been preparing the meeting for a long time. I remember Jeanne had her hair done in a large low bun. She was wearing a yellow silk skirt.

Raoul Costeker was chain-smoking. I opened the French window and went out on the narrow balcony that ran around the apartment.

The night was gray and misty. She came and stood near me, and we stayed there for a while looking out at the trees, the shapes of things, and the Tuileries, ugly now and dusty.

"What about living together again?" I asked timidly.

She was silent. I moved closer and took her hand. She held me close.

"I'd have liked that too," she said. "But no, Karl. You're too wrapped up in yourself and your gambas, and your Bergheim and your books, and your friends who make cellos and bows, and your dealers in autograph manuscripts, and your recording studios and your sound engineers. You're always traveling, you're only at home in the morning, and even then you're not available after three or four o'clock! Believe me, Karl, it cost me a lot. I can still feel the effects. And there's no question of my ever going to live in some freezing little German valley miles from anywhere. Let's just live separately. And when we see each other, let's make love. And when you're not there I can always pretend you miss me or desire me. It doesn't seem to me we'll see each other less if we see each other so little."

I admired her for being so lucid and speaking out so clearly, but it was extremely painful. Love—as soon as you can eat and move about on your own it's best to drop that sentiment. It's born of helplessness and hunger and the most extreme dependence. You hope for things that are infinite. When a man speaks to a woman he appeals beyond her face to a being who no longer exists. And the same when a woman speaks to a man. Men and women aren't made to understand one another. Only music is made to be understood. I'd been reduced to the clichés of farce. And a farce is what it is.

We saw each other. We made love. I abandoned Rue de Varenne and stayed with Jeanne when I went to Paris. She let me have a room in her apartment on Rue du Marché-Saint-Honoré. It's hard to share the love someone else feels for himself. Yet everyone is quite right to love himself a little; it's about the only love we get. Although every so often we do go off ourselves. I found there was some meaning in the universe, a small amount of meaning. Such as, that pleasure is the meaning of desire. I put together a few wise, serene rules.

* * *

I was tired. I was glum. I was at Bergheim. I was going home with a string bag full of shopping—Chinese cabbage and cartons of milk labeled in motherly fashion with the information that the contents should be drunk before February 1984. It was November 1983. I automatically put the canned mushrooms away in the cupboard and the cartons of milk in the refrigerator. I felt mortally depressed. All inclination to go on had collapsed. What was I going to do to occupy myself that evening? I went to wash my hands, and when I looked in the mirror I got a terrific surprise. Inside of a sad face I saw one that was eager and bright. A face like the face of a kangaroo or a hippopotamus. The lines of fatigue or disillusion around my mouth looked completely artificial. The smokescreen of lethargy and pleading in the eyes failed to conceal a permanent eagerness. I gradually started to laugh. I shaved. I ran a bath. Joy and happiness could still exist even if one did live in constant horror and despair. Mademoiselle Aubier would probably have said the absence of hope was very amusing. I called up Klaus-Maria, got out the car, and headed for Stuttgart.

I stopped by at a candy store in the Königstrasse, thinking of Seinecé, and bought some chocolates and caramels and all sorts of out-of-the-way confections. With every mouthful I tasted I said a mental "In memoriam," and I was quite serious. It was a genuine act of piety. As I hurried back to the car I thought, "Happy the friends whose only wreath when they die is a little Magnificat caramel and some chocolate kisses!"

I decided I'd had enough of myths. I bought a cat, a kitten. Her name was Nausicaa. I was quite moved. She wasn't as shy as Dido. But who could ever replace Dido? Cats are not interchangeable like human beings, who are completely interchangeable, at least when it comes to indifference and cruelty.

She used to frown. I'd forgotten how prudent and cynical a cat can be, and how it watches everything that's alive and sounds it with the tips of its whiskers: the wool of the carpet, the china its bowl is made of, the heat of its food. I'd forgotten the extreme caution, followed by the almost invisible swiftness, with which it starts to lap up milk. Then the little slurping noise completely shattered me. I had to go away and leave Nausicaa on her own.

"Dido!"

The cry rose up like some physical pressure within me. I went into the bathroom and stanched my tears one by one with a towel. And in a pretense of celebrating Nausicaa's arrival, and so as not to make too bad an impression on her, I fetched a bottle of Tokay from the cellar.

I gave her some water in a crystal bowl. We sealed our alliance half in fresh salmon and half in smoked. Half pale pink and half orange—it made me think of a Gallé lamp in a darkened room beside a paler candy box that probably contained caramels and Hopjes. We drank. We drank a lot. And we talked a lot that evening, very comfortably.

I'm subject to nightmares. When I woke up shouting and drenched with sweat I switched on the light and picked Nausicaa up. I looked into her eyes and told her all about my suffering and the horror I'd just glimpsed. She's the only one I've told about the secret of the universe. It's too sad to tell anyone else.

I had some excellent sliding cat doors installed at Bergheim.

Delphine was divorced in 1983. Strangely enough, I had a couple of postcards from her that summer, one from Crete and one from Yugoslavia. The same journey Isabelle once made. And after her father died, like him, she signed only her name on the postcards she sent. At the end of November or the beginning of December 1983 she phoned and said she had something for me that she ought to have given me a long time ago. She'd mentioned it years back, at Saint-Martin. She was embarrassed at having taken so long, and that made her anxious to see me as soon as possible.

I was mystified. I remembered that at the time of her wedding, ten years earlier, in Dieppe, she'd mentioned a present she was supposed to give me. What could it be that she was making such a mystery about? Just after the war my sisters and I had seen a fine, gloomy film at the cinema club in Heilbronn in which a lot of journalists tried to make out the meaning of an American newspaper magnate's last words. Only the audience was aware that they referred to a sled he used to ride on when he was a child. I was reminded of this now.

We invited her to dinner in Rue du Marché-Saint-Honoré. She was beautiful, though she looked more childish than before. Her hair was short. She must have just had it cut: she wasn't yet used to it not being in a bun, and her hands kept going to the nape of her neck as if to check on it. With her short skirt and cropped locks, her angular sad face looking larger and her body smaller, she was like an amputee still feeling pain in her phantom hair.

I introduced her to Nausicaa. Then from a fashionable designer tote bag she produced a large object rolled up in magnificent green wrapping paper. But what attracted me was not so much the thing she'd made such a mystery about as her own eyes. Immense, bright, blue, and gold, they were the eyes of Ibelle; waters eternally new and transparent yet impenetrable; small blue, black and gold continents on the huge ocean of the iris. They made me turn my own eyes away, take her in my arms, and bury my face in her shoulder. We hugged. Then we sat down again, and I undid the wrappings.

Finally, amazed and deeply moved, I extracted the statuette that used to stand on the red-veined marble mantelpiece at Saint-Germain-en-Laye and be reflected in the mirror above.

But what really shook me was actually to touch with my own hands a mistake I'd been making for twenty years. I'd always remembered the statuette as representing a naked, sensual nymph pursued by a satyr and turning to him with a sad but consenting smile. But it wasn't that at all: the statuette depicted Psyche, naked and full of admiration, remorse, wonder, and despair, holding an oil lamp and turning toward the infant Eros who is already deserting her. The maker of the statuette had gone to the trouble of carving on the base of the statuette the words "Psyche and Eros."

The same theme was the subject of a large Empire painting at Bergheim—it's in the music room where we used to play as children and where I'm writing now. And my mother, so beautiful, so silent, and not even looking at us, used to sit under it just long enough to hear us play the pieces inflicted on us by Fräulein Jutta.

I'd forgotten about Psyche and Eros. Just as the mistresses of the gods glimpsed their lovers' naked bodies only for an instant, so I had seen both the gods' and their mistresses' naked bodies only for an instant—and had misinterpreted what I'd seen. We long for a light, and it leads us astray. We are fools, flashes of light, who get everything wrong.

One day, said Delphine—it must have been fifteen years before—Seinecé had told her, "This is for Karl. We must give this statuette to Karl."

But she hadn't done anything about it. She'd kept it out of pure revenge, because of an old jealousy. She hated the thought of her father giving anything to the person she saw as the cause of her parents' separation. She admitted that every time she thought of me it was as the person who'd stolen her mother. So she had stolen the statuette that her father had wanted to give me as a token of forgiveness; she'd hidden it among her childish belongings, in a wicker basket where she kept her dolls' paraphernalia—miniature dresses, umbrellas the size of a Pigeon lamp, tin tea sets with cups no bigger than a radish or plum. Similarly, some ten years later, on Rue Guynemer, Seinecé was puzzled at not being able to find, try as he might, any of the things Denis Aubier had given him after Mademoiselle's death. The memory of a woman, of the ghost of a goddess, a lamp that frightens and burns the form it lights up—a more trivial scene had intervened, with characters less strange and distinguished than a satyr pursuing a nymph. But the myth was right. The gods flee as soon as anyone catches a glimpse of them.

Our mouths play a part in the taste of a fruit. But even as I say that I wonder. I find it hard to believe my own mouth capable of making such a contribution. And it strikes me as incredible that the beauty of the universe could be to some small degree enhanced by my looking at it.

Delphine, alone and without her son, found herself at a loss. She often came to dinner whether I was there or not. She'd taken to Jeanne. I no longer loved Jeanne, but I was very proud that she didn't hate me anymore, indeed seemed quite fond of me.

A few months later, one spring day in 1984, by which time Delphine was seeing Denis Aubier and his family regularly, she urged me to go back to Saint-Germain-en-Laye. I didn't care for the idea and declined Denis's invitation to lunch or dinner. But the notion persisted and kept coming up, and one Saturday afternoon we made up our minds. Delphine called up Denis, and he promised to be there in the middle of the afternoon.

Delphine opened the gate. I recognized the creak. I was rather short of breath. I felt as if the air were swirling around my feet as I went through the gate; as if a dog's teeth were surreptitiously pressing on my hand; as if the memory of a dog that was somehow the procurator of Judea and Samaria was making a sign to me. I had to repress a tiny spasm, a tiny sob. The little lilacs that used to grow by the steps were now big trees.

I felt like a perpetual ghost, always returning to scenes of the past, always having visions of everlasting memories. Another little Oriental tale: Once upon a time a ghost met a phantom dog. . . . I wanted to write down these constantly recurring scenes to be able to wrap them up, repudiate them, and throw them far far away. Why did the dead come back? The priest at Bergheim used to say they sometimes came back to ask for masses or prayers, or to get a friend or relation to fulfill some promise they'd been unable to keep; to require a wrong to be righted or something stolen to be restored to its rightful owner. They often visited the houses they used to live in, too: it gave them pleasure to see the places they'd known when they were alive. Places and things they visited in this way were called haunted, and people who were haunted were called madmen. They were said to have hallucinations.

I had hallucinations. Of dogs, old ladies, and cats. Of rose gardens, bow windows, and even brass curtain rods and half curtains. Even of the heavy curves, in claret and crimson, garnet and vermilion, that wound over the variegated or yellow opal surfaces of Quinquet lamps. Of old blouses, watch chains, mists rising up out of the coppices in a little valley in Normandy, cottages and bougainvilleas and mimosas. Even of the faintest sunbeams and the sudden clicks of pike hunting in the Loire in the soft, gray-tinted dusk.

The preacher Ezekiel tells how the people mocked his visions: "The days are prolonged, and every vision faileth." But Ezekiel reversed this. He believed memories and visions grew as day succeeded day—that they gained in strength and bitterness and cruelty. And that has been my experience. The cruelty, I admit, gives me a bitter pleasure.

Denis was suffering from flu, but the great giant and his wife and children were waiting for us with tea and coffee and cakes. I'd brought some piping hot turnovers and various other pastries, not all of them, I fear, quite the genuine article. Delphine stayed with the children but started to miss her son, Anatole, and wanted to leave. She said she didn't feel well and would wait for me out in the little avenue.

I asked Denis to let me look over the house. The furniture was all different, made of Swedish pine and material so brightly colored and cheerful it made you want to weep. The downstairs rooms weren't lived in any more and had reverted to storage and playrooms. When I went into the pink salon on the second floor—where we used to have such indefatigable discussions, Seinecé and I, in the early sixties—I didn't at first feel any great surprise. "Well, well," I thought, "so it was blue after all!" I looked pityingly at the large modern settees, the television set, the computer, the stereo. Denis insisted on showing me some of my own records. I stood numbly in the middle of the room.

"Where's the big table?" I thought. "Where are the wicker chairs that used to stand round the Godin stove? Where is the Godin stove itself? All gone!"

But gradually I came to and grew surprised, even agitated.

"But wasn't the room pink?" I asked Denis.

"No, it's always been blue," he said. "Always that rather insipid blue. I like it. I had them use the same color when the room was repainted—that particular shade must be at least a hundred years old!"

"I knew it, I knew it!" I thought. "I was always so unobservant! It must have been the sunset that made it look pink—that was the time we used to meet here. The color was due to the time, not the place."

I tried to decipher some significance here but couldn't. The room was blue. But something inside me resisted. For some reason I remembered Ibelle's teeth in a restaurant on Quai Voltaire—the resistance of the spoon offering a mouthful of profiteroles, of the cake fork offering a piece of Napoleon and French cream. And I remembered how that resistance had been summoned up one day as I held the handle of the pump at Bormes, when Ibelle and I kissed for the first time. I seemed to feel physically the resistance of another's body at the end of a spoon; its eagerness, its strength, its teeth were the same as the sudden marvelous heaviness of a fishing rod—to go back to the banks of the Jagst or the Neckar when I was a child—the feel of a living creature caught on an invisible hook in river or ocean, struggling and perhaps about at any moment to break the line.

I joined Delphine in the avenue under the still bare lime trees. She talked to me about Anatole, how much she missed him, his body, even his sour smell, even his rages, like the tantrum he threw late the previous summer when he stamped with fury because he'd gotten grape or blackberry seeds stuck in his teeth.

I don't know why, but although it wasn't raining and there wasn't any hay around, I could smell wet hay as Delphine talked to me about her son. I pointed it out to her, and she could smell it too. It made me anxious. The sickly, insipid, delicate, smooth yet revolting taste of sugar beet pursued me, and still does. It was the taste of memories. I thought of young Anatole's rages. A seed stuck in your molars—something overripe and rotting and doing harm. An exact definition of a memory.

Delphine told me how frightened her son was of nettles, and how the thing to do was to rub the sting with a sorrel leaf. It was just like Ibelle, twenty years on. The rivalry with Mademoiselle Aubier. Old rites going back to the Merovingians, the Celts, the cave at Lascaux.

A fine rain began to fall, regular, slow and soothing, on the young lime leaves, bathing their brightness. Its drops stood out warm on my hands, like sweat.

They call such small incidents "cardiac alerts." It happened at Mirecourt during the annual St. Cecilia's Day banquet. I lost consciousness twice. I was given medical attention, warned to be careful, advised to cut down on travel a bit and lead a more regular life. And all this while we were celebrating the feast of St. Cecilia, patron saint of musicians and in particular of organists. She was a terrifying matron who preferred the bosom of her brother-in-law to the body of her husband but yielded her virginity only to the angels. She liked the smell of roses, hated perspiration, even on leaves or plums, and liked to sing hymns to her own accompaniment on the hydraulic organ. The incident I refer to took place on November 22, 1984.

I'd left Rue de Varenne but spent one week of every month in Paris, at Jeanne's place, where I had a bedroom that also served as music room and study. I'd started quite a prosperous little summer school in Bergheim for a few students advanced in the gamba. I'd had the village organ electrified. I took care of my health. It would probably be wise not to come to Paris so often.

I woke Nausicaa, who was reluctant to open her eyes, and talked to her about giving up Paris. She hated these trips but condescended to wiggle her whiskers and stretch out a paw toward me. I understood what she meant. And when I told her I had decided to go to Jeanne's only two or three times a year in the future, she yawned, showing the incredible pink inside of her mouth.

But things didn't turn out as I expected. Jeanne got fed up and broke with me. I had to buy a little pied-à-terre on Quai Anatole-France, where I plan to spend a few weeks every winter.

Playing in unison, if the musicians are at all accurate, produces an extraordinary feeling of exultation because of the way individual defects are lost in the communal effort. Instead of your own inadequacy being reflected back at you, you're absorbed into one great augmented sound. It's like the Homeric plain where birds of ill omen all sing together, a plain that's irresistible even though it's strewn with bones the crows have picked clean. They have emptied the eye sockets, eaten the eyes. It's from these bones that flutes are derived. Playing in unison is love. And friendship. And when the unison is lost your own voice, alone, is no longer your own. It's diminished, out of tune, cracked.

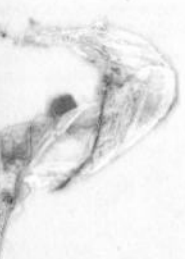

Some men are of indefinite appearance. Their bodies are unremarkable and make no attempt to attract attention. Such men are not envied for their looks, nor are they arrogant in their behavior. Their morals are neither shocking nor overscrupulous. Their faces are timid and open. Their lips and eyelids are delicate. You can read them like an open book, or like a sunlit brook babbling along over poplar leaves and bits of green moss. In company they never speak without being spoken to, and if you ask them a question they never speak loudly or long. There's nothing distinctive about them, and their company has no special appeal. And yet they have a kind of genius. They look melancholy and retiring, as if the daylight had forgotten them—as if they had almost completely forgotten themselves. But they're such geniuses that they leave practically no traces behind. Some of the best of them give off a smell of old books—old books that have fallen to dust. Some of them pass on fragments of rhymes or the memory of a sound, though they've forgotten the song it comes from. They cast only a discreet shadow, even when the twilight sun stretches out all other shadows, lengthening those of the spider and the stalactite to touching dimensions. They know the classics like the back of their hands but don't display their knowledge. Knowing what has been, they have a good idea of what will be, but they never prophesy, as that would mean prophesying woe. They keep quiet and move about almost as little as ferns and flowers. Their company is a true miracle.

I was thinking about a friend. I could see his body and face shining strangely in my memory. And, seeing him, I was sorry I hadn't loved him more. I was sitting in the study at Bergheim. The salon that Heinrich had had painted too bright a yellow. A yellow closer to the excrement of a goose than the feathers of a canary. It used to be the music room and had fascinating art nouveau French windows made of imitation bronze. The frames of the doors had been lacquered gray, and the moldings on the ceiling painted white. Before they were more yellow, though not gilt. I'd been advised to give up tours, rest a bit, do some writing. The table was covered with books, green, blue, and crimson. A little teacup and a sugar bowl stood near the edge. The big blue-shaded lamp cast a pool of light on the books, the rim of the cup, and most of the saucer. Some branches were burning on the hearth, but there weren't any flames.

The more I contemplate the former music room, which I've turned into my study and where I'm writing now, the more it seems to me that it has contained my destiny. Like a seed—crumpled, buried, complex, inward, shy. These big yellow walls contained my first scrapings at the cello when I was six, my banging on the piano when I was eight, the unbearable racket of the brass candelabras, my mother's absent look as she sat under the huge painting in which Psyche forever burned love, the first white drops of desire in the palm of my hand as I hid behind the leaves of the papyrus. And my aloneness. Alone—that's the word in which I feel most at home. The tiny yellow seed, shaped like a breast, or like one of the little pears that grow on the banks of the Loire, or like the other, larger seeds that you spit out when you eat a bunch of Italian grapes, had suddenly split open one day in the blue salon in Saint-Germain-en-Laye, which I thought was pink, and had finally come back here to shrink back into itself again.

I don't make music here any more. I just keep quiet. I concentrate all my attention on the soft faint sound of a pencil on scraps of envelope, newspaper wrappings, the backs of concert programs. I write. Suddenly I have a vision of the soul of a man who writes: I see a little rivulet, first gently lapping, then seething. And then a rather worn-out ghost who only becomes real when he gets up and leaves this room—if perception of the world and the people in it can be called real, when the inner rivulet has gradually grown tepid again and slack; when there's practically no life left in it. We are bodies full of dreams. Bodies always heated to ninety-eight-point-six degrees Fahrenheit.

I went to the museum at Biberach, went down to the banks of the Riss. Wieland said that in order to speak you had to have something to hide. And you have to have something to hide to write a book. St. Cecilia had receded. I'd come closer to St. Helen, who went all over the Empire seeking the wood of the Cross. I collect the air bubbles, all kinds of flaws, in the old windowpanes on the Bergheim estate. For the first time in my life I've given up translating and stopped playing pieces. I myself am the piece. I have transcribed my life.

There's a marble dust statue on the mantelpiece depicting some sort of scene. Is it a satyr pursuing Psyche, who desires him? Is it Eros vanishing at the sight of a nymph who's fleeing him? I remember a very hot day in May or June. The room, distant, huge, and blue, was quiet and looked pink in the dusk. I was gazing vacantly at an unglazed pottery statuette. I was filled with a longing that wasn't altogether fulfilled by driving a postal officer's van.

If I turn around I can still see behind me, over the sofa, the huge, ponderous, academic picture of Psyche and Eros, painted in a melodramatic, unctuous, and affected style and surrounded by a massive frame ornamented with gilt acorns and oak leaves.

It was all too deeply recorded in me. That's why I've recorded it all here. But I might just as well write letters and send them to the fire. I'd throw them on the fire, and the fire would read them by its own light. They'd be annihilated in the process of being read. But it seems to me sometimes that what is consumed in the fire and never leaves any ashes isn't really consumed at all. It may be called light. And light is terrible.

"Charles! Charlie!"

I suddenly heard someone call my name one evening in January 1985 on Rue de Rome. I was on my way to see an instrument maker I knew.

The mere fact of being suddenly hailed like that in the street made my heart miss a beat. Which shows not only the weak state of that organ but also how utterly abstracted I am when I'm trailing endlessly and drearily, as is my habit, around the cities where I happen to be.

I couldn't at first put a name to the big green loden coat that was hurrying toward me from Rue Saint-Lazare.

It named itself: "André! André Valasse!"

And as his face came nearer I saw it was indeed he.

I'd known him before I knew Florent. Our encounter was a pale reminder of army days. Achilles meets Marshal Murat, Grand Duke of Berg, in the underworld, and they talk about poisoned arrows and guns loaded with blanks. I looked at his puffy face, his bald head, his expensive cigar, and listened to his smug voice—all that had been loved by Ibelle and given me Dido.

"Remember your ten days in the clink?" he asked.

I'd never been in jail. Not actually behind bars. I've never had any misfortune to be proud of.

Writing this book at least distracts me from the sadness that suddenly descends on me and makes me invoke these memories. Makes me distract myself from what the present sadness itself distracts me from, by means of a dead sadness that is hard to revive and so is almost happy—careless, peaceful, and without a future. Anyone invoking memories is distracting himself with the dead. He thinks to cheat present anxiety by crouching down and tossing the knucklebones of his great-aunts and ancient cousins. How hard it is to get yourself a little place in which to love and be loved!

I'm at Bergheim as I write these pages. I started them last summer. I thought it would soothe me and make me happy, but it didn't. I had about ten pupils this summer. I hand on the little I know. Those are the best days.

You're at home again, in the country. You put on an old jacket you're fond of, you're in your own body again, that old sheath and talisman, as comfortable as in certain houses, certain languages. Paris and French have never really been the right place or language for me. I went into exile. I put on new clothes and tried to look elegant and speak stiffly and correctly.

Here I breathed with my own tongue, through the lungs of my own language. I could speak without bothering about what language I was using when I played, when I ran about, when I turned somersaults, when I was five or six years old. I could speak without thinking about it. I spoke German less correctly but more naturally than French, with more energy and enthusiasm. But I've never been able to write it. My French was richer but more obsessional, fastidious, melancholy, and painful: it was dedicated to someone I'd vainly gone to so much trouble to please when I spoke it!

* * *

I was invited to spend Christmas 1985 at Delphine's. Madeleine and Ibelle were there, polite and stiff and uptight. Painful though it was, I brought, as I'd always done, all kinds of candies, chocolates, and nougat for Juliette and Charles. For Anatole, whom Delphine had gotten back for the holidays, I'd brought a doll with a set of costumes including a Directory gown, a parachutist's uniform, a Red Cross nurse's overall with a syringe in the pocket, the rather complicated getup of an English executioner (his ax made him resemble the nurse in a way), and a habit like that of St. Francis of Assisi, complete with adhesive stigmata and little plastic birds. I can't tell you how thrilled I was myself by this purchase.

Anatole—with Pilotis in attendance—opened the parcel slowly and methodically, sucking the inside of his cheek just as his grandmother used to do at Saint-Martin-en-Caux, Bormes, Le Vésinet, and Chatou long ago. But now she sat impassively on a divan, holding a glass of whiskey, and answering Madeleine's questions in a loud and affected voice. Anatole seemed quite at ease, but hesitant. Delphine, in a motherly—in other words slightly threatening—manner, told him to hurry up and open the package. He then bent forward with the awful expression of apprehension that makes children look as if they're the prey of the gift that's being pressed upon them. Unpicking the tape on the box with his nails, he opened it, looked at the doll and its wardrobe, then burst into tears and flung it all on the floor.

We were reconciled a couple of hours later. Curled up on my lap and playing with my lighter, he told me he hated presents of any kind, and I mustn't think for a moment it was the doll that had upset him. He insisted on this with a politeness that was the obverse of his own pain; by comforting me he was trying to swallow his own disappointment. Only presents of money gave him pleasure, he said; only using such presents to buy wallets and billfolds gave him a thrill; and the only thing that gave him intense satisfaction was putting any money left over in these receptacles and pretending to hide them away in odd places in the large room he slept in at his father's. Underwear, socks, and boxes inside other boxes were favorite caches. I nodded and got out my wallet, and we settled the matter.

I found Juliette very grown-up now—she was nine—and met her three-year-old half-sister for the first time. Little Mathilde grabbed me by the lapels, pulled me close, and recited:

"There are seven geese. One goose, two geese . . . seven geese!"

Then she whispered in my ear, "Do you understand?"

"No," I said.

"Seven geese! That's you!"*

She did her best to explain.

Dusk had fallen at about four. I began to think of leaving. Delphine insisted on taking me to her room to see a curious halogen lamp she'd just bought, which gave out a diffused light. I suddenly felt old. The light was strong but soft, and the big room looked as if it was full of sun. I wasn't against that, but something inside me felt a painful craving for the weak yellow beams from an old-fashioned overhead light fixture.

I admired the beauty of the new acquisition but hurried out of the room and back to Nausicaa, whom I'd left shut up in the kitchen, seeing she wasn't going to get on very well with Pilotis. I talked to her about Pigeon lamps, Argan lights, Gallé lamps, pink Daums, and Quinquets. She unsheathed her claws, inspected them skeptically, then sheathed and unsheathed them again.

I was cross with her and went back to the salon. She was merciless. Dido—the real Dido—at least condescended to weep and pretend to want to die. I crossed the salon to where Charles was directing a great game of marbles on the rug. Charles, Juliette, and Anatole all lay on their stomachs, shutting one eye and flicking their marbles at a larger one at the end of the rug. Mathilde knelt nearby, sucking her thumb. I asked Charles if I could play. They all said I could, and delighted me by pretending to be very pleased. I lay down on the floor too. I used to be the champion at this game in Bergheim.

We played for a quarter of an hour, and though I lost I wasn't disgraced. Charles was the undisputed winner.

"We're not going to stay here for a hundred and seven years, are we?" suddenly yelled Mathilde, aged three.

* * *

* Untranslatable pun: *sept oies* is a homonym of *c'est toi*.

"Why not?" I thought. Seinecé didn't live half as long. I wrote down 1986 in German. *Neunzehnhundertsechstundachtzig.* It made me think of Niedersteinbach, in France, where my uncles lived. And Pfulgriesheim, where Marga lived.

A family scattered about in Alsace, Baden-Württemberg, the Palatinate, and Caen. In Stuttgart, Neuilly, Saint-Germain-en-Laye, Bormes, and Oudon. Sometimes it seems as if we spend our lives doing things that have been dimly sketched out already in the past: completing old jigsaw puzzles, finishing broken-off sentences, carrying through imperfectly felt emotions. And suddenly, among all these unfinished things, buds blossom or twigs sprout. And then there are leaves or books.

Books share with tiny children and cats the privilege of being held for hours on grown-ups' laps. And strange to say, books even more than children and cats can captivate and silence those who are looking at them, can petrify their arms and legs, and can so govern their features that they seem to express mute supplication, or the fear of an animal on the watch, or incomprehensible and perhaps desperate prayer.

My mother used to read and smoke as she read. She collected engravings, porcelain, and Daum glassware, and didn't speak much. But we amass in vain. I accumulate in vain my scraps of envelope, the bits of paper I write on on my knees. It's a dike constructed in vain.

Time destroys everything. We know the lesson by heart but are shattered by the experience. We die. Time destroys us, and itself with us. Then little by little, in death, as time destroys itself it destroys forever the memory of time. And a kind of miracle happens. What we have lived through is like a dream that we have forgotten. What we have dreamed is like a thing that we have forgotten and then lived through again. I told myself, with all the emphasis that goes with real emotion and perhaps even guarantees its sincerity: "Florent is dead. My friend is dead." I kept repeating it, and was moved as I did so. Then I looked up at the unglazed statuette on the mantelpiece and said, "My friend, I will never see you again. I will never again sit in your salon in Rue Guynemer. No more armchair covered in mouse-gray velvet!"

I put up a deck chair by the little music pavilion at Bergheim and lay in the sun. I lay out there in the garden and suddenly sensed a void. A piece of flotsam tossed like a cork through an endless void. I could almost touch the emptiness with my finger, and I felt drawn to plunge into it. I remembered a June day in Saint-Germain-en-Laye. We were dragging deck chairs over the lush grass. We put them up and stretched out in them. Only a marvelous, merry buzz of insects broke the silence. Now I knew that nothing would ever break or disturb the silence again. I looked beside me, at his absence. When I do that I always sense an infinite void. And a feeling of dizziness, of vertigo comes over me, seeing that void on the grass beside me, in the cool, slightly heavy air, blue-tinged and fresh.

I say silently, "My friend, we'll never meet again. I'll never see you again in the whole of time, you who were almost as dear to me as my own health and sleep. I'll go on loving you as if you were still near me for three or four seasons—as if you were still with me, putting your hand on my arm and whispering something that makes me laugh. Perhaps I'll go on loving you for a year. Then, having already died, you'll fade, and the void that has already devoured your life will devour even your memory. Death will sweep from me even the echo of your name."

At about three this morning, as I was making a hearty meal off the remains of a pork pie and some red currant tarts before I started work—it was still pitch dark outside in the garden—I suddenly doubted whether it had ever happened, whether I'd ever known that man and had that friendship. Though I never doubt that I feel the loss and the shadow it casts on my heart. There are times when all the past seems like an airy cloud, a strange dream one should never have had—all the riches of Sinbad in our grasp, and then our empty hands. And suddenly, on an impulse, as now, I want to remember, to add shade and color, hair and smell and reality, to all the stories I write down. To all the stories that memories, traces, enigmas, dates, and ghosts tell one another in our minds. I feel an irresistible urge to ballast the past with lead shot, steel shot, blood. I write down details, I see lights, I hear sounds.

I write and I dream. I write and write, and I tell myself this spirit must have a body, these eyes must have tears, these lips need some kind of lament. I write, and suddenly I think that also, perhaps, this dream needs a kind of sleeper.

About the Author

Pascal Quignard was born in Verneuil, France, in 1948. He has published three other novels: *Carus, Les Tablettes de buis,* and *Les Escaliers de Chambord,* along with a number of nonfiction works on literature and music. He currently lives in Paris, where he is an editor at Editions Gallimard. *The Salon in Württemberg* is the first of Mr. Quignard's novels to appear in English.

About the Translator

Barbara Bray, who lives in Paris, has most recently translated works by Marguerite Duras, Emmanuel Le Roy Ladurie, and Jean Genet. Among many other awards, she has received the Scott Moncrieff Prize, the American PEN Award, and the French-American Foundation Prize.